T0265995

The Perfect World

The Perfect World

A Romance of Strange People and Strange Places

Ella M. Scrymsour

MINT EDITIONS

The Perfect World: A Romance of Strange People and Strange Places was first published in 1922.

This edition published by Mint Editions 2020.

ISBN 9781513272313 | E-ISBN 9781513277318

Published by Mint Editions®

MINT
EDITIONS

minteditionbooks.com

Publishing Director: Jennifer Newens
Design & Production: Rachel Lopez Metzger
Project Manager: Micaela Clark
Typesetting: Westchester Publishing Services

Contents

BOOK I
THE OLD WORLD

(*Before the War*)

I

STRANGERS COME TO MARSHFIELDEN

An English summer! The birds sang merrily, and the trees bowed their heads, keeping time with the melody. The breeze whispered its accompaniment, and all the glades and woods were happy.

Marshfielden was, perhaps, one of the prettiest villages in Derbyshire. Nestling among the peaks of that lovely county, its surroundings were most picturesque. Its straggling street, for it had but one, was unspoiled by tripper or tourist, for its charms were unknown to the outside world. The road was cobbled, and boasted of no pavement, and long gardens, shining with marigolds and nasturtiums, reached down to each side of it, forming frames to the pretty, irregular little cottages with their gables and latticed windows.

The little church at the top of the street finished the picture. It was very tiny, holding only about one hundred and fifty people; but with its ivy-covered towers, and picturesque little graveyard, the vicar was a lucky man to have charge of such a place. Unmarried and friendless he had come to Marshfielden forty years before, and had lodged with Mrs. Skeet, the cobbler's wife. Still he remained, having grown old in the service of his people.

It was a well-known fact, that "our vicar" as Mr. Winthrop was called, had during all that time never left the precincts of the parish. Children had grown up and gone away married; old people had died; but still Mr. Winthrop went on in his kind, fatherly manner, advising those who sought the benefit of his wisdom, helping those who needed his aid, and still living in the little rooms he had rented when first he came to Marshfielden, a stranger.

Marshfielden was about seven miles off the main road. As they would have to reach it by narrow lanes and rutted roads, motorists never came its way, and it retained its old-world simplicity.

Two miles to the south was a coal mine, in which most of the villagers toiled. It was quite an unimportant one, and not very deep, but it gave employment to all the natives who needed work. Strange as it seems, however, by an unwritten law, not one of the villagers entered Marshfielden in his collier dirt or collier garb. Every one of the men changed his clothes at "Grimland" as the mine district was called, and washed away the coal dust and dirt; so in the evening, when they made their way in a body to their homes, they returned as fresh and clean as they had left them in the morning.

It was, therefore, an ideal place to live in and as old Mr. Winthrop walked down the uneven street, his eyes dimmed and his thoughts were tender as he acknowledged first one, then another of his flock.

He stopped at the gate of a pretty, white cottage with a well kept garden full of sweet-smelling flowers, and greeted the woman who stood at the gate.

She was quite young and pretty, and maternal love and pride glowed in her face as she gently crooned over the sleeping babe at her breast.

"And how's Jimmy, Mrs. Slater?" he asked.

"Very well indeed, sir, thank you."

"And you—how are you feeling?"

"Quite all right again, now, sir."

"That's right. And your husband?"

"Yes, sir, he's had a rise at the mine."

Mr. Winthrop smiled and was about to pass on, when he noticed an underlying current of excitement in the woman's manner. He looked at her curiously.

"What is the matter, Mrs. Slater?" he asked.

"Have you heard the news, sir?"

"No. What news?"

"I be agoin' to have lodgers."

"Really?"

"Well I heard only last night, sir. Bill—he came home and said as 'ow Mr. Dickson, the manager at the mine, had heard from Sir John Forsyth—"

"The new owner of Grimland?" queried Mr. Winthrop.

"Yes, sir. Well, he said as 'ow Sir John wanted both his nephews to go to the mine and learn the practical working of it—and Mr. Dickson was to find them rooms near by."

"Well?"

"Well, Mr. Dickson knows as 'ow my 'ome is clean—" and Mrs. Slater looked around her little cottage with an air of pride.

"And 'e asks Bill if I would take them."

"And so you are going to?"

The woman looked round her fearfully. "I've a spare bedroom, sir, which I've cleaned up, and they can have my parlour. But fancy, sir, two strangers in Marshfielden!"

"It will liven things up," remarked the vicar "we've never had strangers to live here since I came—now over forty years ago."

"No, sir, nor before that," went on the woman in a low tone. "My grandmother used to speak of two ladies who came to Marshfielden when she was a little girl. Artists they were, and strangers. The clergyman's wife put them up—and—and—"

"Yes?" urged Mr. Winthrop gently.

"Well, sir, they were both found dead one day, stiff and cold, sir, outside the ruins of the Priory. They had been painting, and their easels were left standing—but they were dead."

"What has that to do with the case?" asked the vicar with a little smile.

"Don't you see, sir," she went on quickly, the same half-scared look coming into her eyes, "that was the 'Curse' that caused those mishaps, and I am afraid the 'Curse' will be on the two young gentlemen, too."

"Nonsense," laughed Mr. Winthrop, "You don't really believe that the 'Marshfielden Curse' as you people call it, had anything to do with the deaths of those two lady artists that occurred over fifty years ago?"

"Indeed I do, sir," averred the woman. "Why ever since the Priory was dismantled by Henry the Eighth, the 'Curse' has been on this place. That wasn't the only case, sir. There are records of many others—but that was the last."

"Let me see," began the vicar, "It's so long since I even heard it mentioned, that I've forgotten what it was."

The woman's face contracted as if she was afraid of something, she knew not what, but of something mystic, intangible, uncanny—and she repeated slowly:

When the eighth Henry fair Marshfielden's monastery took, Its priory as a palace, its vast income to his privy purse,—The outcast prior solemnly, by candle, bell and book Upon this place for ever laid this interdict and curse:

> *From now until the end of time,*
> *Whene'er a stranger come*
> *Unto Marshfielden's pleasaunces,*
> *To make therein his home,*
> *Troubles—disease—misfortunes—death—*

Upon the spot shall fall.
So—an' Marshfielden folks ye'd swell
With fair prosperity, and safely dwell,
All strangers from your gates expel,
And live cut off from all.

The vicar laughed. "Yes, it's a pretty legend, Mrs. Slater, but remember this is the twentieth century, and nothing is likely to happen to Marshfielden, its inhabitants or its visitors, because of that. Why, I was a stranger when I came, yet nothing very terrible has happened to me during these last forty years."

"Ah, sir, you don't count. I mean, sir, you belong to the Priory; you are our priest. You wouldn't come under the 'Curse' sir."

"And neither will any one else, Mrs. Slater. It's a stupid legend.— Have no fear."

"But," began Mrs. Slater. "How do you account for the case of—" But Mr. Winthrop lifted up a deprecatory hand.

"I cannot listen to any more, Mrs. Slater." And a note of authority came into his voice. "Why, all this is against the religion I preach to you—never listen to tales of superstition. Have no fear, do the best you can for the two young gentlemen, and I think I can promise you that no harm will come to them or you."

The woman shook her head, and disbelief shone in her eyes. The vicar saw it, and smiled again.

"Well, well! It remains to be proved that I am right," said he.

"It remains to be proved, *which* of us is right, sir."

"Very well, we'll leave it at that. When do they arrive?"

"About six this evening, sir; the usual time when the men come home."

"I will call in this evening then, and welcome them. Good-bye, Mrs. Slater, and don't go listening to or spreading idle gossip!" And the kindly old man went away down the street.

That evening, when the bell rang to denote the return of the menfolk, every door was occupied by an eager face, anxious not only to catch sight of the two strangers, but also to take another look at the woman who had dared to defy the "Marshfielden Curse."

For in this little village the "Curse" was a real, poignant fact, and was spoken of in the twilight with hushed tones and furtive glances. Children were quieted and terrified by it, and the fear imbibed by them in their childhood grew with them till their death. Not one of them but Mary Slater would have risked its anger by allowing a stranger to sleep beneath her roof; and even Mary, although outwardly calm, was inwardly terrified lest her action might be the means of bringing disaster and misery, not only on her two lodgers, but on the whole little community.

Dan Murlock, the husband of the little woman at the corner house, was the first to arrive. He came along at a swinging pace, and waved his cap jauntily as he saw his wife's trim little figure at the doorway.

"Hullo, Moll," he cried, when he was within speaking distance "an' how's yersel'?"

"I'm all right," she replied, while their three year old, curly haired boy and only child peeped from behind his mother's skirts and cried "Boo" to his dad. The man looked at them both, with awe as well as pride in his glance. Even now he was often heard to remark, that he could not make out why a clumsy brute like him should be allowed to own such an angelic wife and child.

"Where's the strangers?" asked Moll eagerly.

"Comin' along, lass. Why?"

"Oh, the 'Curse,' Dan!"

"Never mind the 'Curse,' lass; that's done with long ago! Is supper ready yet?"

"Yes, Dan. It's ready." But his wife made no effort to re-enter their little home, and serve the meal her husband wanted.

"Woman, what are you staring at?" he cried. "Why do'ant 'ee come in? I'm hungry."

"In a moment, Dan. I—I—"

"What's thee lookin' at, lass?"

"The strangers, Dan. Think the 'Curse'—" But Dan only laughed good-humouredly. "Thou't a fule, lass. Come in and do'ant bother yer head about it," and he good-naturedly put his arm through hers, and dragged the unwilling woman into the house.

Most of the women outside, however, were still waiting, waiting for the strangers. Then suddenly came a buzz of excitement as the news was passed from mouth to mouth. "They're coming! They're coming!"

The two young men, Alan and Desmond Forsyth, were entirely unconscious of all the attention and interest showered on them. Of the "Curse" they knew nothing, and had they done so, would have cared less.

They were cousins, and on very affectionate and intimate terms, and one day would share equally in the Grimland Colliery, of which their uncle was now owner. Alan, moreover, would succeed to his uncle's title. The future looked very rosy for these two young men.

Sir John was determined that when they left Cambridge, they should thoroughly learn the workings of the mine. The instructions he gave Dickson, his manager, were that he was to "make them work like ordinary colliers until they were competent to take charge."

They had travelled on the Continent for six months after coming down from the 'Varsity, and this was their first day of real, hard work. It had left them both eager to begin another day, for they were anxious to learn more of the wonderful workings of the mine below the surface of the earth. They had walked cheerily toward Marshfielden, eager to reach their apartments and have a good meal. They liked Slater, and felt that they would be comfortable and happy in his home.

"How do you feel, young gentlemen?" he asked them.

"I'm dead tired," answered Alan, the elder, a man of some twenty-five years, while his cousin, Desmond, a year younger, yawned lustily, as he asked, "How much further is that adorable little home of yours, Slater?"

"We're nigh there, sir. There's my Mary at the gate."

"What, the little cottage at the bend?" asked Alan.

"Yes, sir. She's a good lass, is my missus. She'll treat you well, and make you comfortable and happy."

The rest of the short way was trodden in silence, and at length the two young men stepped across the threshold of Sweet William Cottage, as the Slaters' home was called.

The room they were ushered into was old-world and sweet. The lattice windows were open wide, letting in the soft, fresh air of summer. The ceiling was low and beamed, and the furniture was of old dark oak; while the bright chintz hangings took away all hint of sombreness. The table was laid, and within a few minutes of their arrival they were sitting down to an appetizing repast.

Neither of them spoke for some time, and then Desmond laid down his knife and fork with a sigh.

"I'm done" said he.

"I should just think you were" laughed his cousin "You've been stuffing incessantly for over half an hour" Alan rang the bell for the table to be cleared and then they lit their pipes.

"How do you feel?" asked Desmond.

"Very tired—very sore—and very bruised"

"So am I. I think I shall like the life of a miner, though"

"Rather! What a ripping set of chaps they are!"

So they chattered on until it was time for them to retire. At peace with each other, at peace with the world, they slept until a knock at their bedroom door awakened them.

"Yes" sleepily answered Desmond.

"It's four o'clock, young gentlemen, you'd better get up"

Alan woke up lazily to hear Desmond cry out in amazement.

"Surely not yet, Slater?"

"Yes, sir. You must be at the mine by five fifteen. Early shift to-day, you know"

"All right, Slater" cried Alan, who was now wide awake "we'll be down in twenty minutes"

In a very short space of time they had had their breakfast, and were walking across the Grimland fields to the mine, to begin once more a day's arduous duty.

It passed quickly enough, but they were thankful when the bell sounded for them to knock off work, and they were taken up to daylight again by the cage.

When they reached Sweet William Cottage, they found Mr. Winthrop awaiting them, with profuse apologies for his absence the night before.

"I'm afraid Mrs. Slater omitted to give us any message from you" said Alan "In fact we didn't even know you had called"

"I am the vicar of Marshfielden" said the kindly old man "and I should have liked to give you a personal welcome. You see the 'Curse' has made your position here somewhat strained"

The two boys stared at each other in perplexity. The vicar laughed. "None of the women have been frightening you with their child's stories yet?"

"No!" said both boys together, "what is it?"

"Oh, there's a legend connected with this place, that any strangers in Marshfielden will bring disaster on themselves and perhaps on the place, if they take up their abode here"

"Why?"

"A curse was laid on the place by a monk in Henry the Eighth's time, when the Priory here was dismantled"

"Oh, is that all?" said Alan lightly "We are not afraid of old wives' tales like that!"

But Molly Murlock, who was in the kitchen with Mary Slater, heard the words, and her brow clouded. Drawing her child closer, she muttered as she said good night to Mary—

"'Curse' or no 'Curse,' I'd rather be dead, than live to see strangers come here"

II

The Curse

The two men had now been working for three months at the mine, and the villagers had become used to the sight of strangers in Marshfielden. Indeed, as the weeks sped by, and nothing uncanny happened, they began gradually to forget the "Curse" in connection with the two young Forsyths.

Summer was now waning. Leaves were beginning to fall and folks were making preparations for a hard winter. Mr. Winthrop was still going round on his kindly errands and had become sincerely attached to the two youths who had taken up their residence so near him.

Indeed, there was no one else in the village to whom they could go for social intercourse, and nearly every evening Mrs. Skeet's little parlour was full of the smoke and chatter of the vicar and his two young friends. It was now the first Tuesday in October, and the evenings were growing chilly. Mrs. Skeet had lighted a nice fire, and they all sat round it enjoying the warmth of its glow.

People outside, passing by, heard the sound of merry laughter, and Mr. Winthrop's characteristic chuckle, and smiled with him. But Moll Murlock passed the cottage hurriedly and drew her shawl closer round her shoulders, while a slight moan came from between her tightly compressed lips.

Of all the inhabitants of Marshfielden, there was one still who had *not* forgotten the "Curse."

"Well, boys," said Mr. Winthrop, "I suppose you feel used to your life among us now?"

"Yes," answered Alan. "It seems almost like home to us."

"We've never had a proper home," broke in Desmond.

"Ours is rather a romantic story," said Alan. "Our mothers were twin sisters—they married on the same day and went to the same place for their honeymoon. A year later my mother died in giving me birth, and Desmond's mother died when he was only a few months old, so we were both left babies to get on the best way we could without a woman's care."

"Poor lads! Poor lads!" sighed the vicar.

"When I was five my father died," said Desmond, "and four years later Alan's father was drowned. Uncle John then took us to live with him—but as he was a bachelor we were brought up in the care of nurses and tutors, and had no real home life."

"You are fond of your uncle?" queried the vicar.

"Rather!" answered Alan. "Uncle John is the dearest old boy imaginable. He's a bit of a crank though. He has been working for years on what he calls his 'Petradtheolin' airship."

"His what?" laughed Mr. Winthrop.

"His 'Petradtheolin' airship. It's his own invention, you know, but up to now he has been unsuccessful. He has built a wonderful aluminium airship—most beautifully fitted and upholstered—in fact it is absolutely ready to fly, but up to now it won't budge an inch."

"What?"

"He is under the impression," went on Alan "that in the near future flying will be an every day occurrence, and it is his greatest ambition to own the most comfortable, most speedy, and lightest airship of the day."

Mr. Winthrop smiled. "There is a great deal of talk about flying now," said he, "but do you honestly think it will ever come to anything?"

"I don't know," said Alan thoughtfully, "we have conquered the sea—'Iron on the water shall float, like any wooden boat'," he quoted. "We have built ships that can submerge and remain under water and navigate for certain periods of time. I see no reason why the modern man should not also conquer the air."

Mr. Winthrop shook his head. "I may be old-fashioned, but it seems impossible to believe that navigable ships could be built for flying, that were *safe*. I don't doubt that airships will be built that up to a certain point will be successful—say for a few hours' flight, but it seems inconceivable to me that man could so conquer the air, that commerce and travel would benefit."

"Well, Uncle John thinks he will conquer it with his 'Argenta'," went on Alan.

"Surely that was not what you called it just now?" asked the vicar.

Alan laughed. "The 'Argenta' is the name of the ship itself, but 'Petradtheolin' is the name of the power he is experimenting on, that he is desirous of using to propel it."

"The machine itself is complete," went on Desmond enthusiastically, "the balance is perfect, and its engines are supposed to be of wonderful velocity, but no known power will raise it even an inch from the ground.

So he is still experimenting on this spirit. It is a formula which embraces petrol, radium and theolin; these chemicals are blended in some way or other—concentrated and solidified. The engines are made so as to generate electricity in the bonnet part. The current acts on the solidified cubes, which as they melt are sent through metal retorts drop by drop, and then being conveyed to the engines should make the machine fly."

"Well?"

"I know it all sounds very fantastic, but my uncle firmly believes in the ultimate success of his experiments. His ambition is to be able to fly for about one hundred hours with about a cupful of this powerful matter. He expects each drop of the vaporized spirit, as it issues from the retort, to keep the engines going about fifty minutes."

"It all sounds very interesting," said Mr. Winthrop "but is extremely puzzling. I am afraid I would rather trust myself to Mother Earth than to your uncle's very ingenious 'Argenta'."

"So would I," laughed Desmond. "But the dear old boy is so keen on his work, we don't like to discourage him"

"And" finished Alan "there in a most wonderful shed, rests the 'Argenta'; its body of glistening aluminium—its interior richly upholstered and wonderfully arranged from engine room to kitchen, but absolutely lifeless. And there I expect it will remain, for he will never destroy it. It is his biggest hobby after us—sometimes I think it even comes before us. He has the money, he has the brains, he may perfect this power, and if he does, he will have conferred a great benefit upon humanity"

"You stayed with him until you came here, I suppose?"

"Yes" answered Alan "We went to Eton—Cambridge—"

"Cambridge?" Mr. Winthrop's face lighted up "Dear me! Dear me! What College, may I ask?"

"Queens" said Desmond.

"Queens? That was my College"

"Indeed" cried the two boys together.

"Yes, I've not been there for over forty-five years. I expect the dear old place has changed a great deal?"

"Yes. We had rooms opposite each other on the same staircase in the New Buildings" said Desmond.

"That was since my time" said Mr. Winthrop rather sadly "I've never even seen the New Buildings. I was in the Walnut-Tree Court" Then he stopped, and gazed into the fire, his eyes sparkling and a colour coming into his old, worn cheeks, as he thought of the days of his youth. Reminiscences came quickly. "Do you remember this?" "I remember when so-and-so happened" So the conversation went on until they were rudely interrupted by a sharp knock on the door, startling in its unexpectedness. All three rose hurriedly.

"Come in" cried the vicar and Mrs. Skeet appeared breathing heavily, with a look of horror in her eyes.

"Whatever is the matter?" asked Mr. Winthrop in dismay, startled out of his usual placidity by her frightened mien.

"Dan—Dan Murlock's baby—it's gone, sir"

"Gone? Gone where?"

"No one knows, sir. He was playing in the garden, safe and sound, only five minutes before, and when Moll went to call him in to put him to bed, he had vanished."

"It's impossible for the child to have gone far," said the vicar. "Why, he is only a baby!"

"Three last month, sir."

"Has any one looked for him? What have they done?"

"The child can't be spirited away," said Alan. "Why, there's no traffic in the village that could possibly hurt him."

Mrs. Skeet looked scared. "If you please, sir," she half whispered, "the people do say, as 'ow it's the 'Curse' and that he has been spirited away."

The vicar blinked his eyes. "Nonsense, Mrs. Skeet! I'm ashamed of you. Never let me hear such words from you again. Spirited away indeed! I expect he has strayed away into the woods at the back of the Murlocks' cottage. Come, lads, we'll go down and see Dan and his wife, and do our best to help them." Taking up their hats the three made their way down the street, usually so quiet and still, but now buzzing with excitement.

As they reached the Murlocks' cottage, they saw the front door was open wide, leaving the kitchen and garden beyond exposed to view. Curious neighbours, sympathetic friends, open-mouthed children were surrounding the stricken mother, who was rocking herself to and fro in her abandonment and grief.

"Let us go through," said the vicar, and the two boys followed him.

The woman heard the approaching footsteps, and lifted up her tear-stained face to the intruders. She held out her hands pathetically to the vicar, and the tears rolled down her cheeks unchecked. He took hold of

ELLA M. SCRYMSOUR

the toil-worn hands, and was about to speak when she caught sight of the two boys behind him. Her eyes dilated and her body stiffened. Suddenly she uttered a piercing scream, and pointing a shaking hand at them, "Go, go!" she cried. "You came to Marshfielden unbidden—you defied the 'Curse'—now you have taken my baby—my darling, darling baby!"

Dan put his arm about her tenderly. "Do'ant 'ee tak' on so, lass," said he gently. "Sure, we'll find the babby. Already John Skinner and Matt Harding have gone with search parties to find the wee lad. We'll get him back, wife mine." But she only looked fiercely at the strangers. "Go—go—the 'Curse' is on us all!"

Mr. Winthrop silently motioned to the two lads and they quickly left the stricken house, and made their way back to their rooms in silence.

The next morning on their way to work, they missed Dan Murlock. Some of the miners eyed them suspiciously as they asked where he was, and Slater, their landlord, was the only one to satisfy their curiosity. "With his wife," said he curtly. "The wee laddie has not been found."

"Wherever can he be?" said Desmond in bewilderment. Slater shook his head.

"Search parties were out all night, but could find no trace or tidings of him."

"Have you any idea what has happened?" asked Alan. Slater gave a quick look at each in turn, and then muttered something unintelligible under his breath, and the boys had to be content with that.

It was a terrible day at the mine for the two boys; they had to partake of their midday meal in silence, for not one of the colliers addressed a word to them if he could possibly avoid it. They were regarded with suspicion mingled with fear, and the "Curse" seemed to be on every one's lips.

Two days passed—a week, a fortnight; still Dan Murlock's baby was not found, and at last the broken-hearted parents appeared at church in mourning, thus acknowledging to the world that they had given up all hope of ever seeing their little one again.

Murlock was silent about it all, but every one who knew him realized that he was a changed man. He had idolized his wife and child, and at one blow had lost both, for his baby was without doubt dead; and his wife had turned from him in the throes of her grief.

The weeks passed on, Christmas was nigh upon them, and the child was spoken of in hushed tones as one speaks of the dead. The two boys were treated as aliens by the men, and they were beginning to chafe under their treatment. Although nothing had been said openly, they knew instinctively that they were blamed by the superstitious inhabitants for the disappearance of the baby.

"Alan," said Desmond one day, as they were sitting apart from the rest eating their dinner, "I can't stand this. I am going to speak to the men."

"Stand what?" asked Alan wearily.

"Why the whispers and sneers that are showered on us whenever we are near them. They all shrink away from us—treat us as if we were lepers; even Slater avoids us, and the 'Curse' is whispered from lip to lip as we pass."

"You'll do no good, Desmond."

"We had nothing to do with the child's going away, yet they treat us as if we had murdered him."

"Leave it alone," said Alan, "I don't know what it is, but this place seems uncanny. I think I am almost beginning to believe in the 'Curse' myself."

Desmond made no reply, but squaring his shoulders, began to walk toward the miners.

"Look here, you fellows," he began. "What's wrong with you all? Why are you treating my cousin and me as if we were murderers? We aren't responsible for Murlock's little child vanishing away."

The miners moved restlessly and muttered together, each waiting for a spokesman to assert himself, who would teach them the line of action they should take. Desmond continued, "You talk about the 'Curse'! We knew nothing about it when we came here, and to us it seems ridiculous to imagine there is anything supernatural about the whole affair. The river is only a quarter of a mile from their garden gate; I know it has been dragged, but after all it is full of whirlpools and weeds, and if the little chap did fall into it, ten to one his little body will never be found."

Suddenly a leader was found among the men, and Matt Harding stood up.

"Look'ere mates," said he. "We do'ant suppose these young gentlemen actually hurt Dan Murlock's baby, or that they know where he went to, but after all, the 'Curse' tells us *not* to have strangers in Marshfielden, or evil will befall. It may befall *them*, it may befall *us*, but some one will reap ill. Now it's really Slater's fault for giving them lodgings. Let Slater turn them out, and that may break the 'Curse.'"

"Aye, aye!" cried the men in unison.

"Where is Slater?" asked one burly fellow.

"With the shift above," came the reply in another voice. Then came groans from the rest. "Turn them out! Turn them out!"

"There is no need to turn us out," said Alan with quiet dignity. "We will find rooms outside Marshfielden, and leave at the end of the week."

"Leave now! Leave now!" cried a hoarse voice, which they recognized as belonging to Toby Skinner.

That was the one word needed to make the miners obstreperous. "Yes, go now, go now," they cried. "By the end of the week all our babes may be gone."

In vain the signal was given for the men to resume work; but they were free of their pent up feelings, and refused to listen to the strident tones of the bell that called them back to their duties.

Suddenly the manager's voice was heard above the din and babel.

"Get to your work at once," he thundered, "or take my word for it, there will be a general lockout to-morrow."

Gradually the men quieted, relieved of the strain of the past few weeks, and slunk back to work.

"What's the trouble?" asked Mr. Dickson, coming to the boys.

"They think we are the cause of the disappearance of Dan Murlock's baby," explained Alan to the manager with some bitterness.

"Yes," continued Desmond, "and now they demand that we leave Marshfielden. That damned 'Curse' is driving us mad. These people are like a set of uncivilized savages, who believe in witchcraft and omens of the twelfth century."

Mr. Dickson smiled as he answered them. "Our Marshfielden folk are unique. They are almost a race in themselves. As Cornishmen consider themselves 'Cornish' and not 'English' so Marshfielden men call themselves 'Marshfieldens.' It is true they are very superstitious for they believe implicitly in the folk lore that has been handed down to them from all time."

"What would you advise us to do?" asked Alan somewhat impatiently.

Mr. Dickson thought a moment, and then said quickly, "The widow of one of our men lives in a little cottage not a quarter of a mile from here; it stands on Corlot ground—not Marshfielden. She has a hard struggle to make both ends meet. I will send round at once and see if she is willing to take you two as lodgers. If she will—then go to her, for she is clean, respectable, and will look after you well. Meanwhile, neither of you has had a day off yet, so go and arrange about your luggage, and I'll see you are fixed up somewhere with rooms."

"Thanks," said Alan. "I shall be very sorry to leave Marshfielden though. It is such a quaint, old-world place."

"Far too old-world for strangers," said Mr. Dickson significantly. The little village street was buzzing with excitement when they reached Marshfielden. Women were rushing to and fro across the cobbled stones, and the whole place showed signs of some great disturbance.

As the boys approached, a sudden hush seemed to pervade the place, and the women huddled together and whispered "The 'Curse'! The 'Curse'!"

Alan shrugged his shoulders. "I'll see to the things," said he. "You go along to Mr. Winthrop, and tell him of the change in our plans."

"Right, old boy," and Desmond went towards Mr. Winthrop's rooms, whistling and doing his best to ignore the hostile looks that were directed at him.

Alan went into the little room that had become so dear to them both. The cottage was deserted, Mrs. Slater was absent, and as he made his way up to the little bedroom, he sighed as he thought of leaving the dear little place.

In a very short space of time the drawers were emptied and the trunks packed; everything was done except the putting together of the hundred and one odds and ends that invariably remain about.

"That's good!" said he to himself, as he rose from his knees, having finished strapping up the trunks, and he surveyed his handiwork with pride, as he realized the short time it had taken him to complete it all.

"Alan!"—He turned round suddenly—it was Desmond's voice.

"Coming, old chap," but Desmond was in the room, with a white, set face, trembling limbs and a look of horror in his eyes.

"Good God! Whatever is the matter?" he asked.

"John Meal—Matt Harding—" gasped Desmond.

"Have found Dan's boy?" eagerly.

"No. Their children have disappeared too!"

"*What?*"

"It's true! Mr. Winthrop told me. That's what caused the commotion when we arrived here this morning. This news had only just become known."

Alan seemed struck dumb. He looked at Desmond with unseeing eyes; his tongue swelled, and his mouth grew parched, but his lips would not form words. Then suddenly sounds came. "I wonder—is it the 'Curse' after all?"

"I wondered that too."

"When were they missed?"

"The children were all in school safe and sound. Lunch time came and they were seen to enter the playground with the other little ones. Ten minutes later the bell was rung for them all to reassemble.

"When the children did so, it was found that there were five children missing. Harding's three little girls and Meal's two had disappeared.

"The Head Mistress was furious, thinking they had all gone off together, and were playing truant. She sent a message round to the parents, so John Meal left his work in the fields, and insisted on a search being made. He swore it was the 'Curse' and that if he found his children he would find them in company with Harding's, and Dan's boy."

"Do you think it is a band of gypsies at work?" suggested Alan.

"There have been no gypsies near Marshfielden for over five years, they say. Besides that, the extraordinary thing is, the children disappeared from the playground."

"Well?"

"There is a ten foot wall all round it, so it is impossible for them to have climbed over. The only way out is past the Head Mistress' desk. She was sitting there the whole of the break, and declares that for the whole ten minutes of the luncheon time, the hall was entirely deserted and no one passed her. It seems impossible for them to have left the playground that way, and equally impossible by the front entrance."

"Why it sounds like witchcraft," said Alan.

A voice startled them. It was Mrs. Slater; her eyes red from weeping. "I beg of you two young gentlemen to go," she sobbed. "The 'Curse' is upon us."

"We are going," said Alan gently, "but we will do our utmost to discover the children. Now let us have our account." But the woman threw out her hands before her with a cry.

"No-No-Not a penny, sir."

"Oh, come, Mrs. Slater, don't be foolish. Let us have our bill," urged Alan.

But Mrs. Slater was obdurate. "It's only two days you owe me, sir, and I wouldn't touch a penny. You are quite welcome to what you've had, only go—go!" It was useless to argue and they left the house with heavy hearts, and went toward the blacksmith's in order to ask some one to take their luggage away for them.

"Good morning, Jim," said Alan pleasantly as they reached the forge. The man looked up and greeted them carefully, and as he saw Alan about to step across the threshold he gave a cry.

"Do'ant 'ee put your foot inside, gentlemen, do'ant 'ee please! Oh, the 'Curse' be upon us all!"

The boys shrugged their shoulders helplessly, and Alan spoke quickly.

"Send your boy up to Mrs. Slater's, will you, Jim? We want our luggage taken from there to Mrs. Warren's cottage at Corlot."

"You be agoin' away?" asked the man eagerly.

"Yes."

"I be mighty glad, sirs. I do'ant mean to be rude, sirs, of course we shall miss you sorely, but the 'Curse' has hit us sore hard since you came."

"Then you'll send your boy, Jim?"

Jim scratched his head. "Couldn't you manage it yourselves?"

"Surely it won't harm you to help us out of Marshfielden?" said Alan bitterly.

"I do'ant rightly know, sir, but—"

"Well?"

"I'd rather lend you my trolley, sir, than my boy. I do be mighty feared of the 'Curse'."

"All right, Jim, give us the trolley. We'll do it ourselves." The blacksmith wheeled it out, and gave it with half an apology to Alan.

"Don't apologize, Jim. I understand."

But the blacksmith had one more thing to say. "Do'ant 'ee trouble to bring it back to Marshfielden, sirs, leave it with Ezra Meakin. He'll bring it back for 'ee."

"Oh, don't fear, Jim, we won't return to Marshfielden once we've left. Ezra shall return it safely. We'll pay you now."

Jim was not too frightened to refuse payment, and the liberal amount of silver they showered on him touched him.

"I do'ant mean to be rude, sir," he began—but the boys had started on their way and were already wheeling the lumbering trolley down the uneven street.

Jim went back into his forge with a shaking hand. Had he helped the "Curse" by lending his trolley—doubly so, indeed, by accepting payment? And as he beat the hammer on the anvil, sparks flew out all around him like little red devils thirsting for prey!

ELLA M. SCRYMSOUR

When the miners came home that night they were unaware of the double tragedy that had come into their midst. The strangers were gone! They rejoiced, and Matt Harding was among the merriest. Mr. Winthrop and John Meal were away still searching for the missing ones, and no one had dared go to the mine to tell Matt of his loss.

He received the news with a set face, and strong self control. No word of comfort was given him by his comrades; he needed none. Blindly he staggered home, his loving, grief-stricken wife comforting and consoling him, bearing up herself in order to help the man she loved.

Silently the miners prepared for another fruitless search.

"The two young gentlemen are going to help," volunteered a woman in the crowd.

"We do'ant want no help," cried a man baring his brawny arm. "We'll find the chillun ourselves." But the search proved futile, as they almost expected, for as Murlock's boy had vanished completely, so had these other five children. But still stranger things were happening!

Mrs. Skeet possessed a dun cow of which she was very proud. Two days after the disappearance of the children, she tied it up in its stall in the byre, as it was suffering from an inflamed heel. Next morning when she entered the byre the cow had gone, and the whole of the thatched roof had been burnt away. Rushing into the cottage she called Mr. Winthrop, but there was no reply. She knocked at his bedroom door. The room sounded empty. Again she knocked, and fear made her open it. In a second she was out, and shrieking in her terror, for the window was open wide, and the vicar too had disappeared.

III

THE LIGHT

The London papers were burning with excitement. Marshfielden had at last become known to the vast, outside world, for the disappearance of so many of its inhabitants could no longer be hidden under a veil. After the vicar was found to be missing, Mr. Dickson at the mine made Slater promise to report the matter to the Kiltown police—the nearest constabulary to Marshfielden.

The detective officer and his men came over and pompously took notes and asked voluminous questions, but after a fortnight's search came no nearer solving the mystery. Then one of the constables disappeared too, and Sergeant Alken thought it was high time to report the matter to Scotland Yard.

Detective Inspector Vardon, the shrewdest, cleverest man at the Yard, came down immediately, and at once sent for Alan and Desmond Forsyth. He had been working out a theory coming down in the train and these two young men were very closely connected with it.

But after his first interview with them, he realized that his suspicions were entirely wrong, and knew he must look elsewhere for a clue. Alan told the full story without any hesitation whatsoever and explained how they themselves had suffered over the "Curse."

"Pooh Pooh!" laughed Vardon "We will leave the 'Curse' out of the question. These mysteries are caused by no witchcraft, but by a clever, cunning brain."

"Do you really think so?" asked Desmond.

"Of course," and Alan gave a sigh of relief as he murmured, "you don't know how that has relieved me. I was beginning to get quite a horror of the unknown."

"Of course it's an uncanny case," went on the Inspector, "but we'll solve the problem yet." Then he added laughingly, "I came down here prepared to suspect you two young gentlemen."

"Us? Why?"

"Well, all these mysteries occurred after you arrived here, and I found you were none too popular with the natives."

Desmond was indignant, but Vardon soon cooled him down. "See here, my dear sir. It's my business to suspect everybody until I convince myself of his innocence. I know now I was mistaken—therefore I have been candid with you."

The inquiries lasted some time, and every day brought some fresh disaster in its wake, filling the little village with misery and consternation, and the London editors' pockets with gold. Sightseers and tourists came galore to the stricken place, and the carrier between Marshfielden and Kiltown reaped a small fortune from the curious. Every day the papers recounted some fresh loss—perhaps a cow or a pig, but often a human life. Women kept inside their homes, and even the men folk walked about in pairs, so that they could help each other should the "unknown" fall upon them.

The two boys still worked in the mine, and the men, realizing at last that they were not the instigators of all the trouble, admitted them, charily enough at first, into their lives again.

Alan and Desmond were quite happy with Mrs. Warren, but missed Mr. Winthrop's kindly advice and friendship greatly. No trace of him had ever been found, and a younger man now took his parochial duties. Amateur detectives swarmed about the place, but the villagers in a body refused shelter to every one. Even the police officials themselves had to pitch tents in fields near by for their own use, as no bribe was high enough to obtain accommodation for them. Inspector Vardon was beginning to get disheartened; he had formed many theories during his stay, but upon minute investigation they all fell to pieces.

Walking away from the village one day, his hands behind his back and his head sunk upon his breast, deep in thought, he was suddenly awakened from his reverie by the sound of groans. Hedges were on either side of him, but he vaulted over the one from whence the sounds came.

There lay a sheep, its wool burnt away and its body scorched. He examined the helpless creature in pity, and the poor beast breathed his last. He was distinctly puzzled. There was no sign of fire anywhere at all—the poor animal alone had been hurt.

He pondered for a moment, and the thought came into his mind that perhaps this was a sequel to the strange disappearances and mysteries he had been trying to unravel—but after a moment, he cast the thought aside as being impossible, and decided that the accident must have been caused by a passer-by throwing away a match or a lighted cigarette, so he hurried across the fields to tell the farmer of his loss. That night, however, he had cause to think more deeply over the mishap to the sheep.

About six in the evening Ezra Meakin and a companion set out for Kiltown. They intended to stay the night there and come back by the carrier in the morning. At eight a shrieking, demented man came flying into Marshfielden, and fell in a heap across the steps that led up to the church.

Matt Harding was near and ran to his aid.

"Good God, it's Ezra!" he cried.

It was indeed, but a very different Ezra from the one who had left Marshfielden only two hours before. His clothes were scorched and his hair singed, while great blisters, that could have been caused only by excessive heat, marred his face.

"What has come over ye, lad?" asked Matt in concern.

"The fire! The fire!" cried Ezra hysterically. "It's taken Luke—he's gone," and with the words he lapsed into unconsciousness.

Matt lifted him up in his strong arms, and bore him to the nearest cottage. "Fetch the Inspector," said he curtly as he busied himself in trying to restore life to the inanimate form on the bed. At length he succeeded—a tremor passed through the body; the hands unclasped; the eyelids fluttered slightly. Then the lids slowly moved, and Matt stared down in horror at the wide open eyes. Blindly he stumbled out of the room, and fell into the arms of the Inspector.

"What's the matter?" asked Vardon.

Matt looked at him stupidly for a moment, and then gave a harsh, mirthless laugh. "Ezra—he's—he's—"

"Yes?"

"He's blind."

"Blind?"

Matt Harding could say no more, but sank down on to a chair and buried his head in his hands.

For a week Ezra lay delirious, and it was even longer than that before any one could get his story from him. When it came, it was disjointed and almost incoherent. After he and Luke Wilden had walked about a mile, he told them, they suddenly saw in the distance something that looked like a red hot wire on the horizon. Dancing and swaying it drew nearer to them, and fascinated they watched to see what it could possibly be.

Then suddenly, before they realized, it was upon them. It swooped down and coiled around Luke's body, and carried him off into mid-air.

As he tried to drag Luke from its clutches, the end of it, in curling around Luke still more firmly, struck him, and burnt and blinded him. He remembered no more; everything grew dim, and he fled down the long, straight road towards the village, instinct guiding him in place of his sight.

Every one heard the story incredulously, and it duly appeared in the London newspapers, and tended to make the "Marshfielden Mystery" as it was called, still more complicated and unfathomable.

Ezra recovered from the shock, but his eyesight was gone forever.

"Destroyed by fire," was the verdict of the eminent specialist who was called in to diagnose his case.

The story of the "Light" grew daily more terrifying. School children declared they saw it from the windows of their class-rooms, and when closely questioned about it, declared it was "a golden streak of fire, as thin as wire, that came rushing through the sky like lightning."

Then men began to watch for it, but somehow it seemed to evade most of them, and for some time, solitary statements were all that could be obtained with reference to it.

"What do you make of it, Alan?" asked Desmond one day, after it had been seen by three different witnesses at the same time and in the same direction.

"I don't know. Every one is not a liar, and at the same time every one cannot suffer from a like optical delusion. Every one who has seen this phenomenon agrees in every detail about its appearance."

"Yes, even the children," supplemented Desmond.

"Let's go for a walk," yawned his cousin. "I feel very tired to-day."

Mrs. Warren watched them going toward the gate with apprehension in her eyes, and just as they were about to pass through, she rushed to the door. "Be you agoin' out? Oh, do'ant 'ee go—do'ant 'ee—not to-night! I be afeared—mortal afeared."

"Oh, we'll take care of ourselves," laughed Desmond. "Don't you worry."

"But I'm afeared." She shivered as she spoke—but the boys laughed as they walked toward the Corlot Woods, a favourite spot of theirs.

As they crossed the stile leading to the path across the fields, they heard a dog crying pitifully. Alan, always tender-hearted towards dumb animals, stopped and looked round. Again came the mournful cry. "I think it must be across the way," said Desmond. Alan crossed the road, and then called out to his cousin.

"It's Slater's pup"—he bent over it closely—"Why its leg is broken and its fur is singed," he added in an awe-struck tone.

A rustling sounded behind him—an intense heat that nearly stifled him; he heard a sudden shriek—a groan.

Once more the "Light" had found its prey. Alan was alone!

"Come at once. Something terrible has happened to Dez. Don't delay. Alan."

Such was the telegram that Sir John Forsyth received upon arriving at his office the day after Desmond's disappearance. The two boys had kept him fully posted with all the news at Marshfielden. But as he always prided himself upon his strong common sense, he laughed with the boys at the suggestion that the "Curse" was responsible for the strange happenings in the little Derbyshire village.

His face blanched as he read the message, and instinctively he thought of the "Curse," yet put the thought aside as quickly as it came.

Masters, his confidential secretary, almost friend, looked at him pityingly.

"I am going to Marshfielden," announced Sir John.

"Shall I come with you?" asked Masters.

"Yes, Masters, I shall need you."

"An express leaves for Derby in half an hour," went on Masters. "If we book there, I can 'phone through for a car to meet us and motor us direct to Grimland."

"Yes! Yes! You arrange," and Sir John, who had grown as many years old as minutes had passed since he had had the news, sat with his teeth chattering and his limbs trembling.

"A motor car will be waiting for us at Derby," announced Masters as they took their seats in the train.

At last the whistle sounded, the flag waved, and the great engine snorted violently as it left the station.

Sir John, in his anguish of mind, was unable to sit still; up and down the corridor he walked until the passengers began to pity his white, strained face, and wondered what his trouble could be. Derby at last! Then followed a mad ride to Grimland. Alan was awaiting his Uncle at the pit head; he had not attempted to go to bed since the "Light" had taken Desmond from his side. Silently they gripped hands, and Sir John entered the little office and heard the whole story.

ELLA M. SCRYMSOUR

Alan wound up by saying, "Even as I tell the story, it seems almost incredible. As I turned round I saw Desmond in mid-air, with, it seemed, a fiery wire about him—and as I looked he vanished from sight."

Sir John was determined not to look upon it as witchcraft.

"It's man's devilry, I'll be bound," said he. "I'll swear it's not supernatural. Get all the scientists down—let them make investigations. I'll pay handsomely, but discover the secret I will."

The men, when they realized that Desmond had disappeared, were shamefaced, and came to Mrs. Warren's cottage to offer their sympathy. They tried to atone for their past conduct, by inviting both Alan and his Uncle to stay in Marshfielden. But Alan refused. "No, we'll stay here," said he. "Mrs. Warren has made me very comfortable. But perhaps we'll come and visit Marshfielden, if we may, and do our utmost to discover the perpetrator of this diabolical plot."

"Aye, do 'ee sur, do 'ee," said the men, and Alan felt strangely cheered by their friendship.

Sir John stayed with Alan for a fortnight, but as others had disappeared, so had Desmond, and no trace of him could be found. It was necessary for Sir John to return to town, in order that he might keep his business appointments and he asked Alan to accompany him.

"I curse the day I ever sent you to Grimland," said he over and over again.

"Don't upset yourself so, Uncle John! How could anyone have foreseen such a calamity. No, I'll stay here, and perhaps I may be the means of unravelling the mystery."

Police from the Continent, detectives from America, Asiatic wizards and sorcerers all came to Marshfielden—but none solved the mystery. For days no one stirred out of doors, and when at length they did so, it was with faltering steps and bated breath. No one knew who would be the next victim of the strange power that pervaded the place. Summer came again! A year had passed and left its mark on the once peaceful English village. Many white crosses adorned the little churchyard, but of all the new ones, few really marked the last resting place of those whose names they bore. A tiny tombstone in the far corner, under a weeping ash, named the spot consecrated to the memory of little Jimmie Murlock, the first victim of the "Light".

Moll Murlock had gone out of her mind. The shock had turned her brain,—and when, one after another, she learned of the tragedies that were daily coming on the little village, her senses left her entirely, and she was taken to the Kiltown asylum. Dan lived alone, in the little cottage, his hair snow white, and his features old and wrinkled; and none of his comrades dared recall the past to his mind. The new vicar who had taken Mr. Winthrop's place was very unpopular, and on Sundays the church was nearly half empty. Fear had turned their thoughts from Heaven, and while men openly cursed their God, the women whispered their curses in their hearts.

Inspector Vardon was still investigating, but his reports to the Yard were all the same. "Nothing further to hand" and then came the day when he added "Fear this is beyond me" and the chiefs looked at each other in dismay, as they feared it would remain one of the unsolved mysteries of the day. They had no shrewder or cleverer man in their employ than Marcus Vardon.

Then the "Light" suddenly disappeared. No more losses were reported, things went on more calmly, and women began to go out of doors more freely. Children returned to school, and Marshfielden had become almost normal again. For two months there were no casualties, and people hoped that the evil influence had departed for good, or burnt itself out.

And the next Sunday the new clergyman addressed from his pulpit a full church. The people had once more come to the house of God for comfort and to return Him thanks for the cessation of the past horrors. And his voice shook as he gave out his text, from the one hundred and twenty-first psalm:—

"The Lord shall preserve thee from all evil; the Lord shall preserve thy going out and thy coming in, from this time forth for ever more."

IV

THE OUTLET

For over six months Marshfielden was unvisited by the "Light". The inhabitants were settling down and work had begun again in earnest. Alan had been promoted second overseer at the mine, and as he had a firm way with the men, those under him worked diligently and well. Traces of sorrow were left on every one's face. It was impossible to eradicate them in a few months; years would not wipe away the affliction that had come into their lives.

The little village was opened up now. Motors traversed its cobbled streets, and the inhabitants so far allowed themselves to become "modernized" that the sign "Teas provided here" could be seen in nearly every cottage window down the street.

The influx of so many strangers made them forget the "Curse" and as once they believed in it, now they believed just as firmly that the disasters that had come upon them were wrought by some human agency. These six months of peace and quiet they hoped were precursors of the future. Inspector Vardon left the place, and nothing remained outwardly to remind them of the terrible past.

Then suddenly they woke up once more to sorrow. Two horses were found to be missing, and with them the little stable boy who tended them. The "Light" had returned!

Once more voices were hushed and heads were shaken gravely, as every one talked of the tragedy. A week passed, then Mrs. Skeet disappeared, and a few days later Mary Slater. The place swarmed again with detectives; the papers were again alive with the renewal of the tragedies.

The men in the mine worked silently; the only thing to break the stillness was the sound of the picks on the coal seams, or the running of the trolleys up and down the roads. Each feared to think of the horror that might await him when he reached his home at the end of his day's work.

The dinner hour came round, and each man sat silent and glum, eating his bread and meat, and uttering only a monosyllable now and again to his particular chum.

Suddenly there came a dull roar; the men rose to their feet in haste. They knew only too well that ominous sound—it was familiar to them all.

Mr. Dickson appeared, his face ashen. "An explosion in the South Road," said he. "Rescue parties to work at once."

In an instant everything was forgotten but the one desire to help their brothers in distress. With picks and ropes and lanterns they hurried down the main road, just at the bend of which a sheet of flame flared out suddenly, entirely enveloping the first man, and setting his clothing on fire.

In vain they played on the flames—it was useless. The fire had gained too much power. The rescuers were forced back to the cage at the bottom of the shaft, and all had to seek refuge above. Another sorrow had come upon the people of Marshfielden—their cup was full to overflowing as it was, yet Tragedy, the Humourist, was not yet content with his handiwork.

For two days the fire raged, and the willing rescuers were helpless in the face of such odds; on the third it quieted sufficiently to enable a rescue party to descend. Gradually they fought the flames, but not a trace remained of the men who had been caught like rats in a trap when the first explosion came. So Marshfielden was again in mourning, and broken-hearted widows and fatherless children went to the touching little memorial service that was arranged for the lost ones.

Alan was horror-stricken at the calamity that had befallen the mine. The thought of the men who had been burnt to death preyed on his mind; it was his first experience of such an accident, and it left upon him an indelible mark.

The mine was once more in working order, and he was doing some accounts in the office below, when a voice startled him. It was the voice of Mr. Dickson, and very grave.

"Go at once to the third shaft, Forsyth," said he. "The telephone has failed, and Daniels has reported that there is something wrong with the air pumps there."

"What? In the lower engine house?"

"Yes. We can get no further information. Make a careful examination, and if you suspect any danger, order the shift off and close the gates."

"Very good," and Alan, glad to have something to do that would occupy his mind, left the office, and jumped on to one of the empty trolleys that was being run by the cable to the second shaft, and would

　　　　　　　　　　　ELLA M. SCRYMSOUR

take him very near his destination. At the second shaft there were anxious faces.

"Something wrong at number three shaft, sir," said one of the men. "Daniels 'phoned us, but before he could tell us anything definite, the connections broke down."

"Thanks," said Alan shortly. "How many men are working there?"

"None, sir. They've not been working it to-day. Daniels and two other men have been inspecting a bulge that has appeared in the roof, and were arranging to have it fixed up with supports." Mechanically Alan walked down the low road that led to the third shaft. He pushed aside the heavy tarpaulins that hung across the roadways, and kept the current of air from flowing in the wrong direction, and as he passed through each one, he sniffed the air eagerly.

At last! The sickly, choking smell came up from the distance. It was one he knew and feared—a noxious gas. The roof became very low, and Alan had almost to crawl on his hands and knees, for there was no room for him to stand upright. Cramped, aching, he made his way along the narrow roadway. Suddenly he gave a sigh of relief; the roof rose to perhaps ten feet, and the road widened out into a vault-like chamber, perhaps twenty feet square. He heard a cry in the distance. "Help! Help!" It was Daniels—Daniels who came stumbling in and fell on the ground before him.

"Mr. Forsyth," he muttered, "run—save yourself—Rutter is dead— The gas is terrible. There's danger," and even as he spoke there came a dull roar and a flash, a terrible sound of falling—and Alan realized that the little chamber had indeed become a vault, for the force of the explosion had made the walls on either side cave in, and the entrance at each end was blocked up completely.

"Too late," murmured Daniels weakly. "I couldn't get here before." He fumbled at his belt, and Alan bent over him gently. "Water—water," he cried, and Alan unfastened the basket that was slung across his shoulders, and took from it a bottle of cold tea.

But even as he put it to the lips of the sick man, there came another roar in the distance, and Daniels fell back—dead.

Once more the dreaded sound was heard—once more an explosion had occurred in the mine. This time there was little fire—only water— water everywhere.

"Where is Mr. Alan?" asked the manager hoarsely. "Has he returned from the third shaft?"

"No, sir."

"Then he is in the midst of the danger. Rescue parties at once." But all these efforts were in vain. It was water this time—water that drove the men back to the mouth of the pit.

Pumps were put in order, and for hours the men worked to clear the mine, but when at last they were able to get near the spot where the accident took place—they, as they feared, found no trace of Alan.

From the second shaft the mine was in such a complete state of wreckage and ruin, that it would take weeks before it was even possible to get near the third shaft and the original scene of the disaster. So once more a casualty list was sent out, and this time was headed by the name

"Alan Forsyth."

Sir John heard the news with a set face. First Desmond, now Alan had been taken from him.

"Don't take it so to heart, Mr. Dickson," said he kindly. "The boy was doing his duty when death overtook him."

"I am broken-hearted, Sir John," said Mr. Dickson. "I feel that it was I who drove him to his doom. If I hadn't sent him to the third shaft that day, he would be with us still."

"It is fate," said Sir John simply.

But when he reached his office next day, he told Masters to get him his will from the safe. With trembling fingers he tore it across, threw the pieces in the fire and watched it burn. Then he said quietly, "I must make a new will, Masters. But to whom shall I leave my money? There is no one to follow me now." Suddenly he took up pen and paper and wrote hurriedly. "Fetch a clerk, Masters," said he, and when a clerk appeared he added quietly, "I want you both to witness my signature to my will," and with firm fingers wrote his name, and passed the paper over to Masters, making no effort to hide what he had written.

And Masters' eyes grew dim as he read—

"Everything I possess to the 'Miners' Fund' for widows and orphans, rendered such by accidents in the mine."

WHEN ALAN RECOVERED FROM THE shock of the explosion, he found his lamp was still burning dimly, and felt that he had a dull ache in his legs. He was covered with débris from head to foot and stifling from the dust and powdered coal that was all about. With difficulty he extricated himself, and realized that Daniels was completely buried.

Alone in the little chamber, a feeling akin to superstition came over him, and he moved away from the silent form, now shrouded in coal. Scarcely realizing the hopeless position he was in, he leant back, and closing his eyes, his worn out nerves gave way, and he fell asleep. He woke up with a start some hours later; his watch had stopped and he had no idea of the time. Madness seemed to be coming over him; his face was flushed, his head throbbed. He was ravenously hungry, and crossed to the dead man's side and searched about until he found the basket that contained Daniel's untouched dinner, and the bottle of cold tea. There was not a great deal of food—half a loaf, several thick slices of beef, a piece of cheese and some homemade apple tart.

Alan ate sparingly, for although his stomach clamoured for more, he realized that not yet was his greatest hour of need, and that later on he would need the food still more.

When he had finished, he took up a pick and wildly struck at the blocked exit, but only the echoes replied, laughing at his impotence. Flinging his tool down he buried his head in his hands and sobbed in bitter despair. His convulsive outburst left him calmer, and he began for the first time to think out a plan of escape. He knew that rescue parties would be working hard for his release—but could they reach him in time?

There was around him a death-like stillness, and he realized that the buried cavern was far from the bottom of the shaft. Then he suddenly wondered where the air came from. There must be an inlet somewhere, he thought, for the air he was breathing, although stuffy, was quite pure. He walked round the walled up chamber—round and round—but there was nowhere a weak spot. He sat down and tried to think coherently, and laughed aloud in his agony, as he wondered whether he would go mad. He looked up suddenly, and in his weakness imagined that the roof was trying to dance with the floor. He tottered round the place, hardly able to keep his feet in his wild fancy that the floor was moving, and laughed hysterically as he knocked against a jutting piece of coal, and thought the roof had got him at last. Then he quieted a little, and in the semi-darkness the dead figure of Daniels seemed to rise from the place where it lay, and point at him a menacing finger.

In terror, Alan backed to the further side of the little chamber, his eyes distorted, his limbs trembling. He watched the figure come

nearer—nearer—its long claw-like fingers were almost on his flesh—
"Ah!" he shrieked—the fingers were touching him with a cold, slimy
touch. He felt impelled to move forward—with the forefinger of the
dead man pressed to his forehead. He walked fearfully onward—then
his overwrought brain gave way entirely, and with another wild shriek,
he fell to the floor in merciful unconsciousness.

When he recovered, his dimmed senses hid from him much
of the past. His fever had abated, but he longed for water. His
mouth was parched. He crawled feebly to the basket where the
dead Daniels had kept his food, and drew out the bottle of tea.
There was very little left, but enough to take away the first keen
edge of his thirst. A torn newspaper that had been used to wrap
up some of the food rustled slightly. It startled him and he looked
round nervously. Again it moved, and seemed to be lifted up by
some unseen hand.

He watched it fascinated, then suddenly his face lighted up. "A
draught," he cried triumphantly. "Then it is from that direction I must
try and secure my release!" With renewed energy he began to pick at
the coal, in the fast dimming light of his lantern. Tirelessly he worked,
until success met his efforts and he had made a hole big enough to crawl
through, whence came the sound of rushing waters.

He lifted his lantern above his head in his endeavour to discover
where he was, and its feeble rays shone upon a swiftly flowing,
subterranean river that disappeared through a tunnel on either side. The
place he was in was very small and had no outlet except by way of the
water.

The river was narrow, perhaps four feet wide at the most, but with a
current so strong that Alan, good swimmer though he was, would not
have dared trust himself to its cruel-looking depths. Mechanically he
dropped into the water a lump of coal. There was a slight splash—but
no sound came to tell him that it had reached the bottom. He felt in his
pockets, and found half a ball of string. Tying a piece of coal to one end
he dropped it into the rapids, but his arm was up to his shoulder in the
river, and yet the coal had not touched the bottom.

He looked at the water curiously, and dabbled his fingers in the
brackish fluid. Suddenly a pain in his hand made him draw it out
quickly, and by the light of the lantern he saw it was covered with blood.
As he wiped it clean he saw the impression of two teeth on his first
and third fingers. Slowly his lips moved and he murmured—"There is

animal life in this river then—I wonder whither it leads—can there be humanity near too?"

His lantern was nearly out, and by its dying rays he tried frantically to fashion himself a raft, upon which he could trust himself to the waters. A trolley, smashed by the force of the explosion, lay near him. The wheels had been wrenched off and it was all in pieces. He looked at it carefully. The bottom piece was intact with half of one end still in position. He examined it critically. Would it float? Well he must risk that. He thought it would, and the end piece would serve as a hold to keep him on safely.

He was feeling faint—he ate the remains of his food, and with a reverent glance at the place where Daniels lay, he pushed the plank out on to the seething waters. Lightly he jumped on it himself, and, with a tight grip on the projecting pieces of wood, gave himself up to the mercy of the torrent.

His lantern went out; the darkness was intense; there was no sound but the lashing of the waters and the drumming of the raft against the sides of the tunnel. The current was swifter than anything he had ever known. The water just tore along at a breakneck speed, lashed over the frail raft and drenched Alan to the skin. He was faint. In a dim way he thought of his life—how empty it had been. Where was Desmond— and Uncle John? Cambridge came before his eyes, and he could almost see the serene picture of the "backs" with their quaint bridges and fields beyond.

He felt stiff. Mechanically he held on to the raft, even when his senses left him; and the frail wood with its worn burden of humanity, rushed on, down into the depths, carried by the river that was descending lower and lower through the earth.

Suddenly the raft gave a still more violent jerk, and Alan awoke to life once more. The rapids were over at last, and he was drifting along in waters that were as sluggish now as before they had been fast.

The tunnel widened, and he was aware that the intense blackness had gone, and in its place there was a purplish light that was soothing to his aching eyes. As the tunnel began to widen out, a path branched off at either side of the water.

The raft drifted on and at last found a harbour in a little, natural bay hollowed out in the bank. Alan stepped on land at last, his senses reeling. He had no idea of the time that had passed since he first started on that strange journey, and he felt hungry, weak and tired.

Slowly he walked along the river bank, and the purple lights grew stronger—then voices came upon his ear, and as he eagerly bent forward toward the unknown that faced him, above in Marshfielden, the clergyman was saying—

"And for the soul of Alan Forsyth—lately dead."

BOOK II
THE UNDERWORLD

I

A Strange Meeting

The ever present sense of "self-preservation" beats within the breasts of men most strongly at some period or other of their lives. It showed itself to Alan now. A fear of the supernatural came over him, and very quietly he stepped into the shelter of a jutting piece of rock, from which, all unseen, he could take a view of his surroundings.

He realized at once that it was to no mine that he had come, for strange, fantastic figures flitted about in the distance, figures that did not belong to the upper world.

Suddenly several of these figures leapt into the water and with a peculiar roll came swimming towards him at a terrific pace, and with a graceful movement vaulted out of the water and sat on the edge of the bank. He counted five of them, and saw that they were quite naked, and their skins were of a most peculiar purple shade, an almost exact match to the purple that lighted the place. They were talking volubly in an unknown tongue, and Alan leant forward from his hiding place to catch a better view of these strange, underworld people he had come among in such an extraordinary way. Short—he would judge them to be no more than three feet six, at the most, but with muscles that stood out like iron bands across their bodies. Their hair, in contrast to their skins, was of an almost flaxen hue, and in the females hung perfectly straight to their waists. The men wore theirs cropped close, except on the very top of their heads, where it was allowed to grow long, and was plaited and braided, and fixed with ornaments.

Their features were extremely pointed, and their eyes were small, but of a piercing brilliance. From the middle of the forehead, grew a tusk or horn, about ten inches long. For some time Alan puzzled over the strange horn, but its use was demonstrated to him only too soon. It was a weapon of offence. One of the women suddenly rose, and began an unintelligible tirade against her companion. The man did his best to pacify her, but it was useless, and suddenly she bent down, and with a viciousness Alan could hardly realize, thrust her tusk into the man's face, and with a wild shriek dived into the water and swam away. The man was left with a gaping wound on his cheek, from which flowed a sickly, purply-white fluid. With hoarse chuckles, the remaining three swam off, leaving the man alone. Alan watched him intently. Diving to the bottom of the river, the creature stayed there an incredibly long time, and then reappeared with a bunch of purple water weeds in his hand. He laid a handful of these weeds on his wound, to which they adhered by a secretion of their own, and the man swam away also, leaving Alan more alone than before.

His faintness grew still more unbearable and he came out of his hiding place, caring for nothing but to get food; but his limbs were weak, and he fell, and found that he could hardly drag himself along. As he lay on the ground, a sweet smell assailed his nostrils, and looking round he realized that on little low bushes all about him, hung a luscious-looking, purple fruit.

He picked one and examined it. It was like a grape in size and appearance, but was velvet to the touch, like a peach. He tasted it—it was sweet and wonderfully refreshing, so he ate his fill, with his last ounce of strength pulled himself once more into the friendly arms of the overhanging rocks, and fell asleep. When he awoke he made another meal off the fruit that grew everywhere in such abundance—it was filling and seemed nutritious, and the juice appeased his thirst. He looked carefully around him. There was no one about, and keeping within the shadow of the walls, he made his way down the path. It was not an easy road, for the stones were sharp and the way rough, and the constant effort to keep himself hidden tired him. At last he came to the end of the passage, and saw that the river widened out into a large lake, about two hundred yards across. Peculiar craft lay moored at either side, and in the centre was an island on which grew purple vegetation—short, stunted, purple trees, and a peculiar, purple moss, that covered the ground like grass.

It was a weirdly picturesque scene. Purple light shone from purple trees that were planted at regular intervals everywhere. The light seemed to evolve from nothing, as it showed under the large purple leaves that acted as shades—yet Alan believed it was partly natural, and partly controlled by the power of the purple people he had seen.

A wide passage went to the right, and in front of him Alan saw a large chamber, bounded on one side by the lake. Branching off in all directions were other passages which seemed to open out into other chambers and roadways, in fact the whole place seemed like a veritable warren.

Suddenly an awful crash sounded, followed by the beating of drums and the clashing of cymbals and away in the distance he saw a procession of purple folk passing rapidly, all in the same direction. Cloaks of the same purple hue fell from their shoulders, and the women wore veils on their heads. He watched them with interest. The figures passed in quick succession, then they became less and less frequent, until only one or two stragglers came hurrying up. The sound of singing rose on the air, and Alan conjectured that it must be some religious service to which they all were bent. After the last one had disappeared Alan waited some minutes to see if any more would pass, but as no one else came he walked slowly in the direction from which the multitude had appeared.

In a very short space of time he found himself in a street. Peculiar huts lined either side of it, huts with their doors open wide and no sign of life. He looked about him carefully, and ventured inside one. He found it was divided into three rooms—all on the ground floor. There was a sleeping room, for mattresses of that same purple moss, dried, were on the floor; there was also a living room and a kitchen. Warily he looked about him, and then went out into the street. The main street merged into smaller ones and at last, at the very end, a large building rose upon the scene—larger and more impressive than any of the others he had passed on his way. All this time he had seen no sign of life—the inhabitants were content to rest secure in their belief of inviolability.

Cautiously Alan crept toward the building and as he came close to it, he saw that a sentry had been left on guard—a sentry with an evil-looking knife slung across his shoulders, and a scimitar-like instrument in his hand. The man was looking away into the distance and did not hear Alan's approach. "Hullo," said Alan pleasantly. The effect was magical. The undersized creature swung round and faced the strange, white man. For an instant he remained quite still, and then, with a sudden movement that Alan was unprepared for, sprang at him, and commenced to beat his horn in Alan's face. In vain the white man tried to free himself from the savage grip; he was no match for this strange creature of the underworld. His adversary made no sound as he gradually weakened Alan, and at length he swung him over his shoulder as if he had been a child, and marched with him at a quick pace down the street.

The shock, the strenuous time Alan had been through, took his senses away, and when he came to, he found he was lying on a soft mattress and there was a stabbing pain in his arm. A fantastic figure was bending over him, a figure that licked its lips cruelly as it surveyed its victim, and Alan realized at once that he was in an enemy's hand.

The figure spoke to him, but Alan was unable to understand the jargon it uttered. Suddenly it issued a command, and four men, clad in a kind of armour, came up to Alan, and lifting him up carried him once more out of the place into the street. Outside they placed him on a litter, drawn by four men, and at a fast trot dragged him through the streets. The air grew hotter and hotter, until Alan felt choked; at last, however, they came to their journey's end, and Alan was rudely hauled out of the litter, and found himself standing outside high gates. They were very massive, of a gold colour, and heavily barred on the inner side. One of his captors struck a gong affixed to the wall, and in answer to its strident tones, two women, heavily veiled, came running toward them and unfastened the locks. Alan was almost too weak to walk, but was pushed along a passage until he found himself in a place so vast, so wonderful, so awful, that it left him breathless and trembling.

It was a huge temple into which he had been brought—so vast that he was unable to see the further end of it. An enormous high altar stood near him, and at intervals were smaller ones all round the walls. Statues and images, both grotesque and beautiful, ornamented the place, and the atmosphere reeked with a pungent incense that was sickly and overpowering. But it was not only the vastness and weirdness that left Alan breathless—it was a wonder more terrible, more awe-inspiring than his mind had ever conceived.

The whole of the centre of the temple was composed of a fire—a fire that ran down the length of the elliptically shaped building, and disappeared in the distance in a red glow. A glass-like wall rose to perhaps three feet above the level of the flames, and through it Alan could see into the heart of a bottomless pit of fire, whose flames of all hues danced and swerved and shimmered in a wild ecstasy. The substance of the fire he could not guess—but the fire possessed a terrifying appearance that alone was enough to break the spirit of any mortal man.

The heat was intense, yet the natives did not seem to notice it, and they led Alan to a pillar that rose near the high altar, bound him to it by a heavy chain, and then left him there, alone. He watched his captors disappear one by one. His brain was reeling. He wondered whether all he had seen was but the result of fever, and he would wake up presently to find himself in Mrs. Slater's pretty little cottage at Marshfielden.

But no, he knew he was awake and not dreaming,—and looked about him in bewilderment. That there were people living in the centre of the earth he would never have believed—yet here was the proof—for was he not a captive in their clutches?

He looked at the fire. Never before had he seen anything like it. It seemed to go deep into fathomless depths, and its flames danced and sang and crackled maliciously. He wondered whether he would be thrown into its fiery bosom by the purple folk, and shivered to think of it, but then a feeling of relief came over him. After all it would be a quick death, for nothing could live long in those hungry flames.

Immediately opposite him was the high altar. Six steps led up to it, and he looked with interest at them and at the red stains they bore; and with an uncanny laugh, asked himself whether these were blood. If so, whose? Round the walls on pedestals were huge, grotesque figures; and interposed here and there, an image of almost seraphic beauty, that contrasted strangely with the insidious cruelty and hideousness of the place.

To the right of Alan was a still more grotesque figure. About twenty feet high it stood, with cruel eyes looking out across the fire. Its jaws were open wide, and attached to the under jaw was a peculiar slide made of the same transparent glass-like substance that encircled the flames. This slide reached from the idol's mouth to the edge of the furnace, and suddenly drops of perspiration stood out thick on Alan's brow. The meaning of the slide was only too clear. The victims of these underground savages were forced inside the idol, disgorged by it on to the slide, and thrown into the fire—a living sacrifice. Time passed, and Alan wondered dimly whether he would ever be able to reckon it again.

Suddenly upon his ear came wild yells and fanatical shrieks, the banging of drums, the clashing of cymbals followed by discordant singing. Then the din quieted a little, only to reassert itself once more as the natives reached the door of their temple. Alan gasped in horror as a horde of grinning purple men swarmed into the place, two of whom left their places in the procession, and coming to him caught hold of him roughly.

Priests and acolytes took their place in the procession, which was brought to an end by a high priest, who wore the most wonderful purple robes and purple gems; slowly he walked to the high altar, his richly embroidered vestments hanging to the ground, and two acolytes carried the ends of his cloak, which they kissed reverently as they ascended the bloody steps. When he reached the top step he turned his back on the altar itself, and prostrated himself before the fire, the whole company of worshippers following his example. Boys arrayed in vestments almost the facsimile of the ones worn by the high priest, swung censers aloft, which exuded their sickly perfume, and sent the faint, blue smoke mingling with the smokeless flames of the big fire.

Then they rose and the ceremony began, priests intoned; an invisible choir sang; and the congregation chanted, while live pigs, oxen, horses and goats were thrown alive into the flames. There was a wild shriek from each animal as it felt the heat, a crackling—and it was reduced to ashes. Alan wondered when his turn would come, and longed vainly for the blessed relief of unconsciousness.

Suddenly his captors lifted him high above their heads, and strapped him to the altar. And then in front of him was placed a goat, and two priests, disengaging themselves from the crowd, disembowelled the animal alive, flung the still living and tortured creature to the flames, and stood over Alan with their ugly knives, still dripping with blood, suspended above him. Then the steel came flashing down and he wondered that he felt no pain, but he realized that his clothes had been deftly cut away from him, and he was left on the altar slab, naked. Incense was wafted over him, and he was bathed from head to foot in sweet smelling oils. Then he was released from the altar and had to submit to being robed from head to foot in purple garments. Sandals were placed upon his feet, and for a moment he wondered whether these people really meant him well—but even as the thought passed through his mind, the back of the great idol swung open on hinges, revealing a flight of steps within; and Alan knew the hour of his torture had come.

With incense rising to his nostrils and the noisy clangour of bells in his ears, Alan was led, powerless, although resisting, to the open doorway. The steps inside were heated until they blistered his feet, and the pain caused him to mount higher where he hoped to get relief. When he reached the topmost step, and stood in comfort, realizing that it was cool, the door below swung to. He was alone, and saw that he was standing in the head of the idol, looking through its gaping jaws into the heart of the fire. Then suddenly he felt a jolt beneath him, and realized that his ankles were encased in iron bands. Again the idol's body shook, and he was thrown on his belly. Slowly the slide was coming into position; another convulsive move of the idol, and he was half way down it, and smiled as he saw in imagination a tank of water below him in place of the fire, and himself in a bathing suit, ready to descend the water chute!

Slowly, slowly he began to slip, and wondered why he did not go faster. He tried to kick his feet and so enable himself to get over with death—but the iron anklets were holding him fast, and he knew he would reach the flames only when his torturers desired it. The heat was now unbearable; the flames were leaping up toward him; he already felt upon his cheek their fiery breath. His arms were stretched out before him, and he was at too great an angle to draw them up. Then came a feeling of excruciating agony, an agony almost unbearable. His fingers had reached the fire! powerless to take them out, he writhed round and round in a vain endeavour to obtain relief. No sound came from between his clenched teeth to express the pain he was enduring.

Suddenly above the uproar he heard a woman's voice, commanding and imperious. There was a sudden silence, and then, with a terrible jolting of the idol, Alan once again found the slide rising and he was safe inside the belly of the image. Tears trickled down his face, tears of pain. Of course the mechanism had gone wrong. All that excruciating torture would have to be borne again. He held his mutilated hands out in front of him. Numbness had set in and intense cold.

The door in the idol opened and a beautiful girl mounted the steps and came toward him. She was small, like her companions around her, and of the same colour, and the horn in her forehead, painted gold and hung with gems, seemed in some weird way to enhance her beauty. Almost of English mould, her features were small and pretty, and her wonderful hair hung like a mantle of gold far past her knees. Upon her head she wore a crown of gold, and Alan thought she must be queen of the underworld people, for evidently her power was paramount. She placed her cool, firm hands on Alan's shoulder, and led him down the now cool stairs; and once more he found himself in the temple. He was dazed, and could hardly realize that this woman had saved him. From a basket an attendant carried she took ointments and healing lotions, and bathed and bound up his poor, maimed hands. The effect was almost magical. The burning ceased, and a feeling of relief came over him. She then offered him her arm, and led him to the outer gates of the temple. There a small chariot was awaiting her, pulled by a hideous beast that was the beast of burden in the underworld. Small, with an ungainly body and short legs—its head small in proportion, it had immense tusks and a beard covered the lower portions of its face. Indeed, the "Schloun" was a mixture of rhinoceros and goat, and had the bulldog's squareness of build. It was a hideous animal, and Alan shuddered as he took his place in the chariot. The equipage was extremely comfortable, the floor, upon which they sat was laden with rugs and cushions, and side by side, the man and his protector rode through the strange streets of this underground world.

At last they stopped in front of an imposing building, even larger than the one where Alan had originally been captured. The woman led Alan into it, and took him into an apartment that was evidently reserved for her private use. A soft, purple carpet lined the floor, while purple curtains hung across the door. The woman pointed to a cushion and sat down, and Alan, understanding her meaning, sat down near her. She spoke to him slowly and repeatedly, but he was unable to understand her tongue.

"Kaweeka" she repeated over and over again, and at last he understood. It was her name!

Then he rose and went to the door and called "Kaweeka" and the woman smiled and nodded and tapped her heel on the ground to signify her delight.

Suddenly she rose and stood beside him, and putting her arms about him, planted a very English kiss full upon his mouth. Alan who had never flirted, never cared for any girl, when he was in England, felt his pulses leap and a wild thrill pass through him at the touch of her lips. Then a sense of shame came over him. What was she? Why, hardly human. If he succeeded in getting to the upper world again, and took her with him, scientists would want to cage her as a newly discovered animal! Could he wed her?—marriage?—love?—passion?—he knew too well which sense she had aroused when her lips touched his.

He drew away from her in loathing, and a hard light came into her eyes as she imperiously put her lips up to his. Her fascination was undeniable, but there was something unholy, almost unclean, about her; and although passion shook him from head to foot, he turned away and walked to the other side of the apartment.

But Kaweeka followed him. She twined her arms about his neck and drew his head against her breast, and he felt the wild throbbing of a heart next to his. "Kaweeka," he cried, "Kaweeka." And he drew her to him still closer, forgetting all else but that a warm living thing was lying in his arms, and that thing a woman.

ELLA M. SCRYMSOUR

Suddenly Kaweeka disengaged herself, and with a low laugh intimated to Alan that she wished him to follow her. She led the way through a long corridor, up a flight of wide and softly carpeted stairs to a room on the second floor. It was a wonderful apartment, unlike anything he had ever seen, and even as he looked about him, he heard a low chuckle, and Kaweeka disappeared through the door, fastening it behind her.

Alan drew a breath of relief. The air seemed purer for her absence, and he looked round him curiously. Low divans furnished the room, and on a wonderful table of crystal was food and wine. He was hungry and faint from his experience in the temple, and he fell to on the repast that had been provided and felt the better for it.

In one corner of the room stood a large jar of bright yellow porcelain, and it was filled with blue, green, yellow and purple fungi—flowers they could not be called—but as fungi they were almost beautiful. Their stems were long and bare of leaf, and the flower bloomed at the very top. Some of the "flowers" were almost like poppy heads, others like variegated mushrooms—while one or two blooms at least reminded Alan most forcibly of the pretty pink seaweed he had admired when on a holiday at Rozel in Jersey. The vividness of colouring made a wonderful effect against the purple background and if his position had not been so hopeless, he would have thoroughly enjoyed his strange adventure.

There were no windows in the room—at least not what the world above would understand by the word—but there was an opening overlooking the narrow causeway that served to let in light and air. There was no shutter to it, only heavy purple draperies hung at either side, which could be drawn across if privacy was desired.

In two corners of the room were tall braziers, and Alan touched the large switch that protruded from them. Instantly the room was flooded with the soft, purple light that seemed to exude from the trees; and Alan felt that his first conjecture was right—the trees possessed some natural light which the natives had learnt to control, and which they ran along the branches much in the same way that we run electricity along cables. At any rate the result was very pleasing, and the light possessed none of the glare that is characteristic of electricity.

His investigations being finished he inspected a heavy curtain that was draped across the wall nearest the "window" opening. He pulled it aside, and behind it was revealed a door. It was made on the sliding principle, and as it moved slightly he saw revealed before him a room that seemed almost an exact replica of the apartment he was in. Carefully he stepped inside—and there in the further corner, he saw a low mattress, and in the semi darkness he thought he saw it move ever so slightly. He drew back startled, but on his ears came the sound of deep breathing: some one or something was sleeping there. He moved cautiously toward it, and saw the figure of a man lying on the couch. Suddenly the sleeper turned over, leaving his face exposed to view. Alan uttered an exclamation that awoke the sleeping man. For a moment there was silence and then a great cry rang on the air—"My God—it's Alan."

"Dez, old boy!" cried his cousin, his sobs coming thick and fast. "Dez! Thank God I've found you. Steady, boy, steady—it's two against those purple devils now," and the strong man bent low and sobbed as if his heart would break.

II

The Origin of the People

For some time after the cousins met again so strangely, they could only grasp each other's hands—their hearts were too full for words.

"I'm like a silly woman," said Desmond at last "but oh! Alan, I seem to have been in this Hell a lifetime."

"Poor old boy."

"No one to speak to but Kaweeka—no one to look at but Kaweeka—always Kaweeka—until I felt I should go mad."

"How did you get here?" asked Alan at last. "We were never able to discover the origin of the Light. Oh," he shuddered, "I shall never forget seeing you carried off—whirling through space—it was terrible."

Then Desmond began his story in a quick jerky way, as if eager to get it done. "The Light came upon me so suddenly, I didn't realize what had happened. All I knew was—that I had a fearful burning sensation round my waist—and that I was being carried through space. Then came a descent through darkness which seemed to last a lifetime. I seemed to be going on and on—and then suddenly I found myself in the presence of the high priest in the temple here. I have no recollection of how I reached it—I think I must have lost consciousness and then—"

"Well?"

"Well I felt so ill after the journey that the rest seems all hazy. I know I participated in some of their vile religious ceremonies. I was forced into the belly of Mzata—"

"Is that the idol?"

"Yes. I remember the heat was overpowering. Then before I realized anything else, Kaweeka came and rescued me. She carried me here, and—well, old chap, the rest isn't pleasant. The woman is a fiend. Down here there is no one for her to allure, and as I believe I was the first white man to get here alive, she gave me the benefit of her powerful wiles. She admitted me into a kind of harem, in which I am"—he laughed bitterly—"her chief husband."

"My God," said Alan hoarsely, "You have married her, Desmond?"

Desmond nodded. "I suppose that's what it is—but I don't understand much of what she says. At any rate I was taken to the temple and after a long ceremony, she came forward and acknowledged me before the congregation. Time after time I've been within an ace of killing myself, for the situation is unbearable. But she has spies everywhere and every chance has been taken from me."

"Can you understand her tongue?"

"No, up to now I have only managed a very few words. I know her name. I know that Mzata is the god of their temple,—but I cannot get further than that."

"What do you do all day?"

"Nothing! What is there to do? I go out and Kaweeka accompanies me, caressing me the whole time. Should she not come—then I am followed by her spies. The natives watch me with suspicion; they seem to lick their, lips as I pass, and long to fall upon me and throw me to the flames. I've seen sights since I've been here, and heard sounds that would make the strongest man tremble. Alan," solemnly, "I've seen human beings—human beings that we knew in Marshfielden—people we respected and loved—thrown to the fire through the medium of Mzata. I saw Mrs. Skeet brought here—shrieking—sobbing—crying— and I saw her thrown into the belly of the idol. I was in the temple and rushed forward to save her, even if death had been my reward— but Kaweeka gave a signal and I was seized and bound and forced to witness her tortures. She saw me and recognized me, and as she was sent nearer and nearer the flames she cried to me to aid her. 'Mr. Desmond! Save me! Save me!' she shrieked, and do you know, Alan, as the flames closed over her body, I heard 'Mr. Desmond! Save me!' come wailing up through the fire."

"Then that is the grave of all the lost ones from Marshfielden?"

"I am afraid so."

"What exactly is the 'Light'?"

"I don't know—I've tried to find out—but it is some power of their own that they have learnt to control. I think it is some force—something to do with the natural light that pervades this place. It is sent through the earth itself by the aid of some infernal mechanism, and when it reaches the world above, it attracts a victim which it strikes and brings back—a living, sacrifice to this hell down here."

"It is a very terrible menace to our world."

"Indeed it is! Some of the victims arrive mutilated and burnt, and welcome the fire to deliver them from their pains. In some miraculous way I was unhurt by it—at least I was burnt very slightly, and soon recovered. But, Alan! How did you get here? Did the Light bring you too?"

"No, Desmond!" And Alan told the story of the coal mine disaster and how he found the river that brought him to his cousin.

Suddenly their eyes met, and a quick flash passed through their brains simultaneously. Alan was the first to dispel it.

"It's no good, Desmond, we couldn't possibly escape the way I came. We could not battle with the current that brought me here. The water is too deep to attempt to wade, and there isn't so much as a ledge on either side to which we could cling."

"What are we going to do then?"

"Of course we must try and escape—but how? As far as I can judge we must be somewhere near the centre of the earth. How can we get implements to cut our way back again—and even if we did, how long would it take us to do it? No, we are in a tough position, and there isn't even a telegraph pole or telephone wire to aid us."

Their conversation was broken by the entrance of Kaweeka. Unannounced and without deigning to knock she entered the room, and both men rose to their feet hurriedly.

Alan stood with folded arms and a stern expression upon his face. The moment's madness of the yesterday had passed. He knew the woman, siren, devil, call her what you will, to be sensuous and foul—and his passion had passed, leaving him firm in his strength and with power to resist her.

Like a serpent she glided up to them, and touched them playfully on their cheeks, and then, ignoring Desmond entirely, she held out her arms invitingly to Alan. Sickened he turned away, but she came up behind him, and put her arms about his neck. Brutally he pulled them apart and flung her from him with a very British "damn"—which, though the word might be unintelligible to her, left the meaning clear and plain. A look of fury, followed by one of malicious hatred, passed over her features, and she turned abruptly from Alan to Desmond, and in a low monotonous tone crooned in her own language to him.

Desmond fought against her powerful wiles for some time, but he was frail, and her all pervading power drew him nearer and nearer. Once more her arms were open, and Desmond was drawn into them as a fish is drawn into a net.

Kaweeka gave a low chuckle, and turned in triumph to Alan. With a half step forward he raised his hand as though he would strike her, then drew back in time, turned quickly and left them alone. Up and down the outer room he paced and watched from the opening the stream of purple people walking up and down the street—men, women and children, all bent on work or pleasure. In a way they seemed to be civilized, yet it was a civilization unknown to the upper world. An oppression came over him and he rushed to the door and tried it. It was unlocked. That was more than he had hoped for, and he hurried down the stairs to the outer door. But there his progress was impeded, for a sentry on guard drew a peculiar kind of spear and prevented his passing.

Alan cursed and swore at him, and then tried more pacific measures to get his way; but the man was impervious to everything, and Alan retraced his steps and took refuge in a little alcove not far from the main entrance. Suddenly a hand on his shoulder startled him, and turning he saw Desmond looking at him in a shamefaced manner.

"We can go out, Kaweeka says,—at least that is what I understand her to mean. Will you come now, Lanny?"

As he used the old boyish name, Alan felt a sob rise in his throat and he grasped Desmond's hand.

"Come on! old boy," said he, "I want to talk to you."

Kaweeka was standing near the door as they reached it, and she waved to them to intimate they were free to go out—but as they passed her they heard her issue a command to the guard at the door who followed them, and although they realized that he was for them a protection among the wild people of the underworld, yet it stripped them of all hope of ultimate escape.

"Dez," said Alan at last, "Do you love Kaweeka?"

"No," in a low voice.

"Old chap, cut loose from her. When we get to the world again—don't let our stay down here have coarsened us. The life is sordid enough, God knows, but don't let *us* be sordid."

"She has such power, Lanny."

"I know, Dez, but fight it down, boy, I'll help you."

"Thanks, old chap." Then suddenly, "Do you think we shall ever get away from here?"

"I mean to have a try, how, when, or where I don't know yet, but there are two of us now and we must fight hard for our freedom."

"I suppose we really ought to try and gain the confidence and trust of some of the natives?"

"That won't be easy, but we must make the most of any opportunity that may come our way."

Then they lapsed into silence as they looked about them in interest at the quaint places they passed. The streets twisted and turned like a veritable maze, and the boys wondered how the natives could ever remember their way about. There were no shops to be seen—the whole community seemed to live on roots that grew abundantly everywhere, variegated fungi that grew in clusters on low bushes by the water's side, and fruits. Fish too was eaten at times, but it seemed as if it was only allowed to be consumed during certain periods when religious festivals were being kept.

Every home seemed to possess all the necessaries for weaving the moss into garments for wear. There was little difference in the men's and women's dress—a tunic that was worn wide open at the breast and a slightly shorter skirt on the male was all that distinguished them, except of course, the training of the hair.

The families seemed to live in intense domestic happiness, but jealousy made them suspicious of their neighbours, and members of the bodyguard of the high priest and Kaweeka were continually called in to check the bickerings and quarrels that were always taking place.

Alan and Desmond walked on heedless of time; suddenly their guard came up behind them, and in no gentle manner intimated to them that it was time they returned.

Their life grew very monotonous, but they were together—that was their only comfort. Kaweeka had grown sullen and silent. She seemed to realize that her uncanny power was useless now that Alan had appeared on the scene, and she brooded over the slight he had put upon her when he scorned her.

They still lived in her house, but seldom saw her. Food was brought them at regular intervals. Sometimes days passed and they were not allowed to go out. At other times Kaweeka would grow soft and gentle and would send them out in her chariot, and they would take their food and be away all day, wandering by the underground rivers and lakes, or gathering fruits in the quaint dwarf copses, where the tallest tree was not more than four feet high.

Time hung very heavily on their hands, and there seemed no hope of their ever being able to extricate themselves from their terrible position.

They learnt to weave the moss into tunics for themselves, and they made mats and rugs for their apartments. Grasses they plaited into belts—and that constituted the whole of their amusement and work.

Their personal guard, Wolta, was a particularly fierce individual, who had never recovered from his violent dislike of the white strangers. What services he did for them he did grudgingly, and their food was often ill-served and spoiled through his spite.

Then came the day when a new man appeared to wait on them. They could not understand what he said, but Okwa intimated to them that they were to follow him. He led them down to the lower floor and out into a courtyard behind the house.

There in a rude coffin, fashioned of cloth stretched on poles, lay Wolta—dead. The boys watched in interest, for this was the first death they had seen since they had been in the underworld.

No cover was placed over the dead man, no religious ceremony was held over the inanimate form. The coffin and its burden was carried down the dark street by two bearers. On they went until they came to a dark lake whose waters were black and evil-looking. Without any ceremony the body was pitched out into the water. It floated eerily for a few minutes, the eyes open wide and the mouth contorted into a grin. Then there was the sound of a splash and a large head appeared, followed by another and another. There was the snapping of teeth and the sound of closing jaws—and an ominous purple stain floated on the top of the lake.

The boys turned away sick at heart from the horrible sight—and when they did look again—all trace of Wolta had vanished—there remained only the same stain on the bosom of the water. The two bearers calmly folded up the collapsible coffin and slung it across their shoulders;—it was quite ready for the next victim that death might claim.

"It's horrible," said Desmond with a shudder. "I wonder whether they give all their dead to those filthy man-eating fish?"

"I should think so," answered Alan. "Their idea of burial seems worse than some of the rites of the South Sea Islanders."

Their days passed in sickening monotony, and their lungs ached for fresh air and salt breezes. They spoke to no one, saw no one but Okwa, and they were getting into such a state of nerves, they could hardly converse sanely one with the other. Okwa came in one day and intimated that they could go out. Moodily they walked down the streets and made their way to a river near by—a guard, as usual, following close behind. They sat down on the steep mossy banks that led to the water's edge; depressed and wretched they remained moody and silent. Suddenly there came the sound of a scuffle behind them—a startled cry

ELLA M. SCRYMSOUR

and a splash. A little girl had stumbled, and rolling down the slippery bank was struggling in the water. The current was very strong, and the little maid, swimmer though she was, was unable to battle with the rapids. Twice her head had disappeared from sight.

In a second Alan was in the river after her, and diving down, brought her to the surface; but the whirlpools were strong and treacherous and the water deep, and it was only with the greatest difficulty that he succeeded in reaching the bank, where Desmond was waiting, in whose arms he placed the now unconscious child. But the strain he had undergone proved almost too much for him, and even as he saw the child into safety, he slipped back into the river and the boiling waters closed over his head. He rose again to the surface and with an almost superhuman effort clung to the bank, and Desmond and their guard pulled him ashore.

His first thought was for the child who was lying seemingly lifeless on the ground. He knew the elements of first aid, and vigorously moved her little arms above her head, and then pressed them well against her ribs. Gradually the air was pumped into her lungs, she opened her eyes, smiled, and in a very few moments afterwards was able to stand.

"There, run along, little one," said Alan, kindly—but the child put her lips to his and clung to him, and he had perforce to hoist her to his shoulder and march home with her, ensconced there happily like a little queen. The guard prostrated himself before them, and bowed and kissed the ground.

"You've made a conquest," laughed Desmond. "I wonder who she is." As they neared the precincts of the city they heard the clashing of cymbals and the beating of drums. A religious procession was in progress. Alan and Desmond stepped aside to allow it to pass. A long column of veiled temple virgins led the way, followed by priests and acolytes and tiny children, consecrated at birth to the temple, who scattered leaves on the ground. Then an aged patriarch hove in sight, borne on a litter with a canopy of gold.

The little girl became excited. "Abbi! Abbi!" she shrieked, and wriggled to get free from her throne on Alan's shoulder. The priest's face grew livid. He uttered a cry of rage and gave a swift command to two attendants by his side. Instantly the symmetry of the procession was broken, and Alan and Desmond were bound with rope and dragged away. It was all done so quickly that they had no time to resist.

The little girl had watched the scene with wondering eyes, and when she realized the whole purport, flung herself into Alan's arms. The priest issued another quick command, and with the little one holding fast to her rescuer's hand, she obviously told the story of her escape.

When she had finished the priest kissed her tenderly, and then knelt low before the two boys and kissed their feet. Then they were given places in a litter behind the high priests and were taken to the temple—this time as honoured guests.

They were led to the altar, and very suspiciously and timidly seated themselves on the steps, one on either side, which the high priest indicated to them. The ceremonial service was very long and tedious, but was unaccompanied by any sacrificial rites, much to the satisfaction of the two boys.

Then the priest stood facing the people, and held out a hand to each of the boys who stood shamefaced and awkwardly beside him. There followed an address, and the boys knew it was the story being told to the people of the rescue by Alan.

When the priest had finished speaking, he bent down and kissed their hands, and wildly the congregation flocked to the altar rail to follow his example. They were accepted by the whole community as friends. Their lives were no longer in jeopardy. Then the boys resumed their seats and the ceremony of the temple was concluded.

During the service Alan's eyes were riveted on some peculiar characters that were inscribed on the walls, at intervals, as far as eye could reach. It was a group of hieroglyphics repeated over and over again, and there was something oddly familiar about them—yet he was unable to guess exactly what it was. Then the people's voice rose in song—he listened intently. Again and again were the words repeated like a chorus and almost unconsciously he committed the sounds to memory.

Soon the service was ended and in triumph they were led back to Kaweeka's house. She met them with renewed wiles and charm, but the boys were strong and she left them alone with rage in her heart. They ate the food that was placed before them in silence, a silence which Alan broke by saying abruptly, "Could you make out anything of the last hymn the people kept singing over and over again in the temple, Dez?"

"What do you mean?"

"Well, could you understand it?"

Desmond looked surprised. "Of course not," he laughed. "Could you?"

Alan did not answer the question, but asked another.

"Well, they sung it over a good many times—didn't you memorize the sounds?"

ELLA M. SCRYMSOUR

Desmond thought a minute, "I think I did," he replied. "It sounded something like:

"*Har-Ju-Jar! Har-Ju-Jar! Kar-Tharn.*"
"*Har-Ju-Jar! Har-Ju-Jar! Kar-Tharn.*"

Alan pulled a scrap of paper triumphantly out of his pocket and showed it to his cousin. He had written down the exact phonetic spelling of the words Desmond had said.

"All the same, I don't see what you are driving at," he demurred, "you look confoundedly pleased over something."

"I've been working out a theory, and I don't think I am far wrong in the decision I have arrived at. Now look at that," and he handed him another piece of paper on which were written the following signs:

DESMOND LOOKED AT IT QUIZZICALLY for a moment, and then said, "Why, you've copied down the signs that are painted all around the walls of the temple—in the great Fire Hall."

"Right. Now can you translate it?"

Desmond laughed. "Of course not. Can you?"

"I think so," said Alan confidently.

"What?" almost shouted Desmond in amazement.

"Now," went on Alan. "You got your first in Theology at Cambridge— translate this"—and he passed Desmond a third slip of paper with other signs on it:

דתן. אבירם.

Desmond looked at it carefully. "I've almost forgotten," he commenced. Then—"why it's Hebrew—Hebrew for Abiram and Dathan!"

"Now I want you to think carefully, Dez," and Alan placed the two slips of paper on which were written the characters, before him. "Now would you not swear that *this*," pointing to the characters copied from the temple, "is a corruption of *that*?"—pointing to the Hebrew.

"Well it certainly looks as if it might easily be so," admitted Desmond.

"Now think of the few words we picked up of that hymn to-day. Isn't it within the bounds of possibility that Har-ju-jar is a corruption of Hallelujah, or Alleluia?"

"Ye-e-es."

"And Har-Barim and Kar-Tharn a corruption of Abiram and Dathan?"

"Ye-es."

"Well," concluded Alan triumphantly, "this is the conclusion I have come to. The language of these people is a corruption of Hebrew."

"What?"

"I'm certain of it, and I am surprised we never thought of it before. Of course it was our first visit to the temple to-day since I came here, and I never noticed those signs before—but to-day as I looked at them they seemed oddly familiar, and it suddenly dawned on me in a flash. Now we ought to find it very easy to pick up the patois they speak—we both used to know something of Hebrew in the old days at college."

They were almost too excited to say much more, when suddenly Alan brought his hand down on the table with a bang that made Desmond start.

"I've got it, Dez old boy," said he.

"Got what?"

"Why think of your Bible. In the—let me see—oh never mind—somewhere in Numbers, I think, we get the story of Korah, Abiram and Dathan."

"Oh my dear Alan, I am afraid I have forgotten it long ago."

"Never mind," went on Alan excitedly. "It's the sixteenth chapter, if I remember rightly. I'll remind you of it—Don't you remember the Chosen People rose up against Moses—"

"Well?"

"I can't remember the exact verses but somewhere in the chapter it tells you that the 'earth was torn asunder, and swallowed up the three men with their houses and everything that appertained unto them, and they went down *alive* into the pit, and the earth closed over them.'"

Desmond looked bewildered and remained silent.

"Don't you see the connection, Dez?"

"No! I do not."

"Well, here are people living in the bowels of the earth, and in their temple they have inscribed in bad Hebrew, if I may so put it, the names of Abiram and Dathan. What more likely than that these people are the descendants of those poor unfortunates of the Old Testament who perished some fourteen hundred and ninety years before Christ?"

"Is it possible?" asked Desmond breathlessly.

ELLA M. SCRYMSOUR

"Why not?" answered his cousin. "The Bible story ends there. We're simply told that they went into the pit *alive*—we are never told that they died! Now we are convinced that they speak a corrupt Hebrew, we ought to find it very easy to learn to speak to them, and then we will bid for freedom."

"Alan," said Desmond suddenly. "I wonder whether your theory is correct. We've got Abiram and Dathan right enough, but what about Korah? He was the chief offender and yet there is no trace of his name."

"I expect his name has been lost during the transit of time," said Alan. "At any rate I am tired now, and I shan't bother any more about it for the present. Let's go to sleep," and the two boys went into their inner chamber and were soon fast asleep.

There was no night in this terrible underworld; the purple lights never went out; morning and evening were unknown. The place was never plunged into entire darkness—true, the inhabitants went to sleep, but they pleased themselves as to when they slept and for how long. The whole world was never at rest at the same time—truly, indeed, it was an unholy place of unrest!

The two men were fast asleep, the purple light shining across their, faces, and Alan moved restlessly, for his dreams were troubled ones.

Suddenly the door opened gently and a figure appeared—it was Kaweeka. Softly she crept across their room, and halted by the side of their couches. A fierce light came into her eyes as she watched the rhythmic rise and fall of Alan's chest as he breathed heavily. She bent over him, kissed his lips, and murmured savagely as she did so—

"So desired—so desirable—yet I so undesired!"

III

Relating to History

H ow long have we been down here, Lanny?"
"Together do you mean?"
"Yes."
"Oh months and months—I can't count time."
"Neither can I. Days pass—we grow tired and we sleep, only to wake to another day like the last, like every day here."
"How far have you got with the translation, Dez?"
"Nearly to the end."
"Splendid. What do you make of it?"
"Just what we expected—It is a very corrupted version of part of the Pentateuch."
"How much of it?"
"Nearly all Genesis—a minute portion of Exodus—and Leviticus."

Alan gave a satisfied sigh. "That's splendid," he remarked. Many months had passed since they had made the discovery that the language of the underworld was a patois Hebrew, and quickly and diligently they set to work to learn it. They first spelt the sounds and wrote them down, and then tried to translate them into Hebrew where it was at all possible.

Very shortly after the rescue of the high priest's daughter and only child, as the maid proved to be, a house was placed at the boys' disposal, and they gladly left the protection of Kaweeka, and lived together with a couple of servants, who looked after them. They were free to go out among the people, and they began to feel almost happy. With the aid of a few words they picked up they asked the high priest for "reading" and he had given them copies of the "Kadetha" which proved to be the Bible of these strange people.

It was very difficult to read as it was written on parchment in a purple ink that had faded considerably through time. The characters, too, besides being different from the Hebrew they knew, were written from top to bottom of the page instead of from right to left, as are most Asiatic languages.

From what they could gather the "Kadetha" was divided into two parts—the Moiltee—which proved to be part of the first three books of

Moses—and "Jarcobbi," five books written by one of the first priests of the people after their descent into the bowels of the earth. That these strange people were really descendants of the rebels against Moses, the boys had not the slightest shadow of doubt—the proof in the "Kadetha" was only too conclusive. They were now able to converse fairly freely with the people, and were able to understand many of their strange beliefs.

The true meaning of the Light they were so far unable to fathom, but "Har-Barim" the high priest, told them there would be no more offerings to the Fire from "Above" as he called the world. The people began to take more kindly to them, but Kaweeka remained watchful and brooding, and they realized that she was indeed a bitter enemy, and the person most greatly to be feared in the underworld. Little Myruum, the high priest's daughter, spent many hours with them, and they learnt much of the language from her baby prattle.

They were admitted to all the services and religious rites in the temple, and the boys noted with surprise that the fire seemed to be daily losing its power. Its flames grew smaller and smaller, and they noticed the difference in it when they had not seen it for several days.

"Jovah," they said to Har-Barim one day. "Tell us your history, now we understand your language."

The old man smiled at them. "There is little to tell," he said. "It is true we were once of the earth above—once white people like yourselves; but for over three thousand, three hundred and three years we have lived in the darkness of the earth. Our skins are changed—they have taken the hue of the land we are forced to dwell in. Our forefathers burrowed in the earth to make streets and houses and shelter for their families, and they left us the heritage of their labour." He pointed as he spoke to the short horn that protruded from his forehead.

"What became of Korah?" they asked him.

"Coorer?" he pronounced the word differently. "Korah," he told them, was their bad angel. It was Korah, with the devil in his soul who urged them to stand against Moses, and it was Korah they shut away from their lives when the pit had closed in upon them, revealing to them no more the light of the sun.

"How do you mean?" asked Alan. "How did you shut him out of your lives, my Jovah?"

Jovah signified "Father" and was the term by which all the people addressed Har-Barim.

"Why, my sons, when the pit closed down upon our forefathers, all turned upon Korah as the father of all their woes. He was stoned and left half dead—then a wall was built up in front of him and all his family, together with all his possessions, and there he was left to perish. One of his daughters escaped, however, and her descendants have been Princesses of Kalvar, as we call our country, ever since."

"Then Kaweeka—" began Alan.

"Yes, my son. In Kaweeka you see the Princess of Kalvar, and direct descendant in the female line of the unfortunate Korah himself."

"Where is Korah's burial place?" asked Desmond.

Har-Barim shook his head. "No one knows—in the generations of time that have passed the secret has been lost, and the exact position forgotten. No one knows—no one ever will know, until—but there, read from the fourteenth line of the sixth part of our prophet, Zurishadeel," and taking a small parchment from his voluminous pocket he handed it to Alan and left them to translate it for themselves.

Laboriously they copied out the translation—

"For the body of Korah the devil is hidden with those of his household. Their flesh shall rot and their bones become powder, and in a generation their last resting place shall be forgotten. But on the day the secret is no more—for behold a virgin shall in a dream learn the way—the fire shall consume quickly, strange people shall enter the land of Kalvar, and desolation and destruction shall come to all those that inhabit the earth. Yea, the people that are in the belly of it, and they that have been disgorged from it—when the Fire grows less—when the Tomb of Korah is found then shall all in due time perish."

"Cheery old chap, isn't he?" laughed Desmond.

But Alan was thoughtful. "I wonder what the secret of the fire is. They seem to worship it, although they pray to the 'Lord of their Fathers.' It certainly is getting less—I can't help feeling that something terrible will happen if it does ever go out entirely."

For some time they gazed meditatively at the translations they had made when a shadow crossing Desmond's paper made him look up. It was Kaweeka—Kaweeka who had not visited them for months it seemed, and whose presence now seemed to denote some evil. Quietly she watched them for a few minutes, and a curious light came into her eyes. They glittered and shone with an almost fanatical glow—and in fact her whole being was one of suppressed excitement and almost maniacal fervour.

"Come," said she at last, and held out a hand to each. They felt impelled to obey her, and she led them straight to the temple which was curiously deserted. The great fire was burning in fits and starts. Suddenly a flaming tongue would leap out, blazing brightly as if refusing to be killed, and a moment later it would lie dead and dormant among the embers. Then suddenly the fire would emit a passion of sparks which flew upward in a fury, only to fall back within its folds, dull and lifeless.

It was still enormous of course, but the boys realized that its life was nearing the end, and that its power was nearly gone.

Kaweeka suddenly turned on Desmond and in a whirl of passion addressed him.

"Desmond," she cried, "I loved you—I would have made you happy, but he"—pointing to Alan—"he came between us. He tore my heart from its resting place within my breast—he made me love him also, and then stamped on my love and spurned me."

"That is hardly fair, Kaweeka. I never made overtures to you—"

"No," said Desmond, doing his best to conciliate her.

"Enough," she cried and then began a frenzied tirade to which the boys listened in horror, as they realized that almost a madness had come upon Kaweeka—the seed of Korah.

Falling to her knees she clung to Alan and begged him to marry her according to the custom of his world and hers. She offered to make him Prince of the land of Kalvar and possessor of a thousand fortunes if he would but love her—be it ever so little. And when he gently lifted her up and put her away from him, she looked him fully in the eyes, and for a full minute there was silence. Then with a queer gesture of finality, she outspread her hands and accepted the inevitable. Then in a monotonous voice and with carefully chosen words she began to speak again—

"In the world you came from, O Men of the Sun, you saw strange sights and heard strange things. A light appeared in the sky—a light that was the forerunner of tragedy. I propose to show you the Light, O Strangers. I will unfold the secret of its being before your wondering eyes. Know you now, that this Fire is next in honour to the God of our Fathers. It is the Fire that gives us air to breathe, and light by which we can see. From the Fire we obtain our strength, and when it dies out our power will be gone. But know you also, that when our Fire dies and we perish, so will your world die also. You above are dependent for your very existence on the Fire in the Earth's belly—with our extinction will come also the consummation of all mankind. See"—and she pointed to a coil of metal that looked like a silver rope—"See—this is the Light— the Light that brought sacrifices we could offer to our God of all, and that fed our Fire."

Then she began a weird dance. Grovelling on the floor in apparent worship of the Fire, she drew nearer and nearer to the shimmering metal, and taking up one end of it, undid it until it lay in shimmering folds outspread upon the floor. Still, with rhythmic grace, she continued, now advancing, now retreating, until she had coiled part of the writhing mass about her body, and the boys realized that one end was firmly embedded in the heart of the Fire itself. And as they watched they realized that Kaweeka was dancing away from the Fire—away down the length of the great Fire Hall, to where a little door was half hidden behind cherubim of gold.

The boys felt impelled to follow the strange witch woman. Through the little door, they went, down a dark passage which ended suddenly in a small chamber that was bright with light. But the whole of the cave-like place vibrated and shook with a force that was terrifying in its magnitude. They looked around curiously and saw in one corner a large clock-like instrument from which the sound came.

With almost loving care Kaweeka freed herself from the shimmering metal and placed the end of it in the machine. Instantly they saw it gain in strength and brightness—it seemed to quicken and show signs of life.

The two boys gave a cry—"The Light! The Light!" they cried, for this indeed was the mysterious Light that had stricken Marshfielden, and now they were seeing its wondrous power from below.

Kaweeka leaned over the burning metal, and touched a lever on the clock-like instrument's face. Suddenly with a roar and a flash, the Light soared upwards. Through the roof of the cave—onwards—onwards— forcing an outlet for itself by its own power, through rock and earth it tore,—until the watching eyes of the boys were rewarded by a speck of blue. "The sky!" cried Desmond in amazement. The Light had once more visited the outer world! This then was the horror of Marshfielden!

The boys watched the quivering metal in silence. In its deadly folds it had embraced Dan Murlock's baby. Mr. Winthrop had suffered from its caress. Mrs. Skeet—Mrs. Slater—it was impossible to name all the victims of its diabolical power. Some element, mightier even than electricity, had been discovered by these purple savages, to be used by them only for the purpose of destruction.

Long the boys watched until their eyes ached from the intense brightness. Their hearts were heavy within them as they thought of the victim it might bring back. Kaweeka sat in one corner mumbling and muttering to herself, and the boys seemed powerless to leave the place.

Voices rose in song—cymbals clashed—drums rolled—the evening service was being held in the temple. Still they waited! The sounds died away and the temple emptied, yet the Light had not returned.

They were growing cramped, their limbs ached, and then the Light trembled more violently than before. The vision of the sky grew clearer for an instant; they knew the Light was returning—but it was not returning alone! Rigid in every muscle the boys waited as it travelled through the bowels of the Earth.

The heap of metal grew larger on the floor as it made its descent—then the end appeared in sight—a sheep, burnt and dead, was within its grasp. Silently Kaweeka came forward and touched a lever on the vibrating clock in the corner.

The noise ceased. The Light grew shadowed. The aperture leading to the world above closed, leaving only a scar to mark where it had been!

Kaweeka bent over the stricken sheep and unwound the Light from its body, leaving exposed the singed wool and burnt flesh, and as if it had been a child gathered it up in her arms and still holding to the end of the Light danced back into the empty temple.

Without an effort she tossed the dead sheep into the Fire, and the flames devoured it savagely. Then she began again her wild dance and gradually wound the Light up into its original coils until it lay in a heap by the side of the Fire. "According to the prophecy of Zurishadele I speak. Behold, he writes 'Whosoever shall cause the seed of Korah to die shall be hunted by the people of Kalvar—yea until their blood gushes forth through their eyes and they are blind—until their limbs crumple up beneath them and they fall—so shall they be hunted that the people of Kalvar may deliver them up to the Fire.'"

"Well?" asked Alan.

Kaweeka smiled evilly. "It is true I am of the seed of Korah, and you, my Alan, have scorned me. I have given you my love—I would give you all—but you have laughed at me and mocked me. I would have given you my body—but now I give you more—I will give you my life. The Fire is burning low—more fuel is needed to keep it alive. I will give myself for fuel—but in giving my life, I offer two more to the God of our Fathers. For as you are the instrument of my destruction—so will the people fall upon you, and through the mouth of Mzata the Great, will you be offered a sacrifice to the Fire."

Lightly, gracefully, she stepped onto the transparent wall that surrounded the Fire, and then with a piercing cry tore off her jewels and her raiment and flung them into the flames, that were waiting eagerly for the food that was offered them.

Then, naked, her hair falling about her, her dark skin shimmering in the light, she flung herself into the centre of the Fire.

Alan rushed forward, but it was too late—the cruel tongues of fire had wrapped round her, and all that was left of the seed of Korah was a skull, stripped of its flesh, grinning at them for an instant through the flames, before it disappeared.

It was all so unexpected, so sudden, that the boys had not realized what she purposed doing, and now, speechless and bewildered, they stared at each other in horror.

Suddenly a hoarse whisper broke through the silence. "Flee, flee," it said, and they recognized the voice of Har-Barim. "I cannot save you," he continued. "My people will fall upon you and slay you—for although they loved not Kaweeka, yet the prophecy will have to be fulfilled. To-day is the vigil of the feast of Meherut—to-morrow the great feast itself. Till then and then only can I hide the manner of Kaweeka's death. As you saved my Myruum, so will I try to save you. This much can I tell you. Make for the waters that are turbulent and wild, where they narrow to the space of a foot and dash against a rocky wall. Look for the stones that are red.—Now—go."

"But where shall we go?" cried Alan.

"Take always the centre path, my son, and avoid the waters that are tranquil and smooth. The way is rough—thy path must of a surety be rough also, but with courage victory will come to you. Farewell!"

And Har-Barim left them alone in the temple.

Quickly they made their way to their house, there was no time to be lost. Plans had to be made and made quickly. Once more they were in a strange land, where through no fault of their own, hostility and enmity would meet them once more.

IV

Out into the Great Beyond

The boys had no packing to do. They possessed nothing but the clothes they stood in, and a sailor's clasp knife that belonged to Alan; but they put together a store of dried elers, a fruit that was sustaining, and that, down below, took the place of the bread of the upper world.

There were very few of the purple people about; it was the vigil of Meherut,—the most solemn feast day of their strange religion, and all were shut up in their houses with their curtains drawn spending their time in fasting and prayer.

On, on the boys went, always choosing the middle path if a choice was offered them, if not, then taking the path to the right. Gradually they left all sign of habitation and entered a most desolate region where the purple moss grew only in patches, and the purple lights were only few and far between. They stumbled on blindly; they dared not wait for food; every moment was precious to them. Suddenly Desmond stumbled and fell. "I can't go a step further," he cried. "How long have we been walking, Lanny?"

"About ten hours I should think."

"Then for Heaven's sake let us rest! We have a fair start of them— let us rest and have some food." The elers refreshed them, and they drank of the water that rolled treacherously at their feet. It was not very wide, perhaps three feet at the most, but the current was strong and the whirlpools more torrential than ever.

Stretching themselves out on the ground the boys slept, and woke some five or six hours later feeling greatly refreshed. Then they continued their march, now leaving the river behind them, now coming upon it again and walking by its banks.

They had no idea of where they were going. They had only one goal in view—to put as big a distance as they could between themselves and the purple people whom they knew would already be following them. Suddenly the road ended. They had turned a sharp corner and the way had opened out into a small cave, which was bounded on one side by a narrow strip of bubbling, foaming water, that disappeared at either end in a dark tunnel. "What shall we do?" asked Desmond. "Shall we go back?"

"We can't," said Alan decisively. "The road that brought us here was at least five miles long, without a turn in it. By the time we retraced our steps, the purple devils would have caught up to us. No, old boy, I think this is a tight fix we are in, and at the moment I can't quite see how we are to get out of it."

They walked round the little cave examining it carefully. It had only the one exit—the path up which they had come. The tunnels at either end through which flowed the waters were too low to admit the passage of a body, and the walls on the other side of the little river rose sheer from the water itself. "It looks pretty hopeless," said Alan at last, "but at all costs we must not go back."

"How red the walls are," said Desmond suddenly. Alan started, for in his mind he could hear a voice saying, "Look for the stones that are red." It had been Har-Barim's advice to them, and he had said—"make for the waters that are turbulent and wild—where in the space of a foot—" A foot! why the water couldn't be wider than that here. He looked round hurriedly—was it his fancy or were the stones on the opposite side even redder than those about him?

To Alan's strained nerves it seemed as if just opposite him a stone had been worn away by the constant passage of feet. Slowly a thought came into his mind—if that was a footprint then surely it must lead somewhere. His eyes travelled up the rock eagerly—again his quickened senses discovered another foothold a little higher up, and still another and another. Four in all, at perhaps a stretch of a little over two feet. Upward his glance wandered, and in the rugged rock he saw a flat piece of red stone that looked as if it had been inserted there at some time or other, for some specific purpose. He stretched across the raging torrent and with a mighty effort clung to the jagged rock. "Don't touch me, Dez," he commanded, "I think I can manage best alone."

With an almost superhuman effort he placed his foot in the first little cleft, and gradually worked up to the little red stone that had so aroused his curiosity. Desmond watched him in breathless horror. Although the water was so narrow, Alan would stand little chance of saving himself if he fell in, for it was dashing wildly against the sides and sending its spray even higher than where Alan was clinging. He touched the stone—it moved ever so slightly. "God! A secret way!" he cried, and worked feverishly to open it. But although it trembled and shook, it would not disclose its secret.

Then, away in the distance, came the sound of fierce shouting and the beating of drums.

"The people know," cried Desmond. "They are coming up the long passage." Already they could hear the name of Kaweeka used as a battle cry, and they realized that they could expect little mercy if they were caught by the purple savages.

With beads of perspiration on his brow, Alan worked. His fingers were torn and bleeding from his exertions. Still nearer came the cries of the infuriated people, and Alan had not yet succeeded in moving the stone, which he was convinced hid a secret way of escape. Desmond ran down the passage a little way—in a second he was back. "I can see them," he cried. "There are hundreds of them! Oh, what shall we do?"

"Ah!" Alan gave a cry of relief, for suddenly the stone had rolled back, revealing a small cavity beyond, just big enough for the passage of a man's body.

"Follow me in, Dez," he cried, "no matter where it leads—it can't be worse than if we remain here."

Their pursuers were now in full view, and if seemed that only a few yards separated them. Quickly Desmond climbed the steps and reached the hole, and Alan drew him in, and even as he turned to make fast the opening, a head with an evil-looking horn appeared. Alan doubled his fist and gave a mighty blow, and like a log the man dropped into the water, was sucked under and carried out of sight.

They rolled the stone back into its place, and panting, leant against it. The execrations and cries of the natives came faintly on their ears; the great stone trembled, and they knew it was being forced from without. One hurried glance round revealed to them great boulders of rock lying on the ground. Feverishly they piled them up in front of the stone, and they were strong enough to resist the furious onslaught that the purple people kept up. After a time, the cries of the people grew fainter, gradually they died away altogether, and the underworld folk made their way back to the temple to pray that the white men might be handed over to them, and that they might be allowed to punish the slayers of the seed of Korah.

Spent and tired the two boys sank to the ground, for many hours had passed while they were defending their retreat from the underworld people. A faint, natural, ground light shone around. It was like the same purple light that lit the whole of the underworld, but here it was in its natural condition, and was so faint that it scarcely showed them each other's face.

"Go to sleep, Dez," said Alan. "I will keep watch."

"But you are tired too," demurred his cousin.

Alan smiled. "Sleep first, old man," said he, and even as he spoke, Desmond dropped his head upon his breast, and his eyes closed in slumber.

It was a great strain for Alan to sit there in the darkness—in a weird and unknown place—soundless except for Desmond's heavy, regular breathing. His own breath seemed to his quickened senses like the blast of heavy artillery, and the slightest sound was magnified a hundredfold. Nobly he fought against sleep—but he was worn out, and at last his eyes closed—and he too, slept.

Time meant nothing to these imprisoned men. Science they could laugh at, for, from a scientific point of view, their very life was impossible. How in the centre of the earth could mankind live? Yet it was true they had lived, fed, and breathed for months and months in the very belly of the earth. Science said the centre of the earth was impenetrable—that the intense heat of its inner fire would prevent man even seeing that fire. Yet they could prove that they had seen and they could tell the scientists that the fire was waning.

Still they slept.

Fantastic dreams came into their minds, yet there was not so much as the scuffling of a rat or the squeaking of a mouse to awaken them. All was silent and still, with a stillness that cannot be expressed by words.

Desmond woke first—the light did not seem so dim—or had they become used to it? His eyes rested on Alan sleeping soundly by his side, and a tear dropped on his cousin's brow as he leant over him. It was a tear not to be laughed at, nor to be ashamed of, but the tear of a strong man shed in the bitterness of his oppression.

He rose to his feet, stretched his limbs, and wandered round the place where he found himself. It was a cavern, very similar to the numberless others he had passed through on the further side of the rapid river. Its floor was rugged, but was covered with the purple moss, and a few bushes which bore fruit were growing there. Round and round he walked, but the cave seemed to have no outlet at all. Alan woke and watched Desmond in silence for a short while, and then said, "Don't worry, Dez, I'm sure we shall find a way out. This must lead somewhere." But although he too, examined the cave very carefully, there seemed to be no outlet.

How long they stayed there they did not know—fortunately they found some roots which were edible, and whose long bulb-like ends were filled with a pleasant fluid which quenched their thirst. They played games with each other, did everything in fact to prevent the madness they were afraid would come over them.

Nearer and nearer it crept like a beast of prey waiting to spring and devour his victims. With their forced inactivity their limbs became cramped and although the air was pure, their lips were dry and their throats parched. They began to give up speaking aloud; they would sit for hours in silence, only uttering occasionally a croaking whisper, one to the other, as if they were afraid of being overheard. Then the day—but no, it cannot be called that—the time came when Desmond lay quiet and still, and Alan awoke to the consciousness that something was radically wrong with his cousin. He bent over the inanimate figure, and touched him gently with his hand. The eyes were closed and the fists clenched and had he been able to see clearly, he would have noticed the purple lines round the cold mouth, and a pinched look upon the face, that boded nought but ill.

"I must do something," he muttered wearily, and then he burst out into a paroxysm of weeping. That saved his life, for when he came to himself it was as a fresh man.

Plucking some of the purple foliage, he squeezed the stalks and let the cool liquid pour gently on Desmond's brow, then tenderly chiding and imploring him, he managed to bring back a sign of life to his cousin's face. Nor did he stop then, but continued, until Desmond woke to reason and called him by his name.

When Desmond had fallen into a refreshed and tranquil sleep, Alan wandered round and round the little cave, looking still for some weak spot.

Suddenly there came a sound in the distance—a thud that shook the very ground upon which he was standing. With every nerve wound up to concert pitch he waited—listening intently to see if he could hear again the sudden sound that had broken the stillness.

"It's my fancy," said he aloud, but even as he spoke the noise began again with greater fury. The cavern shook—pieces of rock came hurtling down, broken off from their parent wall by the vibrations. Then suddenly came a sound almost like an explosion, and a piece of rock, larger than the rest came tumbling down, and revealed behind it a small passage.

"Dez." cried Alan. "Dez, a way of escape has come."

Desmond opened his eyes and looked round vacantly, and indeed it was some time before he realized the wonderful thing that had happened.

The underworld folk had made one last mighty effort to reach them, and the boys could have gone down on their knees to thank the purple people, for their machinations had given them hope once more.

V

A Friend from the Enemy

Desmond, still weak, raised himself up, and looked about him; and even as he did so, a huge boulder fell from the blocked secret entrance that led to the city of the underworld.

"They are bombarding the place," said Alan looking startled, "let us go through there," and he pointed to the little passage that had been revealed to them so strangely.

"We can blockade it from the other side," said Desmond, "and at least it will give us more time."

A close examination revealed to them a hinged slab of stone that swung easily to and fro, and the spring that fastened it in place was plain to see on the inner side. They crept into the passage, closed the stone after them, and piled rocks and stones in front of it as an extra protection. Again came a weary time of waiting—a time when the cave was filled with wild laughter and hideous ravings—when the furies of Hell itself seemed let loose on the other side. The purple fiends had forced an entrance, but too late. Their prey had escaped them.

Alan and Desmond lay and listened to the babel of their voices, for strangely enough the slightest sound from the other cave was magnified in this inner one. Then a silence fell, and they realized that the purple savages had once more gone. Hungrily they gathered roots and ate them greedily—when a woman's cry, clear and distinct, startled them. Again and again it came—"Ar-lane! Jez-mun!"

Their names were called in the quaint pronunciation of the underworld folk.

"Who is it?" asked Desmond.

"I'll see."—

"No don't go—don't go—it's some trick—" but Alan had already pulled down the stones in front of the hinged stone.

"Ar-lane. Jez-mun." Again the cry came. "Open—open I beg. I come to aid you."

"I am going to speak to her," said Alan grimly, and he put his lips close against the stone.

"Who are you and what do you want of us?"

A glad cry was his answer, and then followed quickly—"Let me through, O Ar-lane—I have come to seek thee."

"What do you want of us?"

"Listen, O Ar-lane, I have fled from my home in the temple of Fire, and have come to thee. Years ago when a tiny child, I found the cavern and knew it well. But Am-rab the Wise, my tutor and priest, forbade me with threats of torture to wander there again. Since then I have not set eyes upon the place. Let me in, O Ar-lane, for the spring is broken on this side, and I cannot find it."

Desmond was listening suspiciously. "What are you going to do?" he asked.

And again came the pleading voice. "Let me in, O Ar-lane. Oh, let me in."

Alan looked questioningly at Desmond and he gave his cousin a quick nod. "If it's treachery we're done," he remarked, as he touched the spring and the stone moved.

As soon as it was wide open the woman entered. They did not know her, but her eyes were swollen from weeping and her face drawn with emotion, and they realized that she had suffered.

"Waste no time," she commanded imperiously. "My flight is already spoken of in the temple. Should they seek me, it will need all our strength, all our cunning to hide from them. Close the door, O Ar-lane, and build up a wall of stones in front, that is strong, and then let us hasten on." So once more the place was barricaded, and only when the barrier was complete did she deign to explain her presence.

"You know me not, O Men of the Upper World, for you have never set eyes upon me before; but I have seen you often. Behold, I am Jez-Riah, seed of the house of Bin-Nab, and hereditary Keeper of the Hall of Fire. It is the custom, know ye, in this land of ours, for the female seed of Bin-Nab to keep veiled after they have reached the age of ten. I cast aside my veil yester-eve, and immediately came to seek thee."

"Why?" asked Alan curtly.

The woman was fair to look upon—her eyes were deep and luminous, and her tear-stained cheeks filled them with pity. Yet to be hampered with a woman seemed to take from them every chance of their ultimate escape.

Jez-Riah seemed to read their thoughts. "No, harden not your hearts against me, for I can help you," said she earnestly.

"Why have you sought us?" asked Alan, this time less curtly.

"I know a road in here—a secret road, said to be a thousand and ten miles long; a stream of unknown depths, races along by the side of it—a stream that is swifter by far than the fastest of waters—there," and she pointed in the direction from which she had come. "It leads to the tomb of Korah, so they say, but torture was threatened to all who would have ventured in search of it. O Ar-lane, you know not what our tortures are."

"I have seen some," said Alan grimly.

Jez-Riah laughed. "Nay, Ar-lane—you have never seen what I have seen. You have never witnessed the Curse of Fire." As she spoke her eyes grew big and her expression distorted as she lived again the scenes she had so often witnessed. "I have seen men roasted alive. I have seen acid juices poured on the sufferers' wounds. I have seen—" but Alan stopped her. "Enough!" he cried. "It's horrible."

She continued. "But tortures even worse were threatened for those who would seek the tomb of Korah. So none tried. I knew you would be safe for a while in these caves—but I knew too, that with some one to guide you, you might go farther even than you dared hope. I am weary of my life, I am an eighth child of a priestess of the direct line of Bin-Nab; but I have the blood of the living in my veins. I want to live the life of the People of the Sun—your people. That is the reason I cast my veil from me, O Men of the Outer World, and sought you. Oh cast not Jez-Riah from thee, but keep her as thy slave, for she will by of much use to thee."

Jez-Riah had cast herself at the boys' feet, and her tears and sobs were coming fast. Desmond and Alan felt strangely moved at the sight of this woman, so different from the women they were used to in the world above.

"I don't think it's trickery, Alan, do you?" said Desmond. In his heart Alan believed in the truth of the strange woman's story, yet he knew from past experience that it was impossible to believe the inhabitants of the underworld.

He looked Jez-Riah up and down. "Any weapons?" he asked suddenly.

Jez-Riah held up her head proudly and her eyes flashed fire and she stamped her foot. "I come 'feula-ri!' Is it likely I am traitor, O Men who Doubt?"

Now the boys knew enough of the customs of the strange world in which they found themselves, that if the sacred word "feula-ri—" was spoken, no treachery was contemplated; for that word meant more to them than does the white man's flag of truce. For in times of war, has not even the white flag been violated?

"I believe you, Jez-Riah," said Alan suddenly. "Show us Korah's tomb and perhaps we in turn may find a way to show you the sun and moon and stars. And green trees—and grass—and the sea—" He drew his breath sharply. His imagination had run away with him, and for the moment he could almost believe he heard the thunder of the waves as they came dashing in on some rocky shore; he saw the foam and the sun-decked beach. The birds seemed to be singing—and above it all came the unmusical cry of the gulls. He sighed.

"Don't Lannie," said Desmond affectionately. "I feel it too; shall we ever see those things again—shall we ever feel the breeze on our faces and the burning sun—"

Jez-Riah stood looking at them hungrily. "You speak your own tongue," said she, "not mine. What say you each to the other that makes the lines of sadness on your faces grow so deep?"

"It's nothing, Jez-Riah," answered Alan.

"You are sorry I am here?"

"No, we are glad—and you must help us with your knowledge of the secret ways."

"See, I will show you at once," and she rose and crossed the cavern. She pressed a stone in the wall in front of them, and a boulder revolved on a hidden spring and showed a yawning cavity beyond. The noise of troubled waters came upon their ears—loud and thunderous.

"It is true," she cried in triumph, "behold all I have said is true. The waters are calling—come," and she went through into the blackness without a tremor of fear. And Alan and Desmond followed their strange companion without any misgivings for the future.

Providence had sent them an unlooked for guide. Hope, the star they had almost lost in the clouds of darkness that had overshadowed them, came back, shining in all the glory and radiance of renewed fervour. With a muttered "Thank God" the two boys stepped forward, lighter of step and gladder at heart than they had been for some time.

"Ar-lane—Jez-mun," came a voice from the darkness. "I am Jez-Riah—Child of the future—Gate of Hope—Guide of Strangers. Fear nothing—the blackness will pass and we shall find the way easy to tread."

And it was even as she had spoken. In a very little time they found themselves in a maze of natural lighted pathways similar to the ones from which they had come. The sound of the water grew louder. It thundered in their ears; it shrieked and roared as if some evil spirit was shaking the very earth itself. Jez-Riah was radiant.

"The stream of Korah is not far. I have heard it told that whoever braves that stream and finds the tomb of Korah, will live to see the sun. The sun that our prophet Zurishadeel sings of, the sun that the God of our forefathers created. The thought puts new life into me—Come."

On, on they went, the noise getting louder and louder every moment, until, upon turning a corner, a wondrous sight met their eyes. Belching forth from the rocks themselves, forcing itself out from regions unseen, falling like a waterfall from some high precipice, the torrent rushed, making a lake of considerable dimensions, which was overflowing its banks—a wild, mad, boiling liquid. The spray rose a hundred feet in height, and splashed all round and the whole place was fearsome and ghostly.

At one end of the turbulent lake was a tiny outlet, perhaps two feet wide, through which the waters ran at breakneck speed. The fearsome noise, the sight of the rushing waters, the intense weirdness of the scene, kept both boys speechless with awe at their surroundings, but Jez-Riah was on her knees, bathing her face in the water, letting it trickle over her hair, drinking it from cups made of her two hands. And above the din and clamour they heard her singing a weird hymn of praise to the accompaniment of the music of the waters. The boys listened eagerly, and again and again they heard the refrain—

"Korah—Korah—father of our people—the waters will lead
us to where thy bones lie,
"Korah—Korah—thou hast not forsaken us—I am bathing
in the waters of faith and purity."

Then Jez-Riah flung off her draperies and plunged into the boiling waters. The boys watched in breathless amazement as she battled with the whirlpools, but she proved stronger than they, and swam on until she reached the mighty waterfall. Round and round she was carried and whirled but she reached her goal at last—a tiny slab of rock protruding out of the waters and under the shadow of the mighty cascade itself. Standing upon it she began a weird dance—a fanatical dance of joy. The foaming waters almost hid her from their gaze, the spray rose in front of her like a filmy gauze. At moments, however, her lithe body was exposed to view, and the boys marvelled at her agility. She did not seem to tire, but danced on, her voice raised in a strange hymn of praise. Praise of the waters, praise of the light, praise to the God of the Sun. Then came a mighty prayer that the secret ways might be opened to her—and that she might lead the strangers to safety. And even as she sang and prayed, her limbs were moving fast in dance and the waters were dashing over her and chilling her.

When she had finished her prayer she sank to her knees in an abandonment of grief and asked pardon for her one great sin—the sin she committed in leaving the temple, where she was Watcher to the Fire.

There was a long silence—only broken by the voices of the torrent raised in its ceaseless dirge.

Alan moved. "Is she safe?" he asked "What will happen to her?"—but even as he spoke the lithe body had dived once more into the waters and was swimming almost with ease to the shore. Jez-Riah stood proudly before them, her dripping hair a mantle that covered her. "Go—rest," she commanded. "I commune with Korah," and fleet of foot, strong in purpose, she darted down one of the passages near by, and was soon lost to sight.

VI

The Lair of the Serpent

"K orah! Korah!" the words grew fainter and fainter, until at length, worn out with religious fervour, Jez-Riah flung herself on the ground and fell asleep. Alan and Desmond gazed after her for some time and then Alan said "Let's lie down, Dez. We are both worn out, and it is useless to follow her. She will return to us only when the spirit moves her."

"Then for Heaven's sake let us get away from this infernal din."

They walked down one of the widest passages until they came to a place where the moss was thick and soft and the noise of the water rose faint upon their ears.

"Ar-lane—Jez-mun." The cry came low and clear and Alan rose quickly to his feet. He had been asleep and his limbs felt rested and his head was clearer.

"It is I, Jez-Riah," came the soft tones again, and silhouetted against the wall he saw the shadowy figure of the strange woman.

"We must go on," she urged "We have far to go and much to do."

"Where have you been?" he asked her.

"I have been in communication with the Spirit of the Waters, O Ar-lane; soon the mysteries of Korah will be unfolded before thine eyes. Come! Come! Tarry not too long." In a second Desmond was awake, and Jez-Riah showed all impatience to start.

"Have you been here before?" asked Desmond curiously of Jez-Riah.

"No, O Jez-mun, but the water of Korah has given me the gift of sight. Before I was blind—now I can see. Come bind up my eyes, O Ar-lane, that clearness of vision may be mine."

"What do you mean?"

"Bind up my eyes," she commanded again.

Alan tore a strip from his purple mantle, and tied it across her eyes.

She gave an exclamation of joy. "O Ar-lane," she cried. "Before I trod in darkness; now my path is lighted brightly, and I can lead you to many strange sights, and strange things." As she spoke, she stretched out her hands before her and started off at a quick pace. In silence the cousins followed her. In their position as prisoners in the earth, buried so far down that they had little hope of ever seeing the sun again, they had no choice but to follow the strange, half mad creature who had constituted herself their leader.

The aspect of the road they were now traversing changed. The sides of the passage were no longer smooth and earthy, but consisted of a hard, rocky substance—the floor, too, was jagged and rough. The passage narrowed until it left only room for them to walk in single file, and the air was musty and stifling; indeed there was a pressure in the atmosphere that made the boys from the upper, world stumble as they felt the noxious gases going to their heads.

They made brave efforts, however, and staggered blindly on, one after the other, following Jez-Riah who never hesitated a moment in the course she was taking. For perhaps five miles they walked until they entered a large cavern, the replica of the many others they had been through. They noticed the change in the air immediately. It was purer, fresher, even cooler and the boys revived under its effect.

Jez-Riah tore the bandage from her eyes. "The place of my dreams," she cried.

"I feel faint," said Desmond in a low tone, but not so low that Jez-Riah could not hear. "He needs food?" she questioned "Here is plenty," and going to the furthermost corner of the cave she pulled up roots by the handful—roots like the ones they had had in the lower world itself.

All the time they had been walking they had been continually ascending—at times the passages were almost like mountain passes, they rose at such a gradient—at other times the ascent was not so noticeable, but all the same they realized that they were mounting upward, and the thought cheered the two white men.

They sat and ate the roots and felt refreshed, when suddenly Desmond rose with a cry. "My God—what's that?" There on the opposite wall, high above their heads, a light shone down upon them, a light that gleamed baleful in the semi-darkness.

"It is the sacred serpent of the Tomb," cried Jez-Riah. "I have heard of it often when I was a child. It has existed throughout the ages—it will always exist."

"Nonsense," said Alan.

"You cannot kill it," she wailed "It is the Guardian of the Tomb."

"What, are we there, at the Tomb of Korah, already?" asked Alan in amazement.

"No! No! But we must cross its path if we would reach the Tomb. In my conceit I thought I was all powerful. I was over-confident, O Ar-lane! I heeded not the snake that is large enough to slay an enormous army and yet retain its power."

The gleaming eyes grew nearer, and already they could see the writhing body as it moved along a rocky ledge.

"How big is it?" asked Desmond.

"I cannot see its length," whispered Alan "but it seems as thick round as a man's body. Let us get out of this cursed place. Which is the way, Jez-Riah?"

"Through that narrow opening yonder," said she.

Flattening themselves against the wall they crept the way she directed, and were but a few steps from it when there came the sound of a terrible hissing, and a long evil-looking shape dropped in front of them, and hung pendulum-wise blocking up the opening.

"We can't go that way now," said Alan "I am afraid it's too large to tackle. Why it must be thirty feet long at least. We shall have to go back." Then came the most horrible experience the cousins had ever had. The most awful. The most terrifying.

"Run," cried Alan. "If we can get into the passage beyond we may be able to block up the way and prevent it coming through after us."

They reached the narrow opening, and all around were huge blocks of rock and stone which they piled up one on top of the other.

"Only one more is needed," cried Alan triumphantly. But he spoke too soon—a large, flat head, perhaps a foot and a half in length, with ugly eyes glowing like live fire, shot through the opening, and watched them. The mouth was open wide and the forked tongue shot rapidly in and out in venomous fury. The smell was terrible, whether from its breath or permeating through its skin from its body, they could not tell, but it made them feel giddy, sick and ill. For perhaps ten minutes (if time could be measured in that awful place) it remained there motionless, and then gradually the stones came tumbling down as it forced its way through the barricade.

The boys watched their horrible foe. They were powerless. Escape was impossible, for behind them was a narrow passage, perhaps a mile in length, that offered no shelter.

Would it never attack them? Why keep them in this awful suspense?

"Knife," came suddenly from between Alan's tightly compressed lips. Then after a moment, during which time he opened the well worn blade—"There are plenty of stones behind?"

"Plenty."

Swiftly followed the instructions. "Pick up the largest you can handle—both of you—when I give the word dash them at the brute's head. It is our only chance—then rush past the head."

"But—" commenced Desmond.

"Don't argue—it's our only hope. The thing is too big to turn round in this small space. It *must* go on. Once we get past it we may stand a chance."

Alan never relaxed his watchful gaze. Suddenly the reptile lowered its head and an ugly hiss came from its mouth.

"Now," cried Alan, and as he hurled the knife, harpoon-like into the open mouth two heavy stones came crashing down on its skull.

The sudden onslaught dazed the creature, and its head dropped to the ground. Quickly they rushed past it, but they all realized that they were not yet out of danger. The passage they were in was very narrow and the serpent was so immense that it was impossible for them to stand without feeling the clammy skin next to them.

Jez-Riah shuddered. "What will become of us?" she moaned "It is too big to kill." And indeed, it seemed to be, for Alan had not exaggerated. The length was quite thirty feet, and the girth of its middle was perhaps ten feet, narrowing to two at the tail.

"You can't kill it," cried Desmond. "Why we haven't even the old clasp knife now." A sudden convulsive movement passed along the serpent's body, and it made them retch to see the tremor coming from its head in undulating movements to its tail. Then it raised itself up, and Alan was right—it was impossible for it to turn—it was far too big and cumbersome. For some time, with its head raised perhaps six feet from the ground, it writhed to and fro in growing anger that its prey should so elude it. As its anger grew greater, its body rolled and moved in convulsive heaps, and the trio sickened as the malodorous mass pressed itself against them and pinioned them to the wall.

"Lannie, what can we do?" asked Desmond. Jez-Riah was almost unconscious with the awful pressure, and the strain was telling on the two boys. The strength of the beast was enormous, and they realized that it had the power, even when at a disadvantage itself, to press the very life out of them against the wall.

Then came a sudden sense of relief, as the serpent contracted itself, but gave way to horror as they realized that it was backing through the opening, and its filthy head would soon be on a line with them.

"Stones," urged Alan hoarsely. "Hurl them at the head. Jez-Riah, you must help too."

Feverishly they worked throwing rocks and stones with force at the monster's head. It withstood the onslaught valiantly for a time—its strength was enormous—but at last a well directed shot of Desmond's caught it full between the eyes, and the head dropped like a stone.

"The serpent—it is dead?" asked Jez-Riah. "But alas, no. The body is twitching all over—it has life still."

A sharp piece of stone jutted out above Alan's head. "Help me," he said feverishly to his cousin. "This is our last hope—this is as sharp as a knife. If we can but loosen it you must help me to imbed it in the brute's head. It is stunned now—we must try and overpower it while it is in that condition." All the time they were talking they were working hard to loosen the stone and at last it fell into Alan's hands. It was not very large, but it had an edge like a bayonet, and was of intense hardness.

Cautiously they forced their way on either side of the twisting mass, until they were on a level with its head. "There," whispered Desmond. "Just between the eyes."

The stone was raised; the huge beast was motionless—then, with almost superhuman power, Alan brought the stone down and embedded it deeply in the flesh, while as Alan let go, Desmond hurled a heavy piece of stone hammer-wise on the top of the stone, and buried the sharp edge still deeper in the gaping wound. The great snake woke to consciousness, and the boys had only just time to get out of the way of its gaping jaws. "Press yourself close to the wall, Dez," commanded Alan, and they reached Jez-Riah's side in safety. Their eyes dilated with horror as they watched the great reptile die, for the boys between them had given it its death blow.

How long the death struggle lasted they never knew. Alan thought an hour, Desmond said two. Blood poured from the wound in its head and a sickly smell rose from the liquid. For some time the stone remained fixed in the flesh of the serpent, but its writhings at last loosened it, and it fell to the ground with a horrible thud, while the blood rushed out of the open wound like a miniature fountain.

Fascinated the three watched its last movements. The body rolled from side to side, dashing first against one then against the other of the unlucky prisoners, but by flattening themselves against the walls, they escaped any big injury—only bruises left their mark to show what they had been through.

The movements became more irregular. For a long time the mighty snake remained quite still, only to wake up again after a rest with renewed energy. At last its spasms became less frequent and less powerful. It was dying. Its breath came like huge sobs that travelled down its body. The stench was almost unendurable. "I think it's safe now," said Alan at last. Slowly they moved from their cramped positions. Their hearts throbbed and their limbs ached. Fearsomely they gave a last look at the head of the dying, if not already dead, monster. A shudder ran through them all. The strain through which they had passed had been terrible, but for Alan, who had engineered the defeat, it had been terrific. His limbs ached, his head swam, and he reeled as he walked on the free ground, unpolluted by the serpent. He laughed a wild unnatural laugh; it sounded strange even in his own ears, and he repeated it, as he wondered whether he was indeed going mad. He felt suddenly unaccountably frightened. Everything faded from him but the memory of the serpent behind. With another peal of almost senseless laughter, he ran madly away into the distance, until the darkness swallowed him up, and only the sound of his wild laughter broke the stillness. Jez-Riah clutched at her throat and spoke to Desmond. "Ar-lane—he is ill—come," said she, and the two followed Alan away into the blackness as he sped on, laughing—laughing—laughing.

VII

ON THE WAY TO THE TOMB OF KORAH

Time passed—time that had no measure—time that seemed an eternity. They had all recovered from their encounter with the Sacred Serpent, but the adventure had left them nervous and irritable. There was food in plenty, and the luscious roots gave them both meat and drink. Always upward they mounted—and as they saw the mountainous paths rise before them, hope held out her encouraging hand, and whispered that one day they might even see the stars. Jez-Riah still led them on, through untold paths and a labyrinthine maze. She always maintained that she knew the right path to take.

Sometimes they had to crawl on their hands and knees through narrow and low passages that seemed to have no end. At other times they found themselves in wide, airy byways with a height almost beyond computation, for far above their heads they could just catch the faintest glimmer of light on the purple growth that covered the roof. Now and again springs bubbled up from the earth and ran along beside them, burying themselves as suddenly as they had appeared. The atmosphere was very sultry and fetid—very different from the air on the other side of the underground river that separated the underworld people from the desolate region they were now in. "How long, Jez-Riah?" they asked her over and over again. "How long before we reach the Tomb of Korah?" And her answer was the same each time. "Oh Men of the World Above, I do not tarry, I am leading you to the Tomb as fast as I can. Be content with that." So the days passed—so the nights came round again. Days which had no night, nights which had no day. Time was measured by sleep. When they were all weary they lay down to rest and sleep. This they called night—when they awoke they called it day. But they had lost count of the times they had slept since Jez-Riah had come to them, they had lost count of everything. They had only one object before them—to reach the Tomb of Korah. Their plans ended there; they had no idea what their next move would be after they reached it. They had grown accustomed to their strange, purple companion—in fact she had become almost a necessity to them both. It was she who passed many weary hours for them, by recounting stories of the life of her people since they had lived below. It was she who told them even more fully than Har-Barim had done, how her people's forefathers had risen up against Musereah, and Har-Raeon, and how they had consequently suffered throughout the ages. And both the boys translated Musereah as Moses, and Har-Raeon as Aaron, and were more than ever convinced that strange as the story was, this new race was indeed descended from the Israelites of the Old Testament and could claim Korah, Abiram and Dathan as its progenitors.

It was Jez-Riah who told them that behind a barred gate was built a golden tomb wherein had been deposited the remains of their first priests—"Har-Barim and Kartharn." It was at their shrine that the ceremonies attached to the feast of Meherut were performed. It was their Holy of Holies, and it was over the bones of Har-Barim and Kartharn that the priests made their vows.

They asked Jez-Riah about the fire and she grew solemn as she answered them—"Ah, Men from Above, Our Fire is sacred—it is Holy. It is the symbol of our Jovah.—It is almost our God. The God of our forefathers took on one occasion the form of fire, so fire is sacred to us."

"The Burning Bush," said Alan in an undertone.

"But," she added sorrowfully, "the power of the Fire is waning. According to one of our prophecies, when the Fire shall die, then, also shall all the seed of Korah die too. In all the ages that have passed since the earth closed against us, no fuel was needed for the Fire—it burnt of itself and never grew less. Then one day noises were heard in the earth—our land shook and trembled, and men fell on their faces in fear. From that day we knew the Fire was growing less. Our priests knew it—all our people knew it and terror was in all our hearts. Then our high priest looked up all the old laws and in the fourth book of Rabez-ka, Queebenhah the Seer writes—

'When the Fire shall shrink, then is the time ripe for the people of Kalvar to rise. Live sacrifices must be offered to appease the God of Anger. Send forth a Light to the world above, and let it bring back men and animals and birds to feed the furnace of Light. Live sacrifices alone will keep the fire quickened—live sacrifices alone will prevent calamities falling on the Children of Kalvar.'

"So our wise men gathered together," she continued, "and by the wisdom of all, the Light was made. The wise men of the temple and Kaweeka alone could handle it—for they were possessed of Holiness, and the Light was made from the Fire itself. Chemicals were drawn from the recesses of the earth, and in secret the Light was made."

"How did they use it, Jez-Riah?"

"When it was sent out into the earth above, it was sensitive only to life. When any warm living thing of the world was near, it swooped down, and coiled round and carried its prey back to us."

"I understand better," said Alan to his cousin. "The Light is some magnetic electrical current with abnormal power. Ugh! It's horrible."

"But why did they stop sending out the Light for fodder to feed the flames?" asked Desmond.

"Because we realized that our time is short. Nothing will keep the Fire alive. The end is near."

So they travelled—and then depression overtook them as their journey seemed endless and they got no nearer to their goal. Even Jez-Riah herself seemed to lose hope, and with tears in her eyes she would say pathetically "O Ar-lane, my senses seem dimmed—the way is dark. Surely we must come there soon!"

The monotony of the way drove the white men nearly mad. The monotony of the food sickened them. They felt half dazed; they forgot the reason of their march; they forgot, even, what the goal was toward which they were going. They knew only that some power within them urged them to go on and on and always on.

At last Jez-Riah's eyes grew bright and her step alert. "Don't speak," she urged, "don't speak!" So they went, until all the passages merged into one long tunnel—darker than the others through which they had come. The natural light shed from the earth itself, grew still more feeble, and they found it difficult to walk for fear of hidden pitfalls. Suddenly the passage ended and Jez-Riah gave a glad cry. "Behold, O Men of the Sun, this is the entrance to the Tomb of Korah."

"Are you sure?" asked Alan.

"Quite, O Ar-lane. The paths we have been traversing were made by our forefathers long æons ago. After they had fastened Korah and all that appertained to him fast within the bowels of the earth, they had to fight their way through to make a place of habitation. They cut paths as they marched along, and when they found the Fire—there they made their home. I knew that when all paths merged into one, the way was near to Korah's tomb."

The place in which they found themselves was very disappointing. Their way just ended—it did not widen out at all, and the end was piled with stones and earth that had fallen through the ages. Their quest was over at last, and they took their first untroubled rest. They slept long and quietly, and it was Jez-Riah who awakened them and placed before them the food they were so heartily sick of. "Nay, eat," she commanded, "your strength is needed more than before," and feeling the truth of her words, they ate until they were satisfied and felt all the better for the food.

"The earth has fallen," said Jez-Riah. "If we are to find the entrance to the tomb we must clear away all that rubble."

Feverishly they set to work tearing their hands to pieces on the jagged stones until the passage behind them was nearly closed with the mass of rock and earth that they had displaced. Twice they slept, and then success came to them, for a solid slab of rock appeared in the wall—a rock that had been made smooth and upon which were carven hieroglyphics.

"I cannot read it," said Jez-Riah, but Alan was already translating, for it was the Hebrew he knew, and not the corruption that had come down through the ages to the purple people.

"Read it aloud," said Desmond, and Alan spoke the words of the inscription reverently.

BY THE WILL OF THE EXILED CHILDREN OF ISRAEL

"Korah, son of Izhar, the son of Kohath, the son of Levi, and his wives and his children and all that appertains unto him and to them, lie buried in this cave. For the wrath of Jehovah fell on his people who sinned against the Lord, tempted by the Evil one— Korah. This is his Tomb—cursed be the ones who open it before the day appointed is at hand.

"Dathan and Abiram, sons of Eliab, the son of Peleth, son of Reuben; Shedur, son of Helon, son of Abira, the son of Simeon. Priests, chosen by the banished Children of Israel in their new land of Kalvar—in the bowels of the earth."

The cousins did little else but talk about the discovery until the time came for them to rest. Their labours had been rewarded; the Tomb of Korah had been revealed to them.

ELLA M. SCRYMSOUR

They worked hard when they awoke to move the massive block of stone. There was no secret spring to assist them—the stone had been placed in position some three thousand years before, and now seemed to defy all the efforts they made to move it. With rocks and stones used lever-wise they worked until after many "days" they succeeded in forcing the solid block of stone to the ground, but behind it was a wall closely built of stones and earth bound together with a rude cement. Their fingers were torn and bleeding in their attempt to pull the stones apart. "At last," cried Alan in delight. For as he worked his hand had gone into space—the tomb was laid open before him.

VIII

The Tomb of Korah

T he Tomb of Korah! They had reached their goal at last! The boys stood back awed at the thought of what might have passed in that selfsame cavern thousands of years before.

"You go first, Jez-Riah," said Alan at last, and slowly, reverently the two boys followed her in. The natural light had grown stronger and allowed them to see quite plainly the mysteries the cave was to unfold. They discovered it to be a cavern perhaps forty yards square. The roof rose above them perhaps a hundred feet, and was marked by a deep, zigzagged line running across it from one side to the other. It was like a scar!

"Dez," said Alan suddenly, "is that where the earth originally opened, when it deposited Korah and the other Israelites within its bowels?"

"If so we ought to be somewhere in the neighbourhood of Palestine," replied Desmond.

The cave had no outlet, and on the floor lay precious stones of every kind and colour;—diamonds, rubies, pearls, emeralds, sapphires—as large as Barcelona nuts—lay strewn about in fabulous quantities. In one corner of the cave were the remains of furniture and household goods, mostly rotted away and eaten by worms; and mingled with the precious stones were human bones—human bones in such quantities that it was impossible to avoid treading on them. Here was a thigh bone, there a skeleton hand or a skull. Everywhere the bones of men and beasts mingled together in a heterogeneous mass.

Quietly, slowly they made a round of the place, There were skeletons of horses, asses and camels lying together in a corner, and piled on top of each other in such a way as proved it had been done by the human agency, were the remains of little children.

Skeletons of females with the remnants of clothing on their whitened bones, adorned with anklets of gold and bracelets set with gems, were everywhere, and the whole scene was like a ghastly wonder story of the East. They picked their way through a bed of grinning skulls to where they saw something shining.

Alan picked it up. "A censer," said he, "one of the most beautiful I have ever seen," And indeed it was of wonderful workmanship.

Even their little knowledge told them it was of pure gold; it was most wonderfully fashioned to represent on the one side a cherub—a cherub so perfect that even the finger nails were represented, and on the other, bunches of grapes and vine leaves—symbols of the promised land.

Precious stones gleamed cunningly everywhere, and the chains from which the censer swung were studded with diamonds. They could scarcely bear to put it down, but gazed at it entranced with its beauty. Every moment they found in it some greater glory.

"I have seen nothing modern even resembling this," said Alan at last. "Why, it is exquisite—think of its value!"

"Its history alone would render it priceless," said Desmond, "apart from its precious metal and workmanship."

"Yes, but of what use is it to us down here?" questioned Alan. "And even if we ever do get out, who will believe our story?"

"I wonder where we shall find ourselves if we do discover a way out," said Desmond. "We have lost all sense of direction down here—of distance and of time. Why, we haven't even any idea of how far we have walked since we left the purple people—how far do you think, Alan?"

Alan shook his head. "It's impossible to say, Dez. How many times have we slept? We counted three hundred times and then forgot—three hundred times is a long while, old boy. We must have walked at least fifteen miles each 'day' we have been on the march—perhaps even more—so we have done a considerable distance."

"Then where shall we find ourselves? Africa? America? Asia?"

"Well, we shall not be penniless when we do get to the world again," and Alan pointed at the wealth of jewels at their feet.

"It is those that make me feel we shall never get out," said Desmond despondently.

"Why?"

"Because it is only in books of romance that such an adventure as ours would culminate successfully, and it would only be in a Romance of Romances that adventurers would come back from the very centre of the earth, laden with such untold wealth!"

"Don't be so depressing, Dez," laughed Alan.

"But it's true, Lanny. With wealth like this in our hands we could command the trades of the entire world. Why, with this we could corner wheat—corner cotton—corner millionaires themselves—if we were permitted to use it."

"Why permitted?"

"Well, it depends on the government of the country we eventually land in; they will want their share. If it's France we may get one half—if it's Spain perhaps an eighth—Russia?—well, nothing at all and the salt mines into the bargain."

"You are very cheerful," laughed Alan, "but as a matter of fact, I've been planning what I mean to do with my share if we do get out."

Jez-Riah had been listening to the two boys speaking and sighed deeply. They were talking in their own language and had forgotten all about their strange companion.

"What will happen to her if we ever do reach the upper world?" said Desmond suddenly.

Alan looked soberly at the quaint little purple creature who had so grown into their lives, who had been so useful to them, who had become almost a friend. They treated her as they would some great, faithful hound who was devoted to them alone. She was like a dumb animal in her unwavering loyalty to them, and indeed would have laid down her very life for her friends.

"She'll have no easy time, poor thing," said Alan, "but I'll use every scrap of my energy to prevent an Earl's Court Exhibition for her."

Again Jez-Riah sighed and a tear rolled down her cheek.

"What ails thee?" asked Alan in her own language.

"I am sad and sorrowful, O Ar-lane," she replied. "The memory of a prophecy has come to me. I shall see the stars of Heaven—the Sun in the Sky—but with pain alone will such sights come to me."

"We'll keep pain from you," said Alan kindly. "If you are to see the stars, then that means we shall all find a way out from here."

The boys set to work to try and find Korah's remains and an outlet to the world above. Many times they slept, and their last waking thought was—"Shall we find a way out to-morrow?" They counted the skeletons and piled them reverently in one corner. They counted the remains of twenty-two women, forty-nine men and about thirty children, some of whom appeared to be but newly born.

They gathered the precious stones, and placed perhaps a gallon measureful in a basket Jez-Riah had plaited out of the roots of the mautzer—her fingers were busy the whole time they were exploring the cavern and its contents.

She had made a covering for the censer, and that had been put carefully aside. The furniture and tenting was all valueless. It fell to pieces at a touch and only small scraps of tinder-like material remained to prove the glories of the silken coverings that had been buried with the Israelites of old. Harness made of leather, and trappings bound with gold lay on the ground mixed up with the bones of the animals they had adorned; chariot wheels lay among the wreckage, and the whole scene was one of utter desolation and carnage.

"Do you know of a way out?" asked Alan of Jez-Riah over and over again, and always she answered "I have brought you in safety to the tomb of Korah, O my friends. Further the way is hidden from me. Now I trust to you."

There was no apparent outlet from the cavern, and the boys hunted for any written record that might have been left behind by Korah or his company. "I want a proof of our statements," said Alan. "When we get to the upper world we shall be looked upon as madmen if we are unable to substantiate our story."

But Jez-Riah would say, "Give up hunting for records of my forefathers, I beg you, and turn your energies to find a way to the sun—"

Alan was thinking deeply on the situation they were in, when his eyes were caught by the scar on the roof. "I wonder," said he suddenly, "I wonder if there is a way out—there."

"Where?" asked Desmond.

Alan jerked his head in the direction of the scar. "It would be madness to try and find out," said he. "The ledges of rock are not strong enough to bear one—don't think of risking your life in such a foolish adventure."

And indeed it seemed almost impossible. The walls of the cavern were jagged and rough, and in many places overhung in a dangerous manner. To climb to the roof would have made even an experienced Alpine climber think twice before he attempted it, and to one inexperienced in such feats it seemed like courting death.

"You wouldn't try," Desmond urged. He knew Alan of old, and feared for him.

Alan laughed. "Is it likely?" was all he said. But all the same the thought remained in his mind, and his brain was working.

It was time to go to sleep. They had supped off the roots of mautzer, and had drunk the liquid from the stems of the elers, and felt refreshed. Jez-Riah was already breathing softly, and Desmond was talking in fitful gusts with drowsy interludes between. Of the three, Alan alone was wide awake. He answered Desmond quietly, and he at last dropped off to sleep too. For some time Alan remained quite quiet, afraid lest a tiny movement of his might awaken either of his companions. Then Jez-Riah's breath came in deep, indrawn sighs, and Desmond lay with one hand over his head and his lips slightly apart. Alan looked at them both closely—they were fast asleep.

Stealthily he rose and stepped past the sleepers through the low way into the Tomb of Korah. He moved with purpose, for his plans were all carefully thought out. High up in the roof, at the farthest right hand corner, the scar seemed its widest. Quickly he walked toward it, and without a backward glance began a long, dangerous and arduous climb. The rocks were slippery, and the foothold almost nothing, yet with tenacious pluck he kept on until his fingers were lacerated and his limbs ached. Pulling himself up by the jagged pieces of rock, he came closer to the roof. Once only he looked below, and his heart pumped and his head swam as he saw the depths beneath. After that he kept his eyes bent upward, and he did not stop until he could touch the roof itself. There was a little ledge, three feet from the top, which was big enough for him to sit on fairly comfortably, and his breath came in hard gasps as he rested.

Then, as his strength came back to him, he carefully put his hand inside the fissure. A stone moved, and as he withdrew his hand, it dropped into the cave beneath, and the sickening thud made him tremble. He heard the sound of rushing waters. Gradually he wormed his way until he was seated in the fissure itself, and looked down on a swiftly flowing river twenty feet below him. It was very swift—he could not tell its depth, neither could he get down to it—for the water had neither bank nor ledge to stand upon. High walls reared on either side of the water as it raced on its mad journey. He watched the swirling depths. The spray at times reached his face, and cooled him. The water was of a different colour from the rivers in Kalvar—it looked cleaner, fresher. "I wonder whither it leads," he muttered, and then he examined his position.

He was inside the fissure on a ledge perhaps three feet wide. There was a sheer drop into the waters below of twenty feet. There was no other outlet at all. If they were to escape it would have to be by the water. It was impossible to go back. Then a daring plan came to him. "If we had the pluck," said he to himself, "Well, it will be do or die." and slowly he turned his attention to the descent.

IX

THE PAPYRUS

Desmond had slept well; he woke lazily and looked round him. Alan had already gone. He turned sleepily over, but raised himself quickly as Alan hailed him from Korah's tomb with an exultant shout. Even Jez-Riah realized that something of import had happened as she watched Alan enter, bubbling over with excitement, and his eyes bright and shining.

"What is it?" asked Desmond eagerly.

"I've found the remains of Korah." Alan made the announcement quietly, but his cousin saw the undercurrent of excitement that lay beneath his words.

"You've found Korah?" he repeated stupidly.

"Listen," went on Alan eagerly, and speaking in the quaint Hebraic dialect, so that Jez-Riah might share his news, he told them of his adventure to the roof of the cave, and of the river beyond. "Well," he concluded, "as I neared the bottom my foot slipped and I clutched at a piece of jutting rock to save me, and I had to use all my strength to keep from falling. My foothold gone, I had to worm my way round the rock to find another place easy of descent. You know the wall is full of cracks and crevices. I came upon a crevice larger than the others. It was big enough to get through, and I wondered why we hadn't noticed it before. I realized, however, the tricks the lighting of this place plays upon us, and I could see that the hole simply looked like a shadow on the wall, so cunningly is it hidden. I scrambled easily through, and found it to be a cave, quite small, in the middle of which is a deep pond of water, and fastened on the wall by the aid of rude nails was this—" and he held out a roll of parchment that crackled at his touch.

Desmond examined it curiously. "Why it's a papyrus," he exclaimed.

"Yes! and written by Korah himself, and placed there just before he died."

"Have you read it?"

"Yes, it's quite easy in parts. Listen," and Alan translated from the old and faded Hebraic characters the following,

Know, then, these four months, as far as it is possible to judge time in this accursed spot, I and all my belongings have remained in this cavern. Abiram and Dathan have sealed the doors of stone against us. Escape is impossible. There is naught for us to do but die. Be it known—I—Korah the Accursed—am sore at heart for my sins of rebellion against Moses and Aaron. Jehovah has inflicted upon us all a grievous punishment. His name be praised. Food there is none except that which came down with us into this pit of terror. Lord of Hosts, I tremble at what I see. Mothers tearing their little ones, women in childbirth crying to the God in Heaven that they may die before they are delivered. I—Korah—alone have remained fasting. It is the only reparation I can make for my sins, and for the unworthiness I have shown as one of Jehovah's chosen ones. I Korah—"

Then came a space that was unintelligible. Time had worked its will and the writing was indistinct, and in parts entirely erased. "How awful," said Desmond, shuddering. "Think—half these skeletons here were perhaps murdered by their brothers for food. What agonies, what pangs they must have suffered!" "Wait—there is more," said Alan, and he went on translating,

"Forty days and forty nights fasting is as nothing to the fasting here. It seems forty times forty since food passed my parched and cracked lips. My people turn not upon me and slay me. Oh that they would! Dead flesh is rotting all around me—the air is heavy with the stench. There are none now left alive but myself. I will fasten this to the wall of the inner cave, and then lay me down to die. Of what use are gold and riches to us here? Poorer am I than the most disease-laden beggar of the world above. O God of Hosts forgive Korah, the son of Izhar, the son of Kohath, the son of Levi."

For some time after Alan had finished reading the boys remained in silence. The whole scene rose up in their minds like a picture, and the horror of it nauseated them. The terrible hunger and thirst of the captives-the scenes of cannibalism afterwards—the child murder—it was revolting. "Now," said Alan. "Come to the real tomb of Korah. This is the tomb of his people—but he lies yonder." So the three of them mounted the rough steps in the rock, and ten feet above their heads was the little opening. Just a little cleft through which they passed, and down a short but steep path into the cave below.

The centre of the cave was taken up by a deep pool of water, but a narrow path ran all round. A huge block of stone lay immersed in the water and round it the water bubbled and sang showing the place where the pond had its birth.

But Desmond saw no sign of the bones of Korah. He looked puzzled. "There is no skeleton here," said he. "Where is Korah?" Silently Alan pointed to the grey rock over which the water was lapping. Desmond looked at it intently-and then understood. In the course of time a spring had bubbled up and the waters had covered the body of Korah. Some chemical property in the water had preserved the dead body and turned it to stone, and in the ages that had passed deposits of lime and other minerals had been secreted on the body, until it was now of gargantuan size. Still plain, however, were the features. A rather long nose, Semitic in shape, protruded from a face that had possessed prominent cheek-bones and deep, sunken eyes. The hair which had been long was now a mass of stone that mingled with the shapeless body. They could just trace the semblance of arms that were folded across the stone chest, and there was the suspicion of feet protruding from a kilted tunic of cold grey stone.

In all, just a shapeless boulder in which could be traced the likeness of what had once been a living man. The waters of the centuries had preserved Korah alone of the Israelites of old who had been imprisoned in the pit.

Jez-Riah had listened in silence. With one finger she had traced the outlines of the once handsome face—now she spoke.

"He killed himself—in the water?" she asked.

"No," said Alan, "I think the cave was dry in those days. He just came here to die; and in the place where his dead body lay, before time could rot the flesh, a spring broke through the floor of the cave and preserved him—a memorial to all time of his sin."

"Praise be to Jovah," said Jez-Riah in a hushed tone.

"*Requiescat in pace*," said Alan as they turned to leave the place. "Amen," whispered his cousin—and Korah was once more left alone.

"Now," said Alan some time later while they were having their meal, "now we must make some arrangements about leaving this place. The only way is by the river, yonder."

"Can we make a raft strong enough to bear us?" asked Desmond. Alan shook his head. "I've already investigated," he said. "There is absolutely nothing. The wood in there is rotten with age. I doubt whether it would even float. There is only one possible way," and he looked at them intently. "We can all swim pretty well. Our only hope is to throw ourselves on the mercy of the waters. The knowledge we have of swimming will enable us to keep our heads out of the water—we must trust the current to do the rest. It may mean death—but are we not in a living death already? At any rate are you willing to try?" They walked into the big cave and Desmond looked fearfully at the terrible ascent which they would have to make in order to reach the river, for it flowed on a much higher level than that on which they were themselves.

"Yes, it's pretty stiff," said Alan grimly. "But it's that or nothing. Are you ready to risk it?" For a moment only, Desmond hesitated, then his mind was made up and his hand gripped that of his cousin.

"Yes," said he. "What about you, Jez-Riah?" And they were both surprised at the calm way in which she took the suggestion.

"It is very high," said she. "How easy it would be to fall!"

They rested and slept and ate before they attempted the ascent. Also they had many preparations to make. There was certain of the jewels to be taken with them—the papyrus and the censer. Jez-Riah plaited a waterproof case for the parchment, and with a plaited rope fastened it to Alan's shoulders. The jewels were divided out between them and placed in little bags that Jez-Riah wove from the root tendrils that grew outside the large cave. The censer proved the greatest difficulty. It was not only heavy, but exceedingly bulky and cumbersome. It was Alan again who decided to carry it. "But it will drag you down," objected his cousin. "I'll manage it," he replied, and he had it fastened securely to his back with the strong rope that Jez-Riah could make so quickly.

So they began their arduous climb. Alan went first, followed by Jez-Riah, and Desmond brought up the rear. "On no account look down," Alan kept urging. "It will be fatal if you do." At last they reached the tiny platform. Alan looked at it doubtfully. Would it hold three grown persons? He shivered—it would be a tight squeeze. His hand went down and met Jez-Riah's. He pulled her on to their resting place in safety, and then Desmond reached it, and for a while they sat in silence.

The rushing of the waters could be plainly heard. Time was passing—Alan dared not move, for Jez-Riah, worn out with the climb, was leaning heavily against him, and he knew that the slightest movement from one or the other of them might send them to their death, for the seat was none too safe. "I think the time has come for action," said he quietly at last. "It is useless to wait here any longer."

Jez-Riah moved restlessly. "What your will is, O Ar-lane, that will I do," said she.

"I am going to plunge in the water," announced Alan. "If you see my body rise—follow me quickly. Do not struggle, let the current do its will with you. Safety lies in submission."

"Why wait to see if you rise?" asked Desmond.

"Because I do not know what whirlpools may be hidden there. If you do not see me after I have plunged in, then you must do as you think best. But surely death is preferable to a lifetime here?"

"Then I shan't—"

"Don't argue, old man. Do as I bid you. God bless you."

The cousins solemnly shook hands, lingering pathetically. It was like a good-bye to the dying.

"Ar-lane, O Ar-lane," came from Jez-Riah.

"Have courage, little sister, be brave and follow me." And before they could say another word, he had swung himself over the edge and had dropped into the foaming water.

The water hissed and roared with fury as it felt the presence of the foreign body—then it quieted a little. Alan's head appeared, his face deathly pale, and before they realized it, he was out of sight, borne on the swift current.

Jez-Riah was trembling. "Be brave, little sister." Almost unconsciously Desmond repeated his cousin's words. She clung to him for a second, and then with a little frightened moan that went as soon as it was uttered, she too dropped into the water below, and was carried out of sight. Suddenly a great fear came over Desmond. He was alone. The cavern seemed to ring with laughter—the laughter of dead men. He hovered at the edge of the little cleft and looked deep into the boiling mass below, but he dared not drop in.

"I can't, I can't," he moaned, and the awful loneliness came upon him and enveloped him in a cloak of terror.

He looked behind him at the yawning chasm below. If he lost his foothold—he shuddered. And then with a mighty spring and a muttered "God help me," he followed in the wake of his cousin. The water closed over him—he held his breath until his lungs felt as if they would burst with the strain. Relief came at last, the waters had calmed a little, and he was floating gently on the current. He was conscious of intense inky blackness, of icy waters and a fetid air above; of a swiftly moving stream, that, although not rough, was running fast; of strange shapes that seemed to hover about him, and long, clammy hands that tried to pull him out of the water. He knew it was death himself he was fighting, and he fought to evade the fingers that were now so near, almost clasped round his throat. Then his senses forsook him and he was only an atom, tossed about on the bosom of the unknown river, a nothingness in a world of mystery and wonder.

X

The Escape

A nd the seventh day was the Sabbath! The Lord rested on the Sabbath! Sabbath! Seventh! Seventh! Sabbath! These words kept ringing in Alan's ears as he lay quiet and tranquil in the darkness. He wondered where he was, but was too tired to make much effort to find out. His senses were dulled and his whole body ached; he could see nothing, for total darkness surrounded him. Then unconsciousness again overtook him, and he dreamed again of the Marshfielden fields and the rippling brooks.

When he awoke it was with a healthy feeling of hunger, and gradually his senses returned and he wondered where his cousin and Jez-Riah were. He called them by name, but there was no reply. He reached out on either side of him, but could feel nothing—he seemed to be alone. The silence was oppressive, the air heavy, and he found a great difficulty in breathing. He tried to think of the mad plunge for freedom into the swift underground river; he remembered feeling the cold waters close over him, followed by an interminable time under water when he could not breathe, when his lungs were bursting, longing to disgorge the used up air within him. Then he remembered a feeling of relief as he drew in a long breath of air, and afterwards—no more. He seemed to have fallen into a never ending dream. Now at last he realized he was safe again, and in his heart he thanked God for having watched over him and brought him once more to safety.

As the past events became clearer, Alan rose up cautiously, but his head came in contact with the roof of the place he was in. He went on all fours and groped his way round the place. It was very small, perhaps twenty yards in circumference, and perfectly dark. Suddenly his hand touched something, something warm. It was Jez-Riah, and, close beside her lay Desmond. He spoke to them each in turn—shook them, but they showed no sign of having heard him. He listened for their heart beats, but neither showed any sign of life.

The water that had carried them all to this new abode ran near, and Alan dragged the two bodies to the water's edge. He dipped his hand in the cool liquid and found that it was only an inch or two deep at the most. He made a cup with his hands and dashed the water into his companions' faces in turn, and at last was rewarded by a heavy sob from Jez-Riah and a groan from Desmond.

"Dez, old man, how are you feeling now? Jez-Riah, are you better?"

So from one to the other he turned, his only thought to bring them back to life and hope.

Suddenly Desmond spoke. "That was a near shave, Lanny."

"How are you?"

"I feel beastly."

"Where are we?" suddenly asked Jez-Riah.

"I've no idea. The river has either disappeared underground or we've been brought up a little side creek and left the main channel itself. There is very little water here—only a few inches at the most and it is running very sluggishly. There is a tunnel to the right up which we must have come, but it is very low; I can hear the sound of swiftly running waters, but I don't feel strong enough to investigate in the dark."

"Of course not, Alan," answered Desmond, and then Jez-Riah said pathetically, "I am hungry, O Ar-lane."

Alan shook his head wearily. "There is no food here. The purple light has gone. I am afraid we are far from the vegetation of the underworld."

They talked in low tones for some time—they all felt ill and weak. The papyrus and all their treasures were so far safe, and the censer still remained fast on Alan's back. Their clothes were nearly dry, so they realized they must have been thrown up by the water for some considerable time. While they talked they suddenly heard the sound of heavy blows from somewhere above their heads. Then the sounds increased and they heard that which it was impossible for them to mistake—they knew it too well—the dull roar of blasting operations in a mine!

Alan's eyes were shining. "Did you hear that?" he asked excitedly. "You know that sound? Haven't you heard that dull roar in the pit at Grimland?"

Desmond spoke huskily. "You mean that we are—"

"We are immediately below a mine. White men are not far away, I am sure. They may be Britishers like ourselves—oh, how can we get to them?"

Wildly they hacked at the roof above them, but the sounds they made were puny and little and made no impression in the distance. Tired and weary they all fell asleep, and when they awoke there was silence everywhere. They were suffering terribly from hunger; could they have seen themselves they would have been shocked at their appearance. Pale, emaciated, with hollowed eyes and deep furrowed cheeks, they looked almost like old men, instead of youths still in the glory of their manhood.

They fell into a stupor, and hardly roused themselves, so weak and tired were they, when all at once there came upon their ears a mighty explosion which shook the place they were in and sent stones and rocks hurtling all about them in the darkness. Then came a rumbling deep and terrible.

"It's all right," whispered Alan. "They are only blasting again." But neither Desmond nor Jez-Riah answered him. Weak and hungry they lay inert and senseless upon the ground. The throbbing overhead began again, and Alan alone in his agony beat at the roof with his hands, but realizing his weakness fell on the ground beside his cousin and gave vent to dry, hard sobs.

He listened to his cousin babbling meaninglessly in the throes of fever, and he heard the pitiful cry of the purple woman as she asked for water to moisten her parched mouth. Then he too gave way. Strong and brave he had been through all their privations, but he cried and chattered insanely to the figures he conjured up in the darkness. Death was hovering near them; the Black Angel was standing by them, and the Reaper had his scythe in his hand only waiting for the opportunity that he hoped would come, and that would enable him to cut down three more sheaves for his well stocked granary.

"I CAN'T THINK WHERE THE water comes from, Mr. Vermont. There must be a hidden spring somewhere. Can I have the pumps going and make preparations for an excavation?"

"Certainly, Mennell, when you like," and William Mennell, foreman of the Westpoint Gold Mines in Walla Balla, Australia, started his preparations.

The part of the mine he was working on at the moment was overrun with water, which made the working very difficult, and was causing a great deal of anxiety about the ultimate safety of the mine. The pumps were made ready, a shaft was sunk, and they began to work.

"The trouble is there, sir," said he, indicating the ground under his foot. "I'll have it all up to-morrow." By six the next morning the men were hard at work, and merrily they shovelled the earth aside, cracking jokes meanwhile. Suddenly one of the men lurched forward and gave a cry as he threw himself backward on the ground behind him.

"What's up, Bill? Tea too strong this morning?"

"Take care," he shouted. "There's a landslip or something. My spade went right through. There's a hole there."

Carefully they examined the place, and found that the ground was not solid beneath, but below yawned a pitch dark cavern.

"Where is Mr. Mennell? What had we better do?"

Mennell came up. "Got a lantern, boys?" he asked. "Let's see how deep it is." They tied a miner's lantern on to the end of a red neckerchief and let it down. "H'm, only about eight feet—during the blasting the land must have slipped. My God," he shouted. "Ropes! Ladders! I'm going down."

"What's wrong?" asked Ferrers, one of his pals. "You look as if you have seen a ghost."

Mennell wiped the sweat off his forehead. "Look down there, Ferrers," said he hoarsely. "Can you see anything?"

Ferrers took hold of the lantern and peered down into the blackness. Then suddenly he stood up and looked closely into Mennell's face. "There is something there," said he in an awe-struck voice. "Something that looks like men."

"You saw too?"

"Aye, William."

"Then it was no ghost."

Down the rope ladder went Mennell, followed by Ferrers. They bent over the inanimate forms of Alan and Desmond Forsyth and gently carried them up into the mine.

"What's that?" Ferrers pointed to a far corner of the cave.

"It's a woman."

Tenderly also was Jez-Riah carried up the swaying ladder. The miners were all speechless. How was it possible for three human beings to have got into such a position?

Reverently they were carried to the office at the bottom of the shaft where the manager was busy writing. Mennell told him what had happened, and the boys were laid side by side upon the floor. But when they looked at Jez-Riah they could not repress a shudder. She looked almost inhuman with her purple skin and protruding horn. They overcame their repugnance, however, and forced brandy between her parched lips.

Desmond opened his eyes first. "Is this Marshfielden?" he asked.

"It's all right," said Mr. Travers, the manager, kindly, and he offered him some more of the stimulant.

"Then I am alive?" He touched Mr. Travers' hand. "God, I am among white people at last," and he fell back again unconscious.

"The doc's above," said a man. "I've been on the 'phone. Beds are all prepared for them."

So the two boys, wrapped in miners' coats, were carried out into the sunlight once again. Alan, however, did not recover consciousness at all. He was worn out from hunger, fatigue and worry. Always the one to have a comforting word to cheer his companions, this last experience had been too much for him and he lay so still and quiet and cold, they feared it would be impossible to save him. And Jez-Riah? She had come to her senses and had called for Alan but the miners did not understand her, and drew away from her in fear.

"What shall we do with—it—her?" asked Mennell at last.

"Take her above and put her in Dr. Mackintosh's care," said Mr. Travers kindly.

"Right, sir."

The day was perfect, the sun shining brightly, the sky was blue, a transparent blue, and the birds were singing gaily. The warmth of the sun's rays came through the coat that was wrapped round Jez-Riah, and she struggled to be free of it. The men put her on the ground, and she stood, hands outstretched and gazed at the sun.

"Jovah. Har-Barim," she cried, and smiled at the brightness all around.

Suddenly a change came over her features and she stepped out on to a grassy patch. A crowd of men watched her, and their expressions showed horror and intense fear. There was perfect silence for a moment, and suddenly a voice cried out in tones so hoarse as to be unrecognizable, "My God" and a man turned and fled. All the rest of the miners followed him, their faces white and strained, and little work was done that day at the mine.

And in a little saloon near by, half the men were drinking deeply, drinking to forget the horror they had just witnessed; and they laughed brazenly and made coarse jests in their fear, but not one of them spoke to the other of what he had seen.

BOOK III
EXIT THE WORLD

(*After the War*)

I

AT WALLA BALLA

Nurse Mavis Wylton looked after her patients cheerfully; she was glad of something to do. Life had been very dull in the little township and although the advent of the two Englishmen had made her unaccountably homesick, it had done a great deal toward breaking the monotony.

In the first year of the Great War she had taken up nursing, had tended the suffering on the muddy battlefields of Flanders, had seen service under the scorching sun of Salonica, had continued her labours in Malta, Gibraltar and Egypt. She was in Cairo when the Armistice was signed, and applied for a post in Australia at the conclusion of the War.

An orphan, she had no ties in the dear old Mother Country; her only brother was sleeping in the company of thousands of others in the battle-scarred region of Ypres. She was interested in her two patients— they had come from the mine in an unaccountable manner: she heard the story of the strange woman who had accompanied them and only half believed it—it sounded so very improbable. How could it be true? What was it Mr. Travers had said? She remembered his exact words.

"Nurse, it was horrible," he told her. "As we watched, it—the woman's face—seemed to dry up and wrinkle until it looked like parchment. The outstretched arms grew thin and bony; the body trembled violently and crumpled up and fell to the ground,—and when I went closer all trace of the woman had vanished and there was only a little patch of brown dust on the ground and a little purple package that she had been wearing fastened to her back." The nurse could hardly believe anything so horrible, so uncanny. Yes, poor Jez-Riah had had her wish. She had seen the sun, had drunk in God's pure air. But the atmosphere was too rare, and she had died. Died? Nay, withered up, and returned to the dust from which she had sprung, and nothing remained of the strange, underworld creature, but a little powdery matter that was blown away to the four winds of the heaven she had just existed to see.

Both Alan and Desmond lay in a semi-comatose condition for many days. Their hardships had been so great, their experiences so terrible, that it was marvellous that they had returned sane to the upper world. As it was, both suffered from brain fever, and were now being nursed back to health and strength. The crisis over, both boys were on the high road to convalescence. Side by side in little narrow beds they lay, and gradually the knowledge of their adventures came back to them.

Mavis had just entered the room one day when Alan broke the silence. "Nurse, what day is it?"

"Tuesday."

"What month, Nurse?"

"It's Tuesday the twenty-fourth of June."

"Midsummer day?"

"Yes," she smiled. "Now you mustn't ask a lot of questions, but I'll tell you this—both you and your friend—"

"My cousin," corrected Alan.

"Well, you and your cousin have been very ill. You were brought here four weeks ago and at first we despaired of your lives. You are both much better now, and we hope to have you up very soon. Now don't talk any more—"

"Nurse," he pleaded. "Just one more question." He pondered a minute. "It was June at Marshfielden when—Why it must be 1915!" he finished quickly, Nurse Wylton frowned. Was this a new form of delirium?

"Now don't ask questions—"

"Nurse, Nurse—I must know! We've been away a long time. If this is June, then it *must* be 1915."

"We are a long way past 1915," said the nurse quietly. "This is June, 1920. You must have mistaken the date."

Alan looked at her in blank amazement. "1920," he muttered. "Desmond"—hoarsely—"did you hear that?"

"Now don't talk any more," commanded the nurse—and she drew the green blinds across the window, and shut out the brilliant sunlight.

As soon as she had gone, Desmond spoke. "Six years in that Hell! I can't realize it. Over six years cut right out of our lives!"

"I don't know how we are to explain our presence in the mine," said Alan thoughtfully. "I don't think it will be altogether wise to tell our whole story. I'd rather Uncle John knew first. He would, perhaps, get old Sir Christopher Somerville to organize an expedition to Kalvar."

"Yes," said Desmond, "a properly equipped exploring party would find it comparatively easy to prove the truth of our story. Why we have made one of the biggest racial discoveries of the century. Historically

ELLA M. SCRYMSOUR

and scientifically we shall have benefited the whole world by our experience."

"Poor Jez-Riah," said Alan suddenly. "What an end!"

The first day the boys were coherent, they had asked about their little purple companion, and it was Nurse Wylton who had broken the news of her "death." The boys had taken it very quietly—and the nurse was unable to form any ideas on the relation she bore to them. But they really felt towards her as they would have done to a domestic animal. They scarcely realized she was human.

In fits and starts the cousins recounted their adventures to each other—even yet they could scarcely realize they had come through safely. Daily they both grew stronger, and the marks of privation and suffering which had so disfigured their features were nearly wiped away. They were afraid to cable old Sir John and tell him of their miraculous escape. "We must break the news gently to him—for he has mourned us both, and it may be too much of a shock for him to learn we are both alive and in Australia," said Alan.

Desmond chuckled. "Australia! Fancy coming out at the other end of the world! It's almost like a fairy story, isn't it? Do you remember we wondered where we should eventually land?"

Nurse Mavis entered—her arms full of flowers. "Now," said she briskly. "There's too much talking going on. I am sure you will both overtax your strength. Besides I have a visitor for you this afternoon."

"A visitor?" echoed both boys.

"Yes, Mr. Travers, the Mine Manager, is very anxious to see you, and he wants to return you your property."

"What property?"

"Some packages you had when you—came—in Walla Balla."

The boys looked at each other blankly. They had entirely forgotten the papyrus and censer and jewels they had brought from the Tomb of Korah. They had been worrying about their financial position, and now, if the jewels proved to be real, they could raise enough money and to spare for their expenses and their fares back to England.

"Mr. Travers will be here in about half an hour," went on the nurse. "Do you feel well enough to be wheeled out in chairs to the garden?"

"Please," said Desmond. "I'm sick of this room." But they felt very weak as they walked across the corridor to where the bath chairs were awaiting them with many comfortable cushions and rugs.

One of the under nurses wheeled Alan out first, and as Mavis tucked the rugs round Desmond, he whispered "Wheel me once round the garden first, Nurse."

The hazel eyes smiled down at the blue ones, and a touch of colour came into the nurse's pretty cheeks. Of the two strangers, Desmond was her favourite. He reminded her of her brother—in many ways he was so helpless, and she mothered him and cared for him, until love had overtaken her unawares.

She wheeled him along the grassy paths, and he asked her to stop and pick him a rose, but when she offered it, he saw only the roses in her cheeks—smelt only the perfume of her hair.

"Mavis, Mavis," he whispered, "will you come back to England with us—with me—when we go? It seems too soon to speak—I'm an old crock—old before my time—but you have brought me back to life and hope. I can't tell you what we have been through, Alan and I. Some day you shall know the whole story. Meanwhile may I hope? I love you with my whole soul. Come back to England with me as my wife!"

The hazel eyes grew tender as Mavis bent over the chair and smoothed the thin hand that lay on the coverlet. "I do care," she whispered tremulously. "I have grown to care a great deal—but are you sure? I know so little of you both. I realize you have been through some terrible experiences. I won't question you, I will trust you, but isn't it wiser to wait? Wait until you are stronger. Perhaps in England there was a girl once," the pretty lips trembled, "a girl you once cared for. She may be waiting still—but you have been ill, and have forgotten."

"No," said Desmond firmly. "There has never been a woman in my life. I swear it—never." Suddenly, as he spoke, there came before his eyes the picture of a purple woman leaping into the flames—Kaweeka. "My God!" he cried, "listen, Mavis! I'm not worthy of you. One day I will tell you everything. It is true there was a woman once—" Mavis stifled a cry. "Listen. She wasn't a woman of this world, but like Jez-Riah, the woman who was with us when we came here. I did not love her—I think I loathed her, but she was like a siren. She exercised an unholy power over me. Mavis—she asked me to marry her."

"Did you?" in a whisper.

A flush of shame came over the white face. "Yes, Mavis," hoarsely. "For weeks I lived in her house—until my cousin found me. When he appeared she did her best to woo him also. She cast me aside, but he was strong where I had been weak. No overture she made was strong enough to tempt him. He it was who brought me to my senses and saved me from everlasting shame."

"You loved her?"

"No! A thousand times no! Mavis—it's difficult to explain. Our whole story is so improbable, so fantastic, that without certain undeniable proofs which we hold, it would be considered as the phantasy of a disordered brain. This woman was nothing to me really; when we were together I loathed and hated her—almost feared her, but I was clay in her hands. It was a difficult situation—at that time I did not understand her language or the ways of her people. Oh, how can I make you understand! She wanted me as a new kind of toy. She knew nothing of morality or life as we know it. Her power was almost mesmeric."

"Is she living still?"

"No. She died—oh, years ago," passing his hand wearily across his brow. "I am sorry, Mavis. I had forgotten. I had no right to speak to you, but all recollection of Kaweeka had faded from my mind until you spoke of another woman. Will you forget what I said? I beg of you, don't despise me too much."

"Dear—I hardly know what to say. I forgive you freely. I nursed you back to life, Desmond. I devoted my whole time to you. While Matron and Nurse Fanshaw attended to your cousin, I watched over you. You grew dear to me. I wanted to see your eyes look at me with recognition in them. I—I—wanted you to—to like me—a little. Then when you first became convalescent I loved to talk to you. Dear, I can forget the past. Life since 1914 has changed. Women have changed. We are no longer the narrow minded stay-at-homes we were before the War."

"The War?" asked Desmond wonderingly.

"Yes, the Great War. The war with Germany." He looked puzzled, but asked no questions, only lay back with his eyes closed, thinking. "We understand the temptations of sex," she went on, "and can forgive. You asked me just now to marry you. I'll marry you most gladly whenever you like, and I'll do my best to make you forget your terrible experiences. Wait—" as Desmond would have spoken, "I'll ask no questions. When the time is ripe you can tell me all. Meanwhile I'll be content to love and trust." There was no one in sight; a tall hedge on either side of the garden walk gave them shelter.

"Kiss me, Mavis," said Desmond hoarsely. "Oh my darling, how I love you." And so the old, old story was told once more.

"Nurse Wylton! Nurse Wylton!" Matron's voice was calling and it was a rosy cheeked nurse who answered.

"Nurse, wherever have you been? Mr. Travers has been waiting over half an hour to see the patients."

Half an hour! Mavis offered no excuse—indeed she had none, and she wheeled her charge to Alan's side. As she turned away to fetch Mr. Travers, she heard Alan say petulantly, "Wherever have you been all this time, Dez?" but she didn't catch Desmond's reply. If she had it would have set her thinking, for he said in an awe-struck tone, "Lanny, old boy, do you know there has been a war—a war with Germany? And we've missed it, old chap, we've missed it."

Mr. Travers was a genial soul and loved by all the miners. He came forward and greeted the boys cheerily.

"Well, I'm glad to hear you are both better. A nice fright you gave every one to be sure. We wondered at first how you had got into such a position." He laughed heartily at the recollection.

"However, the explanation was quite simple after all, wasn't it?"

The cousins looked at one another with questioning eyes. In their opinion the explanation could hardly be called simple! Mr. Travers, however, went on. "After you had been rescued, Mennell, our foreman, gave orders for the men to cease work at that point. He wanted investigations to be made, after consulting me. The following day, however, we found the cave had filled with water, and the pumps were kept very busy, I can tell you. Then part of the flooring caved in, and the walls gave way. Oh, it was a horrid mess! However, it was eventually cleared away, and we discovered the subterranean passage. Very ingenious indeed." And he rubbed his hands together. The boys were frankly puzzled.

"When did you leave Karragua?" asked Mr. Travers suddenly.

"Karragua?" asked Alan.

"Yes, Karragua."

Desmond opened his mouth as if about to speak, but Alan was the first to recover his wits.

"Before we tell you our story, won't you tell us what you discovered?" he asked shrewdly.

"Certainly, my friend. I suppose it was some bet you had on?"

"Something of the sort," agreed Alan, now wholly puzzled.

"I thought so. I knew I was right. I shall take a bottle of rum off Old Man Paterson now. I told him it was the result of some freakish wager—he would have it you had discovered it by accident."

"Do go on," urged Alan. The situation was becoming desperate. Neither of the boys had the slightest idea of what Mr. Travers was talking about.

"Well," continued the cheery manager, "you may be sure it took some time to clear away the débris after the cave-in. When it was clear we saw a passage leading out of it, and followed it about a mile, when it became choked up; and as we had made no preparations we returned and decided to continue our investigations another day."

"Well?" from both boys.

"It was a Thursday. John Cornlake, Bill Watson and one or two other good, all round pick hands came with Mennell and me. It was a long road—two and three quarter miles by our pedometer—pitch dark, as you know. Suddenly we saw a speck of blue in the distance. We moved the boulder aside—how cleverly it is hidden among the rocks and undergrowth! and we realized at once it was the exit of 'Red Mark's Tunnel'."

Neither of the boys spoke—they saw the humour of the situation, but were afraid lest by a word they might give themselves away.

"It must be a hundred and twenty years since it was used. How did you come to discover it?"

"A fellow told us about it," said Alan vaguely after the fraction of a pause, and Mr. Travers was content.

"Of course when the shaft of our mine was sunk, the workmen searched for the entrance to the tunnel, but it was never discovered, and I don't suppose it ever would have been except by a lucky accident. I suppose you were unable to find your way back to Karragua—was that it? You were in a pretty bad condition when you were found. We have already informed the government of the discovery," he went on, "and agents have been sent down to inspect it. We are not sure what the result will be. Every one in Walla Balla wants to have it opened up as a sort of showplace. It would certainly do the township an immense amount of good. Red Mark and his fellow convicts who escaped through it have certainly left a wonderful monument behind them."

So! It flashed on Alan's mind at once. In some miraculous way the entrance to the passage by which they had come from Korah's tomb was again blocked up. Their secret was still their own, but a subterranean passage made by early eighteenth century convicts had been unearthed instead.

"Did Red Mark dig the passage himself?" asked Alan.

"The story goes that Red Mark and a fellow convict escaped and commenced a passage. Walla Balla was a large farm estate at that time, and was employing nearly sixty convicts. Escape was almost impossible, the place was so well guarded, and such brutal treatment was inflicted on those that attempted to escape that few tried. Red Mark and his companion were lucky, however, and they managed to elude the bloodhounds. Their friends helped them with food. Feverishly they worked at the tunnel. It was their plan to burrow to the sea. It took them several years to complete it, but they accomplished their stupendous task at last. The night it was finished fifty convicts vanished. They had ransacked the larders and had taken plenty of food with them. Those that were left talked vaguely about having heard of a subterranean passage, but it was never found—at least not until now. Those convicts were never seen again. But at Karragua Creek a small sailing craft disappeared, and on it doubtless went Red Mark and his friends. But of course you've heard the story before. How did you find the place—by accident? And then I suppose you wagered you'd find your way through to the other end."

Alan smiled. Mr. Travers was extremely helpful. He talked so much himself that he gave no one else the chance of speaking, and he considerately answered all the questions that he put to the boys—himself.

"Yes," said Desmond, who had taken his cue from his cousin. "We told a friend about it, who wagered us one thousand pounds we would find our way through. Unfortunately, our lanterns went out, we lost our way, we had no food and—"

"And I suppose you were a week or more in that cave—hungry and worn out?" finished Mr. Travers helpfully. "Now I've brought you your property back," and he handed them the packages they had brought from the Tomb of Korah. "Oh, you might give me an official receipt for them," and he handed the boys a paper for them to sign. "By the way," he continued, as he put the receipt away, "that woman." His genial face grew solemn. "What was it—? Was it some—some joke you had prepared, or was it—"

"I can't explain yet," said Alan shortly. "We are going home to England where we have a very strange story to tell. I cannot explain the phenomenon you saw, but I may have to call upon you to repeat the story of her death. I suppose I may use your name?"

"By all means. I shall be only too pleased to assist you young gentlemen in every way I can, but I shall be glad to hear about that woman—it was damned strange. By the way, I sealed your parcels with our office seal. I should like you to examine them to see they are intact."

"We won't bother now, Mr. Travers, thank you. We have absolute confidence in you. By the way," he added, as if in afterthought, "could you put me in touch with any one who would buy one or two unset gems? I have some with me, and am anxious to convert them into cash for our immediate use."

"That's easily done," said Mr. Travers. "Our general manager is connected with Messrs. Frimpton, Long and Beauchamp of Melbourne. They are, I think, the biggest dealers in gold and precious stones in Australia. I will get an introduction for you."

"Thanks very much."

"Don't mention it. Now I think I have stayed quite long enough for a first visit. Good-bye, Mr. Forsyth. Good-bye, Mr. Desmond. Take care of yourselves, and don't get over tired," and the kindly man left them.

"We got out of that pretty easily, thanks to you," said Desmond as they saw him disappear down a bend in the garden. "I couldn't think what he was driving at."

"It's extremely lucky the way to Korah's tomb has been hidden again. That heavy fall of rock and earth did us a good turn." Alan remained silent a few minutes, and looked at his cousin quizzically. Then quietly—

"Haven't you anything to tell me?"

"What do you mean?"

"Oh my dear chap—don't think I am merely inquisitive, but we've been like brothers all our lives. I've watched our pretty nurse; I've watched you too. Have you spoken?"

"Yes. My God, Alan! I'm not worthy. Think—Kaweeka—"

"That is past. It's no good worrying over what is done. You were not responsible down there, alone, in that Hell. Have you told Mavis about it?"

"I've tried to make her understand about Kaweeka—but I've told her nothing about our adventures and our discoveries."

"I'm glad of that. I should like Uncle John to be at the first telling of our experiences. I'm glad about Mavis for your sake. I like her very much—in fact I might say I've grown to be almost fond of her. All happiness, old boy."

"I should like to be married before we start for England."

"Will she agree?"

"I think so."

"Well I'll be best man. Ah, Mavis"—as she appeared—"there is to be no formality now, you know. You are going to marry one of the best, and you've got to like me too."

Mavis bent down and kissed his cheek. "There! Alan, see how cousinly I can be," said she laughingly. "Now it's time you both went to bed—you've been up quite long enough for one day."

That night before the lights were extinguished she told them the story of the Great War. "Where have you been?" she asked in bewilderment. "Why every one in the world knows of it. It's been horrible—terrible; white fighting against white; white employing black to help them. Every nation in the world suffered in one way or another."

"I know it sounds improbable, dear, but neither Alan nor I knew the long talked of war with Germany had really come to pass until you spoke of it to-day. Don't ask any questions—just trust me."

"It's all very mysterious and strange," said she ruefully. "But I will possess my soul in patience."

As soon as he was able, Alan sent one magnificent diamond and half a dozen emeralds to Messrs. Frimpton, Long and Beauchamp and received in return banknotes to the value of five thousand pounds. The boys had also chosen some diamonds for Mavis, and had had them set into an engagement ring for the woman Desmond loved.

Already they were well enough to leave the hospital, but as Walla Balla was only a very small mining township, there was no accommodation for visitors, so the cousins remained at the hospital as paying guests.

One day, late in July, a very pretty wedding took place. The bride was dressed in her nurse's uniform and the bridegroom and best man were arrayed in unconventional white duck. The ceremony was performed by the local clergyman, and there was a big spread afterwards at the hospital, to which everybody in the township had been invited.

Alan felt rather sad as he stood waiting on the platform for the train to come in that would carry off the happy pair to their honeymoon. No woman had ever entered his life. His great ideal was a dream still; and he wondered if the time had passed for her ever to materialize.

"You'll arrange for everything, won't you?" said Desmond.

"Rather. Now don't worry. The boat leaves Sydney at noon on the seventh of next month—eleven days from now. It's the Clan Ronald. I'll book your berths and await you there."

"Good-bye."

"Good-bye."

ELLA M. SCRYMSOUR

Their farewells were said, and Alan was left alone. He stayed a few days longer at Walla Balla among the friends he had made, and then travelled by easy stages to Sydney. The country was very beautiful but he longed to get home. He longed to see the smoky chimneys of London, the bustling streets, to hear again the noisy traffic, and at last to enjoy the truly rural beauty of the English lanes and woods. He longed to see his uncle. Was he still alive? he wondered. He was afraid to cable; he was afraid to write. Suddenly an idea came into his head and he wondered why he had not thought of it before. He would write to his uncle's confidential clerk and friend—Masters. He could trust him to break the news gently.

HOTEL MAJESTIC,
SYDNEY

DEAR MASTERS (*he wrote*)

*"You'll be surprised to hear from one whom you no doubt
have long mourned as dead. Don't be afraid—it is no ghost who
is writing you, but a living man. I cannot explain everything
in this letter, but I am catching the next boat home, and I will
telegraph on reaching Plymouth the exact time we expect to
arrive in London. Yes—it's 'we,' Masters, for I have found my
cousin Desmond. It all sounds wildly impossible I know, and
I am writing you that you may break the news to my uncle
that we still live. Tell him we are longing to see him. Tell him
Desmond has found a wife and is bringing her home. I can say
no more—my hand is trembling with excitement as I write. We
have seen strange things, been to many strange places since we left
Marshfielden, but impress upon Sir John, that had we been able to
communicate with him we should have done so.*

"With our renewed wishes to Sir John and yourself,

Yours very sincerely,
ALAN FORSYTH

"There! I think that will meet the case," and Alan fastened up the letter and posted it.

The seventh at last! All the luggage was on board; Desmond and his wife drove up radiantly happy to the quay and waved excitedly as they saw Alan leaning over the bulwarks. The bell clanged, the sailors gave vent to their sonorous cry, "All ashore! All ashore!" The siren sounded. Gradually the great vessel glided away; the smoke belched out in volumes from her funnels; the landing stage grew smaller and smaller until it was out of sight altogether. The vessel had started on her journey to England.

That night after dinner, when Mavis had gone to her state-room, the two cousins had a heart to heart talk in the moonlight.

"It seems impossible we are really going home at last," said Desmond. "I feel like a child again. I have so much to learn. When we disappeared aeroplanes were only beginning to be used—now they are almost perfect, and are vehicles of every day use. The whole world seems to have progressed a century in these last few years."

"There certainly is a great deal for us to learn," agreed Alan, "but we must leave it to Uncle John. He will put us right about everything."

"I wonder how he has progressed with his airship," said Desmond after a pause. "We used to laugh at the dear old chap; he has the laugh on us now."

"He always said that the future of commerce was in the air."

"Have you the papyrus safe?" asked Desmond suddenly.

Alan laughed. "Rather! Or at least the Purser has. I bought a strong deed box in Sydney and packed everything in it; here's the key. When next we open it, please God, it will be in the presence of Uncle John."

Alan looked sadly at the scene in front of him. A brilliant moon had risen and was sending its beams across the phosphorescent waters. The air was sweet and balmy—the Southern Cross was discernible and the whole scene was like a wonderful painting. The chud-chud of the engines and the swish of the water was the only sound to be heard. Somehow, Alan felt very much alone that night. Desmond, his childish playmate, his boyhood's chum, and later his companion in adventure, seemed lost to him. He had married a wife. That was the trouble in a nut-shell. Things would never be the same again. He was fond of Mavis—she was a dear girl, and would be a splendid wife for his cousin—

"Good night, old chap," said he huskily. "I'm tired. I'm going to bed. I've been keeping you too long from Mavis."

"Good night, Alan. I think I will turn in now. I shall tumble to sleep as soon as my head touches the pillow," he added boyishly.

"Good night."

But it was early morning before Alan went to sleep. He wondered what the future had in store for him. Would it prove as adventurous

　　　　　　　　　　ELLA M. SCRYMSOUR

as the past? Or would he remain a lonely old bachelor, a wanderer on the face of the earth? No fixed home of his own—a favourite uncle, perhaps, to Desmond's sons. Yes, he was getting morbid. He was still young, barely thirty and had his life before him. Somewhere, perhaps, a mate was waiting for him. Somewhere, some time he would find his ideal,—and then—

The clock struck five; he yawned, turned over and fell asleep.

II

Home Again

In a lovely part of Perthshire, deep in a valley among the mountains, lonely and hard of access, stood a curious building. Any one with a knowledge of aeronautics would have recognized it as a hangar for an airship. A narrow track led from it to a tiny cottage in which lived three men—Sir John Forsyth, Abel Masters and Hector Murdoch, the latter a trusty and faithful mechanic. Shortly after Alan's supposed death, Sir John gave up everything to the last remaining object of his life—the completion and success of his giant airship. He had grown very secretive about it. He had it dismantled and taken to pieces, and in pieces it was sent to Scotland to await further experiments. A hangar had been built, the workmen had gone—and then the three men set to work to build up the "Argenta" once again. Sir John had disposed of his interest in the Marshfielden collieries, and his London offices had been taken over by the new owners, hence he had no tie to keep him in the great metropolis.

For over five years he had worked, and now success had come. The powerful spirit he had perfected as a motive power was unexcelled and on the morrow they were going for their first trial flight in the great machine.

Sir John rubbed his hand affectionately over the shimmering metal. It meant everything to him since his nephews had gone.

"It's beautiful, Masters!" said he, and there was a note of triumph in his voice. "It's perfect."

"Yes, sir. Three hundred miles an hour we ought to do comfortably, that is the minimum, and from four hundred and fifty to five hundred at express speed."

"You've worked with me very faithfully, Masters. It was good of you to pander to the whim of an old man, and bury yourself up here."

"I was only too glad to come, Sir John," answered Masters. "For forty-five years I worked in your office—your father's it was then, sir. I was the first to congratulate him after Victoria, God bless her, had made him a baronet. For over twenty years I was your confidential servant—"

"Friend! Masters, friend!" gently corrected Sir John.

"Well, friend, if I may say so. I was always interested in electricity and mechanics, and when you started experimenting, it was me you asked to help you. I have never forgotten that, Sir John, and now I am proud to have been the one to see the work of years rewarded by such success."

"Where is Hector this morning?"

"He has motored to Arroch Head for the letters."

"Is it the day?"

"Yes, Sir John, it's Friday."

"Ah, of course, so it is."

Since Sir John had been living at Dalmyrnie, no one had his address except the Poste Restante at Arroch Head—the nearest village fourteen miles away. No persuasion was strong enough to make him reveal his hiding place. He seemed to live in dread of his secret being snatched from him. No precaution was too great to take to prevent such a catastrophe.

"Lunch is ready, Sir John," came a voice from behind him. It was Hector who had returned. The three men all had meals together in the little honeysuckle-covered cottage that had once been a gamekeeper's. There was no ceremony—they were all workers together.

The leather Post Office bag was on the table, and Sir John unlocked it with the key that hung so prominently on the wall.

"What a budget," said he testily. "Why do people bother me?" He began to sort the letters. "One from Freemantle and Goddard—their account, I suppose. That's from Armstrong's with their invoice for those aluminium screws. A wire for you," tossing the little orange envelope across to Masters.

Masters picked it up gingerly. "Who ever can it be from? Oh," as he read it. "I don't understand it. I think it must be meant for you, sir."

Sir John looked up. "Why?" he asked.

"It was handed in at noon yesterday at Plymouth. It was redirected on from the old London offices. It says, 'Landed quite safely. Leaving Plymouth this morning. Arrive Paddington 5:20. Will come straight to you. Forsyth.'"

"Forsyth!" repeated Sir John. "Who on earth can it be? And if it's for me, why did they address it to you?"

"I don't understand it at all, sir," said Masters. "Haven't you a cousin— Dr. Forsyth who went to Canada some years ago?"

"Yes, yes! Malcolm Forsyth! Of course, of course. Well, I can't see him. I won't see him. I don't want to see anyone. But why did he wire you, Masters? He didn't even know your name."

"I can't understand it at all, Sir John," then his face brightened, "unless the clerk who redirected it put my name on by mistake."

"Ah, perhaps that was it. Oh well, never mind," said Sir John testily. "You must write and say I can't see him. Here's a letter for you, too," he went on.

"I expect it's from the Stores," said Masters. "I have been expecting their list of concentrated foods with the highest caloric value. We want them in our flights."

He opened the letter casually. "My God!" he cried and it dropped from his nerveless fingers.

"For Heaven's sake control yourself," said Sir John sharply. Now his airship was complete, his nerves were all on edge waiting for the trial. "What is it? What is it?"

"I'm sorry," said Masters penitently, "but I've had a shock. I've heard from some one I thought was dead years ago."

Sir John showed little interest. "Well let us now get on with lunch," was all he said.

"I don't think I'll have any if you don't mind," said Masters. "I must go into Arroch Head at once and send a telegram. I may have the car I suppose?"

"Why, of course, but do have your meal first."

"No—no I can't wait. I must go at once."

Masters had had a shock. He had received Alan's letter from Sydney, and the meaning of the telegram was clear. Alan and Desmond were safe and had arrived in England. He must wire them at once, and give them Sir John's address. He scarcely knew how to break the news to him, and it worried him as he went into the little village.

"Have you wired your friend?" asked Sir John when he got back.

"Yes."

"Do you want to see him—if so you had better take a short holiday after the trial."

"Thank you all the same, Sir John, but I've wired them to come to Arroch Head."

"The devil you have!" roared Sir John. "I suppose the next thing will be that you want them to come over here and see the Argenta."

"I was going to suggest it to you," answered Masters imperturbably.

"Have you taken leave of your senses? Show my work—the child of my brain to strangers? Never!"

"They are not quite strangers, Sir John. The fact is—" he hesitated, "I told you I had mourned them as dead—so have *you*, Sir John."

"What?"

"I have given them your address and—"

"You've given them my address?" spluttered the old gentleman in rage.

"Yes, Sir John—don't you understand now? I told you that *you too* had mourned them as dead."

Sir John looked sharply at Masters, and as he gazed deep into his eyes he read there the truth. "Alan—Desmond," he said hoarsely. Masters nodded his head and Sir John sank back into his chair.

"Alan!" he whispered. "Is it true?"

"Yes."

"Don't joke, man, for God's sake! Don't fool me! It can't be true. It's six years since the accident. Why the mine has never been in use since—not that part."

"Don't you understand the telegram now, sir?" Masters held it out. "They have been away, but now they are back in England."

"Was that the letter this morning?"

"Yes! Read it."

Sir John was plainly overcome. "I'm sure it's a joke," he muttered over and over again. "It can't be true. The thing's impossible."

All that day work was at a standstill. Hector alone saw to the bodily requirements of the men, and meals as usual were served at their proper times.

"They will be here for the trial," whispered Sir John excitedly. "Oh my God!" and the old man burst into tears. His grief at the loss of his two nephews had been so great, his affection for them so sincere that he could scarcely realize that in some miraculous way they still lived.

"Will you meet the train?" asked Masters as they retired for the night.

"Yes! Yes! Of course! Take the large car. Are you sure everything is ready for them? You see there will be a lady, too. Desmond's wife—my niece."

"Everything is quite all right. We have made the place quite comfortable—we will occupy the two rooms there, and that will leave three bedrooms in the cottage free. Yours, Mr. Alan's, and the largest, at the front, for Mr. Desmond and his wife."

"Splendid, Masters, splendid." It was a glorious, late September morning when the Scotch express steamed in. Alan was out of the train first.

"Uncle," said he, "dear old uncle."

"My boy—my boy! How are you? Oh, how you have changed! Desmond, my boy, welcome home!"

"This is Mavis, Uncle John."

Sir John held her by the shoulders and looked into her eyes. She could see that suffering had left its mark on the old man's face, so she impetuously flung her arm round his neck and kissed him. "Uncle John," she whispered. "I've heard so much about you from Desmond and Alan. I've been just longing to come home—to you!"

It was a very merry party that drove home to Dalmyrnie.

"Eat your breakfasts," commanded Uncle John. "You shall tell me your story afterwards. But have a good meal first." After breakfast, they sat in the old-world garden, among the trees—Sir John and Masters, the two boys and Mavis, and their wonderful story was told.

Desmond began by telling how he was caught by the Light, omitting nothing, and Alan concluded the story. "Now here is the papyrus and here are the jewels and the censer. These, I think, will prove the truth of our strange story."

"And you mean to say there is a race of people living in the centre of the Earth?"

"Yes, indeed, where we have been actually living for the past few years."

"They are actually descended from Korah, Abiram and Dathan?"

"Yes, as I told you, they still speak a patois Hebrew—they possess a copy of part of the Pentateuch—they worship the God of the old Testament, Jehovah, the great 'I am'."

"And yet you say they are savage?"

"I don't think my description can be good, if I left you with that impression," said Alan thoughtfully. "They are not like the black, savage natives of the present day. I should say rather, that they still possess the savage instincts of our forefathers. The sacrifice of living creatures, even humanity, does not revolt them. They are impervious to great pain themselves, and can watch it in others without flinching. The living sacrifices they offered to the Fire must have suffered agonies before life was finally extinct in them; but to their mind the pain they were inflicting made the sacrifice still more acceptable to their Almighty. They inflicted terrible tortures on their Virgin Watchers of the Temple—they were cruel, cunning, vile—yet in other ways they were too cultured to be called savages. Savage yes, but not savages."

"I see the difference you mean, my boy. But didn't you say they worshipped the Fire?"

"Yes. It is itself a part of their religion. I don't think I ever understood it properly myself. They looked on the Fire almost as God himself—not a different God, but just God. Yet at the same time they believed that the God of their Fathers exists in the Heaven above the Upper World. It sounds very complicated, I am afraid."

"No, no, my boy. I understand quite well what you mean."

"They believed they had to offer living sacrifices to the Fire to keep it burning. The strangest part of their belief is, that when the Fire does die out, then will come the consummation of the entire world—not only theirs but ours too."

"Then they know of our world?"

"Oh yes. Dathan and Abiram left written histories about the world they had left—the world they had once inhabited."

"Going back to the Fire," said Sir John. "Is it large?"

"Enormous. We never saw it in its entirety. It seemed to stretch away into the distance for miles. It was walled in with a glass-like substance, and was absolutely unlike any fire we had ever seen before. It seemed to have no real substance—was all leaping, brilliant flames—yet the heart of it seemed solid and firm. During our stay we could see that the Fire was really growing less and less. Imperceptibly at first, but latterly by leaps and bounds."

"I wonder what *will* happen when the Fire does go out," said Desmond thoughtfully. "It has existed on itself for these thousands of years. The only fuel that was ever given it latterly was human or animal life. Surely that could hardly feed a Fire."

"I think some world-wide catastrophe will come when the Fire dies out, if ever it does," said Alan.

"And Jez-Riah just fell to dust," went on Sir John slowly.

"Yes."

Mavis was very excited. "Why our fortunes are made," she cried. "Of course you'll write to the papers?"

"We didn't know what to do," said Alan. "Desmond and I talked it over and came to the conclusion we would tell Uncle John first and get his advice."

"No one else knows at all?"

"No one but us five."

Masters looked up and gave Alan a grateful look. "It was good of you to include me," said he.

"Why, you are part and parcel of ourselves, Masters," laughed Alan. "Nothing would be complete without you," and he shook hands heartily with his uncle's trusty friend.

"We must go back to London," said Sir John at last. "I will wire Sir Christopher Somerville—he's President of the Geographical Research Society you know—and Professor Chard of the Geological Society to meet us in town. I will put the whole matter before them and take their advice. But, my dear boys, I can scarcely yet realize I have you back with me again."

"Have you done any more with your Argenta?" asked Desmond suddenly.

Sir John's eyes shone. "Come with me," said he and he took them to the hangar. "She is complete and I think perfect," said he simply. Very beautiful indeed looked the Argenta. There was a perfect grassy incline leading from the hangar to a large, flat field.

"I shall run her down the slope," he explained, "and the field in the hollow is splendid for both ascending and descending."

"Have you tried her yet?"

"No. We were going to try her yesterday, Mr. Alan," said Masters, "but Sir John postponed it until your arrival."

"And we must postpone it again, I am afraid," said Sir John, rather sadly.

"Is it necessary, Uncle John?" asked Mavis.

"I think so, my dear. Your story is too wonderful to keep back a moment longer than is necessary. We will go to London to-morrow, and after all formalities are done with, will come back, try the Argenta, and if she is as I think she is, we will go for a long holiday in her."

"Shall I accompany you?" asked Masters.

"Just as you like," answered Sir John. "Come with us by all means, or stay with Hector and watch over the Argenta."

"I would rather stay here, sir, if you have no objection. I've no ties that take me back to town, and I would rather remain by the Argenta."

Forty-eight hours later Sir John, Alan, and Desmond and his wife arrived in London. Sir John had let his town house, so they chose a quiet hotel at the back of Berkeley Square for their domicile.

Sir Christopher Somerville and Professor Chard kept the appointment made, and once again the boys recounted their adventures. "Wonderful! Marvellous! Miraculous!" the professors kept muttering to themselves, as the improbable story was unfolded to them, piece by piece.

"Now," said Sir John, when it was at last told. "There are seven people only that have heard this story. What do you advise us to do?"

"I will see the Home Secretary," said Sir Christopher at last. "This is a Government affair, of course. England's to the fore again; lucky they found their way out on British territory. The question will be brought up in the House—an expedition must be formed, and the two young gentlemen would probably like to accompany us, and help us with their knowledge of the place."

"Don't go again," cried Mavis, her face blanching. "Oh you wouldn't take him from me?"

"Don't be afraid," said Alan kindly. "Nothing is done yet, and when it is they will be probably quite contented with me alone."

"Would you go again?" eyes wide open in horror.

"Of course, Mavis, but I'll see that Desmond doesn't go," and he laughed cheerily.

The professors called a general meeting of their associations upon the matter of "The Discovery Of A New And Hitherto Unsuspected People" and the two boys came in for a great deal of congratulation and applause. Everything was settled at last, however; matters were directed through the right channel and a statement was brought up in the House of Commons. The only point that was not made public was the exact place of the entrance to Kalvar. That was kept entirely secret—the Home Secretary having pledged his word that until the necessary arrangements had been made between the two Governments, that of the Mother Country, together with the Commonwealth of Australia, most stringent secrecy should be kept, so that no one could possibly know that Walla Balla was the favoured spot.

All the papers were full of the new discovery. Reporters, ordinary newspaper men, big newspaper correspondents, all found their way to the little hotel. Alan and Desmond Forsyth had become famous! Kings and princes,—commoners and dukes, all vied with one another to meet and entertain the two men who had had such remarkable experiences.

At last the expedition was complete and was due to sail in a fortnight's time. Meanwhile, Alan, who was to accompany it, was to take a fortnight's entire rest. Geologists, historians, geographers, all wanted representatives sent. Mechanics, electricians and a small armed force had to be provided. The Government had already made a large grant to the Mining Company at Walla Balla, and had the entire rights for excavating a mile each way from the Second Pit.

The whole expedition was a voluntary one, and once again Britain and her Colonies came to the fore as the greatest pioneers in the world.

The golden censer had been offered to the British Museum, and had been gratefully accepted. The papyrus had been placed in the hands of experts who pronounced the document to be genuine. Antiquarians from all parts of the world came to see the relics, and the newspapers had paragraphs in them every day, relating to the "Kalvar Expedition."

"Phew!" said Alan one day as he leant back in a taxi. "That is the last public speech I shall make for months, I hope." He and Desmond had been guests of honour at a luncheon given by the Society of Antiquarians. "Thank goodness we leave to-night for Scotland. To-morrow we shall see the Argenta. Nine months since we were there. What a lot we have crowded into our lives these last few months."

"I think we've made up for our lost six years," laughed Desmond.

Masters met them at Arroch Head and was frankly glad to welcome them back.

"Nine months since we were here," said Sir John. "You've seen the news in the papers, of course?"

"Of course, Sir John. The *Cavalier* sails in a fortnight, I believe."

"Yes," answered Alan, "and I am going to take fourteen days real rest, and then—well, off to Kalvar again, only this time of my own free will."

The longed-for moment had come! Hector was in the mechanic's seat, while Masters navigated the great ship down the grassy slope. Gracefully she slid out of the hangar, and down the incline and stopped on the level. Sir John was very excited. "You are sure you want to test her?" he asked. "Remember she has never been up before—you have only my word for it that she's safe. Desmond, don't you think you had better stay with Mavis, in case—"

But Mavis interposed. "Nonsense, Uncle John. This is *the* day of my life. Now give me your hand," and she gracefully swung herself up the ladder and on to the lower deck. Sir John followed suit, and they stood side by side, watching the cousins ascend the ladder.

At last! They were all aboard and the six persons entrusted themselves to the aluminium bird that shone brightly in the sunshine. They hauled the grappling irons in, Masters touched a lever, and they started. Slowly they ascended at first—but climbed higher and higher, faster and faster until the hangar was lost to sight and they saw only broad expanses of country below them.

"Oh!" said Mavis breathlessly. "We're off. Where are we going?"

ELLA M. SCRYMSOUR

"I want to make a circuit of the British Isles, and then home to Dalmyrnie."

"But shall we have time?"

"At express speed we ought to do it in about four hours."

"Only four hours?" in amazement.

"Well, we shall only go from Dalmyrnie—we shan't touch further north to-day."

"Now," went on Mavis impatiently. "I want you to take me all over this wonderful ship. I want to see everything. I want to know how it is possible to navigate and propel such a tremendous vessel by the work of only two men."

"Then we'll start right now," laughed Sir John. "Come, boys, we'll explore the Argenta, and then have some tea."

III

The Airship

"It's wonderful, Uncle John! It's almost beyond belief!" Mavis had walked the whole length of the vessel on the under deck in silence. Her husband's arm was about her waist, her face was radiant, flushed with excitement. Alan, too, was bereft of words; even his wildest dreams had never imagined a vessel so perfect, so magnificent, so sensitive to touch that two men could manage it with comfort and ease, and should necessity arise, even one man could manipulate the tiny levers and navigate it.

With a torpedo body some nine hundred feet long, its nose narrowed to three feet, giving it a grace unusual in such a monster aircraft. The entire body was composed of an alloy of aluminium, the formula of which was discovered by much hard work and research by Sir John and Masters. An upper and lower deck ran round the entire ship, about six feet wide, which was covered with a fibre, and had bulwarks of aluminium.

At intervals round the deck, hatches were open, leading to the hold, which contained the tank for the reserve propelling spirit, the water-tank, larders and cold storage. Three ladders on each side and one at either end led to the upper deck. The bow of the vessel was covered with a kind of thick glass and formed a comfortable smoking room where one could sit in comfort in wet or windy weather and gaze into space. There was a dining room, a drawing room, and five bedrooms; all most beautifully upholstered and furnished with the maximum of comfort. The inside walls were polished like burnished silver, and the windows of the same thick glass were hung with pale blue silk to match the upholstery. There was everything for use and comfort; telephonic communication from every room to every part of the ship—electric light—electric fans—electric stoves—a pianola and there was even a gramophone on board.

Sir John had also remembered a good library of books, novels and serious works, and a wonderful supply of writing materials.

"Why, you have forgotten nothing," said Mavis. "Uncle John, I think you have been wonderful."

Perhaps the kitchens furnished Mavis with most interest. They were so well planned out. In one corner stood an electric cooking stove, and on the wall hung everything necessary for the success of the culinary art. A pipe led from the water tank to the kitchen and there was a very ingenious arrangement by which all waste matter was emptied into an electrically heated tank which reduced everything first to a pulp and then to steam, which escaped through a pipe to the outer side of the ship.

"How much water can we carry?" asked Mavis.

"Well, in cubic feet, my dear—" commenced Sir John.

"No! no! Uncle John! I don't understand cubic feet. Tell me how long our water would last."

"With the utmost care we can carry enough water to last six people two months."

"As long as that?"

"Yes, and then, should any unforeseen circumstances arise, by which we were unable to renew our water supply, I could fall back on a wonderful discovery I have made. See, my dear." and he opened a small press. There, on shelves, were packed row upon row of transparent blocks, perhaps an inch square.

"What ever is it?" said Mavis, laughing. "Why, it's camphor!" Alan picked a piece up and examined it. It was certainly like camphor to look at, but was odourless and of an intense coldness. "It's done me. What is it?"

Sir John made no reply but took from a little stand a small electric heater. Upon this he placed a quart metal bowl, into which he put the little cube. "Very gentle heat at first, my dears," said he. "Ah!" as it began to melt. "Now I think it's safe to put on full pressure."

Fascinated, they watched until the vessel became full of a sparkling, bubbling liquid. Turning on another electric switch, he plunged a metal needle into the fluid. It belched forth a cloud of steam, hissed violently and then calmed down.

"What ever is it?" asked Mavis. For answer, Sir John poured the liquid into three glasses and handed one to each.

"Try it," he suggested. "It's quite cold. That was an electric needle which generates a coldness below freezing point."

"Another invention?" this from Desmond.

"Yes."

"There's no smell," said Mavis, as she delicately wrinkled her pretty nose.

"And no taste," averred Alan.

"It reminds me of something," said Desmond. "I'm sure I've tasted something like it before."

"What is it, Uncle John? Do tell us," pleaded Mavis.

Sir John laughed. "Water, my dear, just plain water. Desmond is quite right, he has tasted it before."

"Water," said Alan in bewilderment, "but surely frozen water has a greater bulk than when it is in a liquid form?"

"So it has, my boy. But I call this 'concentrated essence of water.' There is enough in that cupboard to last eighteen months. Of course we should never want such a quantity, but the experiments pleased and cheered an old man in his loneliness."

He then opened another press and showed that it was packed with concentrated tea, concentrated essence of beef and chicken, concentrated essence of milk; it had everything in it that had been devised for reducing food bulk to the minimum with a maximum amount of caloric value.

"Eighteen months' provisions," he chuckled. "The Argenta could withstand a siege." The boat was sailing beautifully, ten thousand feet up; it was a glorious day, cloudless and fine.

"Now for the chef d'œuvre," said Sir John. "Why, where is Masters? This is his work." He telephoned through: "All going well?" he asked.

"Splendidly, Sir John."

"What speed?"

"About three hundred an hour. We've just sighted Plymouth."

"Plymouth," said Mavis in amazement. "Why, we have only just left Scotland."

"Come along to us, Masters. I want you to demonstrate the working of the atmospheric shutters."

"Will you come into the compressed air room?" said Masters as soon as he arrived.

They found it was quite a small room which held no furnishings of any kind. Levers and switches and strange electrical contrivances were everywhere, and on one side of the room were twelve levers, very like those in a signal box on the railways.

"My idea was this," began Masters. "We have ten engines on board, of which we use only one at a time; the others are reserve stock, as it were, or would be useful if we came up against very nasty weather and needed a stronger power to use against the elements. At the time I

ELLA M. SCRYMSOUR

worked out my theory, Sir John had no interest in life. You two young gentlemen we believed were dead, and I have neither kith nor kin. It struck us, that one day we might try and reach the outside of the earth's atmosphere for experimental purposes. I needn't go into exact figures now, it would not interest Mrs. Forsyth, but you all know after a certain distance up life becomes impossible. Should we ever reach that height, we should have recourse to these levers," and as he spoke he pulled them down one after the other. "Now we will put the electric light on, and I would be glad if you would step out on to the upper deck."

Mavis gave a cry of amazement. Gone was the view of the sky; gone the heavens above and the earth beneath. The entire ship was covered in with an awning of metal.

"Do explain," said Alan.

"This covering works almost on the principle of a Venetian blind," went on Masters. "There are really two coverings, with a space of thirty inches between. The levers release the metal and it unfolds and clips into position by means of strong clasps. By means of another lever we fill the cavity between with a mixture of gases—ether is the chief component, and this makes our little home absolutely air proof and rain proof; and above all it makes the inner vessel impervious to atmospheric pressure or gravitation. We hope later on, by the aid of an electrical device we are still working upon, to generate an atmosphere of our own, outside the vessel, which will enable us to propel ourselves through infinite space, and thus we should be independent of the atmospheric peculiarities around us."

"But how can we breathe?" asked Mavis the practical.

"Masters thought of that contingency also," said Sir John.

"In the little room we have just left are dynamos for generating our own electricity; there is also another dynamo for generating an inexhaustible supply of air."

"You have left nothing to chance," said Alan.

"Nothing, my boy. Remember this is the culmination of over thirty-five years of study and experiment, and the last five years have seen us progress by leaps and bounds."

"Our absence had its good side, after all," said Alan. "Had we been allowed to remain, you might never have got this machine to such perfection."

"I'd rather not have had those years of sorrow, all the same," said Sir John softly. "I'd rather have destroyed the Argenta with my own hands, and never built her up again, than you should both have left me for those long years," and the old man turned away with a sigh. "Now about our air supply," he went on, recovering himself. "As the used up air sinks to the ground, it is attracted into pipes, and by the aid of tiny electric fans is driven to a large cylinder. There it undergoes a kind of filtering process. The purer portions go into circulation again, while the carbonic acid gas is taken down pipes which run along the whole side of the ship to an outlet where it can escape into space. To guard against the extrance of any unknown noxious gases, this pipe has a trap in every foot, which closes mechanically as the gas passes through. The mechanism of these traps makes it impossible for any foreign air to enter. No matter where we are, or through what poisonous air we may pass, we are protected from its entrance by this device; while it is impossible for the ship to collapse while it is protected by its envelope of ether."

"Then you could live as long as your provisions lasted on the Argenta?" asked Desmond. "You are not dependent on the outer world for anything?"

"We are dependent only on ourselves," replied Sir John.

"Why, it's like a fairy tale," said Mavis.

"Tea," said a voice from behind them. "Tea, Mrs. Forsyth." It was Hector. Masters had unobtrusively left while they were all talking, and Hector had turned cook.

"Tea is served in the Bows," said Hector again.

Masters had drawn back the shutters, and once again the little room was flooded with sunshine. The telephone bell tinkled. "Well, Masters?"

"We are passing over Whitby, sir. Do you wish to cut across country direct for Dalmyrnie, or will you go right round by the coast?"

"Time is getting on. I think we had better make straight for home."

"Very good, sir."

"It's been a wonderful success," said Alan. "More wonderful than I could have dreamed possible." Sir John beamed at the praise. "But, Uncle John, leave your atmospheric experiments until I come back from Kalvar. I'd love to accompany you on your adventures."

"Would you really?"

"Nothing would give me greater pleasure."

"Look," said Mavis presently. "We are over Loch Tay. How beautiful it looks from here. Why there is still a suspicion of snow on Ben Lawers."

"We are very near home, now," said Desmond, looking at her fondly.

Within a very few minutes the great vessel tilted ever so slightly, and then with a graceful movement, slanted her nose to earth. There was only the faintest suspicion of a jolt as she touched the ground, and then ran smoothly along the field, coming to a standstill at almost the very spot she had left a few hours before.

The trial was over! The machine had proved her worth.

Science had won yet another brilliant victory.

IV

THE END OF THE WORLD

Four days had passed, four days of glorious sunshine. Every day the whole party had been for a trip in the Argenta. They never landed anywhere, however, for Sir John was still jealous of his secret; he wanted to test her in every kind of weather—he wanted to leave nothing to chance, so that finally her worth could not be questioned.

It was nothing for them to circle over the Outer Hebrides in the morning, come home for lunch, and then run over as far as Paris before dinner. Scarcely any motion was to be felt in the boat.

Alan had made arrangements with Sir Christopher Somerville to accompany the expedition to Kalvar. Desmond was to stay behind and look after Mavis, who intended staying at Dalmyrnie until her baby was born. Her fingers were busy fashioning tiny garments for the little newcomer, whose arrival was expected very soon.

"What shall we do to-day?" asked Sir John. "Mavis, my dear, would you like to rest? You look very tired."

"No, nothing does me as much good as a sail in the Argenta, Uncle John. Let us go up after lunch for a couple of hours." There was a curious stillness in the air, as the Argenta climbed up to six thousand feet,—hardly a breeze, in fact.

"Oh I'm stifling," said Mavis.

"My poor darling," murmured Desmond lovingly. "Are you sure you are not overtiring yourself? Your fingers never seem still. Always working at something or other, aren't you?"

She blushed prettily. "I can't let—him—come into the world and find we've not prepared for him, can I?" and she hid her face on her husband's shoulder.

"You've made up your mind it's to be a—'him'—?" he laughed.

"Of course, Dez. I must have a son first." He laughed at her naïve remark.

"Well if you feel tired be sure and tell me, darling, that's all."

"I shouldn't be surprised if we had a storm later," remarked Masters. "Although the sky is clear, there is the curious oppressiveness that usually precedes a storm."

"Then let us get back," said Mavis. "I am terrified at thunder."

Majestically the Argenta sailed, gracefully she skimmed along the sky. Now above the level of the clouds, now close down above the waters of the Atlantic.

"How beautiful the islands look, dotted about in the water," said Alan. "It is indeed a pearl-studded sea."

Hector came up to Sir John with a puzzled frown. "I don't quite like the look of the weather," said he. "The compass won't work, and the altimeter is frisking about in a most unaccountable manner. There's a bad storm brewing, and I think we shall be wise to turn her nose round and go back."

"If you think it is best," agreed Sir John, and as he spoke the sun burst out in all its glory from behind a fleecy cloud. At the same moment, away on the horizon, where angry blue-black clouds had gathered, came a vivid flash of lightning.

"Oh!" cried Mavis as she covered her eyes, "what a terrible flash." In a few minutes the sky was black and gloomy, the wind rose suddenly to a hurricane, and the big craft was spinning and twisting in a most unsafe manner.

"We'll go back, sir," said Hector. "Now go inside, Mrs. Forsyth. Believe me, there's no danger."

Then followed a most awful experience. The lightning never ceased, but lit up the ship from end to end, the thunder crashed and the Argenta rocked violently. Gradually they steered her round, and to the accompaniment of a most vivid flash of lightning and a deafening roar of thunder, the ship started on her homeward journey. At last they came safely to anchor outside the hangar and Mavis, always nervous in a storm, was now in a state of semi-unconsciousness. Desmond lifted her tenderly out of the ship and carried her to the cottage. Her nerve had completely gone.

That night a son was born to Desmond, and old Dr. Angus, who had been fetched in haste by Alan, spoke very gravely of the chances of saving both mother and child. The slightest shock would be fatal to her, he announced, as he took his leave.

"I'm glad you had a nurse in the house," he added, "a very wise precaution when so many miles separate doctor and patient."

"You'll come again?" said Desmond hoarsely.

"I will be round again in the morning."

Desmond, white faced, his hands twitching convulsively, stood on guard outside his wife's room. The ordeal was terrible, and the perspiration stood in beads upon his forehead. Once he heard a tiny cry, then stillness. He dared not knock—there was a nurse behind that closed door, and he knew he could trust her. Still—.

A hand touched him. "Go to bed, Desmond, and try to get a little sleep." It was Alan. "I'll watch for you, and I'll give you my word I'll call you if you're wanted."

"No, no, Alan. I'll stay here. If she wants me, I want to be near."

So the hours wore on, and no sound came from the sick-room. Dr. Angus motored up, and without a word disappeared within. An hour later he came out and saw Desmond's haggard face.

"You may go in for two minutes only," said he. "Both your wife and son will live."

It was a white-faced Mavis who greeted him. Her face was lined with pain; her hazel eyes were sunk deep into her head. In her arms she held a bundle, a little bundle that was everything to the man and woman beside it. "Dear, he's like you," whispered Mavis weakly, and then, with an almost roguish smile, "I said it would be a boy." Her eyes closed, and with her husband's hand in hers, she gave a contented sigh and fell asleep.

"Whew!" said Sir John, a few days later. "I wouldn't go through last week again for a king's ransom."

"Thank God she has pulled through," said Alan fervently. The two men were sitting at breakfast, the first square meal they had had for a week.

"Any news?" asked Sir John, as Alan was devouring the *Post*.

"Not much, Uncle John. There was a new Housing Bill brought up in the House last night. The Government seems very rocky. There are hints of a General Election. H'm. H'm—A bad earthquake in South America, I see. Five thousand people killed. Oh, and a landslip or something in New Zealand. How shocking," he went on, "ten thousand casualties there. Why, it's as bad as a war!"

"No, it's the States where the earthquake is," said Sir John who had unfolded the *Scotsman*.

"No, South America," contradicted Alan. "Listen—

"A tremendous earthquake has been felt at Lima, Valparaiso, and Buenos Aires. These three cities have suffered great damage. Over five thousand people have been killed outright, while the casualty list is considerably greater. The shock was felt in Bermuda, New Guinea and even as far north as Kentucky."

"Then there has been one in the States as well," said his Uncle. And he read from his paper

"The Meteorological office at Pimenta states that a serious earthquake has occurred in New Jersey."

"Later.

"News has now come through that Tennessee and Vermont have suffered considerable damage also. The loss of life is comparatively small considering the damage done to property. The tallest buildings have toppled over, shaken from their foundations. The electrical supply is cut off, and in many places severe fires are burning."

"It seems all over America," said Alan lightly. "I am glad we don't go in for those merry little sideshows in this country."

"Your time is growing short," said Sir John with a sigh. "I shall miss you very much, my lad."

"I shall miss you too, sir. But of course I am rather looking forward to the expedition."

The weather had been quite settled since the time when the *Argenta* had encountered the terrible storm, on the day preceding the birth of Desmond's son. Slightly sultry, perhaps, but an occasional cool breeze tempered the heat.

The next day all the papers were full of the epidemic of earthquakes that were occurring in different parts of the world. Work in many places was disorganized, and a fear was expressed that influences were at work round Southern Europe which might mean that the earthquakes would be felt nearer home.

Alan was due to sail in two days, arrangements had been made for him to leave Scotland the following morning, when a wire came from Sir Christopher Somerville. "Postponing departure of *Cavalier* indefinitely. Fear unsafe to sail south. Awaiting favourable report from Greenwich. Will advise you at earliest of arrangements."

"Well, it gives us a little more of your society, my boy," said Sir John, and there was a pleased look in his eyes.

Alan picked up the paper. "My God!" said he suddenly, and his face blanched.

"Following the news of the disastrous earthquakes that have been scourging America and the islands of the South American coast," he read, "come accounts of further appalling phenomena. In all parts of America, after violent cyclones, the land has in many places opened up, and swallowed men, animals and buildings. The loss of life is abnormal—rough estimates are given as high as 900,000 lives. Internal rumblings and coastal waterspouts in Tasmania have caused a panic among the population. The sea is too rough for even the largest boat to sail upon. Natives are rushing hither and thither with no real idea of where to go for safety. Volcanic eruptions are taking place in districts where for thousands of years the volcanoes have been extinct. Scientists are at present unable to account for this extraordinary outbreak of nature. As we go to press, news has come through that Sydney has disappeared entirely. San Francisco is in ruins. The whole of Cape Colony has sunk below sea level—and the water has poured over the whole country, sweeping everything before it. A later edition of this paper will be issued at noon, and at intervals during the afternoon and evening with news as it comes to hand."

"It is the worst scourge nature has ever given us," said Sir John.

"What I cannot understand," said Alan, "is why it is in so many places at once. Different latitudes seem to have suffered and different lands."

All that day a deep depression had taken hold of the occupants of the little cottage, and they were all very quiet. "Masters, motor over to Arroch Head," said Sir John, about six in the evening, "and if you can get no further news, ring up the offices of the *Scotsman*. Tell the Editor you are speaking for me. He will give you the latest news, I am sure." Masters was back within the hour, his face blanched, his hands trembling.

"Well?" asked Sir John. "Is it as bad as all that?"

"It's terrible," replied Masters. "It's coming nearer home. Rome has gone entirely—so have Naples and Athens. Spain and Portugal are under water. Authentic news is hard to get, as telephonic and cable communication in many places have failed. Some air scouts were sent to investigate, and witnessed the destruction of Spain. The air disturbances were so great that it was with the greatest difficulty they managed to reach England in safety."

"Do they think this visitation will reach us?" asked Desmond, the picture of his wife and child coming before his eyes.

"The *Scotsman* says that so far the Meteorological Office reports no disturbances within eighty miles in all directions of our coast. They hold out a hope, that being an island, we may escape," said Masters brokenly.

There was no sleep for any one that night; but the morning came and brought with it a blue sky and a gentle wind. There was not even a hint of disaster in the clear atmosphere. Hector got the big Napier out, and all but Desmond motored in to Arroch Head. He stayed behind with Mavis, to keep all breath of disaster from her ears. The little village street was full of white faced men, women and children, children frightened because their parents were frightened, yet realizing nothing of the danger ahead.

"Any news?" asked Sir John, of old Weelum McGregor, the hotel keeper.

"Aye, sir, an' it's no verra guid. Paris is on fire the noo. There was an internal explosion in the neighbourhood of Versailles yestere'en, and soon the roads were running with molten lava. Paris caught fire, and every one is powerless to suppress it."

Three days passed. England and Scotland were isolated—entirely cut off from the outer world. They had just to wait and pray that their time of tribulation would not come. The night was extraordinarily dark, the wind moaned and rose in mighty gusts. The rain came down in torrents. The thunder rolled in the distance, and occasionally flashes of lightning lit up the horizon.

Mavis was very restless. "Is anything the matter, Dez?" she asked, as he sat by her bedside.

"Why, dear?"

"You look worried. You make me feel anxious."

"I've been worried about you, my darling, that's all," and he lied glibly to the sick woman.

Then there suddenly rose on the air a terrific sound, worse than the loudest peal of thunder, and the room was brilliantly lighted from without as though by a mighty fire. Mavis rose up in bed; her limbs were shaking and she drew the sleeping babe still closer to her breast. "What is it, what is it, Dez? No, no, don't leave me," as Desmond was about to leave the room. He put his arms about her and crooned to her as if she had been a baby. The noise was terrible—one long, mighty roar. The room shook with the vibration, and the light from without grew brighter and brighter.

Sir John entered. "Mavis, my dear, you mustn't be frightened. Hector and Masters are launching the Argenta—we are going to take you up in her."

"What is happening?"

"I don't quite know, my dear, but Ben Lawers has broken out in flames. Schiehallion and Ben More in the distance are belching out heavy, dark smoke—I think it's volcanic action. Now, we've talked the whole matter over, and we feel that the safest place is inside the airship."

"But listen to the wind—could it live in such a storm?"

"It is the safest place," said Sir John firmly. "We will carry you and baby down in a hammock. Nurse has already packed you a goodly store of clothes, and then we'll all sail away to a more healthy spot."

"Are you sure there's no danger?"

"No, my dear! It's a magnificent sight to see the grand old Ben belching out smoke and flames. Lava is pouring down his sides into the Tay, and Killin is lighted up so that you can see the houses as if it was day."

Gently Mavis was carried to the ship, and tenderly lifted aboard. There was no time to waste. Sir John had only told half the truth to the invalid. The lava from Ben Lawers was already spreading towards Dalmyrnie. The hot ashes were being carried on the mighty wind, and the men were scorched and burnt while they were launching the airship.

Feverishly Masters hauled aboard packages, and bundles, hasty provisions to supplement those on board. A crash sounded behind them—the pine woods at the rear of the cottage had caught fire! It was an unearthly sight. Ben Lawers roared and hissed and spluttered, the pine trees crackled—the whole countryside was lit up with flames. In the distance the surrounding peaks and Bens were beginning to show signs of fire, and the whole scene was like a page of Dante come true.

"Everything aboard?" asked Sir John hoarsely.

"Yes," said Alan.

"Where's Nurse? Isn't she coming?"

"No! I tried to persuade her, but she wanted to get to Arroch Head to her mother. I told her to take the runabout—she's a fairly good hand with the car."

The flames drew nearer. Already their cruel tongues were licking round the house. The hangar was smouldering. Suddenly there came on their ears a deafening explosion—the reserve petrol had caught fire!

The heat was unbearable. "It's no good," panted Sir John. "Let's leave the rest and get off."

"Please God we shall soon be out of here, and shall be able to land in safety," said Alan.

Scorched, blackened with smoke, Masters made one more superhuman effort. He shipped his whole cargo in safety! He swarmed up the ladder, the grappling iron was drawn in, and the great ship slowly moved, travelling upward with her human freight.

The Argenta pitched and tossed, but Masters and Hector worked steadily at the delicate levers. Now they headed her right, now left; now she climbed above the average ten thousand feet, now dropped low to avoid the nasty air patches. Mavis was in her bed, her eyes wide open in terror. Above the roaring of the engines, came claps of thunder, deafening and awe inspiring.

"I don't understand," she moaned. "What is happening?"

"It is impossible to say," said Desmond. "But I feel we are safer here than we should be on earth to-night." And the night of horror passed.

Below, as they hovered to and fro, the whole country was blazing. Dawn came, but an angry dawn. Dark clouds scudded across the sky; the thunder grumbled in the distance, and occasional flashes of lightning illuminated the angry heavens.

"Where are we?" asked Sir John.

"Over Edinburgh," answered Masters from the other end of the 'phone, "we have scarcely moved for the last four hours."

"What?"

"The engines seem disinclined to work. I can't make it out at all."

The ship suddenly swerved to one side—a terrific explosion filled the air, and they saw the Castle Rock suddenly shiver, crumple up, and fall a shapeless ruin on to the railway line beneath. In a few minutes, Edinburgh, the Modern Athens, Edinburgh the Fair, was a mass of flames! They watched the populace, mad with fear, running aimlessly along the streets. "This is awful," muttered Alan. "Make south if you can. Let us get away from this desolation."

With a great amount of patience and skill, Masters at length managed to get the engines to work. But they came upon havoc and destruction whichever way they went,—indeed, the whole world seemed to have turned upside down. They circled London, but the first metropolis of the world had been the first English city to suffer from the terrible scourge. Blackened, charred, lifeless, London was a city of the dead.

As they swung in space over the dead London, they tried to pick out the familiar landmarks, but in vain—The Houses of Parliament were but a mass of bricks and dust; gone was the Abbey of Westminster, levelled to the ground was the mighty Tower of St. Edward, belonging to the Catholic Cathedral—gone was the Tower of London. There was not a sign of life in the once great city.

Aimlessly they flew in all directions. The whole of England was a flaming mass. They headed for the Continent. It was true, Paris had gone; Brussels was no more; there was not a city left. Denmark was wiped out,—and the sea washed up noisily and angrily over a barren rock that had once been Norway. At short intervals terrific explosions rent the air, and the vibration caused the Argenta to perform many nerve-racking aerial gymnastics.

"Head for the Atlantic if you can," cried Alan in despair. For ten days they had hovered over dead cities, dying lands, and waste voids. Navigation was almost impossible, the hurricanes drove the craft this way and that; now forcing her high, now bringing her low. It was all very fearsome, very terrifying. Mavis was up, and with her baby in her arms she followed the men about, a forlorn pathetic figure. Landing was impossible—there was no place where they could land. They had plenty of water, plenty of provisions, but they ate mechanically, scarcely realizing what it was that Hector placed before them with unvarying regularity.

They watched Europe sinking—the vast Atlantic was slowly but surely washing over lands and countries that had once been great empires.

The Argenta was wonderful; no matter what the atmospheric disturbances were, she always righted herself. The heat, at times, was terrific, and the Argenta was forced to climb out of the reach of the burning wastes below. Then the water of the ocean seemed to rise like steam—the Atlantic itself was boiling, and as it grew hotter and hotter, the ocean seemed to grow less in size.

The heat was so intense that the Argenta rose to a great height and remained among the clouds. After some days she descended, but seemed to be in a new world altogether. There was a large tract of barren land stretched out before them—gone was the Atlantic in its vastness. Dead bodies lay strewn about—the remains of great ships were embedded in the earth. Animals, humanity, fish, lay mixed together in that arid waste.

ELLA M. SCRYMSOUR

Suddenly Alan spoke, very reverently. "And the sea shall give up its dead."

"The Atlantic?" whispered Sir John.

"I think so," answered Alan.

And as they watched there came a mighty sound, greater than any they had heard before. The whole world shook, and for one moment was a living ball of fire. Then it shivered violently, split into a thousand pieces, and from its gaping wounds belched forth smoke and flames. Once more came the terrible sound, the sound of a world's death cry; there was a mighty crash, the flames went out and where the world had been—was nothing.

All was black, all was gone; the earth had returned to its original state; the sea had disappeared entirely; shapeless, dark,—the earth was dead! And in her last convulsive hold on life, she shook the very heavens. The Argenta was whirled round and round in a maelstrom of agony, and then was shot into space.

With a mighty effort Masters released the shutters, and filled the intervening cavity with the ether. It was his last conscious act. On, on went the Argenta, at a terrific speed. The fury of the heavens seemed let loose, and the atom in the firmament was like a wisp of wool in its grasp. Turning, twisting, rolling, the Argenta was borne on the bosom of the whirlwind, and carried with its seven souls of Terra; seven souls that had escaped from, but had witnessed The End Of The World.

BOOK IV
THE PERFECT WORLD

I

In Space

S pace—infinite space! On, on, swept the Argenta through the heavens at frightful speed. The engines were useless; the levers refused to work, and the occupants of the airship sat within the shuttered vessel, helpless.

For days they had eaten nothing—they were unable to move; terror had them fast within its grasp.

"Sir John," said Masters at last, "I'm going to make a cup of tea. Here we are, and here we must remain until our food gives out. Mrs. Desmond,—won't you come and help me?" Mavis rose from an armchair, and tenderly laid the sleeping babe on the cushions of a settee.

"My baby," she murmured, "to think I bore you for this."

"Come, Mrs. Desmond," and Masters led the way to the tiny kitchen.

All sense of direction had gone, and the occupants of the giant airship, had simply to accept the extraordinary conditions that had been thrust upon them, and remain helpless in the Argenta, carried they knew not whither, adrift in the heavens. They had ceased to reckon time, minutes had no meaning; hours and days passed as one long whole. They were just atoms, existing in space, which is infinite—where time is infinite—where life itself is infinite!

Mavis entered with a tray laden with tea and biscuits—the exertion had done her good, and already there was a slight colour in her cheeks.

The airship was ploughing along at a terrific rate, but its motion was steady, and they could walk about in comfort. When first the explosion that had accompanied the end of the world sent them spinning into the infinite unknown, the Argenta had behaved in a most erratic way. Broadside she skimmed like an arrow, throwing them from side to side, then she reared up on her tail, and climbed the heavens almost perpendicularly; then she would roll over and over, porpoise-like, until the frail mortals lost all sense of everything except that a great calamity had come into their lives.

"Where are we?" asked Mavis suddenly.

"I intend to try and find out," said Masters grimly. "Whatever happens we can't be in a worse position than we are at this moment. I intend to move the shutters from the bows and then we may get some idea of where we are."

"But is it safe?" objected Desmond, looking first at his wife and then at his child. "So far we are safe. This mad journey must come to an end some time or other. Why jeopardize all our lives for the sake of a little curiosity?"

"Must it come to an end?" said Sir John thoughtfully.

"Of course," answered Desmond. "We can't go on forever."

"Why not?" continued his Uncle. "Space is infinite. Now time is eternity. We, when in the world—"

"How strange that sounds," interrupted Alan.

"As I was saying, when we were in the world, we often used the expression, 'For ever and ever.' If we thought what it really meant, it dazed our brains; we wanted to probe further, and find out what it was that came after that 'ever and ever.' We puzzled our intellects by pondering on the infinity of time. I realize now, what Eternity is! Since we have been here, I have ceased to count the minutes; I have ceased to think of days, or night, or weeks. Time is! That is enough for me."

"Then you really think we may go on forever?" asked Desmond in horror.

"I don't know. I certainly think it is as likely as not."

"Oh God," Desmond muttered between his clenched teeth.

"Come, dear," said Mavis bravely. "We ought to be thankful that the promptitude of Uncle John and Masters saved us from an awful death below."

"Are you sure it was 'down below'?" asked Alan quizzically.

"Why, of course," Mavis began. Then she stopped. "Oh I don't know. That is all so strange and puzzling."

"Now, Masters," said Sir John. "What were you going to do?"

"I was going to release the shutters from the bow. I can close the patent traps, and leave the ether protection all round the ship," he explained to the others. "But it is possible to leave a small portion of the glass in the bows, exposed, through which we shall be able to see the course we are taking."

"I think it's worth making the experiment," said Sir John, and they all followed him into the comfortable front cabin.

"Now if you see the slightest sign of danger, 'phone me," said Masters, who was going into the lever room.

"How can you tell if danger is near?" asked Mavis with interest.

"This way," said Masters. He pointed to a portion of the glass wall, now covered with the outer sheet of aluminium.

"That portion of the glass is of extra thickness and strength. If the outside air pressure is too great, or the gravitation or any unknown element too powerful for it, that glass will bulge, either inwards, or outwards. Only slightly at first, but it will get bigger and bigger until it bursts asunder. Now, if you see the slightest suspicion of that happening, 'phone through to me, and I will close the shutters again. At any rate, we shall have done no harm, and at least we shall have tried to do something to ease our position."

In breathless silence they waited, watchful in the dark. Suddenly a tiny ray of light lit up the stygian gloom. Bigger and bigger it grew, until the whole of Masters' wonderfully planned "lookout" was exposed to view. Breathlessly they watched. There was not the slightest sign of strain upon the glass. It was certainly capable of protecting them for the present at any rate.

"All serene," cried Alan through the 'phone.

"Everything safe?" from Masters at the other end.

"Quite safe."

"Oh-h-h-h." It was Mavis. "How wonderful!" They were looking into endless space at last! They had no sense of location—no ordinary sense of North or South—East or West. They were in the heart of the Solar system, with no horizon to act as a guiding line! The vastness of space overwhelmed them; there was no landmark to direct them. There was no comforting horizon, with mighty arms outstretched, embracing the world. There was nothing to give them a feeling of security. Here space just "went on" for ever and ever, beyond human comprehension.

Wherever they looked, there was just—no end.

But the scene was beautiful beyond comparison. Away to their right, in the dark recesses of the firmament, was a wonderful brightness.

"It's the Milky Way," said Mavis clapping her hands in ecstasy.

"I don't think so," said Alan. "But all the same, I think that gives us an idea in what direction we are flying. That brightness must be the Greater Magellanic Clouds in the Southern Constellation."

"What, are they only clouds, then?"

"No, just stars. Stars of all magnitudes, richly strewn in the heavens. Even the faintest of the nebulæ are more abundant than in any other part of the firmament."

"It's wonderful," said Sir John. "The illuminating brightness is almost overpowering."

They were unable to take their eyes from the cloud-like condensation of stars—one of the glories of space.

"We don't seem to be getting any nearer to it, although we are going at such a pace," said Mavis.

"My dear," answered her uncle. "We are too many miles away to see any appreciable lessening of distance between us."

"What is that bright star there," asked Mavis pointing. "Just a little to this side of the Magellanic Clouds?"

"I don't know. It certainly is wonderfully bright," answered Sir John.

Alan was searching the heavens. "Isn't that the Constellation of Draco—the Dragon—?" he asked suddenly. "I think it must be. If so, that star, as you call it, which lies between the Greater Magellanic Cloud and Draco must be Jupiter."

"Jupiter?"

"Yes. One of Jupiter's poles lies in the heart of Draco, and the other is close by the Greater Magellanic Clouds."

Mavis puckered her brows. "Jupiter," she almost whispered, "the Prince of all the Planets?"

"Yes."

"We don't seem to know much about him, do we?" she went on.

"No," said her husband. "The astronomers seem much more interested in Saturn and Mars."

"I've often thought," said Alan, "that such a magnificent orb could not have been created just to have shown our old earth light. Its beauty, its grandeur, its magnitude, suggests to us the noblest forms of life."

"You think it is inhabited?" asked Desmond.

"Why not? Surely its beauty and magnitude alone are a convincing proof of the insignificance of our earth. If Terra was inhabited, populated with many fine races of human beings, possessed of glorious scenery, and full of nature's wonders, surely if such a puny world as ours was peopled, why should a far finer planet be debarred from possessing and nurturing higher forms of animal life?"

"It sounds very interesting," said Mavis laughing, "but I wonder whether it's true."

"If people are on Mars, or Saturn, or Jupiter, they would hardly be like us," announced Desmond, grandiloquently. "They would either be like the Mechanical Martians that Wells wrote of, or just animal life of some gelatinous matter as favoured by Wolfius."

"Oh you egotistical, egregious Englishman," laughed Sir John.

"Can you beat him?" said Alan. "No one but a Britisher *could* have made that remark!"

There was a laugh at Desmond's expense, and then Alan went on, "Personally, I feel convinced that ours was not the only inhabited planet. Even our feeble knowledge of the solar system, individually and in bulk, has proved the wonder of Jupiter, the symmetry and perfection of the system that circles round him, the glory of his own being, and he should rank as the world of worlds. I should be inclined to believe that Jupiter is not only capable of producing the highest forms of life, but that his humanity surpasses in intelligence the most cultured, most brilliant, most learned of our earth's philosophers."

"No, no, I won't have that," said Desmond. "Look at the brilliant men of letters Britain alone has given to the world. Think of her eminent scholars, dauntless pioneers—why no other country or world could compete with Britain."

"As I remarked before, the egregious Englishman!" said Sir John. "I admire your courage, my boy, in sticking to your guns. I admire your loyalty to the country that gave you birth. But we are not in the world now, my boy. Our beautiful little planet has vanished, has disappeared into the void from which it came; yet here, before our eyes, we see Jupiter still existing, still a brilliant orb in the sky. Surely now, Desmond, you are convinced of the minuteness of the planet upon which you were bred and born?" Sir John put his hand on Desmond's shoulder. "While you were upon it, it was everything. Now it is nothing—gone—while other planets still exist and shed their brightness over space."

"I think," said Mavis thoughtfully, "that if our own little world possessed such a high form of life, and we measure a planet by its bulk, then surely the Jovians must be the most highly favoured race in the Solar Kingdom?"

A tiny cry came from the cabin behind. "Baby," she cried. "Oh, I'd forgotten him," and she fled to her nursling who had missed his mother's care.

"Such are the wonders of the heavens," said Sir John, thoughtfully. "It's so grand, so massive, so unbelievable, that it makes even a mother forget, in its contemplation, her first-born, her little son."

"Why he is not named yet," said Desmond. "I had forgotten all about that."

"Well, we have no parson here," said Alan. "Now our world has gone, can we call ourselves Christians? How do we rank with the Almighty? Have we become atoms tossed about on an endless sea, or Christians to whom eventual release will come?"

"We are still in God's Hands," said Sir John reverently. "In the absence of an ordained priest, a layman may administer the Sacrament of Baptism. I am getting very old. I have one foot very near the grave. Shall I do it?"

"Please," said Desmond.

And whirling through the Solar system, belonging neither to earth nor heaven, was performed surely the strangest rite ever known from time immemorial. And it was in this strange place, in this strange manner that Desmond and Mavis' son—John Alan—was named.

II

ADRIFT IN THE SOLAR REGIONS

L ife in the Argenta became very monotonous. After the first throes of despair, the glimpse of the glorious expanse of the Heavens served to cheer the prisoners within the ship. They had no clocks that were going. During the terror of the first few days time had mattered so little to them that they had let them run down. They now arranged to set all the clocks, and judge the time accordingly, and plan out their days. Rise at eight; lunch at one; tea at four; and dinner at seven and then to bed. The "night" would pass and they would begin another "day."

They reckoned they had sufficient food to last the twelve earth months, and they could exist in comfort for three hundred and sixty-five days. And with the minutest care, perhaps even longer. "We can't live in space for more than twelve months, surely," said Mavis, but Sir John did not answer her. They had consumed perhaps an eighth of their water supply, and had the supply of concentrated water essence untouched. Still, they were afraid to waste any for washing purposes, and considered it a treat to be allowed to dip their fingers in any fluid that was left over from cooking; even a drop of cold tea proved a boon to them, and they gratefully damped cloths in it and wiped their hot and dry faces.

Alan fixed a piece of paper on the wall of the front cabin, and every night before they retired, he would tick off the number of the day from the time they had reset their clocks and begin to count again. Thirty, forty, fifty, so the "days" passed, and little John Alan grew enormously. The few garments that had been packed in their hurried flight were now too small for him, and Mavis was forced to use some of her own dresses, and cut them up for the growing child. He alone was unconscious of the danger of their peculiar position, and he crowed and gurgled and bit his toes, in complete babyish happiness and delight. If anything, Mavis had grown more beautiful after the arrival of her child. Her eyes glowed with maternal pride, and her cheeks were flushed with joy as she watched her baby, born into such a strange life, grow day by day fairer and more loving.

The library aboard, which Sir John had had the foresight to install in his giant Argenta, proved a godsend to the weary travellers. Every day they read aloud some old literary favourite, and renewed their acquaintance with Sam Weller, Pip, the Aged P, and Little Nell; laughed over the experiences of the "Innocents Abroad" enjoyed again the story of "Three Men in a Boat." But even with these diversions, with chess, dominoes, and draughts; with singing and playing, they grew tired of their enforced inactivity, and chafed at their surroundings.

Their air supply was excellent; the mechanism never failed in its work; certainly the air grew hot and fetid at times but by the aid of electric fans it was freshened and purified. Every day they looked out of the little glass window, and drank in the glories of the heavens.

One day, it was the ninety-eighth according to Alan's chart, Mavis startled them all by a sudden exclamation.

"What is it, my dear?" asked Sir John, looking up from an interesting game of chess he was enjoying with Alan.

"Look at Jupiter! Isn't he large to-night?" said she. "Why, yesterday he looked like a big star, to-day he is like the moon at harvest time."

They all crowded round the little window.

"By Jove, you're right," said Alan. "We must be sailing in a direct line toward him."

"How plain the clouds are upon him," said Desmond. "You can see them plainly right across his face."

The belts across the face of Jupiter were certainly very plain; across the surface of the planet they floated pearly white, like masses of "snow-clouds" as seen in England on a hot summer's day. From the equatorial region they merged, both north and south from a glorious coppery colour, becoming a deep, ruddy purplish tint at the poles.

"Are they clouds like ours?" asked Mavis wonderingly.

"I don't think it has ever been proved what they really are," answered Alan. "I think the general theory is, that those clouds as you call them are, in reality, a vapour-laden atmosphere that floats across the orb."

"I should love to go there," said Mavis.

"Well, it looks as though we were making for that part of the firmament," said her uncle.

"It certainly does," she retorted. "But when shall we reach there?"

At that moment Masters and Hector came in, in great excitement.

"The engines are working," announced Hector enthusiastically.

"What!" from all.

"It's true. Masters and I were tinkering at them this morning, when

ELLA M. SCRYMSOUR

suddenly the little starting cog flew round, there was a roar, a flash of sparks, and they started properly."

This was indeed good news, for ever since the end of the world the airship had been propelled through space by some unknown outside influence; her engines not only refused to work but her steering apparatus refused to act.

"I intend navigating straight ahead," announced Masters. "I'll have eight engines going, and then we ought to get up a speed of over four hundred and fifty miles; that together with the pace we are already travelling should help us considerably in reaching somewhere, if there is anywhere for us to get."

Eagerly they all went into the engine room, and watched first one, then another of the powerful engines set going. They were however surprised to find that they felt no difference in their speed; yet the speedometer registered four hundred and twenty miles, and all eight engines were working merrily.

They went back to the bows, and watched the universe stretched out before them. They passed close to a star, whose name they did not know, and its radiance lit up the little cabin for fourteen days, that were marked off religiously on Alan's calendar. Then came another terrible time, when depression took hold of them all again, and they would sit, silent, staring into space. Their eyes were dull and lustreless; their limbs cramped from lack of exercise, and their brains torpid and sluggish.

Perhaps Alan felt the deprivation of air and exercise most, but he continued to be the cheeriest of them all.

"Oh, for some green vegetables," sighed Mavis one day. John Alan had been particularly restless, and she felt more than usually miserable.

"And plenty of nice rabbit food," went on Alan cheerfully. "Crisp, long lettuces, the rosy radish, juicy tomatoes, and above all the cool, refreshing slices of the unwholesome cucumber."

"Oh, Alan, I'm so miserable," she sobbed. "Will this awful existence never end? Shall we just die here, and this ship become the meteoric tomb of seven unfortunates of the world? A tomb always spinning on, on, through endless space, through endless time, like some lost soul."

"Lost world, you mean," corrected Alan. "You are mixing your metaphors, and when a lady does that, it's a sure sign she wants a cup of tea!"

"I don't want a cup of tea, Alan. I just want to get a breath of air. Alan, couldn't you persuade Masters to open the shutters? Couldn't we just go on to the deck for five minutes—only five minutes?" she pleaded.

"My dear," said Alan gently. "It's quite impossible. Now listen carefully to what I am saying. Long, long ago, we were out of the atmosphere and the gravitation of our earth. In some way or other, the tornado that accompanied the end of our world drove us through space where nothing is! Oh, I know it sounds complicated, dear, but by all the knowledge of science, as taught by the most advanced astronomers, long ago we should have been suspended in space, unable to move or be moved, outside the gravitation of other worlds; just atoms, motionless, still. That hasn't happened. We have defied the great authorities, and are being whirled through the heavens by some power unheard of by the scientists of the earth. Still, dear, we do not know whether there is air outside. Should we lift the shutters that protect us, we might find we were unable to exist."

"That's the word," cried Mavis. "We aren't living now. We are only existing. We don't know from hour to hour what terrible fate may await us. If by lifting the shutters we kill ourselves, surely that is better than this lingering death."

"Mavis, Mavis, don't."

"Do you know we have only a month's supply of food left?"

Alan looked at her in horror. "You don't mean that, Mavis?" said he incredulously.

"My dear Alan, you are just like all men. Sufficient for the day! That's your motto. You never enquired about the food. Since I took over the culinary department, none of you have worried a bit, while day by day I've seen our stock of provisions grow less and less. In a month's time, Alan, our food will be totally exhausted."

"What about the condensed foods?"

"Oh we still have some of them—perhaps with extreme care they would last another four weeks, and then—the end."

"Why didn't you tell me before, Mavis?"

"Oh I couldn't," hysterically. "You were all so contented. Besides I didn't realize the seriousness of it myself until to-day. Our flour is nearly gone. You yourself said the bread wasn't as good this morning. Of course it wasn't. It was just mixtures of every cereal I could think of to try and make it last out."

This news was indeed serious, and Alan walked thoughtfully to his chart. Yes, he ought to have known. It registered five hundred and fifty-five days. Over eighteen earth months they had been flying through the heavens. Their food had lasted magnificently.

"Water?" he queried.

"We finished the tank water long ago. I'm pretty well through with the cubes."

"Let me come and see the food supply."

Carefully he went over every item. Even yet, there seemed to be enough to feed an army, but he knew how little there was in reality. "I think if we have one good meal a day, we ought to make it last longer," said he. "After all, one good meal is better than three small ones, and incidentally, we save over the one transaction. We must sleep longer, that's all. We will get up at noon, and have a cup of tea and a biscuit. At four we will have dinner, and if we retire at eight, a cup of cocoa then should suffice us. The longer we remain in bed the less food we shall require. Come, let us tell the others."

Sir John took the news very quietly. Not a muscle of his face twitched—he might have been receiving a most ordinary announcement. Masters shrugged his shoulders indifferently, and Murdoch went on with his work as if he had not heard. Desmond took the news badly, however. His face grew ashen. "Why should this have come upon us?" he cried. "We had been through so much. Happiness came my way at last, and now—" He drew Mavis fiercely to him. "I won't lose you. There must be some way out."

"There is none, my boy," said Sir John, "so you had better make up your mind to that at once. Here we are and here we must remain, till by some merciful intervention, we die, or are given release."

"Where shall we ever find release?" from Desmond.

"In some new world, perhaps."

"How big Jupiter is," said Alan, looking out into the vastness. "He is certainly a wonderful planet," said Mavis.

"Is it my fancy or are we slowing down?" asked Sir John.

"I've wondered the same thing myself," said Masters. "For the last few days I have noticed an appreciable difference in our speed."

But although the difference was so slight as to be almost undiscernible, the new topic of conversation gave the prisoners new life.

The days passed—the quantity of the food they consumed grew daily less and less, and they were growing weaker and weaker every day. At length they gave up their cup of tea in the mornings—their tea had gone. Then they halved their dinner portions making one day's share of food last two! But all the same the dreaded day came only too soon, and five hundred and ninety-five days after Alan had put up his calendar, they found they had only a few tins of concentrated food left. They were all hungry. Little John Alan grew fretful, his mother feverish. There was silence in the little front cabin, the silence of the grave. The little party were all half asleep, when suddenly Alan rose. "What's the matter?" he asked quickly.

"What is it?" asked his uncle.

"Don't you realize?—we've stopped! We've stopped!" It was true, the Argenta was stationary at last! At the same moment Masters came rushing in.

"We've stopped!" he cried. "The engines have refused again to work."

They all crowded round the little "lookout," but could see nothing. For the first time for nearly two years their vision was limited. Gone was the brightness of Jupiter, gone the glorious Magellanic Cloud—gone, too, the many thousand points of light that enriched the heavens. All about them was a moving vapour. It was unlike clouds, but surged and swirled like heavy snow flakes. It was a whitish vapour that looked like steam—that altered again and took on the hue of thick yellowish smoke.

"Where are we?" asked Mavis. "Can't we get out?"

"We'll see," said Alan soothingly.

But still Mavis went on pleadingly. "Oh surely our chance has come at last. If we opened the shutters now, we might get free altogether."

The next morning, Murdoch was missing. His bed had not been slept in. "Where's Murdoch?" asked Alan of Masters.

"I don't know. I've been expecting him to relieve me in the engine room every minute. Is he in the kitchen?"

"No. I can't find him anywhere."

"Good God! Then I know what he has done," said Masters brokenly. "He was very upset over Mrs. Desmond yesterday. She wanted me to open the shutters. Come."

At the stern of the ship and on the lower deck was a little trap door in the metal covering. "He's gone through there," said Masters hoarsely. "He asked me a lot of questions about it last night. I told him about the mechanism of this trap and he suggested we should go out on deck, and see if it was possible to breathe out there. I laughed at him and thought no more about the matter."

As he was speaking he deftly wound a scarf about his nose and mouth, and stuffed his ears with cotton wool saturated with oil. He touched a spring and a sheet of metal unfolded and when it rested at

ELLA M. SCRYMSOUR

last in position, it formed a tiny air tight closet outside the trap. "I shall open the trap as quickly as I can," said he quickly. "On the other side the deck is opened up and there is a space left large enough to test thoroughly the outer air. But by the aid of this "cubby-hole" we still have our ether protection kept safe all round the ship. Now I am going out to see if Murdoch is there. If I don't come back, don't search for me. It will be too late."

"Masters, don't go!" urged Alan.

"I must go," grimly, "but I beg of you, if I don't return in ten minutes, forget I ever existed."

Without another word he slipped into the little boxlike chamber, and the door snapped to after him. They heard the sound of a click, rushing air, and then, silence.

Five minutes passed—six—seven—eight. Sir John, Desmond and Mavis had come up in time to hear the trap close, and quickly Alan explained the position.

"Why did you let him go?" cried Mavis.

"Murdoch went for you, my dear," he answered sternly. "Masters went to save him."

Mavis covered her face with her hands, and the tears trickled down her face.

"My dear, don't take it to heart," went on Alan kindly. "If anything happens to Murdoch, he will have given his life for his friends."

Then a muffled cry came from within the little chamber. Quickly Alan touched the lever, the folds of metal rolled back, and two figures fell forward on their faces.

"Water," commanded Alan, and Mavis rushed to get some.

"Have you any brandy left?" asked Sir John.

"A very little."

"Bring some too," he cried as Mavis disappeared into the kitchen. Tenderly they wiped blood and sweat from the faces of the unconscious men.

Masters opened his eyes. "Out there," said he hoarsely. "Terrible smell—sulphuric—can't breathe properly—whirling clouds—eyes smart—don't go again."

"He'll do," said Sir John. "How's Murdoch?"

"He's so terribly cold," said Mavis.

Alan took his place by the still form. "Brandy," said he. He looked at the man on the floor. Thick veins like whipcords stood out upon his forehead. Blood trickled from his nose, his ears, his mouth. His lips were swollen, and were blue in colour and cracked.

"He's gone," said Alan.

"Dead?" cried Mavis in horror.

"Quite dead." Gently they carried the dead man, who had risked his life for his friends, to his little sleeping cabin. Tenderly they laid him on his bed, covered up his face, and closed the door softly behind them. Then they went back to Mavis who was watching over Masters.

"How is he?" asked Desmond.

"Better, I think. He asked for water. I think he is sleeping now."

Alan bent over their old and valued friend. The look of pallor had vanished, the veins subsided, he was breathing naturally.

"Poor Murdoch," sobbed Mavis. "I feel it was my fault. I was always worrying you to open the shutters and let us go outside."

"Don't worry, little one," said Sir John. "He died like an English gentleman."

"Oh how terrible everything is," she sobbed hysterically. "There seems no end to our torment. Oh this horrible place, this horrible ship of doom!"

III

The Vision of a New World

Perfect silence, perfect stillness, and the clouds whirled round and round outside.

In vain they tried to move the ship. The engines worked smoothly, and with perfect rhythm, but were powerless to propel the Argenta.

The death of Murdoch had a terribly depressing effect on every one—they all missed his kindly brusqueness, his forethought and stolid help.

When Masters was sufficiently recovered he told his story. "I got through the ether all right," said he. "I was through in a second and was standing on the exposed deck at the mercy of the elements. The cold was intense—I've never before experienced anything like it. In those few seconds it just cut through me. I could hardly see—my eyes filled with water, and smarted terribly as the gaseous vapour touched them. I lowered my handkerchief for the tiniest fragment of a second, and drew a very slight breath. The effect was terrible. My lungs felt as if they would burst—my mouth felt as if it had been seared with hot irons—my senses reeled; I felt as if I should fall. Then I became conscious of Murdoch lying huddled at my feet. I pulled him into the cabin after me, and well,—you know the rest. Poor Murdoch—I was too late."

The excitement following the loss of Murdoch and Masters' adventure after him, had made the hungry prisoners forget the emptiness of their larder. They all sat down to a hearty meal, and it was only at the end they realized it meant their being on still shorter rations in the future. And only too soon the larders were indeed empty! Mavis grew too weak to move, and lay helpless on her bed, her baby at her breast. Masters was the last to give in, and as he walked unsteadily to his cabin, he had visions of Sir John on one chair and Alan on another, each vainly trying to whisper words of comfort to the other.

Still the ship remained motionless—the stillness was of the grave.

Suddenly a whitish beam of light shot out through the clouds, and Alan saw a new moon rising. And as he watched he saw another skim the heavens, and another, and yet another. He looked at them in perplexity—four pink tipped crescents in the sky!

"Four Moons! God!" he cried. "The four satellites of Jupiter! Or should there be eight? Four—eight—eight—four." His brain muddled. Four Moons visible at once! Jupiter! He was witnessing the rise of four of the planet's moons! He was watching them through the misty clouds—then came a blessed sense of oblivion, and he too, lost consciousness. When he awoke again, it was with a feeling that the Argenta was again moving through space—moving slowly, but with a speed that was gradually quickening. He staggered to his feet, and bent over his uncle. Sir John was still breathing, but there was a curious greyness in his face, and Alan moistened his lips with a drop of brandy. The old man moved, and opened his eyes. "Drink a little," said Alan kindly. "It will do you good."

Sir. John managed to swallow a little of the burning fluid, and sighing naturally, closed his eyes in sleep. With difficulty, Alan managed to reach Desmond's room, for he was very weak. He found Mavis lying on her bed, hardly breathing: the babe lay in her arms sleeping peacefully. She had given the very essence of her strength to her child, and he had scarcely suffered at all.

Desmond was breathing heavily, jerkily, the breath came like sobs from between his clenched teeth. Alan forced some of the brandy between his lips and said huskily, "Dez, old boy: don't leave me, old chap; we've been through some tight corners, don't give up yet."

Desmond struggled to a sitting position. "Good old Lanny," he muttered.

"I must see Masters," said Alan. "Keep up, if you can, till I return."

Alan reeled from side to side in his weakness as he struggled on to Masters' cabin. It was empty! He was almost too weak to think or act coherently.

"Masters," he moaned. "Where are you?" Slowly he made his way back to the little room in the bows, and as he neared it, a brilliant beam of light shot across his path. The unexpectedness of it threw him off his balance, and he would have fallen, had not Masters rushed forward and put his arm about him.

The light was strong. So strong that they could feet the heat of its rays through the little glass window.

"What is it?" he asked.

Masters could hardly speak. His lips were swollen and blackened, and his tongue parched. "Help," said he thickly. "That light is like a magnet—it is drawing us somewhere. It's sent out by human agency I am sure. See how it flutters and fades, only to come bright again." They watched the ray—it was focussed directly on the bows, and it seemed to be drawing them closer and closer to some harbour of refuge. Still they were going through the encircling clouds, which had suddenly turned to a most beautiful roseate hue. Then without any warning they emerged and found they were gazing on the most wonderful scene they had ever beheld.

It was more wonderful than their thoughts could have expressed. Imagine hovering over the most wondrous piece of natural scenery—double—treble its beauty, and even then you could have no idea of the grandeur, the poetry of the picture they gazed upon.

They were, perhaps, three thousand feet up. Mountains rose all round with rocky crevasses, and wonderful waterfalls dashing down their sides. Foaming waters trickled and bubbled and laughed by the sides of grassy paths. An inland lake glowed in the glory of the sunshine. Trees of all kinds nestled in the valleys and climbed the hillsides.

A sea—a glorious azure sea—with dancing waves and white flecked foam rolled merrily in and out on wonderful white sands. There were rocks and caves, and velvety grass slopes along the sea shore; babbling brooks merged into the blue, blue waters; tall lilies, virginal white, mingled with roses, red like wine, and grew in clusters at the water's edge. All was nature at her best—unspoiled by man.

Wooded islets were dotted about in still more wonderful bays; birds white as snow, birds with plumage rainbow-hued floated idly on the waters, and added to the picturesque beauty. They could see little buildings nestling among the trees here and there, buildings that, like the châlets of Switzerland, only added to the beauty of the scene.

The airship had stopped suddenly, and they were unable to move her, and still they hovered over the wonderful land. Sea—sky—both of a most glorious blue; the verdure of this new land was green—"The same as our world," murmured Alan.

"But with what a difference," whispered Sir John.

"I never knew what the sea was until now," said Alan. "I never realized what 'colour' was—what blue or green meant, until I looked down yonder."

New life was born in the three men. "I'll call Desmond," said Alan. Mavis was lying as he had left her—white, inert, silent. "Leave her," he told his cousin. "She will be quite safe; but we've news at last—we are in sight of land."

When he reached the bows again, he saw they had dropped a few hundred feet, and were now well below the summit of the mountains.

Below them, in a fertile valley, they saw what they thought were six giant birds running along a field. They rose, soared straight up, and flew directly toward the Argenta. They were like swans with outstretched wings, and necks like swans; but never had they seen birds of such a monstrous size.

"They are as big as a small plane," said Sir John wonderingly.

"By Jove, I believe that's what they are," said Alan.

As the "birds" drew nearer, they could see that the body was in reality the car of the plane. Soon six were circling round the Argenta, and the prisoners within could see figures standing in the cars of the strange looking aeroplanes.

The Argenta gave a jolt, and quivered from stem to stern, and they felt themselves sinking. The newcomers had thrown out some kind of grappling rope and were pulling them to earth. They were nearer to this wonderful country. Already they could see the brilliant flowers—trees laden with wonderful fruit and bright plumaged birds fluttering about without any sign of fear.

"Release the shutters," said Alan hoarsely.

"No," said Sir John with decision. "Remember we have on board a defenceless woman and her child. We don't yet know if we are in the hands of friends or enemies. I'll get my revolver. Dez, my boy, I'll give it to you. Stay in your cabin and be prepared. You understand?"

"Shoot—her?" asked Desmond hoarsely.

Sir John bowed his head. "Surely you would rather do it than me?"

"Yes—but—"

"There is no 'but,' my boy. Rather death than horrors unnameable. Stay in the cabin with your wife and child. If I think we are in good hands I will call you. Otherwise, I will give our whistle—the one we used when you were boys—the three sharp calls, and a long minor note," and he illustrated it softly. "If you hear that,—don't hesitate, my boy." They gripped hands, and Desmond, dazed, speechless, walked unsteadily out of the room, and they heard the click of his cabin door as it closed behind him.

Slowly, but surely the Argenta was being dragged down to the field below. At last they touched solid ground—there was a scrunch and a grating—they were on some earth at last.

"Alan," said Sir John grimly. "I have two other revolvers on board.

Masters, if the worst comes to the worst, and I give the warning whistle for Mr. Desmond, go in to him. If he does not turn the weapon on himself do it for him—and keep a spare bullet for yourself."

"I understand, sir."

The six white "birds" had also reached land, and from out of the bodies they saw strange figures appear. The figures were like themselves—yet how different! The men approaching were perhaps under average height, but they were beautifully moulded, muscular with a symmetry of form that was glorious to behold.

All but one wore white—a garment that reached to their feet, and which resembled in shape a Roman toga. This white garment was embroidered with richly coloured silks at the neck, wrists and hem. On their heads, they wore fillets of gold. The leader was garbed in a garment of the same shape, but of a glorious blue bound with gold, and his fillet was studded with gems that shone and flashed in the sunlight. All walked up to the Argenta and smiled through the little window at the occupants. Then the leader opened his hands—held them up empty, and with a charming smile, bowed low before them. Then he seemed to issue a command, and all the others, there were altogether perhaps thirty of them, followed his example, and bowed before them.

"They look friendly," said Sir John. "Masters, let the shutters be raised—then stand near Mr. Desmond's cabin. If I shout—'view halloo!' bid him to come out on to the upper deck, but—"

"But if I hear the whistle, sir, I shall know what to do."

"Keep your revolver hidden, Alan," said Sir John, and they made their way to the upper deck.

They waited in silence for the ether to be pumped back into its cylinders, and for the shutters to lift. Gradually light came creeping in through chinks here and there—higher and higher was lifted the moving metal, until at last the two men drank in fresh air and bathed in glorious sunshine once again. They found they could scarcely move along the deck—in fact it was with the greatest difficulty they could keep their balance. They felt horribly material and gross.

"What is it?" whispered Alan.

"The law of gravity, my boy. Wherever we are, I should say it is about three times the strength of that we were used to when we were on Terra. I think we have about trebled our weight."

The strangers had advanced—the leader was smiling graciously. He gave another command, and his band of followers came to a sudden halt, and he approached the Argenta—alone. He addressed them in a language they did not understand.

"I do not understand—" commenced Sir John, but before he could say any more the stranger spoke—haltingly it is true, and as if unused to it, but he spoke in English.

"Where are we?" cried Sir John in amazement.

"You are on, what I think you would call—Jupiter."

"Jupiter?"

"Yes. And may I welcome you strangers to our land of plenty. I know not who you are or whence you come—but you are welcome—very welcome. But you look tired—"

"You are not enemies, then?" cried Sir John.

"Enemies?" repeated the Jovian. "I understand not the word."

"You are friends?"

"Friends of course—we are all friends. Can you find a more beautiful word than friendship?"

"Thank God! Thank God!" cried Sir John, and with a wild "View Halloo" issuing from his lips, he fell senseless to the ground.

IV

Jupiter and the Jovians

The sweet toned bell in the Observatory at Minnaviar rang violently, and startled the students out of their usual calm and placidity.

Kulmervan looked up from his studies. "What is it, my Waiko?" said he in his own language to his friend.

"I know not, my Kulmervan. Let us go to the Turret Room, and see." The two astronomical students at the most important meteorological college on the whole of Keemar, went swiftly up the wide, marble stairway to their Djoh's room. Before they were half way up, the bell rang louder than before.

"Haste, my Waiko," said Kulmervan. "The Djoh is anxious." As they reached the archway leading into the experimenting room, the Djoh met them.

"At last," said he testily. "At last you are come. I summoned you as there is a most remarkable phenomenon registered by the sensitive disc. After we recorded the destruction of the planet 'Quilphis,' you will remember, we discovered a new comet or meteor that seemed to have separated from the planet itself. We witnessed this extraordinary 'star' whirling toward us, daily nearer and nearer. Our learned Ab-Djohs consulted together as to the meaning of this extraordinary thing. At last I was consulted, and by the aid of every scientific means we possessed we tried to discover the substance of this new moving orb. You recollect?"

"Yes, my Djoh," answered Kulmervan, the senior student.

"Look," said the Djoh triumphantly, and he led the way to a large disc that stood in front of the large window. This disc was of glass, and was connected by etheric pipes to a large telescopic tube fixed outside the window. It was by the aid of this that the Keemarnians studied the solar system, and learnt about the other worlds in the sky.

As Kulmervan looked into the disc, he saw, by reflection, a peculiar body suspended in the heavens—stationary it rested near Wirmir and Kosli, the twin stars of Gorlan. "What is it?" he asked eagerly, while Waiko, the younger student, stood silent, listening eagerly to the conversation.

"It is the meteor of Marfaroo," said he. "It is the strange body that detached itself from Quilphis, when the life of that unfortunate planet was run."

"But it is still now, my Djoh."

"The four Meevors have not yet risen, my son. In fourteen permos from now, they will be bright and shining. When they are at their full, they will draw that orb within our surrounding vapours. Then we must direct our light rays upon it, and draw it within our atmosphere. It is a wonderful thing, my son, and will aid us in our knowledge of science. My theory is, that it is a minute portion of the planet Quilphis itself. Oh, very small, hardly as big as the Rorka's palace; but the knowledge of its composition will help us in our research. Take turn and watch with me, my sons, and at the right moment we will direct our Ray upon it."

Eagerly the students watched. The honour was great the Djoh had put upon them, and they were eager to be present when the light of the four full Meevors should shine upon the strange presence in the sky.

"But the time the Kymo sinks to rest, my sons, the fourth Meevor will be at the full, and we will watch the developments with interest."

The three surrounded the little disc; the pale beams from the Meevors shone distinctly on the glass; there was a movement—the foreign body moved slowly toward them.

"The Ray," cried the Djoh. "Summon the Ab-Djohs."

Ten Ab-Djohs appeared at Waiko's call. They were all dressed in the green tunic and vest and short cloak—the symbol of their calling as the highest astronomers in the land, bar one, the Djoh himself, who wore a voluminous cloak and tall, conical hat in addition. The wise men adjusted the focussing apparatus and directed the nozzle toward Wirmir and Kosli. A whirring noise sounded—and then suddenly shot out a most glorious ray. "When Kymo has risen but four thoughts, the orb will be here," announced the Djoh. "Waika, go call Waz-Y-Kjesta. Tell him the Djoh has words of import to utter."

Soon Waz-Y-Kjesta appeared. He was a handsome man, fair-haired, long-limbed. He wore his blue toga as became him as Waz of the air birds, the vessels which were used by the inhabitants of Keemar to journey by the sky.

"Fetch in that strange star, O Waz," said the Djoh. "Bring it to earth, and I will await its arrival here."

Waz-Y-Kjesta bowed low. "Your will shall be done, my Djoh," said he, and he went swiftly to the place where his air birds were housed.

"Mashonia," said he to his Waz-Mar, or Lieutenant. "Order out six air birds, we go on a mission for the Djoh."

In a very short space of time, six beautiful "birds" rose from the ground and skimmed toward their goal which was now approaching very rapidly.

"My Waz," cried Mashonia suddenly. "It is part of no planet that we are approaching. See, there is glass in front, and men like ourselves are looking toward us!"

"They are like us, yet unlike us," said Waz-Y-Kjesta. "They are habited in sombre clothing—they look dark and gloomy."

"Where can they come from?" asked Mashonia wonderingly. "All sons of Keemar would signal us. They are strangers from another world, I fear."

Gradually they circled round the Argenta, and brought her safely to the ground. They watched the lifting of the shutters curiously. This was indeed the strangest "air bird" they had ever seen. When Sir John gave his wild cry, the Keemarnians realized that the strangers who had come in so wonderful a manner to their land, had suffered acutely. "Send for six Bhors," said Waz-Y-Kjesta quickly, "these friends are ill."

In the shortest space of time, the Bhors, the Keemarnian carriages, appeared. They were comfortable litters like vehicles, laden with rugs of silk and downy cushions. Above were canopies of silk which shaded the occupants, who swung hammock wise from a wheeled frame, into the shafts of which were harnessed magnificent colis—beasts very similar to Shetland ponies, only with long curly hair.

At a command from Waz-Y-Kjesta, Mashonia and another leapt nimbly over the bulwarks of the Argenta, and without a word, in turn carried all the erstwhile prisoners of the airship, and placed them on cushions in the comfortable Keemarnian equipages. As Alan was carried past the Waz, he murmured feebly. "A guard for the Argenta, please."

A look of surprise passed over the Keemarnian's face. "What meanest thou?" he asked.

"A guard," urged Alan. "The Argenta contains all our possessions."

"A guard?" answered Kjesta. "Nay, why should we do that? It is safe there. It does not belong to us. Fear not, no one will touch it, my friend."

Gently the colis stepped out, drawing easily the Bhors and their occupants. "Drive to the palace of the Jkak," said Waz-Y-Kjesta. "We must acquaint him first with the news of the arrival of these strangers."

The weary travellers saw nothing of the country through which they passed. They were too weary and worn to raise themselves on the cushions and look around. The cool breeze swept across their faces and refreshed them, so they were content to remain as they were and not think or worry about the future.

A runner was sent before to acquaint the Jkak of their near approach, and as they stopped at his beautiful palace, men came out, unhooked the hammock part of the Bhors, and carried the occupants into the Jkak's presence. He was awaiting them in the cool reception hall, and regal and patriarchal he looked, in his robe of loose green silk, with his golden fillet low upon his brow.

"My brothers," said he in a low musical voice. "Welcome to Keemar, the land of all good. Eat first from yonder viands. They will revive you."

Trays daintily laden with food and wine were placed before the hungry travellers. The Jkakalata, consort to the Jkak, attended to Mavis. "A child," said she, "and a woman, too. Come, Persoph," to her husband, "give me that glass of friankate—it will revive her." She moistened Mavis's lips with the fragrant wine—Mavis opened her eyes, and as she looked at the kindly woman's face, she burst into tears. "Who are you?" she cried.

"I am Mirasu, the Jkakalata," she replied. "Drink this, it will do you good."

Mavis drank long of the sweet liquor, and ate the strange fruits that were placed before her. Alan, as usual, was the first to recover and made a movement as if to rise from the Bhor.

"Nay," said Persoph. "Do not move, I beg you. Rest, and later you can tell us your story." Then he turned to Desmond. "She with the babe—she is yours?"

"How did you know?" asked the perplexed husband.

"By the look in your eye when my Mirasu handled your babe," said the wise old man sagely. "It was the look of possession."

"Yes, she is my wife," said Desmond.

"Wife—ah! that is the word. Now rest among the cushions of the Bhors. Rooms are prepared for you. Sleep, my friends, until the Kymo rises twice again. Then refreshed and strong we will welcome you among us, and listen with interest to your story."

The Jkak's palace was of a glorious green marble, highly polished. In the entrance hall was a huge fountain. Six beautiful maidens, their garments chiselled out of coloured marble, held large shells from which poured water into the basin beneath. The figures were life size, and gracefully moulded. Lovely water flowers grew all around, and coloured fish swam in and out among the pebbles and plants.

Up a wide stairway, which branched out into large galleries, the strangers were carried, the Jkak himself leading the way, as if he were doing homage to the Rorka himself. They wended their way through a narrower passage which widened out again into a spacious loggia. In the very centre of this space four malachite pillars, highly polished, supported a crystal shell out of which poured sparkling waters into a pond beneath. There were six doors round the loggia; at the first the Jkak stopped, opening it himself, led the way in. With gentle hands Desmond and Mavis were transferred to soft, downy beds. "Rest, my friends, and sleep until Morkaba brings you wine and food." Then the other three were taken to separate sleeping apartments, where their weary limbs rested in contentment on the soft, downy cushions.

Desmond and Mavis's room was perhaps the largest—a glorious room with a wide balcony upon which were growing the most beautiful creepers and plants—with wonderful perfumes and flowers. An enormous four poster bed stood in the centre of the room, with its back immediately in front of the door. A canopy of silk was overhead; there were no sheets or blankets upon it, but there was an abundance of cushions, and silken rugs of all hues. Easy chairs, plenty of mirrors and a dressing table furnished the room. The walls were of a polished pale pink marble, and the fittings, tapestries and silken hangings were all of colours that blended and made one harmonious whole. All the other rooms were similar, except in the colouring, and on the polished marble floors were spread rugs of exotic colours.

A silver bell tinkled! To Mavis, it sounded like the Angelus on a summer morning. She opened her eyes; again the bell sounded. "Where am I?" she cried, and with sudden remembrance. "Baby—where's Baby?"

Desmond woke. "Where's Baby, Dez?" she asked again piteously, and even as she spoke she heard the sound of a tiny chuckle, and by her side on a bed, the miniature of the one she was on, lay her baby, crooning with delight. The bell tinkled again. Desmond went to the door and opened it slightly. A smiling girl was outside with a table on wheels. "Your mushti," said she wheeling it toward him.

"To eat?" queried Desmond.

"Of course. It is pleasant on the 'vala,' outside among the flowers—have it there with your friends."

"Thank you. It's breakfast, Mavis," said Desmond. "Look out on the balcony and see if Uncle John is there."

Mavis was almost too bewildered to ask any questions, and obeyed. There was a tiny gate dividing their balcony from the next, and she went through. "Uncle John," she called softly.

Sir John, Alan, and Masters appeared at the window of the next room.

"You're awake then?" laughed Alan.

"Yes."

"Have you had any food?" asked Desmond.

Alan laughed. "A table each—and chock full. Shall we wheel ours along and all have it together?" In a trice the six were sitting down to the first real meal they had had since they had so miraculously escaped from the end of the world.

The tables were of different coloured glass, and were laden with food very different from that to which they had been accustomed. There were jugs full of steaming liquid, neither tea, coffee, nor cocoa, but with a reminiscent flavour of all three, and extremely refreshing. There were wines—fruits whole, and fruits compote. There were cereals served almost like porridge, and there was bread too. Bread and tiny, crisp rolls, biscuits sweet and biscuits plain, and pats of golden butter. It was a delightful meal, refreshing, invigorating, and so different from the stodgy, unwholesome tinned meats they had been living on for so long. There was also a tiny tray for the baby—a bowl of fresh new milk and some rusks. A plate of a kind of arrowroot mixture was greatly appreciated by little John Alan, who cried out "More—pese, mum, more."

"The little beggar likes it," said Sir John. "He appreciates the change too. Well, here we are all on land again at last, and among friends."

"What are you going to do?" asked Mavis.

"We'll throw ourselves on the mercy of the Jovians of course; make up our minds to settle down in a new world, and live the remainder of our lives in peace and contentment."

"Shan't we ever go home again?" Mavis's eyes widened, and she looked imploringly at the others. The truth was forced on her mind at last. She had no home! Gone were all her pretty possessions—gone her trinkets, her books, her silver. Gone also her delicate trousseau—her frocks, lingerie, jewels.

Everything was gone. The world itself had vanished.

ELLA M. SCRYMSOUR

"Now, my dear," said Sir John. "We must acclimatize ourselves to this new life. After, all, we can easily do that. We have been treated as honoured guests, so I must speak to the Jkak, and find out our future standing in this world."

"They speak English!" said Alan wonderingly "How is that? Surely we are the first English people who have found their way here? There can't be a colony of Britishers in Jupiter!"

The bell sounded again, and Alan went to the door. Waz-Y-Kjesta stood outside. "The Jkak is eager to see you," said he. "If you feel strong enough and sufficiently rested, come with me and I will lead you to him." They followed him down the stairs to the entrance hall, and through into a spacious apartment.

"The Reception Room," said the Waz. "The Jkak wishes not to be on formal terms with you—he bade me bring you to his garden room."

Through a doorway they went and out into the most glorious garden they had ever seen. Fountains splashed in the sunlight—tiny brooks gurgled over white stones, as they wound round beds of flowers. There was a riot of colour in this wonderful garden—glorious, flowering trees and shrubs abounded—creeper-covered archways were everywhere, and at the further end they could see a creeper-covered arbour, hung with exotic blooms. Inside this were easy chairs, settees and comfortable lounges. The Jkak, and Mirasu, his Jkakalata, were seated there awaiting their arrival, and rose to greet them.

"Now tell us your story," said the Jkak, "for wonderful it must be."

"First," said Alan, who at Sir John's request, acted as spokesman, "how is it you can understand our language? Surely English isn't spoken here?"

"English?"

"Yes. We are English. We come from that part of our world that was known as England, you know."

"We have the 'gift of tongues' my friend," said the Jkak. "Until we spoke to you, we had never before heard your tongue, but the moment you spoke we understood. I cannot describe our gift—it just—is. We of Keemar all speak one tongue. No confusion is here. Until you came, we had never had the opportunity to benefit from this gift we all believed we possessed. To-day, all Keemarnians are thanking Mitzor, the Great White Glory and Tower of Help, for His graciousness in having conferred upon us this gift, and for allowing us to have the means given us for using the 'gift of tongues'. We understand, all of us. We may not understand every expression you utter, for things are different in other worlds, and we ourselves no doubt possess peculiarities of our own—still we can converse freely with you."

"It is a wonderful gift to possess," said Sir John.

"Now your story," insisted the Jkak gently.

So Alan told the whole story of his life since the time when he and Desmond first went to Marshfielden. He told of the Light, and the people of Kalvar—of their wonderful escape from the bowels of the earth, and of the end of the world.

"So Quilphis is no more," said the Jkak. "Indeed, we witnessed its destruction, and thought that your airship was part of the planet itself. And so," he went on, "you believe that the end of the world was caused through the failure of the fire in the centre of the earth?"

"I feel sure of it," said Alan. "During our stay in Kalvar, we noticed that the Fire grew daily less and less. And the purple people prophesied that when the Fire went out, then would come the end of the world. I think that, in its last dying gasp, it tried to get a new lease of life. In its gigantic death struggle, it burst its bonds, and earthquakes, volcanoes, and water spouts were the result."

"Oh, it was horrible," said Mavis shuddering.

"And your ship—the one you sailed in—you must invite me to see it," said the Jkak.

"Why, of course," said Sir John. "Have you not been?"

"It is not mine," replied the Jkak. "It would be an impertinence to pry into your affairs without an invitation. Now, with regard to yourselves. I must see that you go to Hoormoori and pay your respects to our Rorka. Hoormoori is the chief place in this world of ours; it is there that our Rorka has his palace."

"Rorka?" asked Mavis "What is that?"

"Our Rorka rules over the whole of Keemar."

"Have you only one Rorka or King over the whole of Keemar?" asked Sir John.

"Why, of course. Why should we have more?" asked Mirasu smiling. "Keemar is one world—with one Rorka. Then we have one hundred Jkaks, and one thousand Moritous—that is enough, surely, to govern a world?"

"Are you only one nation then?"

"Naturally. We are all Keemarnians—just one great nation, divided into many families. We all speak the same language—all worship in the same fashion Mitzor, the Great White Glory and Tower of Strength, and all live in peace, friendship, and harmony, one with another. But now my friends, strangers though you are, you are welcome here. I will put at your disposal houses and serving men."

"We possess nothing," said Sir John. "We have no property, no valuables—nothing but the Argenta. How shall we repay your kindness to us?"

"Repay?" said the Jkak, "nay, that is another, word I know not the meaning of."

"But," began Alan.

"Nay, you are strangers in a strange world. It is our duty to make you all feel at home here. I can see you were of high estate in your own country—you must be of high estate here also. Know you, we are wise in this land. Our Rorka is first, and his spouse, the Rorkata, ranks second. Their offspring and nearest blood relations come next; then come the Jkaks and Moritous; our Djohs and Ab-Djohs; the Wazi, Captains of our air birds, our learned men and students, down to the serving men and maids, and the builders of our homes and our ships. From highest to lowest, all share 'pro rata' in the good things of the world. We are all satisfied—the laws of our land have fixed the rates that are to be paid to each household from the common fund. I assure you, there will be enough and to spare for you."

Masters spoke for the first time. "I am Sir John's servant," he began.

"No," corrected Sir John. "Masters is my faithful friend and adviser."

"Then you would like him to dwell in the same house with you?"

"Please," said Sir John, "and my nephew Alan, also."

"And you, no doubt," went on the Jkak turning to Desmond, "you would like to have apartments to yourselves."

"Thank you," answered Mavis for her husband and herself.

"Good. I will summon Waz-Y-Kjesta. There are several new houses near at hand. Go with him—you can take your choice," and with a wave of the hand and a smile, they realized that they were dismissed from the presence of the Jkak and his charming wife.

Waz-Y-Kjesta was hovering near and came toward them. He had received his full instructions beforehand. "Come," said he. "The houses that are unoccupied are quite close—come and take your choice."

"How is it," asked Alan, "that we can walk so easily now. When we first came out on to the open deck of the Argenta, our limbs were as heavy as lead. We could not walk an inch, and we were so top-heavy we could hardly stand."

"That is easy to explain," replied the Waz. "Eight Kymos have risen since you arrived here."

"Kymos?" asked Mavis. The Keemarnian names puzzled her.

"Sun?" suggested Alan.

"Ah, you call it—sun. Yes, since you first came, the sun has sunk seven times. You have slept—breathed in our air. While you were sleeping, our men of science administered medicinal gases through your nostrils. These gases lightened you—took from you the heaviness of your earth. You will find no difficulty now," and he led the way through the garden to the most glorious street it was possible to imagine.

"Now you will see our country," he continued, "and compare it with your own. You are not too tired?" he asked Mavis.

"No, of course not. I feel too excited. I want to see your beautiful city—your beautiful country. May I first see that my baby is all right?"

He gave the necessary permission, and soon she returned. "He is sleeping peacefully," said she. "Morkaba is watching over him. Now I'm ready," and they all went down the marble steps of the Jkak's palace, eager for their first sight of this new, strange land.

V

Death in Jupiter

They walked down a lovely avenue to the outer gates. It was grass-covered, soft and velvety and cool. Birds with the gayest plumage hopped among the branches of the trees, and came fearlessly up to the strangers. One bird, perhaps as big as an English bullfinch, of many colours and with a fan-shaped tail, perched on Mavis' shoulder, and chirped prettily to her.

"How wonderful!" said she.

"Did not your, birds do that?" asked Waz-Y-Kjesta.

"No, they were too nervous."

"Nervous?"

"Yes—frightened—terrified," she explained.

"I understand the meaning of the word you utter," said he, "but you will not find the sensation of fear known on Keemar. We live in harmony with our birds, our animals, and even our fish. They are all our friends."

At the end of the avenue they found themselves on a broad road. Hills rose up at the side, steeply in some places, while in others the rise was more gradual, leaving moorland and valley in view. Houses were built at intervals along the roads, all of wonderful, coloured marbles, but they were all surrounded by beautiful grounds, and added to the scene.

"Oh," said Mavis suddenly. "There's a shop."

Waz-Y-Kjesta looked puzzled, and followed her gaze. "Oh yes, you mean our Omdurlis. How else should we get food to eat and clothes to wear?"

"How then do you manage about your coinage? Do you have money?" asked Alan curiously.

"I know not the word."

"How do you buy things—what do you give in exchange?"

"Oh, we have laika—royla, suka and minta," said he; and he drew from his purse that hung satchel-wise across his shoulders, some coins. The first was square, as large as a five shilling piece, and green in colour.

"This will purchase the most," he said. "Five roylas make a laika." The royla was exactly the same, but no bigger than a florin. "Then there are ten sukas to a laika, and twenty mintas." The last two coins were of a bronze hue and as big as a shilling and a sixpence.

"I expect those five coins are equal to a fiver, a sovereign, a two shilling piece and a sixpence," said Mavis thoughtfully.

"How do you get your money?" asked Sir John.

"Oh, from the Rorka," explained the Waz. "I am a Waz—I receive one thousand roylas or two hundred laikas a murvin. The Jkak will get a thousand laikas, while little Morkaba, who is born of the workers, gets but ten and her food."

"I suppose the shopkeepers make a lot of money," said Desmond.

"Oh no. All members of the Omdurlis get one hundred laikas. All that they make above that they are bound to send to the Rorka. He places all the surplus in the general fund which is held in reserve for all Keemarnians. As each male Keemarnian reaches the age when he has seen the Kymo rise three thousand and thirty times, he journeys to Hoormoori, makes his bow to the Rorka, and receives from him his manhood. According to the station in life in which he has been born, and from which he has sprung, so he learns to take his part in life."

"It is a wonderful system in theory," said Sir John. "But how does it work in practice?"

"It is our custom," was all the reply the Waz made.

"But don't you sometimes find you get dissentient spirits? Don't they rebel against this formality? Don't they want to make more money than is allowed by custom? Don't you sometimes have trouble from these spirits?"

Waz-Y-Kjesta smiled. "In our books of science we have read that in other places than ours—there were troubles like those you name. That man fought man—brother hated brother—women sorrowed, and children were rendered homeless. We, in Keemar, know not the meaning of such things. We are happy; we are content with our life; why should we complain?"

There were no ugly streets and lines of shops in this wonderful city; but the Omdurlis were to be found here and there at the edge of the grass covered paths, while the houses lay further back. Everywhere were to be seen happy-faced men and women, and laughing children. Bhors driven by colis, and bhors driven by the etheric power that was used for lighting and propelling purposes, thronged the streets, and the whole scene was gay and beautiful.

Although the sky was a wonderful blue, and all the buildings were of white and brilliant coloured marbles, the whole effect had none of the tawdry or bizarre appearance of the cities of the East, in the world; but the whole was soothing and pleasing to the jaded nerves of the earth folks. They turned a corner and found themselves in a short road ending in a cul-de-sac formed by high gates and marble pillars.

"This is one of the houses," said Waz-Y-Kjesta. "Come, and see it." The garden entranced Mavis before she saw the house. It was like a picture out of the fairyland she had dreamt of as a child—the fairyland she had dreamt of as a woman! For are not all true women half fairies at heart? Is not the mysticism of life itself a fairy gift to a pure woman's mind? Mavis had lived her life among the fairies. As a child she had played with them in bluebell woods and primrose glades; and when she renewed her own childhood in her baby, she renewed through him her acquaintance with the fairies.

Trees overhung the grassy path which was on a gradual upward slope. Burns ran down on either side—rushing, laughing, maddening burns. Tiny flowers peeped out among the grass; lichen-covered rocks reared up majestically from the centre of still pools. Gnarled trees lined the way, and their twisted roots formed steps up the hillside. The top spread out plateau-wise, and a blue marble house was built in the very centre. It was not very large; a verandah ran all round it on both floors, and the foliage and creeping plants added to its beauty. The door was open wide, and the splashing fountain in the entrance hall looked inviting and cool. Apart from the kitchen and servants' quarters, there were on the ground floor only two living rooms and the entrance hall. Each of the six bedrooms on the upper floor had magnificent bathrooms leading from them. They were like miniature swimming baths, shallow at one end, deepening to six feet, and the water was hot and cold in the pipes. The whole house was decorated in a delicate shade of blue, and was absolutely ready for use. Mavis was entranced. "May we stay here?" she asked.

"I will acquaint the Jkak with your decision," answered the Waz. "Now," turning to Sir John, "through the garden yonder, and down a short woodland path is a garden house. Would you care to see it? It might suit you, and you would be all near to one another."

"It sounds most attractive," said Alan.

They walked through the garden and down the hill on the other side of it, and saw, nestling among the trees, the tiniest house they had so far seen on Jupiter. It was an absolutely perfect bachelor establishment, and the three men decided at once that it was an ideal spot to live in.

"The Jkak is eager to see your air bird," announced Waz-Y-Kjesta. "When may he go?"

"Why I'd forgotten all about the Argenta," said Alan. "Can't we go now?"

Mavis looked from one to the other. "Do you want Dez?" she asked pathetically. "I seem to have seen so little of him lately. Dez come— come home, and Baby, you and I will have a long, happy day together."

So it was decided that Sir John, Alan and Masters should go back to the Jkak's with the Waz, and arrange about the trip to the Argenta. "Waiting men and maids have already been dispatched to your houses," announced the majordomo, Marlinok by name.

"Is the Jkak at liberty?" asked the Waz.

"He is, my Waz."

"Tell him, if it is his desire, the strangers will show him their air bird now."

A few minutes passed and Marlinok returned. "The bhors are ready and waiting, my Waz. The Jkak has already started."

Outside they found two double bhors ready, and Sir John and his faithful Masters travelled in one, while Alan and Waz-Y-Kjesta occupied the other. Alan was now able to enjoy the scenery through which he passed. The path by which they travelled ran by the side of an island lake, with tall mountains towering on the further side of the water. The woodland nature of the scene with the twining paths and overhanging branches reminded Alan forcibly of the bank of Loch Lomond between Tarbet and Ardlui; yet the almost tropical colouring of the flora—the wonderful brightness of the birds' plumage, the waving palm-like trees that were interspersed here and there, were unlike anything he had ever beheld. This place seemed to possess everything to make it perfect— mountain—moorland—water—and woodlands. Nothing was missing from this panorama of glory.

At last the Argenta hove in sight, and somehow its beauty seemed to have lessened in this land of glory. The silver brightness of its aluminium looked dim in the golden sunlight; the torpedo-shaped body seemed ugly and sinister in comparison with the beauty and symmetry of the Keemarnian air birds. The Jkak waited for the strangers to alight, and the Waz whispered his instructions. "Welcome the Jkak, my friend," said he. "It is our custom. Ask him to honour you by boarding your craft. Let him bring peace and prosperity to your house by stepping across the threshold of your boat."

ELLA M. SCRYMSOUR

"My Jkak," said Alan, going to the side of the state bhor, "will you honour us all by boarding our Argenta, and bring us joy and peace?"

"You have learnt your lesson quickly and well, my son," said the Jkak in reply. "I will come with pleasure." He walked aboard and was extremely interested in the vessel. "But how do you move it?" he asked. "How does it rise into the heights of the heavens?"

"This is the spirit," said Alan, "but alas, it will not work in your atmosphere. There seems no power in it. Perhaps later on, we might experiment with your etheric current?"

The Jkak and his suite were enchanted with the fittings of the Argenta—the electricity, the furniture, the hangings. As they made their way toward the sleeping cabins, Masters suddenly spoke.

"Poor old Murdoch—he's in there," said he. "I am afraid I forgot all about him."

"Poor chap," said Alan, "so did I," and he quickly barred the way. "May I suggest, my Jkak, that you do not go in there," said he. "A very dear comrade of ours risked his life for us all. He is in there—dead."

"Dead?" asked the Jkak.

Sir John bowed his head sadly. "Dead," he repeated, "and one of the truest servants that man ever had."

"But if he is in there," said the Jkak with a puzzled frown, "why does he not come out?" He looked at the others in turn. "Why does he not enjoy life with you? Ah! He thinks the Argenta would not be safe without him? That is foolish. I will enter—I will assure him he has nothing to fear."

"But he is dead," urged Alan.

"Dead?"

"Yes, he died before we reached Keemar."

"I know not the meaning of the word. The 'gift of tongues' fails me here. Explain—dead."

Alan looked at him in amazement. Death was such a common word in the world; one met with it at every turn; it was strange that it should remain unknown to the Jovians with their wonderful "gift of tongues."

"His life has gone," said Alan simply.

"But life is eternal, my son."

"Surely you do not live for ever on Keemar?" asked Alan incredulously.

"Ah, no. We do not live for ever on Keemar it is true—but our life is eternal."

It was impossible to explain—they had no knowledge of death—yet they, on their own showing, seemed to expect to leave Keemar at some time or other. Surely death alone could remove them?

"I beg of you, do not go in there," urged Alan, and he barred the door of the death chamber.

"My son," said the Jkak. "I must know all things in my country. If what you call 'death' has entered—then I beg you, acquaint me with it."

"But it is horrible—"

"Let me meet it face to face—"

"It is loathsome," urged Alan. "I pray you, do not go inside."

The Jkak made no reply, but raised his right hand high above his head—palm outwards, and even as he did so, Waz-Y-Kjesta and his suite bent low on one knee.

"The sign of the Jkak," said the Waz. "His wishes must be honoured, his commands obeyed."

Alan moved away from the door, his head bowed in acquiescence, and Marlinok turned the handle of the door, and stepped back to allow the Jkak to enter. There was a tense silence for a moment, then from the darkened chamber came a startled cry, a cry full of poignant horror, and with an ashen face the Jkak appeared at the door.

"I have seen Death," said he. "I have seen the horrors of sin. Death, until now, has never entered Keemar. Death brings its own punishment. Death brings horrors and adversity. Death! Oh Great, White Glory, Tower of Help, Mitzor of our Fathers—I have seen Death in its hideousness. Mitzor the Mighty, grant preservation to thy people—grant help to thy faithful." Persoph the Jkak was trembling. His face was white, his hand was shaking as he pointed to the door.

"What will you do with—with—that?" he asked, almost inaudibly.

Alan answered him. "Bury him, poor chap."

"Bury?"

"Yes. Do you not dig graves for your dead?"

"We have no dead, my son. I pray Mitzor, that the entrance of this—soul—may not bring disaster on our land. But how do you bury?"

Alan explained, and as he finished the Jkak's face was more horror-stricken than before. "Nay, my son, bury you cannot. That would be impossible here." He turned to the Waz. "Does not the Sacrament of Schlerik-itata take place within eight Kymos?"

"Yes, my Jkak," answered Y-Kjesta. "Ak-Marn sent cards for all to attend it. It will be the biggest feast I have ever known. His seed is mighty, his seed is great. Five thousand and ten cards have been issued, and yet five thousand and more still clamour for admittance."

"Good," answered Persoph. "This," pointing about him, "all this must go. Summon me Misrath, the High Priest. Bid him bring his 'waters of purity' and his smoke of sweet odours. Bid him bring his choir of young voices, and bid all prepare. A sacrifice will be offered to Mitzor; the Great White Glory must be appeased."

Alan and Sir John were very mystified over the whole scene. These Jovians did not seem to understand Death—yet they spoke of sacrifice!

"I am sorry, my son," said the Jkak. "I can save nothing for you. All must be burnt and offered to Mitzor. Come now, I will draw a ring around the contaminated spot, and we will witness the destruction from without."

Sir John and Alan were both loth to have the Argenta burnt—but being dependent on the Jovians for their entire future, they were unable to demur. With a silent prayer for the friend who had given his life for them, they left the ship and stood some way off. After an interminable time of waiting, a mighty blast of music burst on their ears, and they saw a procession of etheric bhors coming towards them. The first stopped, and Misrath the High Priest alighted, followed by priests and acolytes in quaint garments of ecclesiastical cut.

A procession formed—two acolytes with censers led the way, and wafted the glorious perfume from side to side. Then followed one of the most mystical and picturesque ceremonies it was possible to imagine. Almost of Mosaic grandeur, it thrilled the watchers. They were unable to understand what was being said—all was in the language of the Keemarnians—but the meaning was plain. The High Priest offered the Argenta and its contents to Mitzor, the Great White Glory. He offered it, with its fine workmanship, its precious metals—and its body of sin. He asked that through the mediation of the sacrifice, any evil might be averted, that the entrance of Death might bring. He consecrated the Argenta to Mitzor—he consecrated the ground it contaminated. He poured the "waters of purity" across its bow, and named it "Meeka," the Bringer of Knowledge.

Then the Argenta was sprayed from stem to stern with a milky fluid that dried like little curds all over the vessel. A torch was lighted and applied to the ship. Little flames ran along meeting each other until they merged into one great whole; there was a roar and a noise like thunder, and the Argenta, the hobby of a life time, the fruit of patient labour, was no more!

Sir John watched with a set face, but as the fire died out, and he saw that the whole had been swallowed up, had consumed itself entirely,— he crumpled up, and lay inert upon the ground.

VI

THE SACRAMENT OF SCHLERIK-ITATA

Alan bent over his uncle, but the High Priest waved him away. "Touch him not," said he sternly, and such command rang in his tones, that Alan stepped back involuntarily.

Again the scene was repeated—Sir John was prayed over, sprayed with the "waters of purity," and incensed. As the sweet fumes found their way up his nostrils, he stirred. Alan rushed to him and embraced him. "It was only foolishness, Alan," said he brokenly. "But the Argenta—my ship—I was so proud of her. Masters, you know how I felt? She was my all in my days of sorrow. And in my days of joy, when reunited we sailed in her, she was my joy."

"I understand, Uncle John. But try not to mind—when one is in Rome—you know the rest. We are in Jupiter and we must do as the Jovians wish."

Persoph the Jkak, came up to them. "Nay, grieve not," said he kindly. "We have cleared this place of sin. An air bird to take the place of the one that has gone shall be placed at your disposal. Go you home. Cards will be brought you for the Sacrament of Schlerik-itata. I beg of you all—attend it. Nay, I command you. We will meet again within eight Kymos. Farewell. Farewell."

Waz-Y-Kjesta, motioned to their bhor. "Come, my friend," said he. "I will drive you back another way—we will drive along the shores of the secti, and watch the breakers roll in." The sea shore was wonderful; the sea was blue, a deep, deep blue, and the breakers, flecked with foam, rolled in to a golden shore. They passed bays, promontories, caves and rocks—and they found the drive of bewildering beauty.

Alan asked, "What is the Sacrament of Sch—"

"Schlerik-itata?" supplemented the Waz.

"Yes."

"My friend, you must wait until you witness it. You will understand us more fully when you have been to the home of Ak-Marn. Now to-night, there is a small party being given by Kulmervan and his fellow students at the Observatory. I have been asked to bring you all. Will you come?"

"With pleasure," said Alan.

"The Jkak is sending you all a complete outfit, my friend. Your clothes are old, travel-stained and torn—they are sombre too. If you accept his present, wear to-night your brightest garments."

"Will you help me to adjust them?" asked Alan.

The Waz drew himself up with a haughty air, but it as soon passed. "I was forgetting, my friend, that you know not our customs. The serving men will assist you. When you reach home, you will find your house fully staffed, and Quori, a most efficient steward and adviser."

"What about meeting to-night for the party?"

"I will call for you as the Kymo sinks. You will have bhors sufficient for your use."

When they reached home they found a note awaiting them from Mavis, asking them to come over and have lunch with her and Desmond, and they walked through the garden to the other house. Mavis was waiting for them, her cheeks dimpling and her eyes sparkling. "It's a wonderful country," said she. "I've nothing to do all day; the cooking and cleaning seem to go by clockwork. Morkaba is Baby's personal attendant and mine; she has arranged my frock. How do you like it?" and she twirled round on one foot showing the soft draperies of Keemarnian dress.

It was of a soft green, embroidered with coloured silks and her hair was left loose flowing around her shoulders, and caught above her ears by a narrow fillet of gold that gleamed as she tossed her head.

"I like it much better than the frumpy old English fashions," said she. "Desmond is not quite ready yet—he will look splendid."

"We shall change later," said Sir John, "and I shall be glad to get out of these stuffy and dirty garments. All the same I don't fancy myself a cross between an imitation gladiator and a stained glass twelfth century saint."

They thoroughly enjoyed their meal; eggs served in a wonderful salad of fruit and vegetables proved to be the staple part, and this course was followed by a baked grain, similar to barley, but of a bright green colour, deliciously creamy and sweet. There was milk to drink, and plenty of heavy cream.

"They seem to be almost vegetarians here," said Mavis, "for although we have had plenty of milk, eggs and cream, I have not seen a sign of fish or meat."

"All the better," said Sir John, "after all that tinned stuff while we were on the Argenta—ugh!"

They drove in state to the students' party. The Waz had constituted himself their guide, and they were very thankful for his services. The large ground floor of the Observatory had been converted into a veritable bower of roses. At one end, almost hidden by flowers, were the musicians—playing dreamy music on soft-toned, stringed instruments.

The Host in Chief, Kulmervan, with Waiko, stood on a raised dais at one end and received their guests, who were all announced by an usher who wore a kilt-like shirt and a flowing cape. As the strangers entered he announced from a card they gave him, first in his own language and then in English, "Sir John, Alan, Desmond, Masters, and Mavis." No surnames were known on Jupiter, and so far they possessed no Keemarnian title. To Sir John they gave his prefix, although they did not quite understand it.

A great silence reigned when the announcement was made— Kulmervan left the dais and advanced toward his guests, and this mark of homage was acknowledged by clamorous cheers from all the others who were present.

"Welcome," said he. "I witnessed your descent upon our land. Indeed, it was I who helped to focus our ray of attraction upon your vessel and helped to draw you into our atmosphere."

"What are your rays?" asked Alan. "Surely you had never any cause to use one before?"

"Indeed, yes, my friend. Some time ago, some of our Keemarnians, while experimenting in the Heavens, found themselves outside our atmosphere. They never returned. Across the roadway between the red planet 'Mydot'—Mars I think you call it—and ourselves, are many rapidly moving meteoric bodies. We fear that our gallant brothers met one of these, and were destroyed. Many men of science went after these lost ones but none ever returned. Through our wonderful glass, we saw one of our air birds in space; it was unable to reach home. Then was the great magnetic ray discovered. In the shortest space of time it was perfected, and played on the silent air bird. Gradually it was drawn nearer and nearer to our shores until it was within our atmosphere, and was able to land in safety. Since that time, if air birds venture too high, we have nearly always been able to save the adventurous spirits, and in your case, we brought you safely here."

"It's a wonderful invention," said Sir John, "and I can imagine would have been of immense value to our airmen on earth."

Kulmervan then presented them to Waiko, and Mavis was led to a seat of honour on the dais.

They spent a most enjoyable time, and the whole entertainment was very like what they were accustomed to on earth. Games were played,— games with balls and racquets, and balls and hoops, and between the games there was singing and dancing.

Refreshments were served in a hall adjoining, and consisted mainly of luscious fruits and dainty cakes and pastries. The many Keemarnians they met, invited them in turn to parties and entertainments, and they felt they had more invitations than they could safely accept. "Never accept," whispered Waz-Y-Kjesta to them all, "unless you mean to honour your host with your presence. A refusal never offends, but to accept and then to disappoint, is unforgivable." Suddenly in the middle of the dancing a trumpet blew loud and clear. The band ceased and the couples stood still. Then rang out a fanfare of royal welcome, and the guests rushed to the entrance hall in great excitement, waving and cheering. "It must be some one of importance who is coming," said Desmond. "Perhaps it is the Rorka," suggested Mavis. There was a roll of drums, and then, on a litter carried by six stalwart men, entered a girl of perhaps eighteen years. The cortége stopped and Kulmervan bent low before her, and kissed her proffered hand. She bowed ever so slightly, and he assisted her from her cushioned throne. She stood beside him, and proved to be quite small, not more than five feet in height, but of a beauty almost indescribable. She was very fair and fragile. Her eyes were purple-blue fringed with long, black lashes. Her fillet was of gold, and was enriched with gems the colour of her eyes, while her robe of blue hung in folds about her. Perhaps it was her lips that impressed the watchers most. A perfect bow—they were of a vivid scarlet that contrasted strangely with the delicate pink flush of her cheeks. Self possessed, calm and regal she looked as she graciously acknowledged the plaudits of the guests.

"Who is she, Alan?" asked Mavis. But he was unconscious of her question, he could only gaze and gaze at the beautiful apparition who had come so unexpectedly upon the scene.

Waiko bent in turn before the stranger who whispered something to him. Immediately he came toward Mavis. "We are honoured to-night," said he. "The Ipso-Rorka Chlorie has journeyed from Pyrmo to welcome you. She heard of your presence and came at once."

"Who is she?" asked Mavis.

"Why the highest lady in the land—the only child of our Rorka."

Mavis went toward where the girl stood, and the Ipso-Rorka held out both her hands to the English girl. "Welcome," said she, in a voice musical and low. "I hear you start soon to honour the Rorka, my father, with a visit. May I welcome you first?" In turn the others were presented to her, but her attention was all for Mavis—it was Mavis the woman she wanted to know.

And Alan? He had seen his ideal! Years before, he wondered whether he would ever meet her—and now he had. And a King's daughter! And he a stranger in a strange world! How dare he even lift his eyes toward her. Yet he dared—and his pulses leapt madly as his eyes feasted on her beauty. Not once did she address him—not once did she even seem to notice him. Chlorie put her hand lightly on Desmond's arm. "I will dance with you," said she smiling, and Alan watched them lead the merry throng of dancing couples. The demon of jealousy, earth jealousy, was in his heart.

"Why are you looking so—how can I put it—so sad?" asked Kulmervan.

Alan laughed. "He has a wife," he muttered. "Why does he take her from others?"

"But she has honoured him. It is not for us to choose for the Ipso-Rorka," said Kulmervan.

"Yes, but she is so beautiful, so sweet, so glorious," began Alan. Then he stopped suddenly. "Oh," he continued, "what do you people of Jupiter know of love or hate? Your lives are too quiet, too humdrum to know aught of passion—"

"Teach me! Teach me!" cried Kulmervan leaning toward him. "Your face is drawn—your eye hard. Yet you look as if you could battle with the world. What is it?"

"Love and hate," said Alan grimly. Then he laughed. "What a fool I am. Desmond is my cousin; we love each other like brothers. He has won Mavis—why should he not dance with the Ipso-Rorka? Mavis does not mind."

But Kulmervan turned away in silence. Knowledge had come to him in a curious way. He saw passion, love, hatred, anger, jealousy all raging within a human heart. Unconsciously the feelings were photographed upon his too sensitive mind. Love that had only smouldered was now born in all its fury for the Princess Chlorie, the fair. And with love was born the twin, hate—hate for Alan, the man he feared might supplant him.

It seemed as if death, although burned and purified, had brought into Keemar unrest and sin. The prayers of the High Priest himself were unable to wash it away, until scourged and purified the earth folk themselves became less material and more godlike and true.

The day for the Sacrament of Schlerik-itata arrived at last and the strangers found themselves on the way to Ak-Marn's palace.

Although the Aks had no administrative powers, as had the Jkaks, they were held in the highest esteem, for they were princes of royal blood.

Ak-Marn greeted them warmly. They saw that his dress was different from the usual male costume. He was in unrelieved white, and wore neither jewel nor ornament. The material of his robe, which hung with a long cloak to the ground, was almost like plush and there was something almost bridal about the costume. Yet Ak-Marn was an old man, with a beard of white, and grandchildren in plenty. Surely Schlerik-itata could not be the same as matrimony, thought Mavis.

The guests were eight thousand in number, and all wore their brightest jewels and their finest raiment.

There was singing and dancing and much gay chatter, and the whole scene was one of wonderful gaiety and joy. Refreshments were brought in, and Ak-Marn began to speak. The English people could now understand the Keemarnian language fairly well. It was easy, its grammar simple, and its pronunciation almost Latin.

"Friends," said Ak-Marn. "I break bread with you. Two and ten Kymos have sunk since I quenched my thirst or satisfied my hunger. I've prayed to Mitzor, the Great White Glory and Tower of Help, to prepare me for my journey. My call came eighty and five Kymos since—I saw the figures in fire. I heard my call, and am prepared. I go with hope in my heart—with joy in my breast. I am to be envied, my friends, for my days have been long upon Keemar. I leave my loved one, Viok, and our children, and our children's children in your care, my friends. When I am gone, cheer her with loving words—help her with kind counsel. I leave you with love in my heart. I leave you with the knowledge that our parting is not for long. Soon you will join me in the home of the Tower of Help. Remember that the eternities of time cannot be measured."

Then bread was broken, and there followed the "Feast of the Sacrament," and the most intimate friends of Ak-Marn drank to his "future"—drank to his coming "joy." And Alan and Sir John were no longer mystified. They realized that what they in their materialism knew as "Death" was nigh—but not Death, the slayer of happiness, Death, the dread reaper, but Death in a kindly form, a death that gave life—a death that was glorious.

"I thought at first that the Jovians were of a finer nature than ours," said Alan.

"If they have conquered Death, they must indeed be high," said Sir John thoughtfully.

"Who is Mitzor?" asked Mavis.

"The God of our Fathers, my dear. The God of Abraham and the God of the New Testament. Whatever their religion and ritual is, they worship the same God as we do," said Alan.

"Are you sure?"

"Quite."

When the feast was ended, the guests, one by one, bade farewell to their host. It was a long tedious business, as no one was permitted to pass without at least a few personal words from Ak-Marn who was seated on a raised chair near the doorway. And as each woman passed out, she was crowned with a wreath of beautiful, freshly cut flowers, from which hung a filmy white veil, while the men were given long white cloaks with hoods which they drew over their bare heads. Mavis bent her knee, and held out her hands to the kindly old man. "My child," said he. "Our beautiful ceremony is so far meaningless to you. Go home—pray to Mitzor the Mighty that He may refine and cleanse you, that when your time comes you may be reincarnated to Him, through the medium of his Sacrament. Farewell."

To Alan he spoke long and quietly. "My son," said he, "you are in a strange world, you are young, you are carnal. Ah," as Alan would have protested, "we of Keemar, my Alan, are not as of your world. We know not sin as you know it. Our first parents, Menlin and Jorlar, were placed in a garden—" Alan started—"Yes, my friend, as your parents were. They succumbed not to temptation—so they lived in happy solitude for many years. Then Mitzor in His great kindness gave them the knowledge of Love—Love without sin. They mated. Their love grew. Children of love were born sinless into our world. Child bearing was a glory; motherhood the highest estate. They knew neither sin nor sorrow, and so in love our populace grew."

"Do you mean to say you are sinless here?" asked Alan incredulously.

"My son, it is not an estate for us to glory in, for the merits do not belong to us, but to our first parents. No—real sin has never entered here, but we live in dread of its coming. In a far off country—in Fyjipo—there is built a large palace behind high walls. If anger, or lust, or impatience is shown by any one of us, an order is given and the offender is taken to the Hall of Sorrows to purge away his sins. Should a madness come upon us, for such we reckon these failings to be—we are kept safe until it has passed, and until we can no longer contaminate our fellow creatures."

"It's a wonderful country," said Alan. "Where we come from, is all sin and misery and—"

"Nay, tell me not. I go on a journey. I shall face my Mitzor. I charge you, should you or your friends feel this madness coming on you, hide yourselves, I beg, in the Hall of Sorrows. Stay there until it has passed, and preserve the purity and happiness of this land. Farewell." The cloak was fastened round Alan's shoulders, and he too left the kindly presence.

Waz-Y-Kjesta was waiting for them at the outer hall. "Go home," he whispered. "Your bhor awaits you. I beg of you, eat no more this night, but in the early dawn, while Kymo still sleeps, put on your cloaks, and the Lady Mavis her veil, and go you to the Temple of Mitzor. Farewell." It was a very solemn party that retired to their rooms that night, yet the full mystery of the Sacrament had not been unfolded to them.

It was dark when they arose, and in a dim twilight they drove to the Temple. They had never before been inside it, and it was with much trepidation that they waited on the threshold. It was a very beautiful building of pale blue marble—the colour of the sky. An enormous dome rose up in the centre of the square body of the Temple, and at the four corners, minarets with gilded tops finished the picture. A flight of fifty steps led up to the doors which were of a burnished metal, and studded with precious gems. Just inside was an antechamber, where the guests waited in silence until they were ushered to the seats that were allotted to them. The inside was wonderful. Mosaic walls representing allegorical tales gleamed in the dim light; the roof was of gold, and marble pillars supported it down the long aisle. An enormous altar rose up at the further end upon which were carved in marble cherubim and seraphim. In the sanctuary, if such it could be called, was a small white throne of marble, with heavy, white curtains draped at either side. It was placed in such a position that although it did not intercept the view of the altar, which was high above the nave, yet it could be seen by every one in the building.

The seats allotted to Alan and his party were very near the front where rails of gold separated the Sanctuary from the people's part of the Temple. Music floated on the air—soft like babbling brooks and the song of birds; now bursting out into thunderous praise and mighty worship.

Suddenly there came a solemn hush; a bell tinkled; the organ played softly, and there came the sound of boys' sweet voices raised in ecstasy: from a door at the side of the choir a dozen acolytes walked dressed in their garments of white. The procession started down the nave. After these boys came priests and deacons, and then Misrath, the High Priest walked in front of a raised throne. On this sat Ak-Marn, his eyes closed and his hands clasped in prayer. Behind him walked his wife and their children. Their faces were radiant, it is true; yet there was a touch of sadness in his wife's gait. Then followed more priests and acolytes, all singing hymns of joy.

The procession wound round the Temple, and back through the middle aisle, and through the rails into the Sanctuary. Ak-Marn was led to the marble throne; his wife alone of his family had followed close behind, and now his arms were around her. Their lips met in one long kiss, then with a bowed head she left his side, and took her place with her family in the very front seats.

The organ thundered. Voices rang in a mighty pæan of praise. Then silence! Misrath came forward and offered prayers to Mitzor—prayers of offering, prayers of supplication. A mighty wreath of freshly cut flowers was placed upon the altar. It was to be a burnt offering, and as the smoke of the sacrifice arose on the air, the white curtains were drawn around the figure of Ak-Marn and he was hidden from view. Then singing rent the air; the acolytes incensed the throne, until it was entirely covered by the perfumed smoke, covered like a pall.

Alan watched in wonder. The grandeur of the prayers, the singing, the mystic curtains drawn around Ak-Marn appalled him. Misrath's voice rose above the music.

"Children of Keemar," he intoned. "One more brother has been caught by the mantle of Mitzor, and has left this world for ever. He has gone to Glory, gone to Happiness—gone to Mitzor Himself. Peace be unto his house. Peace be unto his wife. Peace be unto his seed for ever. We bid him—farewell."

There was a great silence. The censers were stilled. Gradually the smoke of the incense cleared away from the marble throne, now gleaming in the rising rays of the Kymo.

Misrath touched the cords of the enveloping curtain, and drew them back. The little white throne was empty! Ak-Marn had returned to the bosom of his Creator! But stay! On the floor, as if shed in the hurried flight of its owner, lay the bridal robe of Ak-Marn. The High Priest raised it, blessed it, sprinkled it with the waters of purity, and Ak-Marn's wife received it in her arms. Then the mighty congregation rose and sang one last song of praise, and at the end, quietly left the building. And the last view Alan had of Ak-Marn's wife was of a solitary figure, dressed like a bride, clasping the little white throne that was the last resting place of her loved one.

"I don't understand," whispered Mavis hoarsely, as they were being driven back to their home.

"My dear, he is dead," said Sir John.

"Dead? If that is Death, then it is something to welcome and not to dread," she answered softly. There was a faraway look in her eyes. "What a wonderful Sacrament! Death that is no sorrow—only a parting for a little while, and then—reunion." She clasped her husband's hand. "Belovèd," she murmured, "if Death comes to us like that, then can we have no real sorrow any more. Its shadow cannot cause us pain or grief. What do you think, Alan?"

But Alan did not answer. He was thinking of two deep blue eyes, a laughing mouth, wilful golden curls that flirted on two soft, pink cheeks. He was longing to crush the lithe and sweet body close to his, and smother her roses with kisses. The knowledge and fear of Death had lapsed; Jupiter had eradicated it,—but with its extinction had come love. Love, stronger a thousandfold than Death. He looked upward to where the Sun, Kymo in all his glory, was shining. The whole world was bathed in a glory of light. Yes, Jupiter had conquered death, and before him lay life and love!

VII

HATRED ON KEEMAR

M arlinok, the Jkak's majordomo, called on Sir John and Alan a few days after they had witnessed the Sacrament of Schlerik-itata. "Will you be ready," he asked them, "when the Kymo is at the full, to start on your journey to Hoormoori to render homage to the Rorka?"

"Are we all to go?" asked Alan.

"But one of you need go," he answered. "The Rorka will visit Minniviar later, and then the other strangers may make their bows."

"I am glad of that," said Sir John, "for I should like to stay here in quietness and retirement for a little while. I am beginning to feel the burden of my age, and am worn out with the strain of the last few years."

"I will go to Hoormoori," announced Alan, "I can start at whatever time the Jkak thinks best."

"He has prepared incense and jewels for you to take as gifts from the absent ones," said Marlinok, "if you will now see Waz-Y-Kjesta all your arrangements can be made."

"I'll go now," said Alan.

Alan was going down a pretty lane toward where the air birds were housed when he suddenly became aware of footsteps behind him. He turned—immediately the footsteps ceased, and he could see no one. Thinking he must be mistaken, and fearing nothing from the Keemarnians, he went on his way blithely. The air was deliciously warm, and the fresh breeze, balmy with the scent of flowers, tempered it. Still the footsteps followed with monotonous regularity; as he hastened, so they became quicker; as his died down, so they ceased altogether. Yet he had no sense of fear, no feeling of impending evil; the thought of peril on Keemar was impossible to imagine. The Keemarnians were of a breed as different from the earth to which he belonged, as he was from Heaven! He passed delightful homely fields, gleaming with buttercups and daisies. Friendly cows chewed the cud in sleepy enjoyment. They did not rise as he drew near, but only raised their sleepy heads, and looked at him out of their liquid eyes with interest and friendliness. A pig grunted in a corner as she suckled her squealing young; a donkey brayed; a couple of goats were nibbling the grass while their kids frolicked near them. He saw strange animals too. There was the gorwa of the deer family, a beautiful creature, the colour of a Scottish stag, and its counterpart in miniature, but with none of its brother's timidity. All the animals on Keemar were of a smaller build than those he had been accustomed to. The cows were even smaller then the little fawn Jerseys so valued in England. He had seen terriers and bull dogs, dalmatians and spaniels in this strange world, and the bigger breeds were all represented on a smaller scale. The Jkak had a dog—a Borzoi, Alan would have called it, yet perhaps it was no bigger than a small Irish terrier; but strangely enough, its beauty was not diminished by its minuteness. So Alan went on. The way was strange to him, but he was enjoying the calmness of the scene, and he knew his excellent bump of locality would sooner or later lead him to Y-Kjesta. Again the footsteps beat time with his own, and anxious for companionship, he stepped into the shadow of a tree, and hoped to waylay a shy, but friendly stranger. A second passed. The footsteps had ceased—then came a rustling, and the head of Kulmervan the Student appeared over a honeysuckle bush. Silently he came forward, alert and watchful until he was on a level with Alan.

"Hullo!" said Alan amiably. "Where are you going, Kulmervan?"

The effect was magical! Kulmervan jumped as though he had been struck, and his face whitened. He remained silent. "I'm going to see Waz-Y-Kjesta," went on Alan. "Are you coming my way?"

Kulmervan did not reply, but a baleful light gleamed in his eyes, and his mouth twitched.

"What's the matter?" asked Alan curiously.

Suddenly Kulmervan spoke, and there was a wealth of passion in his tones. "Why did you come here, you strangers? I was happy until you came. I was contented. You have made me want—want the unknown. You have stirred my heart and filled it with longings that I cannot yet fathom. Why have you come to stir up misery among a happy and contented race?"

"I don't know what you mean," said Alan, "I have done nothing."

"You've done everything. You dared to raise your eyes to the level of Chlorie, our Ipso-Rorka. You put thoughts about her into my head. Oh—" as Alan would have broken in—"I read your thoughts, it was easy, my friend. You dared to think of her as a woman—even your woman. It was an impertinence, I tell you. I love Chlorie with my whole soul, and before Mitzor the Mighty, I'll carry her away into some far off land, before she

ELLA M. SCRYMSOUR

can look with a favourable eye on a man, not only of another world, but a man of a coarser nature than our own."

Kulmervan was breathless when he finished, for his words had come thick and fast, tumbling over themselves in his great excitement. Alan was speechless, and looked as he felt, absolutely uncomfortable and ill at ease. "Why your very pose proves guilt," continued Kulmervan.

"Why should I not love Chlorie?" demanded Alan, "Why should my love for her cause strife between us?"

"Because, my stranger, I am a Prince of the Rorka's House. I am not only Kulmervan the Student; but Taz-Ak of the House of Pluthoz. Why else would Chlorie have honoured my party—why else come to the dance of a student? There are but four Keemarnians that Chlorie can marry, and I rank second."

Alan wondered at the time why the Princess should come in so natural a manner to the Student's reception. He wondered at the time at her familiarity with Kulmervan. She had patted his hand, smiled into his eyes, and had honoured him more than once with a dance.

But Alan, too, was in love. Idiotically, insanely in love with a woman who had not even troubled to raise her eyes to his, at his presentation. His pulses throbbed at the remembrance of the touch of her fingertips as he raised them to his lips. He loved her, and in that moment was born a desire to overcome all obstacles, and princess or no princess, to win her. But he knew too that in this pleasant land of Keemar an enmity had come upon him, and wondered whether the Curse of Death had brought it. He wondered whether the dead and decomposed body of their faithful Murdoch had indeed brought sorrow to this fair land.

"I've spoken to your Ipso-Rorka only once," said he. "The night of your party. She has called on my uncle and Mavis. Mavis has been out driving with her several times. But I, unfortunately, have missed her each time. Surely you are not jealous because I—"

"Because you love her? I am," said Kulmervan thickly, "and I say this—if you so much as dare to raise your eyes to her, if you dare to address her, I'll make you suffer for it—aye, even though I also suffer eternally for it," and with that he turned on his heel and walked quickly away.

Alan was very perturbed about this meeting, and felt inclined to tell the story of it to Waz-Y-Kjesta,—yet the sacred feeling he had for Chlorie was not to be spoken of, or bandied about from man to man.

No, he would keep it to himself, and trust to time and common sense to cure Kulmervan of his strange hatred.

He walked quickly on, and already could see the air birds in the distance, circling above their houses. The little lane turned quickly at right angles— there was a steep descent, and hedges rose at either side to a height of six or seven feet, while the overhanging branches of the trees met in the middle and formed a leafy arch. The grassy banks were carpeted with flowers, and the scent hung sweet on the air. Again the narrow path turned sharply to the right, and before Alan realized it, there almost at his feet, stretched across almost the full width of the path, lay a lion, full grown, with his shaggy mane stirring in the breeze. Alan stopped suddenly, and his heart beat quickly. The lion's eyes were closed—he was sleeping.

The Englishman was almost afraid to move lest the savage beast should spring upon him and devour him. He looked round to the right, the bough of a tree hung low over the path. He leapt up the bank, and with one mighty spring caught hold of it, and swarmed up to a topmost branch.

He was safe—but the sudden sound had startled the lion, who rose up and with a low growl prowled backward and forward beneath the tree.

It was an uncomfortable position to be in—the tree bough was very thin, and bent and twisted and crackled ominously. Still the King of Beasts remained sentinel underneath. Alan felt the perspiration on his face as the limb shivered and bent, yet there was no other to which he could move. Still the animal remained near, his quickened senses no doubt wondering at the noise he heard, and waiting to see what had caused it.

The minutes dragged by—the branch was weakening perceptibly— he could already see the white of the inside where the branch was gradually tearing away from the parent trunk. There was no one in sight, and still the lion walked restlessly to and fro.

The Kymo was sinking rapidly. It was already low down on the horizon, and Alan knew he had been about two English hours in his perilous position. He saw a branch above his head, and he wormed his way along to see if he could in any way reach it. Carefully he went— slowly—suddenly with a scream and a crash the branch gave way, and Alan felt himself being hurled to the ground.

The distance was not great, and he landed in the centre of some sweet-smelling, soft bushes. He was dazed, and wondered when the lion would pounce. He knew he was powerless to help himself. He

ELLA M. SCRYMSOUR

heard the pad, pad, of its feet; he could hear the sharp intake of its breath—then the thing was upon him. He shut his eyes and waited.—Nothing happened but the snuffing of the wild beast, and a gentle nosing as it examined the stranger.

Alan opened his eyes. The animal was sitting on its haunches surveying him, and he felt there was amusement in the beast's eyes as it watched him. He moved slightly—still the beast watched motionless. He raised himself up from the encircling bushes and clambered down. He knew he would have to face the inevitable.

Suddenly a voice hailed him, and he saw Waz-Y-Kjesta coming round the bend in the lane. "Stand back," he cried. "There's a lion here—he may spring!" But the Waz came on fearlessly. Alan was petrified, his tongue was parched, no sound came from his lips. He watched the Waz in frozen horror.

The Keemarnian was smiling. "Where have you been, my friend? You are late—very late. I thought you had missed your way, so I came to seek you." He was now within three feet of the lion. "What is the matter? Why are you so grave? Has aught affrighted you?"

Alan pointed to the tawny beast. His hand was shaking. Surely the farce must end soon, the lion spring, and tragedy culminate the play.

"Why Maquer," said the Waz affectionately, "what are you doing here? You seldom visit us, you know."

The lion moved toward him, and rubbed his great head against the Keemarnian's leg, while Y-Kjesta talked to him and petted him.

"He's tame then?" gasped Alan with a rush of relief. "You know him?"

"No, my friend. I've never seen this Maquer before—they generally stay in rocky places."

"But he is so friendly."

"All beasts are friendly here, my Alan. What—would Maquer have hurt you on your Earth?"

And Alan laughingly told of his fright at the lion. He had learnt one more truth about Keemar—there were no savage animals upon it. Of a truth, it was a perfect land!

Waz-Y-Kjesta was highly amused at his friend's story, and together they went toward the air birds. The Keemarnian airships were indeed wonderful creations. White and gold, they were shaped like swans, with graceful wings outspread, gleaming in the light. They were made of a mixture of wood and metal, and contained accommodation for perhaps forty passengers, as well as the Waz in command, and a staff of ten.

Although not as big as the ill-fated Argenta, the Keemarnian airship was possessed of a speed nearly thrice as great.

"This is the Chlorie," said Y-Kjesta, "and our fastest bird. The Jkak has given orders that you are to choose your own vessel, so perhaps you would like to see over some others?"

"No," said Alan, looking at the blue hangings, and seeing in them the reflection of his love's eyes. "No, this one will do beautifully." And the Waz was impressed by the easy way in which his friend was pleased. He little realized that it was the name of the vessel—the Chlorie—that attracted him. And in the strangeness of it Alan tried to read his fate.

"We'll go for a short cruise," said the Waz, "and go back to the landing stage Minniviar."

There was not a cloud in the sky, and the warmth from the sun's rays was pleasant.

"I can't understand how you benefit so considerably from the sun, your Kymo," said Alan. "Let me see, you must be at least five times further away from the sun than we were on our earth, yet instead of your light and heat being reduced to about one twenty-fifth of our supply, you appear to benefit to exactly the same degree."

"Ah, my friend, that is easy to explain. Dark clouds hover outside our globe—"

"Yes, bands of vapour," corrected Alan.

"Well—vapour. These bands completely encircle our world. They are saturated with a composition of gas, sulphuric ether I think you would call it. Well, this gas acts as a trap to the sun's rays. It admits the solar rays to our planet but prevents their withdrawal. Therefore it permits the heat to enter, but prevents its escape."

"Well?"

"Consequently we get the maximum of light, and an equable temperature."

"Do you then, have no seasons here?"

"Seasons?"

"Yes, Spring or Winter."

"Oh yes, it is cold at the poles—very cold, but as we get nearer to the equator it becomes warmer, and hardly varies. You see, my Alan, our world differs from yours. The axis of rotation is almost perpendicular to our orbit, consequently we are not subject to seasons as you were in Quilphis."

"I didn't know that before."

"We too, are more flattened at each end—indeed, there are many differences between our world that is, and yours that was."

"Do you ever have rain here?"

"Yes, my Alan. How else would plants live and crops thrive? But again, we do not suffer from excesses."

"But don't you have hurricanes that last from six to seven weeks? Surely those are excesses."

"Hurricanes? I do not know the word."

"Hurricanes—winds—tornadoes."

"Why they affect only the polar regions, and nothing lives there."

"Well," laughed Alan "I think your world is a great improvement on ours."

The scenery they passed on this pleasure trip was very varied, but very similar to the world he knew at its best. Here he could imagine he was in the highlands of Scotland with its crags and hills and torrents. There in Southern France with its vineyards sloping to the river's edge. Again, the warmth of colouring suggested the tropics, and the next moment they were flying over great inland arms of a sea, that were reminiscent of the fjords of Norway.

They descended at last, and went to the Jkak to bid him farewell. There a surprise awaited Alan.

"My son," said the Jkak. "Our Ipso-Rorka has decided to travel in the Chlorie to Hoormoori. She desires to reach her father's side without any more delay. Taz-Ak Kulmervan has obtained permission from his kinswoman to attend her on her journey. But you need have no fear, my Alan. I doubt whether you will even see the Princess. She will keep within the precincts of her apartments, and will be attended exclusively by her maid."

Alan felt distressed. Should he tell the Jkak of his encounter with Kulmervan? Had he obeyed his first impulse and confided in the kindly old man, he would have saved both himself and Chlorie from much suffering. As it was—well, who can tell which is always the right course to take? Errors are made, and paid for in suffering, even in a Perfect World.

"Is it far, my Jkak, to Hoormoori?"

"Forty Kymos will take you there."

"Forty Kymos—about twenty of our earth days! It is quite a long way then?"

"Ah, my friend, you have no idea of the size of our planet."

"And yet you are all one nation—with the same customs and religion and speech! It is hard to comprehend, my Jkak, for at home on our little islands, we were composed of four distinct races."

"The Ipso-Rorka will board the Chlorie immediately," said the Jkak. "Now Mitzor be with you. Farewell."

There was no sign of the Princess when Alan boarded the ship, neither was Kulmervan to be seen, but he was surprised to find Waiko lounging on the deck. He gave Alan a cursory nod of recognition as he passed, but did not rise or offer any greeting.

"Don't you know Waiko?" asked Y-Kjesta in some surprise.

"Why of course. I met him at Kulmervan's party."

"Then why does he not rise and greet you according to Keemarnian custom? You have broken bread with him—"

"Please, Y-Kjesta, don't say any more. I—I think I understand, and perhaps it's my fault. Let it pass."

"As you will, my Alan." The Chlorie rose, soared gracefully over the marble buildings of Minniviar, then tilting her nose, climbed swiftly.

The Princess remained in her cabin, her doors were closed, and the balconies round her apartment shuttered.

"Ought I to pay my respects to the Ipso-Rorka?" asked Alan.

Waz-Y-Kjesta looked at him in horror. "Nay, my friend. It is not seemly to address our Ipso-Rorka unless she summons you first. She has given strict orders that she is not to be disturbed."

So! Kulmervan had begun his work of revenge. Darkness fell, and Alan retired to his little cabin. There were few on board, ten souls in all, and the whole place was wrapped in stillness. All the same he felt very restless—the four moons of Jupiter were shining brightly; they were now passing over a sea, and the moonbeams were playing on the rippling waters. He rose, dressed himself, and was about to leave his cabin, when he heard a faint movement outside. His senses were quickened, he felt for the first time since his entrance into this new world, a feeling of impending danger.

In a second his mind was made up—quickly he placed a cushion on his couch and covered it over with rugs: in the semi-darkness it almost showed the curves of a living body. The door latch rattled softly, and Alan slipped behind the folds of a heavy silken curtain. Softly the door opened, until it was just wide enough to permit the passage of a man's body. Alan peered through the curtain opening and saw that it was Kulmervan who had entered.

The Keemarnian stepped over to the couch and touched the coverlet. "He's asleep," he whispered in his own language, and Waiko entered softly. "Have you the spray?"

"Yes, my Kulmervan—but is it necessary? I'm afraid—"

"Fool," hissed Kulmervan. "The spray."

Waiko handed him a long piece of tubing, the end of which was fastened to a small bulb. Kulmervan laid the nozzle end on the bed—there was a slight hissing sound, and the room became sweet with a subtle scent.

"Quick," whispered Kulmervan to his accomplice, "hasten, lest the fumes overpower us," and the two hurriedly left the chamber closing the door tightly behind them.

The air was already heavy, and Alan felt a drowsiness coming over him. With a mighty effort he opened the window and leant out. It was a battle royal between the fumes and the fresh air. Alan felt his head reel and his senses swim, but the pure night air conquered, and the little cabin was soon free of its poison.

Silently Alan sat until the dawn broke, thinking over the strange problem that had presented itself to him. He had made an enemy, unwittingly it is true, but an enemy who would stop at nothing in order to further his ends. He wondered what effect the powerful fumes would have had upon him. In a land where there was no death, could life be taken? What would have happened to him had he inhaled them? He was determined to ask Waz-Y-Kjesta at the first opportunity. Suddenly from without a cheery voice hailed him. It was the Waz.

"How did you sleep, my friend?" and he entered the cabin.

"Very well indeed," said Alan, glibly lying.

"I slept badly, my Alan. I had evil dreams of you. I saw you lying—serquor—oh!"

"What is serquor?"

"It is the worst thing that could befall us on Keemar, my friend. Seldom it happens—but once in a lifetime. The body stiffens, sleep comes from which one never awakens. Life is, to all intents and purposes, extinct. Yet the body does not melt into nothingness, as at the Sacrament of Schlerik-itata. It remains on earth, cut off from the living, cut off from those already in glory,—useless, desolate, alone."

"What causes it?" asked Alan eagerly.

"Sometimes a blow or a fall—or it can be produced artificially by inhaling morka, a gas used in the weaving of our silks. The workers wear shields over their mouths when using it, and are very careful. Never have I known such an accident to occur, but it could. It was thus I dreamt of you, my Alan."

Alan smiled. He had come across as strange proofs of telepathy as in the old world between kindred spirits. Whatever happened he knew Waz-Y-Kjesta was his friend. "Perhaps I am in danger, my friend," said he. "If so can I count on you?"

"My Alan, I would suffer even serquor for you," he answered fervently. And Alan knew he spoke truly.

VIII

The Unforgiveable Kiss

The day passed slowly. Still the Princess remained in her cabin. Alan passed Waiko with his usual cheery smile, and the guilty student trembled and turned white at sight of the healthy man, who he thought had been doomed to serquor. Kulmervan remained in his cabin near the princess, and had his meals served him there. Waz-Y-Kjesta realized that something was wrong, but as Alan did not confide in him, he made no effort to find out the cause of his friend's restlessness.

"My Waz," said Alan suddenly, "is it possible for me to see the Ipso-Rorka? I wish to speak to her."

"Not unless she sends for you, my friend. It is impossible else."

"It is a matter of grave import," said Alan earnestly. "To me, to her—"

"Nothing can alter custom, my friend. If she sends for you—well. Otherwise—" and he shrugged his shoulders expressively. Alan, however, was determined to speak with Chlorie by foul means or fair. Her cabin was situated in the front of the ship, and round it was a tiny balcony railed in just above the level of the deck.

He paced round this portion of the ship the whole day, resting only at mealtimes from his self imposed watch. Never once did the Princess appear. The Kymo was setting, the sky was bright with sunset colours; the sea was unruffled and calm. A fish leapt out of the water leaving rings of glistening fluid, roseate in the glow. Alan sat, out of sight, still watching the cabin door. Suddenly it opened and Morar, the Princess' personal attendant appeared. She looked around hastily. "All is quiet, my Princess," she cried. "No one is in sight. The sinful stranger is in his cabin, no doubt plotting ill against you and yours." Chlorie came through the doorway. Her hair was gleaming, and her flowing draperies of blue showed up the fairness of her skin.

"I am stifled, Morar. 'Tis ill to spend so many hours without a breath of air. Watch you the other side, and should you see the evil one appear, appraise me, and I will again take shelter within."

With a low bow Morar vanished, closing the cabin door behind her. The Princess paced up and down the tiny balcony, singing a Keemarnian lullaby. Still Alan remained silent and watchful, hidden from sight beneath the covering rail. Morar returned. "There is no sign of Alan the evil one," said she, "but Taz-Ak Kulmervan begs an audience."

"Bid him come hither," said the Princess with a sigh. "Tell him I am weary, and must beg of him to be quick about his business." She seated herself on a swinging lounge, just above Alan, who could almost feel the sweetness of her presence, the fragrance of her breath.

"Sweet Cousin," said Kulmervan entering.

"Nay, Kulmervan, say what you have to say quickly. My head is tired—my eyes weary."

"You have not been out to-day, my Chlorie?"

"Not until this evening. I have carefully obeyed your instructions. Were my father here, I should not care. But I dare not run any risks in his absence. How is Waiko?"

"Still very weak, my Princess. This evil one, this Alan, had contrived his evil work well. When I discovered Waiko a bandage was drawn tightly round his mouth, his nostrils were plugged with wool, and had I not entered when I did, serquor would have set in and Waiko would no more have laughed and played."

"Oh, it's terrible," breathed the Princess. "Why has sin thus entered our beautiful land? I have heard of treasons, and plots and miseries; but so far we have escaped. What is this stranger's object, my Kulmervan?"

"I know not all his treachery, my Chlorie, but—"

"Why bring sorrow on Waiko's family, and upon you, his friend?"

"I do not understand, but his intentions are evil throughout. I heard him tell his kinsman Desmond, that even the person of Chlorie herself was not sacred to him, provided he worked his will."

"That is enough, Kulmervan," she interrupted haughtily. "I will keep my cabin as you advise. Had I known in time, I should not have travelled home in his company. The Rorka, my father, will deal with this stranger, and the Hall of Sorrows will hold him safely, until he has been purged clean. Now good night."

"Chlorie," said Kulmervan passionately. "I dare say much to you to-night. Will you not offer me the flower of love? I dare not ask you to wed me—you are Ipso-Rorka—'tis for you to choose. But know I love you, love you with all my soul. Will you not honour me by choosing me for your mate?"

"Kulmervan," said the Princess gently. "Why make me sad by all this useless talk? It can never be. I can place my hand in only one man's—him I love. Him, alas, I have not yet met, but I do not love you, my

Kulmervan. I never shall. Think, we played together in Hoormoori as babes, built palaces of sand by the sea, picked flowers and fondled our pets. We grew as brother and sister until you went to study with the Djoh, and I had to learn the lesson of royalty. No, my kinsman. I love you 'tis true, but not as a maid should love the man she mates, not as wife for husband, lover for lover. Let this be the last time you speak of such things, my Kulmervan. I will forget, and—"

"But I want you—you—you—," and Kulmervan strode close to her and placed his arms about her.

"Let me go," breathed the girl—but his lips were seeking hers.

"No—no—no," she cried. "Not my lips—Kulmervan be merciful. My lips are sacred until I wed—spare my lips." But Kulmervan's reason had gone. "My beautiful one," he murmured, and ran his fingers through her glorious mantle of hair. He held her head between his hands, and drank in the glory of her face. Her eyes were open wide in terror, her lips tightly compressed, her power of movement gone. Nearer, nearer he drew. His breath came in hot gusts upon her cheek. Her eyelids quivered under his scorching kisses. Her cheeks reddened as his lips touched them. With one mighty effort she tried to release herself.

"In the name of Mitzor the Great, leave my lips," she cried, but the madness of passion was upon him. He revelled in his power, laughed at her struggles, mocked at her impotence. Roughly he clasped her still closer to him, but the Princess was inert in his arms—the strain was too much for her, and blissful unconsciousness had come to soothe her. There was the slightest of sounds. Alan, the athletic still, vaulted over the rail, and swinging Kulmervan by the scruff of his neck threw him on to the ground. Tenderly he lifted the Princess in his arms—she was as light as a feather—and went into her cabin.

"Morar," he called. "Morar." The serving maid appeared, trembling as she saw her beloved mistress in the arms of "the evil one."

"Your mistress has had a fright," said Alan thickly. "Show me her couch." Without a word the little maid led the way into the tiny sleeping apartment, and tenderly he laid his burden on the silken coverings of blue. "Look after her," said he, "she has fainted." With arms folded across his chest and his breath coming in spasmodic jerks, he waited outside the door. Presently Morar appeared. "The Ipso-Rorka has recovered," she said, "and has now fallen asleep. What shall I do?"

"Allow no one to enter her apartments at all. I will send a letter to her in the morning. Can I depend on your giving it to her?"

"Yes. I can see you are not evil," said the little maid. "Some mistake has been made. You are her friend."

"I am her friend," said Alan grimly. "Remember, Morar, no one is to enter these apartments without the Ipso-Rorka's permission. You understand?" and he strode out on to the balcony. Kulmervan had gone, and he vaulted lightly over the balcony rail and went straight to his cabin. As he opened the door he recognized the sweet, sickly odour that he had smelt once before. So! He must be on his guard. Kulmervan and Waiko would stop at nothing—a madness had indeed come over them, a madness of the earth!

Holding his breath he went swiftly across the room, and opened the windows, then shutting the door behind him, went into the big saloon. Waz-Y-Kjesta smiled as he entered. "Where have you been, my friend? I looked for you everywhere."

"Resting," said Alan grimly. That night he never went to bed, but waited grimly for what might happen. He was left in peace, however, and toward dawn slept fitfully. When he woke, he wrote this letter to Chlorie.

> *Chlorie—The Ipso-Rorka*
> I beg of you, see me, just once before we alight at Hoormoori. I overheard the conversation of Kulmervan, and implore you to see me, if only to clear myself of the imputations your kinsman has made against me. In any case, believe that I am your devoted servant always. Command me—I will obey.
>
> Alan

He took the letter to Morar himself. "I will wait while the Ipso-Rorka reads it," said he.

In a moment she had returned. "She will answer you later." There were only four more nights to be spent on board the Chlorie, but much might happen in that time. There was no sign of the enemy—all Alan could do was to wait patiently for their next move.

That night, again, he had no sleep. Soon after he retired, the same sickly odour permeated the cabin. Again he leant out of the window until the fumes had passed; this time they were stronger and took a longer time to dispel. He smiled—it was to be a duel to the end, and he needed all his wits about him. Certainly, Keemarnians possessed of the "madness" were more formidable, more crafty, more callous enemies, than men belonging to Terra. Another night passed—no communication had come from Chlorie. Alan, weary of his vigil, tried to keep awake, but drowsiness overcame him, and his last conscious effort was to drag himself to the window, and rest with his head breathing in the pure air. Again the sweet fumes entered the room, but Alan had safeguarded himself. The next night passed without the enemy showing their hand. They doubtless thought him proof against "serquor" and would take other methods to rid themselves of his presence. Suddenly in the darkness of the night, a noise interrupted his musings. There was a jerk—a crash—and the vessel shivered. Alan flew out of his cabin and met Waz-Y-Kjesta.

"What is it?" he cried.

"Nothing to be alarmed about, my friend. Something has happened to the engine. I have not discovered what, yet—we shall be forced to make a descent. Luckily there is an island near; we will anchor there, and put the matter right. We shall be delayed only a very short time, I think."

The machine descended in jerks and jumps with many creakings and groanings, but reached the ground in safety.

"I will seek Morar, and tell her to acquaint the Ipso-Rorka with this news," said the Waz. The whole day passed, and the Y-Kjesta called Alan in dismay. "I cannot understand it," said he. "There is a screw missing here, and that waste pipe has been filled with refuse. It means taking the whole of the mechanism to pieces, and two days delay at least." But Alan guessed who had planned this sinister work, and that night he kept vigil—not in his own room, but outside the Princess'.

Waz-Y-Kjesta was frankly puzzled. "Yesterday I fixed up the screw for the outer valve," said he, "yet to-day it has gone again. Surely I couldn't have dreamt it—yet it could not go without hands."

"Perhaps some one has moved it, purposely, for spite," suggested Alan.

Y-Kjesta laughed. "Not in Keemar. Besides what for? Who could do such a foolish thing?"

True, the faith of a Keemarnian was wonderful. Alan longed to confide in him—yet dared not. For the second time he made a mistake. Alan saw Morar and asked her if the Princess' apartments were quite safe from intruders.

"Quite," said she. "There is only a very small window, and the doors have heavy bars."

"She always keeps them locked?"

"Always."

That night Alan remained in his own cabin, and worn out with continual watching, fell asleep at his open window. He had a dream so vivid that he thought it was real, and awoke with a start. Chlorie—the lady of his heart had appeared to him, arms outstretched, eyes swimming with tears—"My Lord," she whispered. "The Cave of Whispering Madness—the Cave—" Her voice trailed away, something dark came before his eyes, there was the sound of a scuffle, a small cry, he felt a stabbing pain, and he awoke. It was broad daylight, and his door was flung open wide and Waz-Y-Kjesta, usually so placid and calm, was staring at him and calling him in excited distress.

"My Alan! Awake! I beg of you—"

"What is it?"

"The Ipso-Rorka—is gone."

"Gone?"

"Gone! She has disappeared."

"Are you sure?"

"Morar, her maid, left her as usual last night. This morning she knocked as usual for the Princess to open the door, which by the way, she always keeps barred, but she could get no answer. Thinking her mistress had overslept she went round to look in at the window. The bed was empty—Chlorie was not there"

"Where is Kulmervan?" asked Alan thickly.

"Kulmervan?"

"Yes. Is he on the boat?"

"I do not know"

"Go and see at once, and I'll go to Morar"

The Ipso-Rorka's little maid was crying bitterly. Without any ceremony Alan forced the door. The bed was rumpled and rough; the silken coverlets twisted and torn—Chlorie had not gone without a struggle!

Waz-Y-Kjesta came to Alan, with consternation written all over his face. "Three are missing altogether" said he "Can some evil spirit have taken them? Kulmervan and Waiko are nowhere to be found"

"I thought as much" said Alan savagely. He glanced rapidly round the room. A pile of papers lay on a desk. He smoothed them out. There, in a little blue envelope addressed to himself, was a letter from his dear one. He opened it quickly.

My Lord, (it ran)

Since you saved me from my kinsman, Kulmervan my cousin has once more forced himself into my presence. He is possessed of a madness. I beg of you save me from him. I have looked at you often and I know now I was deceived by him when he whispered tales of your evil doing. I trust you implicitly. I do as you bid me. I command your help.

CHLORIE

Then underneath was written,

"He has spoken to me again through my window. He threatens me with dishonour—disgrace. He talks of the Cave of Whispering Madness. Come to me on receipt of this"

"The cur" muttered Alan. He turned to Y-Kjesta. "Where is the Cave of Whispering-Madness?"

"I have never heard of it, my Alan"

"Listen. I am going to find Chlorie. Wait for me here with the air bird. Should I fail to come by the time the Kymo has sunk ten times—go at once to the Rorka, and ask him to send his aid here"

"Where then, is Chlorie?"

"I don't know, but I'm going to do my best to find out. This island isn't very big—ten miles square at the most, and I intend to search every bit of it if necessary, to find her"

"What about Kulmervan and Waiko?"

"Should you see them, put them under restraint. Bar their windows, and prevent their escape. They are both possessed of the madness—but there, I doubt if you'll see them. Where Chlorie is—there shall I also find Kulmervan and Waiko"

"Can I come too?"

"No, my friend. You stay here and watch in case Chlorie comes. I go now—I shall take no provision with me—fruit will be my meat, and the sap of the water tree my drink. Farewell" and Alan leapt over the bulwarks and disappeared from sight in the thick brush and undergrowth of the island.

IX

ALAN—THE KNIGHT ERRANT

As Alan leapt over the bulwarks, his quick eye caught sight of footmarks, two going one way, and two the other, with perhaps five feet between them. "So," said he grimly to himself, "they were carrying her between them. Poor little Chlorie." The tracks were easy to follow, they led down to the sea and along the seashore. Steadily they went on and Alan followed dauntlessly. There was no attempt made to cover their traces. On they went, carrying their burden between them.

They had about ten hours start, and although night was falling, Alan continued at his self imposed task. Darker and darker it grew, until at length it was impossible to see the footmarks, so he sat down hopelessly to wait for the dawn.

The night was chilly and the rain poured down, so Alan was soaked to the skin, and shivered violently as the grey dawn rose. The rain had almost obliterated the marks, but they showed up faintly here and there on the wet sand. He had no time to look at the scenery through which he was passing—his one thought was Chlorie—not the Princess, but Chlorie the woman, Chlorie his love.

On, on he went all day, and still the footprints showed here and there. Night came, and again he was forced to rest and wait for the light. He was colder than ever, he shivered violently, and longed for the warmth of the sun. That night he never slept at all, and he rose in the early morning light stiff and tired. His head felt light, his limbs ached, and the one thing he could think of coherently was Chlorie.

Suddenly all traces of the marks vanished. He hunted high and low, but all to no purpose; they ended as abruptly as if the pursued had been snatched up into the heavens.

Two nights and two days he wandered to and fro. He was chilled to the bone, and was in a high fever. At last he had to give in, and lay under the shelter of a tree. The warmth of the sun revived him, and he crawled weakly to a bush on which grew luscious plums, ate his fill and slept. When he awoke he felt better and stronger. Perhaps he had been dreaming—the footprints *must* go on. But no, they came to an end at a grassy edge, and there was no mark to show that human beings had

ELLA M. SCRYMSOUR

passed that way. He spent that day hunting for a sign of the fugitives, but was unsuccessful, and wearily retraced his way to the air bird.

The scenery was beautiful. The island rose to a chain of peaks in the centre, and beautiful passes and wooded valleys led through the mountains to the further side. The vegetation was purely tropical. Palms, breast high, grew to the edge of the sea shore; the undergrowth showed no sign of any animal inhabitants; not a twig was broken, not a leaf trampled upon, to mark the passage of a foreign body. Alan made the return journey quickly, and soon found himself at the edge of the bush. But the "Chlorie" had gone! There were the signs of where she had rested; the mark on the sand of her wheels; an oily patch on the ground showing where her engines had been lubricated—but all sign of her had vanished. Had Waz-Y-Kjesta failed him, or had Chlorie returned? He felt in his pockets—there was a scrap of paper and a pencil. "I am going inland," he wrote. "If you come back, search for me. Alan." He pegged it to the ground close to where the Chlorie had been anchored, and turning his face westwards, retraced his footsteps.

Time passed without his reckoning. When the nights came he lived for the day; and in the day time he dreaded the coming of the night. He reached the place where the footsteps ceased at dusk, and for the first time for days, slept through the night peacefully. His fever had abated, but he still felt curiously weak. Yet his brain was clear, and he set to work again to hunt carefully for the missing ones. Yard by yard he worked, and at last his patience was rewarded. There, on a bush low on the ground, he saw a piece of something blue that fluttered on the breeze. He stooped and picked it off the twig—it was blue silk, and with a thrill he recognized it as a piece of Chlorie's dress. Feverishly he looked round him; alas, there was no other piece to act as a further guide. A thought came to him, and he lay flat on the ground and peered under the bush. There, a grassy avenue unfolded itself before his wondering gaze—it had been completely hidden by the dense woody undergrowth. So it was under this bush they had made their escape, and it was probably in dragging the unconscious girl through, that her dress was torn.

Alan wormed his way under the bushes, and gasped in wonder at the vista opened out before him. A straight avenue—bordered on either side by thick bushes and overhanging trees, ran perhaps two miles in a straight line. The grass underfoot was soft and velvety, and a narrow streamlet ran over white stones at one side. The bushes were laden with fruit, but even a cursory glance showed that a quantity had been picked quite recently. Twigs bearing fruit had been roughly broken off, and trampled under foot. On went Alan until he reached the end of the avenue, where four paths branched out in four different directions. He hesitated for a second—all four looked like virgin ground. But his eyes were quickened by love, and only love could have noticed a small patch of damp earth close to the water's edge from where a stone had been kicked aside in a hasty transit. He looked round and saw the stone, its under side still damp—and knew that the fugitives were not too far off.

Down the path he went which twisted and turned, now narrow now wide again. Suddenly the path also came to an end, and thick bushes and low growing vegetation barred his way. Profiting by his past experience, he tried to peer under the bushes, but could find no sign of an outlet anywhere. All at once there came the sound of voices so close that he turned quickly, expecting to see figures behind him. But there was no one in sight. He listened intently—the voices came again—the Keemarnian tongue which he could understand quite well by this time— "—will leave you here," "—spare me, I beg"—"leave you here"—"Kulmervan have mercy—mercy."

It was all very disjointed, and the sounds seemed to come from every direction. Again he heard his loved one's voice—distorted it is true, but even in the hoarse tones, he recognized that it was Chlorie speaking. "—get away.—help me. Waiko help—my father will reward—Waiko—" The voice trailed off. Alan was frankly puzzled. The voice came first behind, then before him—then it seemed to come from Heaven itself. A hoarse laugh sounded—Kulmervan's. Alan was on the near track at last. Again the maniacal laugh came, fading away in the distance. Alan realized the trick nature had played him. He was listening not to the tones of his loved one, or her abductor, but to an echo. The originals might still be many miles away.

Madly he tried to force his way through the undergrowth. It was impossible. All night long he stayed in the little cul-de-sac, and at intervals caught fragments of conversation.

"prevent her escaping.—torture her if need be."

"—love me Chlorie, just love me," "—save me, Waiko!"

"—keep you with me always."

The madness indeed possessed Kulmervan and his friend.

When the sun rose Alan made one more attempt to leave the enclosure. Crawling on his belly, he wormed his way round the roots

ELLA M. SCRYMSOUR

of the bushes. At last he discovered an opening. He crept through it, low upon the ground. When he got through, a network of pathways confronted him, but it was quite easy to discover the pathway Kulmervan had taken. Feeling secure in his flight, he now refrained from attempting to cover his tracks. By the broken grass and branches, the general upheaval of the soil, Alan was convinced that through this part of their retreat, they had dragged their unwilling victim along the path, so he ground his teeth and swore softly under his breath.

Twisting and turning the path opened out into a valley—a valley of rocks and stones between two mighty mountains. The scene was desolate, awe inspiring, dreary—almost terrifying in its grandeur. For perhaps two miles he followed it, until again it narrowed and the character of the scene changed. Once more it was a leafy lane he was traversing, that might have been in Devonshire, with its red earth and dainty ferns.

At intervals during the day he heard the echo, and it led him on—on—to his love.

A sound came upon his ear; it was that of voices—real voices, this time—no longer an echo. Cautiously he crept from tree to tree. There in the centre of a clearing sat Kulmervan. His robe was torn, his skin scratched—his eyes held a look of madness. At his feet stretched Waiko, listening eagerly to his friend's counsel. And tied to a tree, her fair hair covering her, her garments lying strewn on the ground beside her, torn from her body by her half mad kinsman, Kulmervan—was Chlorie. Her head was sunk on her breast. She was breathing heavily.

Alan dared not move—it was two against one, and he had to save himself for her. Silent as a sleuth hound, he watched and waited; and even as he did so Chlorie lifted her head and gazed across the bodies of the two Keemarnians. Through the leafy spaces their eyes met. Into hers came recognition, followed by a flush of shame, as she shook her hair closer still about her gleaming body. Then she smiled a trustful smile, and dropped her head once more upon her breast.

The Cave of Whispering Madness

Throughout the night Alan watched. Never did Kulmervan move from his place in the clearing—never did his eyes close nor did he show the slightest inclination to sleep. Towards morning Waiko raised himself from the ground. He was pitiable to look upon. Led on by a stronger will the madness had come upon him also. But it was a weaker madness than that which affected Kulmervan—it was a madness that chattered and gibbered in the sun, that laughed and cackled insanely—a madness that was pitiful to behold.

Alan watched through the leafy branches, and as the dawn rose, many times he met Chlorie's questioning gaze with looks of encouragement and help. And she knew that when the time was ripe, this strange Lord from another world would save and deliver her.

As Kulmervan still made no attempt to move, Alan wondered whether it would be possible to overpower him. He made a movement and the slight sound was heard. Kulmervan sprang to his feet and looked round, and Alan saw he was clutching the huge limb of a tree—a formidable weapon in a madman's hands. He was evidently not satisfied, and peered round the tree trunks carefully. Quietly Alan crept behind a large bush, and dropping on his belly he wormed himself underneath it until he was completely hidden.

The crackling of a twig was heard by the madman, who, with his dormant passions aroused was a dangerous enemy. He spoke sharply to Waiko. "What sound is that, my Waiko? Is it the stranger that tracketh us?"

"I know not," said Waiko shuddering. "Oh, Kulmervan, my friend, let us leave the Ipso-Rorka here, and flee from the wrath of her father."

"Nonsense, my Waiko! When the Rorka is told that his daughter, Chlorie the Fair, Chlorie the Pure, has spent forty and one nights with us in the darkness, he will be glad to give his soiled goods into my keeping for ever. Then in good time, I shall become Rorka. Shall I not punish my Chlorie then, for her indifference and insults?"

Waiko shuddered.

"My Chlorie," cried Kulmervan suddenly, his manner changing. "Will you not promise me your hand? Oh, my darling, forgive me—I love you so—I love you. Give me your hand—swear before Waiko that you'll take me for your mate. I'll be so good to you—I'll love you so" His voice was pleading. His earnestness could not be doubted, yet Alan knew it was but a moment's lull in the disordered brain.

Chlorie never answered a word, and her silence drove Kulmervan again to threats. Tearing a handful of withes from the side of a running brook, he lashed the captive Princess across her legs with the stinging rushes. With an oath Alan burst from his hiding place, and was on the back of his enemy, before Kulmervan could recover from his astonishment.

Then followed a terrific fight. Alan with all his knowledge of the scientific sport was unable to get in a knockout blow. He parried and thrust, and landed Kulmervan a heavy blow under his jaw. His opponent tottered for a moment, but the blow had no lasting effect, and the heavy Keemarnian struck mightier blows still at his enemy. Waiko was entirely demoralized. He stood watching the fight—his breath coming in gasps, his blue eyes staring, his teeth chattering. As an ally, he was useless to Kulmervan; as an enemy he counted as naught to Alan.

Chlorie, tied tightly to the tree, was unable to move. Her wide open eyes followed the fighters in an agony of spirit; but not a sound came from her lips. True to the tradition of her land, the daughter of the Rorka gave no audible sign of her terror. Alan knew he was weakening. Imperceptibly at first he lost ground, but gradually he realized that his blows had no effect upon the Keemarnian. His hasty rush into the field of battle was worse than useless—he could no longer help his love. The Keemarnian gave him one terrific blow in the stomach. His wind went— he gasped, choked for breath, crumpled up and sank to the ground.

Kulmervan left his vanquished enemy's side and went to Waiko who had been stupidly watching the scene.

"Watch him," he commanded. "If he show any sign of awakening, give him a blow with this. It will be sufficient to put him to sleep again," and he tossed the heavy stick beside the prostrate body.

Brutally he untied the ropes that bound Chlorie. She was stiff and weak, and the agony as the blood once more coursed freely through her veins, was almost more than she could bear. Still she remained silent, and with a noble gesture of majesty, stooped, and drew her mantle of blue about her naked body. Two other garments still lay on the ground—with a sudden thought she caught one up, and drew it within the folds of her cloak. She had a plan! Love had been born to her, in that exquisite moment of agony when she saw Alan knocked down. Her soul cried out within her that here was her mate at last. Her fine sense of belief and trust told her that it was impossible that he was sleeping the sleep of serquor. Sometime he would rise again—bruised, bleeding, torn, perhaps, but rise he would, and come to her aid.

Kulmervan took her roughly by the arm. "Come," said he. "Waiko wait until the Kymo is full in the Heavens—it is but a short time. If Alan the Evil has not moved by then, follow me quickly. Always to the East, my friend. Always take the most easterly path, and you will find me."

"Where are you going?" asked Waiko in horror.

"To the Cave of Whispering Madness," said he, and involuntarily Chlorie shuddered.

"Do you know where it is, my Kulmervan?" asked Waiko.

"Yes. Have I not been there often? Ah, my friend, I arranged that the engines should fail. Ah, oft times should I have been in the Hall of Sorrows, but I came here instead, and of my own free will. I know the place I intend taking you to—I will show you sights—sights I have seen—ha! ha! ha!" and with a wild burst of laughter he dragged his unwilling captive through the bushes, and made his way Eastward.

Waiko remained silent, watching his vanishing friend. His mind was working strangely. The madness had left a deep sense of fear in the heart of Waiko. The inanimate body of Alan seemed to point to his undoing. The blood trickled slowly down the unconscious man's face till there was a little red pool shining wickedly on the green grass. With a cry, Waiko picked up the club and swung it once, twice round his head. But as he would have swung it a third time, it slipped out of his nerveless fingers, and went spinning a hundred feet away. With a cry at his loneliness, Waiko turned and fled after Kulmervan. In a short space of time he had caught them up, and noticed with surprise that Chlorie was walking almost willingly with her captor. There was a rope passed round her body, it was true, but it was slack in the centre, and although she lagged somewhat behind, there was no need to drag her along.

"Alan?" questioned Kulmervan, as Waiko reached him.

"Is serquor."

"Good."

"I struck him, as he rose to hurt me. With one mighty blow I felled him to the ground. The heavy weapon you left with me I dashed on his

ELLA M. SCRYMSOUR

head.—Now he lies quiet, and cold and bloody." Waiko almost believed his story, and as he recounted it, he looked upon himself as a hero.

"'Tis well, my Waiko," said Kulmervan. "What say you to that, my Chlorie? Alan is serquor—never more will Kymo rise upon his smiling face. Never more will he force his presence upon the people of Keemar. He is gone for ever from our sight."

But Chlorie made no reply—only from beneath her mantle could be seen a slight convulsive movement, and from underneath came a tiny tatter of blue, that caught on a rose bush and fluttered in the breeze.

Birds singing—sweetly smelling flowers—a sense of hunger and thirst. These were the first conscious thoughts Alan had, as he opened his eyes on the world once more. He rose from the ground. His head was sore, but the bleeding had ceased. He plucked some luscious fruit that grew low to the ground. It revived him. Then he tried to think. Chlorie had been taken from him once more—but he would find her yet. He tenderly touched the tree to which she had been bound—and stooped and picked up the silken garment she had left behind. It was just a piece of soft, blue drapery that crumpled into nothingness in his hand. He kissed it reverently—it was part of his love.

He looked round wearily—there, attached to a bush was a piece of something blue—he bent over it—it was part of her gown. Further down, in the very centre of the path was another piece, while in the distance he could see yet a third. It was a sign. Chlorie was directing him the way she had gone. The trail was difficult to follow. The breeze had blown many pieces away altogether—others it had carried away playfully into a wrong direction, but by careful watchfulness, he discovered the right way, and there were always the little pieces of blue to guide him.

Then he lost the trail altogether. The last piece of blue was caught on a stone at the bottom of a mighty face of rock. No matter where he looked, there was no shred of blue to cheer him. He ran his hand over the surface of the rock, it was of a reddish sandstone and quite smooth. All around was a low-lying valley with neither a stone nor a tree behind which any one could hide. He could see for about ten miles, and there was no sign of the fugitives. Backward and forward he walked by the mighty wall of rock, and always his journey ended by the last little flutter of blue. The cliff rose sheer perhaps three hundred feet, and the solid wall extended as far as eye could reach. It was unthinkable that Kulmervan had scaled the wall—yet whither had he gone?

Suddenly he heard a rumbling noise; the sound of a thousand people whispering, and in front of him a huge slab of rock swung back, revealing a cavity within. The whispering grew louder and louder. He looked round for a hiding place. There was none—so without a moment's hesitation he leapt inside the darkened cavern. A narrow path led downwards, and it was up this path the whispering seemed to be coming; whispering that sounded like a veritable army speaking in hushed tones. There was a piece of rock jutting out—Alan slipped into its embracing shadows, and waited. The sounds came nearer and nearer—then Kulmervan appeared with Waiko at his side. "The voices whispered that a stranger was coming. The voices are never wrong. See, my Waiko, see yonder if Alan the Evil is approaching." The voice whispered and rolled in the darkness. The whole place was unwholesome and terrifying.

Kulmervan followed Waiko into the sunlight. Immediately they were out of sight, Alan slipped from his hiding place and ran swiftly down the narrow passageway. The faster he ran, the faster he drew in his breath, and it seemed as if a thousand men were mocking him. He sighed as his breath caught in his throat—immediately there were a thousand sighs behind him. Quicker, quicker he tore down the passage, to where he hoped, somewhere he would find his love hidden. The path was steep and narrow and was in total darkness, and he risked his life in his mad rush through the whispering horrors. He heard the voices again! Kulmervan and Waiko had returned. Blindly he rushed on— stumbling here, tripping there, in his haste to reach the Ipso-Rorka.

The path took an upward turn—he tripped over something. Putting his hands out before him, he felt on the ground. Rough steps had been cut out of the rock. Steadily he mounted upwards—upwards—the darkness was intense—the whispering shadows terrifying; but he never ceased his mad pace, so eager was he to reach Chlorie.

Steadily he ascended the stairs—they seemed interminable. Then in the distance, he saw a yellowish spot of light. As he rose higher, it became bigger, until it ended in a blaze of brightness. He had reached the top and was in an enormous cavern lit by torches in sockets all round the walls. The awful grandeur of the place startled him. In the very centre was a huge figure, twenty feet high. It was seated on a throne and had its hands outspread as if in benediction. It possessed a terrible face, cruel, hard, sensual,—and the incongruity of the posing of the hands struck Alan at once. Round the cave, at equal distances, were other

ELLA M. SCRYMSOUR

figures, all enormous in stature, and possessing in their features the same bestial cruelty and lust. Stalactites hung from the roof. Stalactites forty feet long—Stalactites fifty feet long. Stalactites glorious, yet like deadly serpents with heads outstretched ready to strike. In one corner of the place was a huge beast in stone. Once it had lived, no doubt, now it was fossilized and cold. It was similar to the ichthyosaurus of prehistoric days—an evil-looking beast in its life, but infinitely more terrible in its stone period.

Every movement Alan made was intensified a thousand times in this Cave of Whispering Madness. He realized what the name meant. It could indeed, drive the sanest man mad. He realized that he had a fair start of the two Keemarnians, and hurriedly hunted for his lost love. Softly he called, but although her name reverberated from floor to roof, no answering cry took up his challenge. Then whispering voices sounded nearer. Silently he slipped behind the stone monster that had once lived and mated. He was only just in time. Still louder grew the whisperings, and Kulmervan and Waiko appeared at the top of the stairway. With the greatest difficulty Alan was able to distinguish their words. The whisperings were so loud, so sibilant, that the voices sounded like one long hiss.

The two Keemarnians came close to the big carved figure in the centre of the cave. Kulmervan bent low on both knees before the hideous figure. "Spirit of our Fathers," he cried out. "Humbly I pray, take my soul into thy keeping. It is thine—thine for ever—but in return, I pray you, grant me Chlorie's love. See, I sprinkle thee with my blood in ratification of my bond," and with a short knife he severed a vein in his arm and sprinkled the statue with the warm, red fluid.

Waiko was whispering, "Mitzor the Mighty, have mercy! Have mercy!"

"Fool," cried Kulmervan. "Why mention that name here? I have bargained with Pirox the Killer—I belong to him. Chlorie shall be mine. You have come thus far with me, my Waiko, but further thou shalt go. Down, down on thy knees before Pirox—admit that he is great—greater than Mitzor! Ask a favour—nay demand a favour—seal it with thy blood."

Waiko went down on his knees. His face was ashen—he was trembling in every limb. Then came a strange duet, intensified a thousand times by the whisperings. "Mitzor the Mighty." "Pirox the Killer." "Pirox." "Mitzor." "Mitzor." "Pirox."

In a passion Kulmervan arose, and struck Waiko, down. "Lie there, thou dog," he cried. "May thou sleep for ever in serquor. I alone am mighty. Pirox alone is great." Waiko never moved, he showed no signs of breathing. Had he indeed fallen into the trance-like state that the inhabitants of Keemar so dreaded? It seemed hopeless to Alan, that he would ever find Chlorie in this cavern of horror. He realized at last that Kulmervan was a degenerate. The entrance of poor Murdoch had not caused the madness. No doubt he had posed as a good Keemarnian, but he suffered from the madness, and deep in his heart even denied the existence of Mitzor the Mighty, the Great White Glory, and indulged in devil worship and fetish honour. What this Cave of Whispering Madness was Alan could not conjecture—perhaps in some far gone age, fallen Jovians had met here; made the Temple for their abominable worship, and lived a second life, unsuspected by their friends.

That the image in the centre was their god, Alan was convinced. But how had Kulmervan discovered it? Had it been handed down to him from his childhood, or had he in some way found it for himself? If was pitiful to see—a young Keemarnian of noble lineage, saturated with heathen mythology and heretical dogma. In truth he was a menace to his companions, living a life of deceit and sin. His was a complex character, for there was much that was sweet and lovable about him, and he was much to be pitied, for when his secret was discovered he would indeed become a pariah and an outcast. At the moment he felt he was safe, and continued his "Black Sacrifice."

For Chlorie's sake, Alan was forced to witness in silence the horrors that followed. At the foot of the statue was a slab of stone—raised perhaps ten inches from the ground. Upon it were ominous red stains. Quickly Kulmervan set about his business. In one corner of the cave were piles of brushwood—these he piled high under the stone slab. With a mighty effort he lifted the senseless Waiko upon it, and rested his head in a tiny curve at one end. Alan shuddered to see how it fitted the neck. The use of the slab was plain to see. He set fire to the wood by one of the torches, and the smoke curled up and the wood hissed and sizzled.

When the fire was safely alight, Kulmervan went to a corner of the cavern, and touched a hidden spring. A door opened, and revealed a flight of steps inside, leading below. As soon as he was out of sight, Alan rushed from his hiding place, lifted Waiko from the altar and hid him behind the mammoth fossil.

But the noise of his movements was magnified a thousandfold by the hideous whispering echoes of the place. Waiko was still and quiet—he scarcely breathed, and Alan dared not try to revive him. Kulmervan returned bearing in his arms a precious burden in blue. Alan started, and leant forward; his darling was not unconscious, but was submitting to the indignity put upon her with her usual patience. At the altar he stopped in frozen amazement. The stone was beginning to show red,—the deadly fire should have begun its work—but the altar was empty. He looked round—there was no one in sight. With a cry of rage he let go the rope to which Chlorie was fastened, put her to the ground, and darted to the head of the stairway leading to the cave's entrance. And the yells of his curses and imprecations rose on the air, in volumes of sinister whisperings.

Alan was but six feet from his dear one. With a mighty rush he leapt from his hiding place, and caught Chlorie in his arms. He made for the secret door through which Kulmervan had brought her; Kulmervan heard the sounds and was just in time to see two figures disappearing through the little door. With another oath he strode across the cave—but the figures had a big start. They had closed the door behind them, and his fingers hesitated over the secret lock; so he was delayed by his own impatience and anger.

Chlorie had given herself up for lost, and when she felt two strong arms encircle her a vague terror came over her, but even as she was lifted up, a voice whispered in her ear—"Have no fear. 'Tis I—Alan. Trust yourself to me and I will save you." Her emotion was too great for her to speak, but she let herself nestle in comfort in the arms of the powerful stranger.

The door clanged behind them—more stairs, very narrow. Down Alan went, and the darkness gave place to a faint light.

"Where are we?" asked Alan.

"I don't know—but there is a cave down here which is kept padlocked—it was there I was imprisoned."

Alan looked round quickly; the passage had widened and openings led off on either side. Immediately in front of them seemed to come the daylight.

"Can you run?" he asked tenderly.

"Yes—yes. Oh, to be free of Kulmervan!" Through the dim light they went. The whisperings were not quite as bad as in the upper cave, but still they were quite fearsome enough. They seemed to people the place with dead men—men who laughed, and jeered, and pointed their clammy fingers at their victims. But upon the whisperings came a more fearful sound—Kulmervan's laughter!

"Hurry—hurry, my Princess."

"I cannot," she breathed. "My heart beats—it hurts me to talk." Without a word he picked the light burden again up in his arms and made off at a still greater pace; she flung one arm round his neck and clung to him confidingly. Nearer came the laughter. It was so close that it seemed almost on the top of them. Alan never forgot that journey; with his precious burden in his arms he hurried onward, always following the light. And nearer and nearer came the footsteps of the madman. At last they turned a corner—the cave opened out and they saw Kymo, shining in all his glory; the sea was breaking gently on the golden shore.

There was plenty of shelter near; rocks abounded and the vegetation was thick. Alan ran to where a dozen rocks, man high, rose from the seashore. There was in one a crevice that was wide enough to admit Chlorie.

"Stay there," he whispered.

"Oh, don't leave me."

"I won't leave you for long I promise you—but I want to watch for Kulmervan."

"Take care of yourself," she pleaded. "Oh, run no risks, I pray."

With a quick glance round Alan left the shelter of the rocks. No one was in sight—Kulmervan had not shown himself. Quickly Alan made his way to the cave from which they had emerged. He entered it, and to his amazement found it had no exit. Solid walls blocked his way—it was just a hollowed out rock on the sands, going inland, perhaps ten or twelve feet only. Alan was perplexed. He had marked it as he thought by a big coloured boulder at its entrance; but upon careful examination he found there were dozens and dozens of such boulders all over the beach. Stepping from his hiding place he walked to the next cave; that upon examination proved to go deep into the earth, but it was not the cave from which they had escaped into the open. Wildly he rushed up and down. Twenty, thirty caves he encountered all like, very like, the one he was seeking. Some had narrow passages that twisted and turned and ended in a cave next door. Others went further, and after many serpentine turnings, brought him back to the place from which he had started. He knew he was in a dangerous position; any one of these caves might hold Kulmervan—an observer, but unobserved. Rapidly

Alan made up his mind. With Chlorie he would leave the cave district altogether—they would strike inland. If they were still on the island, they would endeavour to find their way back to where the air bird had been anchored. That Waz-Y-Kjesta would return Alan was convinced—and when he did so, they would be saved.

Having made up his mind, he began to retrace his footsteps—but a hoarse burst of laughter startled him. He rushed to the mouth of the cave. There, sailing away to sea in a frail craft, was Kulmervan. It was just a raft he was on, with a tiny makeshift sail. But it was not at Kulmervan that Alan was staring horror stricken—incredulous. But at a blue figure near the helm—a little blue figure that was tied to a post to which the main-sail was fastened; a little blue figure that held out her arms imploringly to the shore. Alan could only stare and stare, incredulous, unbelieving—but the little craft grew smaller and smaller as it was tossed on the waves. Alan rushed to the rocks—the crevice was empty—Chlorie had once more been snatched from his arms.

XI

The Wraiths of the Rorkas

A lan remained motionless, watching the little craft vanish from his ken. He was thinking hard. Kulmervan had so far got the better of him, but the game was not yet won. It might be check to the King, but Alan was far from being mated. His eye searched the beach—there was nothing in sight; neither boat, nor sailing craft. He looked behind him at the many yawning cavern entrances. He was still in doubt as to the one which led to the Cave of Whispering Madness. He clenched his hands together till the knuckles showed white—there he was, alone on an island, impotent, useless—while the woman he loved was in the hands of a madman, and in danger, not of death as he knew it, but of dishonour, disgrace, and perhaps serquor itself.

There was a mist at sea, and already the little barque had been swallowed up in its grey folds—nothing was in sight on the broad expanse of water. He looked above him—he saw no air bird in the heavens, its body gleaming in the light. On the island there was no trace of humanity but himself. Hope seemed far away. Then suddenly he remembered Kulmervan's words. "Take the most easterly path, my Waiko. Always to the East." Unconsciously he turned to the left, and walked quickly across the sands. A great promontory of rock stood out before him, hiding from sight the next little bay. He strode towards it, and found it was impossible to get round it. Already the water was too deep, so he made up his mind to scale it. Clambering up the slippery rocks, he at length reached the top. There before him lay the whole stretch of coast line. Tiny bays; little rivulets coming down narrow valleys and emptying themselves at last in the sea; rugged headlands, and grassy slopes all took their place in the picture. None of these things, however focussed themselves upon his mind; one thing only he saw, and one thing only drew him helter skelter over the rugged rocks. A tiny boat, almost like the Rob Roy canoe he favoured in his 'varsity days, lay drawn high up on the beach, and near it, a little log cabin was built at the water's edge.

Hurriedly he made his way to the little hut, and knocked loudly on the door. There was no reply and he tried it; it opened at his touch.

He entered it—it was deserted, but he soon had proof of its owner. Upon the wall hung a beautiful painting of Chlorie—and it was signed "Kulmervan, from his kinswoman. Chlorie." On a table by the window was a pile of books, and on the fly leaf of nearly every one was written in a strong hand, "Kulmervan, Taz-Ak of the House of Pluthoz." Mostly the books were on Astronomy and Alan noticed with amusement one was called "Quilphis, or the most important unimportant Planet." Quilphis—Terra! His world, once his all—now nothing.

He looked round the room, a door led on one side to the sleeping apartment, and on the other to the kitchen and offices. The whole place was tastefully furnished and showed signs of frequent use. Alan hurried to the seashore—the little craft was called the Chlorie. He sprang into it, and pushed off. In the bow he saw a tiny engine with three levers. He was already slightly acquainted with the simple Keemarnian machinery, so he pulled one down with assurance. Instantly the boat skimmed along the water at a terrific speed. Hastily he touched the second, a slower pace resulted, and the third stopped the boat altogether. With the first speed on, he ploughed out to the horizon. He could see no trace of Kulmervan. The sea was desolate and bare. He felt hopeless. Had Kulmervan swamped the boat, and were he and Chlorie now lying dead at the bottom of the sea? Death! He knew the Jovians had no death—yet surely they were not immune from drowning? Perhaps they would remain on the sea's bed—serquor. The thought maddened him, and savagely he turned the boat first this way, then that, in his hopeless endeavour to find the fugitives. Kymo had sunk, darkness was setting in—he could see the faint outlines of the hut. Suddenly two beams of light shone out from its windows, which were as suddenly obscured. Kulmervan had doubtless returned. Quickly he turned the boat towards shore; he drew close in and beached her without a sound. Quietly he crept up to the open window and moved the heavy curtain ever so slightly.

There was Kulmervan in his easy chair, reading a book—but he was alone. A knock sounded and a man appeared.

"Do you want refreshment now, my lord?" he asked.

"Yes, Arrack. At once."

"Shall I take refreshment to the lady, your mate?"

"No, Arrack. But stay—take her a glass of wine, and," fumbling on his table—"melt this pellet in it. She will fall asleep. When she is asleep, carry her hither and place her in my room. 'Tis my wedding night,

Arrack. I have an unwilling bride it's true, but before Pirox the Killer, my mate shall she be this night."

Arrack smiled evilly. "'Tis well, my lord. I will do thy bidding."

"When you have brought her hither, stand sentinel at the rocky ledge. If Alan the Evil should appear, strike him down, bind him and acquaint me. Should that happen to him, then Pirox the Killer again will have a victim."

Silently Arrack left the room to return almost immediately with a tray laden with food.

"Where did you go this midday, Arrack?" asked his master.

"To the Cave of Whispering Madness, my master. I built the sacrificial pyre beneath the altar. Everything is in readiness. I hardly expected you so soon. Two Kymos should have passed before you came."

"The pyre is ready? Good! But what did you with the Chlorie?"

"'Tis on the beach as it always is."

"Nay," said Kulmervan, "when I landed at the covered bay, I dragged my unwilling bride by way of the beach. The Chlorie was not there, and I thought you must have sailed to the mainland for food."

"It is there I swear, my lord."

Kulmervan looked puzzled. "Could Alan have found it and—" he began—then—"Go quickly, Arrack, and see."

Alan slipped round the corner of the hut, and in the darkness stood flush with the wall, completely hidden. He saw the figure of Arrack run lightly down to the beach, heard him get into the boat, and as quickly return. He reached his coign of vantage in time to hear Arrack say, "It is there, my lord. I saw and touched it. It has moved its position slightly, but the wind has been rather high to-day; otherwise it was as I left it."

"That puling girl has taken my senses away," grumbled Kulmervan. "I can think of naught but her. Go, Arrack, fetch her here. But remember, give her the wine first. When she awakens, she will have become my mate," and he chuckled hoarsely.

Alan was in a quandary, he scarcely knew what to do. Was the secret way into the place where Chlorie was hidden, in the cabin or not? He wormed his way round the hut, and as he did so, he saw a door open, and in the ray of light a figure cross to a little lean-to shed, that had been built against some high ground. He gave Arrack a moment or two of grace and then followed him in. There on the floor was an open trap door with some steps leading from it into the unknown below. A length of cord was in a corner of the shed, Alan picked it up and then followed Arrack. At the foot of the steps, a subterranean passage led for some distance, and then opened out into a large cave. He remembered it—it was the one immediately under the secret exit in the Cave of Whispering Madness.

He saw Arrack in front of him—he had taken a key from his waist and had undone a heavy, metal door. Silently Alan crept nearer and nearer to him. He heard the sound of liquid being poured into a glass. He heard Chlorie's gentle word of thanks. Now he could see the grim tragedy. Chlorie had finished the wine, and was now swaying to and fro; she tottered and fell on to a low couch in a corner of her prison. Arrack watched her until he was convinced she was fast asleep, then he put the wine bottle down and bent over the prostrate girl. He remembered no more—a mighty blow rendered him unconscious, and Alan tied up his unresisting foe, and left him helpless upon the ground.

Tenderly he raised Chlorie and bent over her—he was aching to kiss her sweet lips, but he remembered her anguished cry, "Not my lips, Kulmervan, not my lips." No, until she offered them of her own free will, they should remain sacred to him. He knew she would sleep deeply for some time, so he examined his quarters. Chlorie's cell was hewn out of the solid rock, with nothing in it but a chair, a table and a settee. There was the passage leading to the log cabin; the one with the glimmer of light that led he knew to the sea shore; and the one to the cave above. To the right, there was a tiny passage that looked almost like a crack in the rock. He peered through—it led on into the distance, and he was determined to try that. Arrack had carried a lamp which gave a good light. Alan picked it up, lifted Chlorie gently, and started down the passage. He wondered whether it would lead to safety, or to adventures even more horrible than many of those he had been through. He held Chlorie tightly; he was determined not to lose her again. Again the passage opened out into a cave—narrowed, and a still larger cave came into view. He saw a niche high up in the wall, and with his precious burden, he managed to reach it in safety. He found himself on a high narrow ledge, where they could rest in safety from the machinations of Kulmervan.

Chlorie woke to find her head supported by a strong arm, and her hands held between two firm ones. She looked up. "Alan," she breathed, and made a tiny movement towards him. "My Chlorie," he murmured, and their lips met in one warm long kiss. "Oh, my darling, you really love me?" he said brokenly at last.

"My Alan, I know not the customs of your world. In mime, it is shame to a maid who offers her lips before she is wed. Indeed, a maid would never be thus," and she slipped from the circle of his arm—"even were she sworn to wed. I know not your customs, my Alan, but I am Ipso-Rorka, and my father's child. I—I love you, Alan—"

"And you'll be my wife?" he asked tenderly.

Shyly she hid her face on his breast "In truth, my Alan,—'tis sweeter far to be asked, than ask. I am glad you are of a different world—for your wooing is stronger and yet more sweet than ours. Oh, willingly, willingly, Alan, will I marry you."

Alan had at last met and won his ideal, and he caressed and murmured sweet nothings to her, until they forgot they were fugitives—forgot that a madman would soon be on their trail—forgot aught but the joy of the present, and the hope of the future. Chlorie recovered herself first. Shyly she slipped her little hand into Alan's. "My loved one," said she. "My father the Rorka knows naught of Kulmervan and his sin. We must escape, reach him, and for the safety of the community, for the traditions of our dear land, we must send Kulmervan to the Hall of Sorrows."

"My Chlorie, nothing will purge him of his sin. He is mad—quite mad."

"But he must go away all the same. See what unhappiness he has caused already—see what he may do in the future!"

"You are right. He must be put away. He has money, position and cunning."

"Where are we, my Alan?"

"I know not where this leads," said Alan, "but it is the only road I dared take."

Hungry, tired and worn, they crept on along the little narrow ledge. Suddenly a cave, lighted from without through slits in the wall, burst on their view, and Chlorie gave a startled exclamation. "The Hall of our Fathers," she cried, "I have been here before."

"What is it?"

"This is the place where the regalia of each reigning Rorka is placed, together with his throne, when he has left the fair land of Keemar, through the Sacrament of Schlerik-itata." Round the cave were thrones of all descriptions—some in heavy marble—others in gold adorned with precious jewels; others just simple, wooden thrones, that showed their antiquity.

"Down, down on your knees," cried Chlorie, and Alan realized that the cave had become alive with living figures. The thrones were occupied by men who wore crowns of gold and jewels, and who carried sceptre and orb in their hands. The cave that had been dead and cold only a minute before, was now alive. But there was no sound; all was hushed and still, and the figures were shadowy and unreal. "Oh my Mitzor," breathed Chlorie. "The joy! To think I should have been permitted to witness this scene—to see the wraiths of my forefathers. My Alan, watch—read a meaning in this visitation, for it augurs well."

Alan felt unable to move. He was petrified at the sight before him—at the ghostly pageant of years gone by. Slowly the Rorkas— kings of æons past—rose from their thrones and walked in single file to the end of the cave. There they ranged themselves on either side of a slightly raised platform of rock. They prostrated themselves, and Alan saw a thin vapour rise and like a curtain shut out from sight the little stage. Then it lifted, and through the shadowy film he saw strange figures disporting themselves amid the strange scenery. Then, all at once, he realized that he was watching shadowy figures of himself and Desmond and Mavis. He saw their little cottage at Arroch Head; he witnessed their hasty flight in the Argenta; once more he saw the destruction of the world, his world. But this time it was different. Like a tiny star it shone white and bright, then it shivered, turned red like a tiny ball of fire in the sky, burst into a thousand different pieces, and then disappeared from sight. And as it disappeared the scene clouded again, and the filmy curtain of haze shut out the picture from his sight. The scene changed—once more he saw himself as an actor on the stage, but this time he was a minor character in the drama. Kulmervan was the villain, and played the chief character. He witnessed their meeting in the little lane—he watched the flight of the air bird, Chlorie—the descent, and the abduction of the Ipso-Rorka. So the play went on until one more picture showed clearly before him. He saw Chlorie—Chlorie in a gown of diaphanous white with a crown of gold upon her head. By her side he stood, crowned and with orb in hand; and between them stood a child—a man child who bore traces of his mother's beauty and his father's strength. Then darkness came upon the scene, and Alan drew his trembling love still closer beside him.

Then the wraiths of the Rorkas became faint and misty, and when next he looked, they had vanished from sight.

"We shall win through, my Alan," said Chlorie. "The wraiths of our Rorkas never show themselves except to the favoured few."

"Do you know the way out from here?"

"Yes. Straight through yonder archway a passage leads to the sea. We are not far from Hoormoori. The island is Waro—the Isle of Joy. It is a safe place for Kulmervan to have chosen for his madness—no one would have sought for evil here."

"How far is Hoormoori then?"

"From where we emerge into the light, we shall see the citadels and towers of my home. Oh Alan—the joyous moment when I can take you by the hand and lead you to my father—my chosen one—my love."

"How shall we reach the mainland?"

"We must light a beacon on the shore. Fire is a signal, and some one will row across to us."

In a short while they emerged through a tiny door out on to the beach. They gathered sticks and laid them crosswise upon each other until they were man high, and then set the pile ablaze. At length came a sign from the distant shore where white minarets gleamed in the light, and golden cupolas rose high in the air. There rose against the whiteness of the scene tall tongues of flame and curling smoke.

"Their answer," said Chlorie. "Some one will soon come now."

They watched a craft put out to sea—they saw the pale green sails grow clearer and nearer. Soon they could distinguish the crew. Chlorie ran down to the sea's edge, and stood gaily clapping her hands.

The little launch beached with a groan and a rattle and a Waz stepped out. "We saw your signal," he began, then a look of recognition came over his face and he fell on one knee and clasped the Princess' hand and impressed a loyal kiss upon it. "Oh my Ipso-Rorka," he cried. "We have mourned you as serquor. No tidings could we get of you. Mournings and tears have been in Hoormoori for ten and one Kymos. The Rorka has shut himself within the precincts of his palace, and neither eats nor drinks; but sits always alone—silent, and quiet, and drear."

"Thank you for your welcome, my Waz. I have had strange adventures since I left my father's house. These I will tell my people when the right moment arrives. But first lead me to my father."

The journey to the mainland occupied a very short space of time, and Waz Okoyar obtained a bhor for the Ipso-Rorka.

"I shall not forget you, Waz Okoyar," said Chlorie. "Reward shall be given you for your speedy assistance to me."

"Nay, my Princess, it is a joy to have served you."

Hoormoori proved to be even more beautiful than Minniviar—the streets were wider and the buildings more magnificent. The bhor stopped outside a marble building. "I told him to stop here," whispered Chlorie. "It is better that I break the news to my father myself, of my safe return." They passed through a noble courtyard into a lovely garden. "Our own private apartments. I shall be able to get to my father unnoticed."

Through a little door, up a short flight of stairs, and down a narrow corridor. A heavy curtain of blue hung outside a doorway. Chlorie lifted it gently. Alan drew back. Much as he loved her, he could not intrude at such a sacred moment.

"Father!"

"My child! My child!"

There was the sound of kissing—a whispered conversation, and then Alan heard his name. Slowly he entered the room, and at last was face to face with the Rorka—King of all Jupiter, but above all, father of his loved one. The majesty of the Rorka overwhelmed him, and he bent his knee in homage.

"Nay, rise," said a gentle voice, musical, benign, soothing. "Rise and greet me, oh my Alan, for Chlorie has told me you are to be my son."

XII

The Fate of Kulmervan

Hoormoori was rejoicing! Their Princess, Chlorie the Ipso-Rorka, was found. Not only was she alive and well, but she had found her mate. True he was from another world, but she loved him, and the Jovians, like the men of Terra, dearly loved a romance. The wedding day was fixed, telepathic messages had been sent to Sir John, and he and his party were coming to Hoormoori as guests of the Rorka.

The Rorka was very troubled over Kulmervan. Never, in the history of Keemar, had such a terrible tale of iniquity been told. His cunning, his audacity, his double life was a terrible blow to the proud old Keemarnian.

Waz-Y-Kjesta was thankful to welcome Alan back. Day after day he had circled over the island, and sent search parties to find the missing ones. The Isle of Waro, which was joined to the larger isle by a narrow strip of sand, they left unexplored. It was holy ground—consequently they missed the log cabin of Kulmervan. Waz-Y-Kjesta, Alan, and a staff of twenty men embarked on the Chlorie and flew to Kulmervan's retreat. They landed close to the hut, and although firearms were unknown on Keemar, they, on Alan's advice, protected themselves with heavy sticks and carried thick silken ropes.

They found the hut empty and signs of a hasty retreat. From the little house they crossed to the "lean-to" and descended into the subterranean passage. They ascended the steps to the Cave of Whispering Madness, and forced the door open. The Cave was empty. Alan looked behind the huge fossil animal and hoped to find the body of Waiko—but it had gone. Ominous foot prints on the sandy floor proved that his body had been found, and Kulmervan and Arrack had dragged him back to the Altar. As they reached the slab of stone Y-Kjesta gave a cry of horror.

"See, my Alan. Mitzor have mercy!"

There on the Altar were the charred remains of what had once been a man. The bones were twisted into horrible forms, as if, in their last convulsive agony, they had writhed in vain on the table of fire. One bony arm hung over the side. Every scrap of flesh had been burnt from it— even the tips of the finger bones were missing. The skull was hairless—

the eyes had been scorched from their sockets. It was a horrible sight and Alan shivered.

"Who is it?" asked Y-Kjesta.

"I am afraid it was Waiko. Heaven grant he was serquor when that madman found him."

Gentle hands attempted to move the charred remains from the bed of pain—but they fell to powder as they were touched. The whisperings in the Cave served to make the horrors more intense, and the Keemarnians turned their heads as they passed the human sacrifice.

Down the steps they all travelled, but no trace of Kulmervan could they find. They forced the outer entrance to the cave, but although they hunted through the leafy byways and hidden avenues, he continued to evade them. Again the cave was searched, and the Waz was inclined to give up the task.

"Is it possible," asked Alan at last, "that he is hiding in the place of the Wraiths of the Rorkas?"

"No. Nothing evil could live in the presence of our holiest men."

"Nevertheless, I'd like to go there," suggested Alan.

The Waz shrugged his shoulders. "As you will, my Alan. Remember, of all Keemarnians, only the Rorkas can visit again the home of their life. They would not show themselves to such a thing of evil as Kulmervan has become."

But at the entrance to the Holy Place they saw Kulmervan. Stiff he was standing, and upon his face was a frozen look of horror. Y-Kjesta fell to his knees. "The Wraiths," he cried.

A cloud of haze had passed away, and upon the little stage was being enacted a drama. High in the air a great white cloud hovered. It was pink tipped with a golden glory shining through; at either side were lesser clouds, but all tinged with the glorious roseate hue. And in chains beneath them stood the astral figure of Kulmervan, surrounded by Keemarnians who had gone before. And as they watched, his clothes melted away, and naked and ashamed he stood before his judge—the great white glory. Gradually a dusky shadow seemed to come over the gleaming body, darker and darker it grew until it was jet black. Not the black of an African native, but a cruel black; a thick black that was horrible to look upon, so evil was its appearance. Then all the Keemarnians shrank away from the solitary evil figure standing alone before the glory. The shadowy figure of Kulmervan looked round him wildly, and threw out his hands in supplication. It was no use. His prayers were too late. A yawning pit showed up bright with flames. Yellow tongues of flame licked round the mouth—long, red flames danced together in riotous harmony. Then out of the terrible place appeared a figure, so terrible that Alan closed his eyes and strove at once to forget it. A figure that was neither man nor animal, but part of both. A creature with bloodshot eyes and a baleful smile, with teeth that looked like fangs, with arms that twisted and twirled like evil serpents. Nearer and nearer the figure drew, until, radiating with heat, it drew close to Kulmervan. There was a mighty noise—the Great White Cloud vanished leaving the scene in a pitchy darkness—only the fiery cavern gleamed and glistened. The venomous figure put a sinewy arm about the form of Kulmervan—there was a crackling noise—the hideous smell of burning flesh, and the picture vanished as the two figures disappeared into the fiery jaws. Then Y-Kjesta spoke. "The Great White Glory has judged. We cannot punish now."

There was a fearsome shriek, and Kulmervan rushed from the cave, and fell prostrate on the ground outside. Y-Kjesta stooped over him. The body was rigid—the eyes fast closed.

"Serquor has descended upon him," said the Waz. "Righteousness has spoken."

With an awed feeling, Alan watched them pick up the body and carry it to the air bird, and as they did so a mighty roar filled the air. There was a sound as of thunder—a blinding flash—then silence. The Cave of Whispering Madness had gone! Shivered to atoms, there was nothing but a hillock of rocks and sand to mark the last resting place of Waiko the Unfortunate. The little passage to the Sacred Cave alone remained perfect. When the last shock of the earthquake had subsided, Arrack the servant came out from his hiding, and threw himself upon the mercy of Alan. Firmly he was bound, and taken to the Chlorie, there to await the judgment of the Rorka.

"My son," said the Rorka, when he had been told the whole story. "Kulmervan was shown his future punishment. He may not be suffering now, for he is in the unhappy state of serquor—but some day, when he leaves this world, his time of pain will come. A case of glass shall be made to hold his cold and rigid body. In the Hall of Sorrows shall it be placed as a living testimony of the fruit that is garnered by evil. To Fyjipo the accursed shall be taken—there to remain, until he changes the state of serquor, for his lasting punishment."

XIII

THE SENTENCE UPON ARRACK

Sir John, with Masters, Desmond and Mavis arrived at Hoormoori in time for the trial. They were much interested in Alan's adventures, and were looking forward to witnessing the spectacle of Jovian justice. Mavis and Chlorie were already warm friends, and the Rorka insisted on the strangers occupying suites of apartments in his palace. Baby John Alan had grown into a fine boy. Now nearly four, he toddled about the palace and chattered away in a quaint mixture of Keemarnian and English. The grown-ups seldom used English now—their past life seemed to be fading away entirely; they were already acclimatized to Jupiter and looked upon it as their home. Mavis at the bottom of her heart, however, did not forget all the pretty customs in which she had been brought up from childhood and she it was who introduced a trousseau as a necessary adjunct to a wedding. Chlorie took up the idea with fervour, and in future all society weddings had trousseaux, cakes and honeymoons as essential parts of their festivities.

Chlorie's mother had heard the call of Schlerik-itata when she was but a small child, and possessing no near feminine relatives, the Keemarnian Princess was glad to have Mavis helping her at the happiest time of her life. All was bustle and rush at the palace. The wedding was to be a grand affair, but before it took place, Arrack had to answer publicly the charges that were brought against him. In the large Justice Hall, on the day appointed, the Rorka took his seat wearing his purple robes of Justice.

A fanfare of trumpets announced his arrival, with his postillions and servants and attachés. All wore full court dress, and the whole scene was picturesquely brilliant. Alan had not yet been admitted to the highest circles in Jovian society; his honour was to come on his wedding day—so to meet the exigencies of the case, a special raised seat had been placed at the right hand of the Rorka, and there Alan sat in state and watched the proceedings. There were neither lawyers nor barristers in this wonderful land of harmony. The case for the defence, if so it could be called, was taken by the High Priest—and for the prosecution by the highest Djoh in the whole of Keemar.

The Rorka listened to the statements made on both sides, and gave his sentence as he thought fairest. No appeal could be made afterwards; his judgment was final. Never had there been such a case as this one. Arrack had broken the traditions of his land. If the Rorka adjudged him guilty, he would take his punishment stoically. The Rorka rose, and the silence in the court was profound. "Bring in Arrack the Miserable," he cried, and Arrack appeared in the prisoner's garb of an ugly neutral tint. This garment of shame was worn only by prisoners, when charged with some heinous offence. It was something of the shape of a Jewish gaberdine. About his waist the prisoner wore a hempen rope; his head was covered with a hood, and there were sandals upon his feet. "O Arrack," said the Rorka, "take your seat upon the Penitent's Chair, for you are accused by this court of most grievous dealings. If you are found guilty, a terrible fate awaits you. Speak first, Lamii, Djoh of all Keemar, read your charge first." And Djoh Lamii, a dignified old greybeard, stepped forward and read from a parchment.

"Rorka, most mighty, by the grace of Mitzor, Keemarnians one and all, I charge Arrack the Miserable with grievous sins. Whether he alone is responsible or whether responsibility rests with another—unnamed, but now in a state of serquor—remains to be proved. First, I charge Arrack with idolatry and devil worship,—nay more, I charge him with the greatest offence of all against Mitzor—the offence of offering black sacrifices, the sacrifice of living bodies, to Pirox the Killer, a graven image of hideous aspect. I charge him with acting as assistant in that Temple of Sin and Death. I charge him as a heretic and a heathen. He, a born believer in the one and only Creator, is a deserter from his faith. I charge him with aiding the unnamed, now serquor, in his horrible, nefarious practices. All these charges are with regard to his sins against Mitzor. Now I charge him with attempting to lay hands on the precious person of our loved Princess; with offering her wine that was drugged, and being a party to keeping her a captive against her will. Above all, I charge him with trying to aid the unnamed, now serquor, to soil her purity, and thus to cause her to wed one she did not love. These, O Rorka, are the sins in brief, and a more hideous category of evil, I have never before had to repeat. Although I am old, and my call must come soon, this is the saddest day of my life to think I have to utter such things against a true Keemarnian."

He sat down, and then rose up Misrath the High Priest. "O Rorka, the mighty and the just. I cannot deny the charges that Lamii has brought. Long have I talked with Arrack the Miserable, and it is hard to offer even a word in his favour. Yet because of thy justice I beg of you to hear me out, and I will tell the tale of sorrow and shame. Arrack and the unnamed, now serquor, were foster brothers. The mother of the unnamed received her call while her babe was yet a suckling, and these two babes, suckled from the same breast, drew the food of life from the same woman. As toddling mites they flew their kites together, and threw their balls. Then the sire of Arrack, Meol, now serquor, took these suckling babes to the Temple of Pirox the Killer. It is he I blame, not the innocent ones. He, with two others, lived a life of lies. Respected Keemarnians, wise fathers, loving husbands, they lived unsuspected of their evil practices; for they were all devil worshippers and offered up the black sacrifice. But serquor took them all into his bosom. These tender nurslings grew in the ways of sin. He, the unnamed, possessed brains and cunning. He was the leader. He it was who took Arrack the Miserable on to our Isle of Holiness—made him build him a hut, and left him there, a tool to work his will and prepare his heathen rites. Since he was of tender years he has led this life—hating it, yet loving it; fearing it, yet welcoming it. Then the time came when he, the unnamed, whispered words that affrighted even Arrack the Miserable. Whispered words of passion for a Princess. The Ipso-Rorka was named—and even to that length of degradation would Arrack have assisted, so deep was he in the toils of sin. Then the day of reckoning came. Mighty thunders shook the Cave of Darkness. The wrath of Mitzor tore it asunder; no more shall these perfidious practices be handed down from father to son. No longer shall sin creep out unseen in Keemar. The Great White Glory has spoken. The Temple of Sin is in ruins, and under the mass of rock and stones lies the tortured body of Waiko. Whether he, too, had practised the sins of the unnamed also, we know not. But we do know his character was weak. We pray that his suffering on the Black Altar may have purged his soul and that soon he will be sitting in the warmth of the Tower of Help."

Misrath sat down, and the Rorka rose. "I have heard your case, O Arrack, in silence. I have listened to your tale of shame. One thing only is in your favour. You sought not an evil life, but sin and its sorrows were taught you when you were yet a child. But—" he paused. "You lived the life of Keemar. You attended our services of joy that were offered to Mitzor. You knew sin was abhorrent to us. From the time when our first parents populated our world, we have fought to keep Keemar perfect. Thanks to Mitzor we nearly succeeded. It is to prevent the occurrence of sins like yours that I pronounce sentence. Misrath, High Priest of our Temples—our Mediator on earth between Mitzor and man, robe the sinner in the garments of shame."

Immediately the grey tinted gaberdine was torn from Arrack, and in its place was put a long robe of black. The covering was taken from his head, and the sandals from his feet. His head was bowed in shame, and in shame he was led to the Sentence Bar, there to hear his fate.

"Through the streets of Hoormoori shalt thou be led," said the Rorka. "A rope round thy middle shall direct thee the way to go. Neither man nor woman shall speak to thee. Neither beast nor bird shall be permitted to fawn upon thee. Alone and an outcast shalt thou be sent upon thy way. Lonely shalt thy days be. Lonely shalt thou be taken to the Hall of Sorrows at Fyjipo. There thou shalt live until thy beard grows and turns white with age. Should thy call come early, alone wilt thou have to meet the Great White Glory. No Sacrament shall help thee on thy way. Neither incense nor prayers shall assist thee in thy last moments here. Alone and wretched thou shalt leave this world. But should thy call not come soon, then shalt thou stay in the Hall of Sorrows until thy beard covers thy face and thy middle, then—when that time arrives, shalt thou be free to leave the place of sorrow. But thy life will be lonely all thy days for the sins thou hast committed."

Misrath rose. "Oh my Rorka, thy wisdom is sound, thy judgment just. May I ask but one favour for the guilty Arrack? During his time of sorrows, should he perform two noble deeds wouldst thou reconsider thy verdict and allow him freedom?"

"Yes, Misrath. Should he perform two noble deeds, deeds that mark him as a true son of Keemar, then publicly shall his punishment be remitted him, and once more shall he take his place among the people he has wronged. I have spoken."

The Rorka rose from his seat of justice, and with another fanfare of trumpets took his place in his state bhor and drove to the palace. Alan waited to see the end. The wretched Arrack was led from his place, and taken through a side entrance out on to the highway. There a rope was twisted round his waist, a rope that had six ends. Six men took hold of each end, and dragging it taut, led him through the streets. On he went, a misery to himself, and to those that saw him.

An air bird was made ready for the journey to Fyjipo. Alan begged that he might accompany it. He wanted to see for himself what the Hall of Sorrows was really like. He had no conception of it. Was it like a Pentonville or Portland in England, or did it possess some horror that no ordinary human mind could conceive?

"Go then," said the Rorka to Alan. "Swift be thy journey there, and as swift return. Just time shalt thou have before the day arrives when Misrath shall make my child and thee—one. One on earth and one in Heaven."

"Farewell," said Chlorie, when Alan told her of the journey he was to make. "'Tis customary in Keemar for a bride to withdraw herself from all for twelve Kymos before her wedding day. During that time she thinks and meditates on her future state. I go into silence to-morrow, Alan, and my prayers will be all for you. May you return to me in safety. Farewell."

XIV

The Hall of Sorrows

The air struck cold and Alan was glad of the heavy cloaks that the Rorka insisted on his taking for the journey. They had passed through glorious scenery, but now it was changing. No longer was the air sweet and balmy; no longer were the fields below covered with beautiful flowers. Great stretches of bare and rocky country took the place of the fields, and snow-topped hills looked down on the desolation.

Then Fyjipo hove in sight. One great building dominated the scene. Of a dark grey stone it looked gloomy and forbidding. Kulmervan, still in the state of serquor, had been brought in a coffin of glass, and Alan felt the awful loneliness of the place, when he saw the coffin being unshipped, preparatory to being placed in the Hall of that dreadful abode. The Waz, who was in command of the journey held the only key to the heavy gates, and as he unfastened them, a drear wailing rose from within.

Arrack was dragged along, pushed inside the gate, and then left— to learn how to fend for himself in that gloomy place. Carefully was Kulmervan placed upon a huge pedestal in the hall. His face had lost its youthful candour, its beauty of outline and its peace. The visage seen through the glass, was the face of an old man worn with sin; evil and sinister. Alan shuddered as he turned away from the coarsened form. The state of serquor as known by the Keemarnians was a very dreadful thing. Struck down in life, the victims assumed a trance-like form from which they never recovered. Real death the Jovians knew not; a far happier parting was permitted them. As in a dream a voice told the sleeper that his time had come—that so many more Kymos would pass before he would have to bid his world good-bye. Then in the Sacrament of Schlerik-itata his body and soul were rendered astral, and in a cloud of smoke the favoured one disappeared from sight, and entered into dwelling with his God. It was a wonderful end; there could be no great sadness at such a departure; no corruption was to be the lot of the departing Jovian—he was just carried into glory. But those poor souls that suffered serquor remained in their comatose condition. Alive yet dead! Dead yet alive! Useless to themselves, and of use to no one! No wonder it was the one dreaded thing in this land of all good.

There were but fifty bodies in the condition of serquor on the whole of Keemar, and most of them had been there for many ages. None could remember some of them as creatures full of life; their names were written on tablets and placed above them—their only connection with the generation of the present. In a small, underground chapel in the Temple at Hoormoori were these poor ones kept. Niches, cushion-lined were made in the walls, and in these the victims were laid. There they would remain until Jupiter itself returned to its first void, and emptied its population into the lap of Heaven.

"I beg you stay not long here, my Lord," said the Waz to Alan. "'Tis an evil place, and I would fain hurry and leave it far behind me".

"Nay, my Waz. Stay until the Kymo rises full in the Heavens—'tis but a short time now, and then I shall be ready to accompany you".

There were no separate degrees of punishment in the Hall of Sorrows. The real punishment lay in its awful loneliness. The Keemarnians who were there were paying dearly for their faults. Utter loneliness—comfortless—cheerless—it was desolation personified. Those were the first impressions that Alan received. Food was let down from the air at certain intervals. There was no division, and only just sufficient to go round. It was a question of first come, first served, and the man who appeared last received little if any of his portion. No lighting was arranged in the place, and as it was near the Pole, half their time was spent in total blackness. There was no warmth; it was cold and draughty; no privacy; no comfort.

The Keemarnians who offended purged themselves clean in this dread place of sorrow. Once they were free of it, they never put themselves into the position to be sent there again. Their terms of incarceration varied. For some it might be for only six Kymos; for others sixty or even six hundred! The worst sinner there had nothing on his conscience one quarter as bad as Arrack the Miserable; but he was sent there too, to consort with them.

Alan could not bear to stay in the place. The atmosphere stifled him—the sight depressed him. His last view of Arrack, was of a lonely figure in a gown of black, sitting drearily in a corner of the big Hall, watching intently the still form of his late master. His hands were clasped, his expression hopeless—his whole attitude one of despair.

"It's very terrible," said Alan to the Waz as they sailed away from Fyjipo.

"What is, my Lord?"

"Your Hall of Sorrows."

"But why, my Lord?"

"Surely it must do more harm than good?" The Waz looked amazed. "I know if I were sent to such a place, I should come out hardened and defiant."

The Jovian smiled. "That is where we differ, my Alan. The Keemarnian hates evil of every kind. This dread is born in him. He offends—ever so slightly. The Priest remonstrates with him. He makes promises to atone, but offends again. No second chance is given him. Straight to the Hall of Sorrows he is sent, there to live in discomfort, cold and solitude. He is too ashamed to mix with his fellow creatures; so his sin is purged and he comes out a better man."

Alan laughed slightly at the Keemarnian's earnestness. "I am afraid, my friend, that the world I came from was more material than yours. A life in such a place would have led to worse sin—it would not have cured it."

"Then I am glad I belong to Keemar," said the Waz simply.

They made the return journey in record time, and Desmond and Mavis were waiting for Alan on the roof station when the air bird sailed in.

"Welcome home," said Mavis. "We have missed you badly. However everything is ready for you, and in three more Kymos we will have you safely married."

"Are you so anxious to get rid of me?" laughed Alan.

"No," answered Mavis with a happy smile, "but I've tasted the joys myself, and I want you to find your happiness also, my brother."

"That's very nicely put, Mavis," said Alan tenderly. "I could wish for no one but you for Desmond. At first I was a little jealous when I thought his affection for me would be halved."

"Not halved, Alan."

"No, that's not the right word. But Desmond and I had been everything to each other from our childhood, and then you came—"

"Well?"

"Now I understand what it means, and am glad I am going to partake of the same kind of happiness that Desmond enjoys."

"I'm sure you'll be happy, Alan. Chlorie is so sweet—so human, so understanding. But—" there came a perplexed note into her voice. "I'm afraid of only one thing, Alan. You are sure you are not too—too material—for these Jovians. You are going to mate with a girl almost—

spiritual, if I may so put it. Now—the time is drawing near, I'm so afraid—"

"Don't be afraid, little woman. I've learnt a great deal since I came here. The past is growing dim. My love for Chlorie is so great that I think it is cancelling all my earthly senses. I have only one fear for the future."

"And that is?"

"My inborn dread of death. Not that I fear death for myself, but dread its coming and separating me from my love. She will not have that fear. Until I can comfort myself in the belief of Schlerik-itata, I shall have that fear always with me."

"Death!" Mavis looked dreamily into the distance where her son and his father were romping together. "I think I, too, have a tiny bit of fear left," said she, "but I am trying to put it away. We have left the old world behind us. I was wrong to put doubts in your heart, Alan. You've chosen wisely, I am sure. Good luck and good fortune be yours!"

XV

The Triumph of Ak-alan

The populace of Hoormoori were wildly excited, for the time had come when their Princess, the Ipso-Rorka of all Keemar, was to wed. Every place was full, the streets were thronged with visitors, for people had come from all parts of Jupiter to witness the long ceremonies and jubilations that preceded the actual wedding. Parties came from the warmth of Xzor, from the heat of Paila, from the temperate breezes of the Isles of Kalœ. Every dwelling house in Hoormoori was full; every public guest house had used every available space for their overflowing guests. The streets were gaily decorated; the trees were adorned with coloured lights, and across the wide boulevards silken flags were hung. There were festoons of flowers and leaves everywhere. Every window was bright with silken rugs; the whole scene was gay and brilliant.

The first ceremony of interest was the admittance of Alan into the bosom of the Rorka's family. In a wonderful golden robe Alan stood at the foot of the Rorka's throne in the great white Throne Room in the palace. The whole apartment was thronged with guests, and by the Rorka's side sat the Princess. She had on her face a grave, sweet smile, and in her court robes of blue and gold she made a regal figure.

A majordomo handed the Rorka a golden fillet of beautiful workmanship studded with diamonds. This was placed on Alan's head by the Rorka himself, who said—"Oh Alan, known hence forward by the Royal prefix of Ak—I salute thee. Thou hast taken the oaths of allegiance to me, your Rorka. Thy fidelity and love thou hast offered me. I salute thee, Oh Ak-Alan," and he took him by both hands, and kissed him on either cheek, and raised him to the topmost step of the throne. Then Alan faced the people.

"Behold him," said the Rorka. "Ak-Alan, a noble of the House of Pluthoz. Acclaim him as your own, for he is indeed a Prince of the House of your Rorka."

How the people cheered! With one accord they shouted and surged forward to the foot of the throne, and stretched out their hands to their newly made prince. Alan was delighted with his reception, and had an individual word to say to nearly every one who came near him. The story of his adventure for Chlorie had been widely told; Kulmervan's treachery was known; and every one welcomed the newcomer royally. But this was only the beginning. Ak-Alan had to become a Djoh of the Outer Shelter, and to receive the blue ribbon of his office. The Golden Circle of Unity of Keemar was placed on his finger—The Star of Joy—The Order of Hope—all these ceremonies took their time. But they were all picturesque and interesting.

Many times had he looked upon Chlorie, but never had an opportunity been given to him to speak with her alone. But at his ardent gaze, the shy colour would mount her cheeks, and her eyes would drop in sweet embarrassment.

Waz-Y-Kjesta had been appointed to the Royal Household of Ak-Alan, and was delighted to have the opportunity to remain by the side of the friend he had made. Persoph the Jkak, and Mirasu the Jkakalata had sent handsome presents to Alan and Chlorie, and had expressed their sorrow when Desmond had announced his intention of settling down in Hoormoori.

"We want to be near Alan," explained Sir John.

"We shall miss you of course. We are grateful for your kindness to us all since we arrived so strangely in your land. But we should miss the society of our kinsman, we must stay near him."

"We understand," said Persoph. "But visit us, my friends, and allow us to visit you. Your friendship is dear to us—your esteem we prize."

Several orders had been offered Sir John, but he stuck to his prefix throughout. "My father earned it," he explained. "I honour him by using it. Please allow me to keep it," and the Rorka gave his permission. During all this time Masters had scarcely left Sir John's side. A devoted friend, a loyal servant, he remained always at hand in case the old man needed him. And when Alan had been appointed Ak of the House of Pluthoz, Masters received the shock of his life. Suddenly the majordomo cried out, "And I command Masters of the household of Sir John to kneel at the foot of the Rorka's throne."

Masters turned dead white, and looked appealingly at Sir John.

"Go forward, my friend," said Sir John, and Masters obeyed him.

The Rorka rose, and touched him lightly with the Silver Staff of Office of a Waz. "I promote thee henceforward, Waz, to the house of Sir John. Waz-Masters shalt thou be, with all that appertains thereto. Accept this staff, Waz-Masters, for thou art a faithful friend."

Masters was unable to express his gratitude, the honour was so unexpected that it rendered him speechless; but a few moments later Alan smiled as he saw him talking earnestly with Zyllia, a kinswoman of Y-Kjesta's. And as Alan watched the luminous eyes that smiled at Masters, watched the parted lips and the colour that came and went in the olive tinted cheeks of the beautiful Keemarnian, he foresaw, and foresaw truly, that soon Masters would forsake the lonely role of bachelor; and another love match would be made in Keemar—the land of all good.

Then came the feasts and banquets; a pageant and procession through the streets of Hoormoori. Bhors gaily decorated, fancifully costumed bands, dancing children dressed like wood nymphs, fair-headed, slim youths with pipes like the pipes of Pan, woodland fairies, ladies in court attire, all took part in this wonderful procession.

And Alan sat on a balcony in the Royal Palace and watched it. But half the time his eyes were feasting on the features of his bride of the morrow. Occasionally, under cover of the cheers and the darkness, his hand would stray out, and for a moment clasp hers in the darkness. But no chance had he of speaking with her alone, and her nearness maddened him with passionate longings. He longed to be alone with her, away in the woods and fields, along the seashore, just they two together, communing with nature in all her glory.

"May I not speak to Chlorie a moment alone?" he begged earnestly.

The Rorka smiled. "In your world, perhaps, it would be allowed. But I cannot sanction it. To-day she belongs to me—to the people. To-morrow she will be yours for ever. It is custom, my son. But to-morrow—" he stopped, and looked shrewdly at Alan. "I have been converted to your—'honeymoon'. It is a strange idea to us of Keemar, but a beautiful one, and will, I think, prove popular with my countrymen. To-morrow you take her away—alone. No duenna's guiding eye will follow you. The House of Roses in the Wyio Forest is at your disposal. It is ready—prepared. I have given way on many points, my son, but on this one I am firm. You cannot speak alone to Chlorie to-night. Now I wish to speak to Sir John." Alan bowed his head and moved away, so that his uncle could take his place. He was further away from his love, but sat in the shadow and gloried in her as the light shone brightly on her profile.

"Sir John," said the Rorka, "I have heard much about your wonderful airship that carried you safely to our world. Would you be prepared to build another as like it as possible? I will place men, material and means at your disposal. You need want for nothing, and I should esteem it a personal favour if you would at least consider my proposal."

Sir John's eyes shone. "O Rorka, you have put new life into me by your suggestion. I felt I was growing old—but my heart is still young. To be of use in your world will make my last years happy; to feel I am not wasting my time will strengthen my life. Masters and I were planning another Argenta on paper only to-day. He has been examining the metal you use, and he says it is even lighter and stronger than our aluminium. My whole time is at your disposal, and Masters' as well."

"Speak for yourself, Sir John," smiled the Rorka. "But unless I am much mistaken, Zyllia will have more to say about Waz-Masters' affairs than you have dreamt of."

"Zyllia?" repeated Sir John looking puzzled.

"Look behind you," said the Rorka. In the room behind were two figures—Masters and a woman. The woman was delicately beautiful. Darker than most Keemarnian women, with blue black hair and flashing eyes.

"So he has found a mate," said Sir John softly. "I never thought of Masters and marriage. He seemed too mature. In our world he would have been called 'middle-aged' He has seen forty and three summers."

"But Zyllia is mature," said the Rorka. "She looks a girl, but although her soul is young, she and Masters are not far apart in years."

"You will not object to the match?"

"Nay. I have a great opinion of Waz-Masters, but I like not his name." He touched a bell. "Waz-Masters and the Lady Zyllia. I desire them here at once." The girl bowed, and in a moment the two were standing before him. "My friend," said the Rorka kindly, "I like not your name. Waz-Masters sounds crude and harsh. In our language we have a far softer word that means 'Master' Henceforward shall you be known by that. Waz-Aemo, for now and ever." Masters remained silent. He was embarrassed and hardly knew what to do. "So you are going to mate with Zyllia?" said the Rorka. Zyllia bent on one knee, her hands extended in supplication. "Oh Rorka, most noble. Have I thy permission? Him have I promised to wed, if I have thy permission. For I love this stranger dearly."

"My consent was given long ago. I have watched your play with pleasure, my child. Tell Waz-Y-Kjesta he can give you the use of an air bird for your—your honeymoon."

"Oh how can I thank you—"

"That is enough. See, the procession has resumed—how beautiful are the flowers—the silks—" and taking these words as their dismissal, they bent on one knee, and then passed from the balcony to the room beyond.

The last vehicle had passed, the last burst of music had died away, night fell. But one more ceremony remained to conclude the time of rejoicing—the wedding on the morrow.

Alan woke early on the morning of his wedding day. His personal attendant had placed all his wedding clothes ready for him, and he donned the golden robe and swung from his shoulders the blue velvet cloak. It was lined with gold, and caught up at one corner with a beautiful jewelled buckle. His fillet of gold was on his head, and as he looked at himself in the long glass he saw the romantic robes fade away, leaving in their place a worn and shabby, but nevertheless very comfortable golf jacket. The shadowy figure was carrying a bag over his shoulder—golf clubs. Alan sighed. It was a very long time since he had teed up, and with a mighty drive seen a little white ball sent skimming along at a terrific pace. He could see the ascent to the approach of his favourite green; the green itself, smooth and velvety, resting in a little hollow below. Well, he would get his game of golf on Jupiter. He would plan a course, have clubs made, and he and Chlorie would—No, he didn't regret giving up the old and ugly garments of the earth. He regretted nothing. He wouldn't have altered his fate if it had been in his power to do so. Life held nothing for him but Chlorie. Life and love were before him, and he felt fitted for and happy in the new world.

His golden, sandal-like boots were on. The ring for Chlorie was in his satchel purse. The Crown of Wifehood with which he would presently crown her was in Y-Kjesta's possession. The Waz also had taken care of the gifts, which according to the rites of the Temple he must present to his wife. The coins, to represent that he endowed her with his wealth. The loaf divided in two—to denote that she would share in everything. The fresh cut flowers, a symbol of the joys they would find in each other, and lastly the basket of fruits that were to be laid on the Altar and offered as a burnt offering to Mitzor the Mighty. As they were reduced to ashes, the High Priest would waft them to the four winds of heaven, and the nuptial pair would swear to love each other until such time arrived as the burnt fruits regained their virgin freshness. A poetical way of vowing their eternal fidelity each to the other.

ELLA M. SCRYMSOUR

Waz-Y-Kjesta entered. He was plainly nervous at the thought of the part he was to play in the day's ceremony. "The time has come, my Alan. Your bhor awaits you."

"I am ready," Alan smiled at the Waz. "I don't know how I should get on without you to-day." The streets were thronged with people. Alan sat alone in the State Bhor which drove slowly down the decorated streets, and immediately in front of the bridegroom's equipage rode Y-Kjesta, on a magnificent white coli.

Sixteen Keemarnians, appointed by the Rorka for his personal staff, rode behind him. Sir John and Desmond were already in the Temple. A beautiful blue carpet spread from the door to the street, and the whole way was lined with flowers. Slowly Alan walked up the flowered aisle and took his place at the altar rails. The organ was playing softly. Suddenly it burst out into the Ipso-Rorka's personal air—The Bride had arrived. On the arm of the Rorka she walked up the long aisle. Her bridal gown of blue brought out the colour of her eyes. Upon her hair was draped a thin veil of gold, and her long train was carried by little sturdy John Alan! At the altar rails they stopped, and the High Priest demanded—"Who giveth permission, that this woman shall leave her home and her people, and live in peace with the mate of her choice?"

"I do," said the Rorka.

"You are convinced that happiness and joy will be the woman's lot?"

"I am."

"Thanks be to Mitzor. I am content." Thereupon the Rorka took his seat upon his throne, and the ceremony commenced.

Mavis, who had followed the bridal procession, now took her place on Chlorie's left, to assist the bride. It was a beautiful ceremony, and the incense, the priest's vestments, the music, all helped to make it awe inspiring and impressive. The gifts were offered—Chlorie accepted them—the moment was almost at hand that would make them one. Alan was repeating softly after the priest—

"May this ring, with which I encircle thy finger, be a lasting proof of the unity of our affection. May the circlet with which I crown thee, prove that I honour thee as my loved one, and install thee as Queen of my House."

And Chlorie answered softly, "I accept this ring, and from my finger it shall never slip. I accept the crown that thou offerest me, and in return I pray Mitzor the Mighty, that I may rule my household wisely and well."

Then came the vows of love and fidelity; each repeated the words with hands clasped.

"Before Mitzor the Mighty, the Great White Glory, I promise to let naught come between my chosen spouse and me. I promise to love him (her) and honour him (her), share his (her) troubles, and smooth away his (her) griefs. Lastly, I ask Mitzor, the Tower of Strength, to crown us both with the glory of our union."

Then, kneeling, the High Priest blessed them.

"May Mitzor, the Great White Glory, bless you both, and keep you both in the paths of righteousness. May he make thee, Oh Ak-Alan, a tender husband; and thee, Chlorie, a loving wife. Thy vows are made—kneel and pray while the sacrificial fires are lighted, and the dust of thy offering is thrown to the winds."

Hand in hand the newly married pair knelt. Into a tiny tabernacle the offering of fruits was placed—the doors closed upon it. A second passed, and by the aid of etheric heat there was nothing left but a little powdery dust.

Slowly the priests and the acolytes walked down the aisle, the bridal pair following. With prayers and exhortations the dust was scattered, and wafted out of sight by the breeze. The ceremony was over—a hymn of joy was sung, and Alan and Chlorie were led to their bhor that was waiting.

They drove together in the open bhor, and Chlorie could not speak—her heart was too full of emotion. The excitement, the cheering, the crowds tired her—and yet there was still the reception to get through.

Not a word had she spoken to her newly made husband, but as they alighted he whispered—"You don't regret, my darling?"

She gave him a quick, shy glance, but it satisfied him. They had to wait for the congratulations of the intimate friends and guests, but at last Mavis whispered, "Come, dear, it is time for you to change into your other frock." Quietly the bride left the reception and changed into her other gown. Tenderly she bade her father good-bye.

"Good-bye, my little one," he murmured, "Mitzor take care of you. In forty Kymos I shall come for you. Be happy in your new life."

"Good-bye, my father."

"Good-bye."

"You will find everything in readiness at the House of Roses," said Waz-Y-Kjesta.

There were renewed cheers, the band played—and the comfortable equipage drove off, bearing the happiest couple in all Keemar.

"My darling," murmured Alan, when they were at last outside the town, and running swiftly through quiet country roads. "Are you sure you won't regret this day?"

"Never, my Alan," she replied, her eyes smiling as she nestled close to her husband—"but Alan, I think I am a little frightened all the same."

For answer he crushed her in his arms, and rained passionate kisses on her unresisting lips—and it sufficed her. She was content.

XVI

The Perfect World

Many hundred times the Kymo rose and set, and Ak-Alan and his wife, beloved of all Keemarnians, lived in peace and happiness. A son and daughter had been born to them, and now the time had come when the Rorka had received his call, and through the Sacrament of Schlerik-itata would make his exit from the world, and enter into glory.

"My son," said he, "the voice came in my sleep last night. My room was bathed in a wonderful whiteness when the messenger from Mitzor called me. 'When the Kymo reaches the full for thirteen days make ready—for on the fourteenth thou shalt meet the Great White Glory.' I must now set my house in order. You will reign jointly with Chlorie. I can safely leave my country in your hands."

"Father," said Alan, "must you really leave us?" He was troubled. "Oh it's terrible."

"But why?" said Chlorie. "I shall miss my father it is true—for I love him dearly. But how can I wish him here, when his happiness lies yonder?"

"I don't understand," said Alan miserably. "Death is so sad."

"But it is not—death—" said the Rorka. "I am simply—'going away'."

"That's just it. You are going away, and you are never coming back."

"That is true, my son. *I* am never coming back—but you will eventually come to me. Why mourn? To mourn is selfish."

"It's no good," said Alan. "I suppose I am of coarser clay. I can't believe that I could ever 'pass yonder' through the Sacrament of Schlerik-itata. I come from another world. Suppose I die—oh you don't know death as I do—but suppose it comes to Keemar through me, and afterwards through my children."

"Have no fear," said the Rorka, "that day will never come." And so the last few days had passed, and Alan saw him enveloped in the incense, and vanish from sight.

Alan marvelled at his wife's fortitude. He had felt the knife of death on Terra; this glorious parting was so different. He longed to believe that he, too, one day, would vanish thus, material and earthy though he was. And so Alan the Rorka, and Chlorie his wife were crowned, and occupied joint thrones in the land of Keemar.

Their joy in their unity, in the completeness of their life, was a constant wonder to them. They renewed their joys in their children—their life was almost perfect. Sir John was growing feeble. Part of the time he spent with Mavis and Desmond, and part with Alan. But wherever he went, Masters and Zyllia always accompanied him.

Mavis' three children and Alan's two, grew up like brothers and sisters; indeed, their parents were all like one big family. Alan had not long been on the throne of Keemar, when an urgent message was brought him, that Waz-Mula, humbly begged an audience.

"Who is he?" asked Alan.

"He is holder of the key to the Hall of Sorrows," answered Y-Kjesta, "and sails the air bird, that plys to and fro from Fyjipo."

"I remember him well. Bring him in."

"O noble Rorka, I beg a favour of you," said Mula.

"What is it that troubles you?"

"You remember Arrack the Miserable?"

"Well?"

"He has done a most noble thing, O Rorka. A most terrible scourge has come upon the Hall of Sorrows. A fire broke out. How or where it started no one can tell, but when I reached the place, it was a raging furnace, and the poor captives were beating against the gates in their frenzy to get out. The heat was intense—their skins were blistering. I landed safely, and rushed to undo the gates. But even as I did so, great tongues of fire curled out and licked round me. See, O Rorka, my hands are burnt—my hair is scorched. Three times I essayed to unlock the padlock, but the flames drove me back. Suddenly I heard a cry, and Arrack burst through the flames. 'Throw me the keys,' he cried, and his tone commanded and I obeyed. I watched him as he touched the red hot metal—the flames were fiercer than before. He never trembled or grew hasty. Although his clothes were in flames, and the flesh burnt from his fingers, yet still he strove to open the prison door. At length he succeeded. Five figures fell out on to the ground, burnt and still. I called to Arrack to save himself, but his only answer was to beat his way through the avenue of fire. Minutes passed and he did not return. We looked at the poor burnt things at our feet—their souls had departed, but as we looked their mutilated bodies disappeared. Then through the smoke and grime Arrack appeared bearing in his arms a burden which he laid at my feet. He returned again and again, and yet again. Five women's lives he saved, and he returned again to save the life of a pet animal. Then, O Rorka, he fell at my feet. His face was burnt beyond recognition; his poor hands useless; his body one mass of blisters. He, and those he saved we brought to Hoormoori. The women are now in safety, but Arrack says his call has come. Oh, my Rorka, this then is my prayer. His one wish now, is to enter into glory through the Sacrament of Schlerik-itata. Will you grant him pardon, and answer his prayer?"

Alan was much moved. "Go, return to Arrack. Tell him Misrath shall come and administer the Sacrament himself."

"May I say that?"

"Yes. Where is he now?"

"On board the air bird. He is in great pain, but I think I could get him taken to the Temple in safety."

"See to it at once, my Waz."

Hurriedly Alan sent for Misrath, and told him the news.

"He has purged his sins indeed," said he.

So, with the rites of Schlerik-itata, Arrack left Keemar. He bent and kissed the hem of Alan's garment, and sank back exhausted in his chair. And as the incense covered him, his voice could be heard murmuring— "Great White Glory, I come—I come."

"And so there is to be no more Hall of Sorrows," said Chlorie softly.

"No, my darling."

"It's gone for ever?"

"Yes. It has served its purpose, but I don't think its omission will bring more sin into Keemar."

"I believe you are right, Alan. It was a terrible place, and sometimes I think the punishment was too great for the sin."

A blue-eyed curly-haired girl ran into the room. Breathless and flushed, she clasped a doll in her arms, and hugged a pink-cheeked apple. She was followed by a bright, eager-faced boy of twelve or thereabouts.

"No, John Alan, I won't marry you," said she. "I am Acuci, and Ipso-Rorka, and you are only Ak."

The children did not see the grown ups who were hidden by a curtain, and their childish chatter went on unheeded.

"You must marry me, Acuci—I love you, and papa says that love is everything."

The little maid pouted. "I love you, John Alan, and I think I'll marry you after all."

The two children embraced fondly, and ran out of the room hand in hand.

"My wife," said Alan. "Don't ever leave me. Teach me to know the real meaning of Schlerik-itata—teach me to believe."

Chlorie offered her beautiful lips to her husband. "Love teaches everything, my husband. Love is powerful—love is mighty. Love will teach you even that."

He strained her to his breast. "My wife—my wife—I love you so. The terror of parting is always with me. Teach me to believe—you see, dear, even in this Perfect World, there is a grain of sadness—of earthly discontent."

"My husband—I have no fear—listen—." And from outside came the merry laughing voices of their children at play. "In your children you will learn belief."

Envoi

The time came when Sir John himself heard the Call. Half believing, half fearing, he bade farewell. The prayers were said, the incense rose about him, and he, like the Jovians themselves, was taken to the Great White Glory and was seen no more. And in that moment, Alan believed and was content.

"My wife," he cried, "no longer is there any sadness in my life. I believe. Jovians we have become in body and in soul, I no longer fear— death."

And hand in hand they sat, married lovers ever, and watched their children at play.

THE END

A Note About the Author

Ella M. Scrymsour (1888–1962) was a British actress and writer. Born in London, she was the daughter-in-law of C.A. Scrymsour Nichol, a science-fiction writer who wrote *The Mystery of the North Pole* (1908), a well-regarded utopian, lost race novel. Not much is known about Scrymsour beyond her authorship of two novels: *The Perfect World: A Romance of Strange People and Strange Places* (1922); and *The Bridge of Distances* (1924). The former, thought to be a fixup novel—a combination of two initially standalone stories—has been recognized as a highly imaginative work of science fiction incorporating utopian, lost race, biblical, and apocalyptic motifs and themes.

A Note from the Publisher

Spanning many genres, from non-fiction essays to literature classics to children's books and lyric poetry, Mint Edition books showcase the master works of our time in a modern new package. The text is freshly typeset, is clean and easy to read, and features a new note about the author in each volume. Many books also include exclusive new introductory material. Every book boasts a striking new cover, which makes it as appropriate for collecting as it is for gift giving. Mint Edition books are only printed when a reader orders them, so natural resources are not wasted. We're proud that our books are never manufactured in excess and exist only in the exact quantity they need to be read and enjoyed.

Discover more of your favorite classics with Bookfinity™.

- Track your reading with custom book lists.
- Get great book recommendations for your personalized Reader Type.
- Add reviews for your favorite books.
- AND MUCH MORE!

Visit **bookfinity.com** and take the fun Reader Type quiz to get started.

Enjoy our classic and modern companion pairings!